the Barbershop Girl

ALSO BY GEORGINA PENNEY

Fly In Fly Out

Summer Harvest

'Verdict: lots of humour.'
Gold Coast Bulletin

'Georgina Penney is definitely an author you need to seek out.
Her books are guaranteed to give you lots of reading fun and leave
you with hope in your heart and a smile on your face.'
Book Muster Down Under

'Plenty of humorous moments.'
Canberra Times

'Laced with self-deprecating Aussie humour, peopled with
appealing and entertaining characters . . . and set in a
beautiful part of Western Australia.'
Write Note Reviews

'An entertaining read with both lighthearted moments and
some that bring you to tears.'
Weekly Times

'Moments that have readers astounded one
moment and elated the next.'
Talking Books Blog

'Full of Ms Penney's signature humour and wit.'
My Written Romance

'Funny, sassy, suspenseful.'
The Blurb Magazine

'Will appeal to lovers of romance and family dramas.'
Aussie Reviews

'Another exceptional read.'
Australian Women Writers

the Barbershop Girl

GEORGINA PENNEY

MICHAEL JOSEPH
an imprint of
PENGUIN BOOKS

MICHAEL JOSEPH

UK | USA | Canada | Ireland | Australia
India | New Zealand | South Africa | China

Penguin Books is part of the Penguin Random House group of companies
whose addresses can be found at global.penguinrandomhouse.com.

Penguin
Random House
Australia

First published as *Irrepressible You* by Penguin Group (Australia), 2014
This edition published by Penguin Random House Australia Pty Ltd, 2017

1 3 5 7 9 10 8 6 4 2

Text copyright © Georgina Penney, 2014

The moral right of the author has been asserted.

Cover and text design by Louisa Maggio © Penguin Random House Australia Pty Ltd
Cover photograph by Jelena Simic Petrovic/Arcangel
Typeset in Sabon by Louisa Maggio, Penguin Random House Australia Pty Ltd
Colour separation by Splitting Image Colour Studio, Clayton, Victoria
Printed and bound in Australia by Griffin Press, an accredited ISO AS/NZS 14001
Environmental Management Systems printer.

National Library of Australia
Cataloguing-in-Publication data:

Penney, Georgina
The barbershop girl / Georgina Penney
9780143797333 (paperback)

Man–woman relationships – Fiction
Journalists – Fiction
Betrayal – Fiction

A823.4

penguin.com.au

For Tony

Chapter 1

'WHAT DO YOU think her deal is?' Alex Crane asked over the heavy roar of rain on the awning of the The Norfolk pub's beer garden.

Ben Martindale toyed with the packet of Gitanes he'd just placed on the ale-polished table while covertly studying the lady in question.

She appeared to be the end product of an improbable romantic liaison between a kewpie doll and a fifties Barbie. Her artfully curled platinum hair was pulled into a high ponytail that framed apple-cheeked features, and her rather delectable little body was decked out in a red and white polka-dot dress cinched at the waist, red cardigan and black patent leather heels. In the dimly lit surrounds, she stood out like a rare bird of paradise lost in a penguin exhibit.

If Ben and Alex had been prudent men, they'd have taken all that red as one of nature's warning signals, but Ben had always been fascinated by things that didn't quite fit – in fact, he'd made it his business – and Alex . . . well, Alex was full to the brim of that unique blind optimism possessed by a certain brand of Yank who travels abroad. As far as Ben knew, there was no known cure.

'Actress? She's certainly gained herself an audience,' Ben replied in clipped British tones. He poured himself a glass of a passable Cabernet Sauvignon, inhaling its earthy aroma, and leaned a little further back in his chair, projecting the boneless placidity of a big cat at rest.

'The sailors?' Alex looked around the outdoor bar, which was currently infested with an entire battleship's worth of American sailors on shore leave, some in uniform, some in civvies – all on the prowl. Or as on the prowl as they could be clustered around a bevy of upright outdoor heaters spaced at random. Over the past hour or so, Ben and Alex had watched as they'd approached the lady in packs of twos or threes. Without fail, they'd all been given a double-dimpled smile designed to charm before being sent on their merry way.

'Mmm hmm.' Ben took another sip of wine.

Alex frowned. 'No, man. If she was an actress she'd be playing it up more.'

'I wouldn't be so sure. She's certainly entertaining. By the way, if you're thinking of going over there, just remember, Australian women are a tougher breed than the sensitive plants you're used to. You're getting yourself to the hospital if she beats you to a pulp. I prefer my car seats free of blood spatter.' Ben's bare-knuckle boxer's features momentarily took on the menacing aspect the British tabloids had frequently remarked upon of late.

Alex chuckled, his liquid-gold voice almost, but not quite, drowning out the rain. 'Why would she do that? I love Aussie women. They love me too.'

'I know. Too much. Have I told you how little sleep I managed last night thanks to your stellar full-volume performance with . . . Susan?'

'Sarah.'

Ben waved a hand dismissively. 'Forgive me. *Sarah*. When I said *mi casa es tu casa*, I didn't mean you and whatever banshee you pick up after your show. And I certainly didn't request the encore performance, either.'

Alex shrugged unapologetically. 'Is it my fault you bought a place with amazing acoustics?' He narrowed his eyes at the cigarette Ben had just tapped out of the packet and lit. 'Put that out or you're a dead man. They screw with my vocal cords.'

'I know,' Ben said with a wicked grin, but stubbed his cigarette out on the bottom of his Italian loafer without taking a puff. He'd quit seven months ago and only carried the French cigarettes around out of habit. They were long past stale. He'd throw them out one of these days. Not yet, but one of these days.

'You coming tomorrow?' Alex asked, casually belying the fact he was referring to a sell-out performance of *Pagliacci*. Opera Australia had paid an obscene amount to lure him across the Pacific to play the lead, Canio, and they were getting their money's worth if last night's packed house was any indication. Alex possessed the heady combination of pretty-boy Filipino–American features, a golden voice and the grace of Astaire. He was the opposite of Ben, who couldn't sing for shit, had the features of a hardened criminal and used his tongue to wield words like weapons, usually for comic effect but sometimes for the hell of it.

'Of course. How else will I be able to tell you what you did wrong?' Ben's smirk transformed to a scowl as Alex levelled a punch at his shoulder. 'Bastard. That's my writing arm you know.'

'You don't need it.'

'I bloody well do.'

'Just phone your column in.'

'How about you phone your performance in tomorrow? Oh, wait, you always do,' Ben shot back, only to see his friend hadn't caught the dig. Instead, Alex's attention had been snared by the little blonde again.

Ben sighed. 'Can you be a little more obvious? You're looking at her like she's a postman's leg and you're an amorous Labrador. Down, Fido.'

Alex ignored him, his expression turning thoughtful. 'You know . . . I'm gonna go for it.'

'At your own risk. What do you think you're going to achieve? Well, other than being thoroughly humiliated when she sends you packing?' He returned his gaze to the lady who was currently peering at a small handheld mirror and wielding a tube of lipstick with the precision of a Dutch master. He had to admit he was just as intrigued as his friend was. His fingers twitched in the way they always did when he sensed a good story about to unfold. 'And please make this amusing. I do have a word count to fill for next week.'

Alex ignored him, his brow creased in a frown. He was obviously working out what he was going to say to impress the lady, which was both ridiculous and rather endearing. Given Alex's appearance, success and celebrity, he should have had all the confidence in the world; still, he remained stubbornly oblivious to his own appeal. Ben, on the other hand, knew he could be a charming bastard when he wanted to be and rarely questioned his attractiveness to the opposite sex.

'Watch and learn.' Alex pushed back his chair, then sauntered with painstakingly deliberate nonchalance over to the woman's table.

To Ben's everlasting amusement, the kewpie doll was now too engrossed in playing with her phone to notice Alex immediately, which was understandable since the heavy rain and the increasingly raucous sailors had taken the noise level up a couple of notches. When she finally looked up, she went through the same routine she'd performed earlier. She politely flashed teeth and dimples before saying something Ben couldn't quite hear. Within a matter of minutes Alex had returned wearing a bemused smile.

'Forgive me, but what did I just learn, exactly?' Ben asked, feigning confusion.

'That she's waiting for someone.'

'And?'

Alex reclaimed his seat, his cheeks flushing enough to see even in the pub's muted outdoor lighting. 'And that she thinks I would look handsome in uniform.'

Ben stared at his friend for a few seconds as the words sank in then howled with laughter.

'This is *priceless*. The great Alex Crane just got pegged as a sailor. You're not thinking of doing a bit of Gilbert and Sullivan any time soon, are you? I could see you as a pirate. Oh wait, on second thought, don't. I don't think the world could take it.' Ben took in Alex's frown. 'Oh come on. You can't be offended, surely? You *are* American. And you know, you all *kind* of look the same and sound the same to the uninitiated. Why don't you just go back over there and correct her assumption?' If it were possible, Ben would package up this moment, put it in a box and bring it out on special occasions when Alex was proving particularly difficult.

He got to his feet, fully intending to introduce himself to the woman just so he could thank her for the best laugh he'd had in months, only to sit down again when a familiar-looking bloke with long ink-black hair strode over to her table. Rather than receiving the brush-off like so many before him, this contender received an enthusiastic hug and a kiss on the lips.

Ben nudged Alex with his foot. 'If it makes you feel any better, the someone she was waiting for is prettier than you and just as well known, if I'm correct.'

'Yeah? Who is he?' Alex looked around to catch the newcomer taking a seat at the lady's table, much to her obvious pleasure.

'What?' Ben asked, distracted momentarily by the woman's smile. It lit up her face, damn near lit up the entire beer garden.

'Ben?'

He recovered. 'If I'm not mistaken that's Scott Watanabe. He's a photographer. Just completed a big show in London. *Women in War*, I think it was called. There was a big write-up in the *Times* a couple of weeks ago if you bothered with any news outside the fatherland.'

'Huh.' A flash of chagrin crossed Alex's features before he shrugged philosophically. 'Win some lose some.'

'Were you fighting? I missed that.' Ben abruptly pushed his chair away from the table. 'Another pint?'

'Sure.'

'Scott!' Amy Blaine's baby blues widened in surprise, seconds before she launched out of her chair and threw herself into her friend's open arms. Standing on tippy toes, she wrapped her arms around his neck and planted a warm, platonic kiss on his lips before firing off a barrage of questions. 'What are you doing here? When did you fly in? Why didn't you call me? I would have picked you up from the airport!'

'Hey, squirt. I'll answer you but you've gotta let me go. I'm losing oxygen here.' Scott contradicted himself by pulling her tightly against his broad chest.

She allowed herself to revel in the sensation. They'd known each other since she was eight and he was ten. He'd been her older sister's best friend for nearly twenty years and her own surrogate big brother for just as long. She always missed him whenever he went overseas for work, but his absence had been especially hard this last week.

'Your lungs are big enough so start talking,' she said, not caring if her meticulously applied make-up was getting smudged against his shirt.

'I flew in late last night and would have called but Jo said you've been flat tack this week.' Scott let her go with one final squeeze and took the seat across from hers.

'That's an understatement.' Amy rolled her eyes. Her hair salon and barbershop had been the cause of a great deal of wailing and gnashing of teeth of late. 'It's been insane. Mel's quit because she and Kate broke up *again*, so it's down to just Kate, Roslynn, Marissa and me. I've had to turn people away.'

Scott winced in sympathy and she waved a hand, not wanting to dwell on the negative. 'But enough about me.' She leaned forward in her chair, chin resting on her hands, as she drank in his too-handsome Eurasian features with a rush of pleasure. 'What are you doing out on the town when you could be enjoying my company?'

He gave her a wry smile that didn't quite meet his eyes. 'I was here to meet someone just now. I promised I'd catch up with her the minute I got back but it looks like that's not gonna happen. You?'

Amy echoed his expression. 'Same. I've just been stood up.'

Scott scowled. 'Jesus, Ames. That really sucks. Where do you find them?'

'More to the point, where do they find me?' Amy's eyes glazed over with a flash flood of tears that she wiped away quickly with her fingertips, careful not to smudge her mascara.

'Aw, babe.' Scott reached over and ran a long finger over her up-tilted nose. 'How about I get us a drink and you can tell me about it? You want another one?' He nodded to the perspiring glass of house white she'd been nursing for the past half hour.

'I won't say no.' Amy allowed herself a small sniff, then forced a smile. 'Actually, gorgeous, bring us a bottle.'

'That bad, is it?' Scott asked in a quiet rumble, his eyes sympathetic, his mouth tensed at the edges.

'Yeah, but don't get all serious on me. Go get us a drink. Make it a bottle of red since I don't have to worry about scaring a guy off with red wine teeth tonight. Then I want to hear how your show in London went. I can't believe I haven't seen you for three months!'

'Three months? Yeah. Probably. Far out, that went quick.' Scott leaned back, obviously stunned.

'For you maybe, mister, but it was snail's pace from my

perspective. Anyway, wine first, conversation later. Hop to it.'

'Yes, ma'am.' Scott stood up, saluted and about-turned.

Smile fading, Amy watched his back as he walked towards the bar, side-stepping the puddles formed by the odd hole in the make-shift roof overhead as the rain pummelled on.

A few seconds later her phone chirped, signalling an incoming message. She ignored it in favour of looking morosely down at her new Bernie Dexter dress. She'd spent ages beautifying herself tonight, just to end up being ditched by text message half an hour *after* her date was supposed to meet her. It was enough to leave her feeling a little teary, but she refused to dwell on that right now. She looked up and caught sight of the two men lounging at the table nearby.

The friendly, drop-dead-gorgeous American sailor she'd just brushed off was laughing at something his friend had to say and she felt a sharp stab of longing. Sometimes she wished she was the kind of woman who could have a one-night stand. Over the past couple of years she'd entertained some pretty racy fantasies on the subject but knew she'd never act on them. There was no quality control. She'd never be able to guarantee the man wasn't a violent lunatic or just another inconsiderate bastard. Given her tendency to attract that particular species of male, she didn't want to tempt fate.

The sailor's friend caught her watching them and raised his wine glass in a salute. Unlike his friend, this man resembled a well-dressed thug. His head of black hair was closely shaven to almost the same length as the stubble on his jaw. His pale eyes – maybe blue, maybe green – were watching her from under heavy lids, and his incongruously sensual lips were pulled into a faint, mocking smile.

Amy found herself squirming in her seat, uncomfortable with the attention. She knew it didn't mean anything and she should be used to it by now, but that didn't make it any less cringe worthy.

Every time an American naval vessel pulled into the Fremantle port, the entire city of Perth was flooded with horny sailors who tried to chat up any woman – and a significant number of men – who looked even vaguely available. They usually left without much trouble when Amy told them she had a boyfriend. They had definitely never watched her like this guy was.

She picked up her phone again to mask her discomfort, only to find another message from her absent date. Bastard. When did it become okay to ask someone out, cancel late without a call and then try to confirm an appointment for a haircut and shave a few minutes later?

'There ya go. One bottle of wine as ordered.' Scott set a bulbous red wine glass in front of her. He looked pointedly at her phone. 'Am I killing someone?'

'Nope.' Amy waved her hand dismissively. 'Just helping me stick pins in a voodoo doll later tonight after we get a bit more drunk and debauched.'

'Fair enough.' Scott searched her features for a few minutes before pouring them both a generous helping of rich oaky red, then set the bottle on the table between them. 'So d'you want to tell me why you just gave Alex Crane the brush-off?'

'Hmm?' Amy was too busy focusing on the wine bottle to take notice of his words. It was an Evangeline's Rest shiraz. Scott's family owned the winery. 'You get this stuff for free m'love. Why are you ordering it at a bar?'

Scott shrugged and looked entirely unrepentant. 'I missed the taste of home and I haven't got down to the farm to pick up another case yet. So back to Alex Crane.'

'Alex Crane? Who's Alex Crane?'

'The famous guy who was chatting you up when I walked in.' Scott ran his thumb along the base of his glass.

'Famous? How?' Amy's eyes narrowed on the American sailor at the next table. With looks like his, she was sure she would have recognised him if she'd seen him in one of the trashy magazines at her salon, not that she'd had the time to look at them lately.

'He's a popular opera singer. Tenor. He's only on all the bill-boards and flyers in the bloody city. You been sniffing the perming solution again, Ames?'

'Opera singer? I thought he was a sailor.' The mouthful of wine Amy had just swallowed turned to acid in her empty stomach.

'A sailor? Look at him, babe. If he's a sailor, I'm Popeye.' Scott paused, then his eyes widened. 'Oh Jesus. What did you say to him?'

'Only that I had a boyfriend like I always do. He's a *sailor*,' Amy insisted, even as she realised the man hadn't said as much. She'd not given him a chance. The minute she'd heard his American accent she'd run on autopilot. 'Bugger.'

This time Scott couldn't contain his booming laughter and she gave him a glare dark enough to singe his socks off before twisting to furtively study the men at the next table. The sailor, maybe opera singer, was looking the other way, but his friend was still openly scrutinising her with a cat-that-ate-the-cream smile as if she were part of a joke. If what Scott had just said was true, she probably was.

She twisted back around. 'Scott, tell me I didn't just insult an international celebrity? Please, please, just tell me you're joking. That would top off a truly crappy day.'

'Dunno.' Scott drained his wine glass in one go and filled it up again. 'Chill. I hear Crane's a pretty nice guy. And he's not looking pissed off right now, so I doubt it. Can't say the same about his friend, though. That's Ben Martindale. By all accounts, he's a total prick.'

'Ben who?' Amy dared another look at the thug who had now turned back to his friend. Something about his features reminded her of a more rugged, younger Clive Owen.

Scott's expression turned incredulous. 'You *really* don't get out much, do you squirt?'

'No time.' Amy's mind whirred at the implications of commit-ting such a major social faux pas. Her professional reputation, her livelihood, relied on keeping famous people very happy so they, in turn, recommended her businesses and made *her* very happy. Pissing off an international celebrity was not a part of the plan. With Perth being such a fishbowl, it wouldn't be hard for this Alex Crane guy to find out who she was if he was the vengeful sort.

'Do you think I should apologise?'

'Wouldn't hurt, but don't stress. I don't think it's as big a deal as you're making it.' Scott swirled the wine around his glass and regarded it for a few seconds before raising his eyes to hers. 'You know I missed this. Missed you too.'

'Yeah. Love you too, sweetie. Give me a sec.' Amy kept watch on the men at the next table, who were now engaged in conversation. She was going to have to make this right.

She took a deep breath, pushed her chair back abruptly and bridged the short distance as quickly as her four-inch heels allowed, ignoring a twinge of pain as her feet protested at having to work again after sixty hours on the job over the past week.

Neither man noticed her approach until she was standing at their table.

'Hello again,' she chirped, forcing a cheerful smile, deliberately keeping her eyes on Alex Crane, while surreptitiously smoothing her sweaty palms over her dress. She immediately found herself the centre of attention.

'Hi,' Crane replied with a surprised, weaken-the-knees grin.

The thuggish friend was another matter entirely. He nodded at her in greeting but a sarcastic smile played at the corner of his lips. Maybe it was just the contrast of short hair, heavy black stubble and icy pale green eyes that set her nerves on edge. To Amy, he looked dangerous, moody – definitely someone she didn't want to know. Not that she could dwell on that right now. She turned back to Crane, who was looking anything but offended by her earlier mistake. Still, best to be sure.

'Take a seat.' He gestured to the spare chair at their table.

Amy winced with feigned regret. 'I'd love to but I can't. I came over to apologise.'

'Yeah? Why?' Alex Crane's smile slipped a little as his forehead wrinkled in a frown. Now that she looked at him clearly, Amy kicked herself for her earlier assumption. This man was far too polished to be a sailor. His clothes – a soft-looking moss-green jumper and black jeans – screamed money, and his immaculately groomed curly black hair had no doubt been styled at a top salon. Never mind that his friend Mr Neanderthal was wearing a black suit that had to have been tailored to his lean, hard-looking body. She'd never met a sailor who wore a suit. How had she missed that?

'I thought you were a sailor. That's why I told you I had a boy-friend. I don't. Not that that's important and you're not . . . a sailor, I mean. My friend just told me you're a musician. An opera singer?' Amy drew a deep breath. 'So yeah, I'm really sorry. I'd love to make it up to you. If you want to come to my barbershop on Monday I can offer you a free cut-throat shave. My place is called Babyface. It's not far from here. Most people know about it.' She darted a glance at the thug friend, who was still watching her while flipping a packet of foreign cigarettes over and over on the table in front of him. It felt like he was laughing at her. The sensation wasn't pleasant. It was even less pleasant when he spoke.

'What time Monday?' His voice was sharp, his diction precise. Educated English. Expensive English. While waiting for her answer, he ran his eyes over her new dress as if tallying up every little fault so he could laugh about them later. It was an extremely rude gesture and Amy's hackles began to rise.

'Pardon?' she asked, doing her best to keep her expression friendly for Crane's benefit.

'What time?' the man repeated, as if she were slow.

'Be nice.' Crane gave Amy another warm smile. 'Ignore him, he's not house trained.'

'I'm always nice.' The thug's eyes narrowed and his mouth quirked, almost imperceptibly, at the side. Now Amy knew for sure he was playing with her. She'd watched her sister's cat wearing that same expression when lying on his back asking for a tummy rub. It was always a trap.

'It's alright.' Amy turned back to Crane. 'I open at nine.'

'I didn't catch your name,' he prompted.

'Amy.'

'Amy. You know, *damn*, thank you so much for your offer, but I'm flying out to Sydney on Monday. My name is Alex.' He held out a hand and Amy automatically shook it. His palm was large and warm, his fingers long and narrow, enveloping her hand reassuringly, momentarily putting her at ease.

'I know. My friend just told me.' She darted a look back at Scott before gently disengaging her hand. She could be imagining it, but Alex seemed disappointed at the loss of contact.

'Well, great. I'll be back in town in a few months' time. I'd love to see you.' He flashed her another thousand-watt smile.

Amy felt a surge of happiness as her usual unfailing optimism returned. This incredibly handsome man wanted to take her out? Maybe dolling herself up tonight hadn't been such a tragic waste of time after all. 'That'd be great. Just wait. I'll give you my card.' She returned to her table as quickly as dignity allowed, ignoring Scott's enquiring expression, and retrieved a business card from her bag.

'Here you go.' She handed it to Alex moments later, her voice a little breathless.

'Great.' He took it, immediately tucking it into his wallet.

'Oh well. Great, then. I, ah . . . I have to go.' Amy gestured to her table where Scott was monitoring the proceedings with a faintly protective air. Relieved to have avoided a disaster and elated by Alex Crane's obvious interest, she spun around and began to walk off.

'Ben.' The thug's cut-glass voice stopped her dead in her tracks.

She turned. 'Pardon?'

'It's what you should write in your appointment book for nine on Monday.' With that, he nodded curtly before turning to Alex, dismissing her. Amy was tempted to walk back to their table and pour Ben's glass of wine over his head.

'Want to tell me what went on there?' Scott asked, having heard that last exchange and noticed Amy's quicksilver change of mood.

'I'll tell you after I've finished this glass.' Amy threw back a mouthful of wine. Scott was right. It did taste like home, dark and full of swirling, faintly acidic memories.

'So.' She swallowed with a grimace, then curved her reluctant lips into a tight smile that didn't reach her eyes. 'I missed you too. Tell me about London.'

Chapter 2

'HARVEY, WHY ARE you doing this to me now?' Amy considered the drips of water splattering her bare knees with a morose expression. Harvey had another leak.

Damn.

She peered up at the corrugated tin roof of her antiquated stone outhouse with a long-suffering sigh. Outside, rain was still pelting down, nearly drowning out the sound of thunder overhead. Much of the water hitting the roof was managing to find its way through an assortment of rusty nail holes to land in her lap.

She groaned and stood up, balancing on her beloved hot-pink mule slippers – complete with damp pompoms – and brushed the water off her knees before flushing the toilet. Pulling her black lacy matinee wrap tightly around her in a completely ineffective gesture to ward off the rain and cold, she tottered out the door, across her treacherously slippery, mossy courtyard and into her warmly lit kitchen.

The sweet smell of coffee brewing and chocolate cake baking greeted her senses, as did the sight of a shirtless Scott in the jeans he'd been wearing the night before. He was casually leaning against her kitchen bench slathering a slice of toast with honey, impervious to the faint chill in the house. He shook his head at her soggy appearance.

Amy held up a hand and narrowed her eyes. 'Don't start.'

'Didn't say anything,' he said around a mouthful of toast, shrugging his shoulders.

She washed her hands, then retrieved a butter plate from a bright red kitchen cupboard, handing it to him.

'You didn't have to. Put a plate under that or you're gonna be my maid for the day, and put on a T-shirt while you're at it. You're giving me a lady moment with all this nudity.' She nudged his flat stomach with a playful fist, then poured coffee into a pink and white spotted mug, ignoring Scott as he began to choke on inhaled crumbs.

'And if you're going to die, make sure you call emergency first.' She settled herself on one of the two mismatched ladder-back chairs at her small square kitchen table and took her first sip of heavenly caffeine for the morning.

'You're all heart, Ames,' Scott wheezed. He poured himself his own mug of coffee, then disappeared off to the tiny spare bedroom that abutted the kitchen.

'That's *Princess* Amy to you, mister. There's a brush and an elastic band in there somewhere if you want to tie your hair up. If you're lucky, it won't be pink!'

'Cheers, big ears,' he called back, reappearing wearing his fitted black shirt. His hair had been pulled back into a sleek ponytail and not for the first time did Amy wish she had some of Scott's Japanese–Australian genetics. The man didn't have to try. She, on the other hand, had to use the threat of industrial machinery to get her shoulder-length hair to even listen to her, let alone behave.

'How's your head?' she asked when he took a seat across from her, stretching out his legs to take up most of the kitchen.

He winced. 'Great, now I've downed a few aspirin. Not so great when I woke up. How much did we drink last night?'

Amy shrugged and smiled perkily. 'Three and a half bottles.'

'Jesus.' Scott ran his hand over his eyes, then looked at her incredulously. 'You've gotta be the eighth wonder of the world. How is it that you're half my size and you don't get hangovers?'

'I just don't. You going to stick around this morning for some chocolate cake, or are you headed home?'

'Home, babe. Jo's dropping by for a late breakfast.' He reached over and tugged at her sleeve. 'Was last night just a bit of a vent or do I have to be worried?'

Amy bit her lip, not meeting his eyes. 'Just a vent, sweetie.'

'You sure? Because it didn't sound like it. I haven't seen you cry like that for years. Not since Liam.' His words hung in the air for a few awkward seconds.

'Well, I was due then, eh?' Amy slipped her foot out of her shoe and nudged him on the thigh with her toe.

'Yeah?'

'Yeah, sweetie. You don't need to worry.'

His eyes searched hers for a moment, then he nodded. 'Alright. I'll leave it then.'

'Thanks.' Amy gave him a relieved smile. Around about bottle number two, she and Scott had taken a taxi from the pub back to her little Fremantle house and she'd poured out her tale of woe, going through half a box of tissues in the process.

The past week had been a slow-motion film of how sad and pathetic one woman's life could be. Like all films of that nature, it had commenced on an absolutely peachy note. On Monday morning, Tom Draper, Perth's most loved TV weather man, had given her a call at her barbershop and asked her out for a few drinks. Assuming her sparkling wit had worked its magic on him during his monthly visits to Babyface, she'd immediately said yes. She should have known better. Not once had she had success with a man who had a dry scalp, and Tom's was drier than the Sahara.

Tom's careless rejection had just amplified the ever-present aching sense of loneliness she liked to pretend didn't exist. Once alcohol and Scott's reassuring presence were added to the equation, it was inevitable that she'd find herself curled up, bawling buckets against his shoulder at two in the morning until he put her to bed and stumbled off to her spare room.

'You want a ride to your place?' she asked, derailing the train of self-pity before it could build up a full head of steam.

'What? Yeah, actually, that would be great . . . you sure?' Amy had a strong feeling he wasn't just referring to the car ride.

'Yeah,' she said firmly. 'Just let me get changed. I've got to do a bit of shopping anyway.' What she didn't tell him was that her shopping involved a trip to her local hardware store.

Later that afternoon, buoyed by a break in the weather, Amy cheerfully clambered atop Harvey's roof with a tube of silicon sealant in one hand, holding her rickety wooden ladder in place against his blue-painted stone walls with the other. Although it had stopped raining, the leaves and debris on the corrugated iron roof made it difficult to work out which of the rusty holes she was looking at was responsible for her cold shower that morning. She'd just located the most likely culprits when her sister's loud, husky voice startled her and nearly caused a fatal accident.

'What the hell are you doing?' Jo bellowed from the kitchen door before stomping out into the small jacaranda-lined courtyard. Just over six foot tall and strong from her former job as an engineer working on offshore oil rigs, Jo was able to reach up and easily wrap her hands around Amy's waist, supporting her as she placed her feet back on the second-from-top rung, ready to climb down.

'Hey.' Amy grinned, ignoring her sister's fierce frown. 'If you could just hold me steady for a few more seconds, I'll finish, then make you a hot chocolate.'

'You're insane. You know that, right?' Jo tightened her grip as Amy leaned backwards to survey her handiwork. 'High heels on a bloody ladder. Don't you own a proper pair of boots? What idiot wears heels on a ladder? No. Don't say anything. The answer's right in front of me.'

Ignoring Jo, Amy calmly capped the sealant, dropped it into the front pocket of her cheerful, daisy-printed apron and climbed down.

'Thanks,' she chirped as her feet touched the ground. She spun and pulled her sister's head down for a kiss on the cheek. 'I was fine, but I love you for caring.'

Jo ran her fingers through her short, bright red hair in obvious exasperation. 'At least find yourself some decent work boots like mine. Or get in a pro.' She looked from Amy's two-inch-heeled ankle boots to Harvey. 'Why don't you just tear this thing down and put a toilet inside like a normal person?'

Amy drew herself up to her full five feet and one inch. 'You and Scott are just as bad as each other. He was having a go this morning too. What did I tell you about hurting Harvey's feelings?'

'Settle, petal. I take it back.' Jo lifted up her hands in feigned surrender. 'You want me to put the ladder away?'

'Yes please,' Amy said pertly. She walked across the courtyard and opened the kitchen door, pulling off her boots and sliding her feet into the slippers waiting just inside. She took the time to untie her apron and hang it on the back door. The heavy screwdrivers and various other tools in its pockets made a satisfying *thunk* as they bumped against the wood.

While Jo stopped at the back door to unlace her old beaten steel-capped boots, Amy began heating milk on the stove, breaking in chunks of Lindt chocolate and adding honey, a cinnamon stick and a tiny pinch of salt for flavour.

Jo was silent as she wandered into the kitchen and took a seat at the table, stretching out her Levi-covered legs in a pose that echoed Scott's from earlier. She began idly playing with the pages of a French cookbook Amy had left on the table.

Normally Amy would be chattering away happily, but she knew her sister wouldn't be visiting today if Scott hadn't squealed. So instead of talking, she settled for stirring the hot chocolate into a satisfyingly rich brown sludge, and braced herself.

'Want to tell me what's got you so upset that you cried buckets last night?' Jo asked eventually.

Amy stifled a sigh and finished pouring her luxuriously thick brew into Jo's special blue and white striped mug before filling up her own. 'I knew I should have poisoned Scott's coffee this morning.' She placed both drinks on a bamboo tray, added two generous slices of just-iced chocolate cake, then made herself comfortable at the table.

Jo laughed softly, accepting her hot chocolate, running it under her nose and sniffing appreciatively. 'Ta. Wouldn't have worked. One look at you and I knew you were feeling flat.'

Amy frowned.

'You only wear those old jeans when you're pissed off or have PMS.' Jo shrugged. 'The rest of the outfit gave you away too.'

'What?' Amy looked down at her bright yellow hoodie with a smiling Tweety Bird on the front. 'How?'

'It doesn't go with your lippy or nail polish. It's a sad, sad day when Amy Blaine isn't colour coordinated.' Jo shook her head with mock gravity, pursing her lips to hold back a smile.

Amy scowled down at her nails, which were painted a bright coral. Damn, Jo was right.

'I bet you're wearing black undies too. You only wear those when you're *really* pissy.'

'Am not.' Amy checked all the same, sticking her nose up in the air when Jo was proven correct. 'Smarty pants.'

Jo chuckled. 'I'll take that as a compliment. So what's bugging you?'

'Nothing. Everything.'

'Man trouble?'

'Yeah, or more to the point, lack of man trouble.' Amy pushed a marshmallow around her hot chocolate before raising her finger to her lips, licking off the icing sugar that clung to it.

'Want to talk about it?'

'Nope.' Amy smiled to take the sting out of her rejection. After a truly epic fight nearly a decade before, she and Jo had come to an agreement that her love life was off-limits. 'You can tell me how the wedding plans are going instead, though.'

Jo smacked a hand over her eyes. 'Thanks, Ames. Stick the knife in and cut me to the bone, why don't you? Tell me, why did I agree to get married in the first place?'

'I dunno. From memory it had something to do with falling for an awesome, lovable lug and having spectacular sex on a regular basis, but what'd I know?' Amy grinned widely at Jo's obvious distress. 'You know it's not really the drama you're making it out to be. Stephen'd get married in a shearing shed to make you happy. You're just upset because you know I'll insist you wear a frock.'

Jo grimaced. 'Yeah, you would too. Bitch.'

'Love you too. Come on, it can't be that bad.'

Jo averted her eyes. 'It's not, but setting up the brewery has taken up all our time lately and it's still gonna be another few years before we start making any kind of decent profit. The thought of arranging a wedding right in the middle of it all is giving me the willies. That, and . . . I dunno . . . it's awkward, you know? Stephen's got such a big family and on our side there's just you and me. Not that I'd want Mum and Dad there in a million years after what they did . . . but it kinda seems a bit sad, eh?' Jo scuffed her foot across Amy's floor, scowling at her big toe poking through a hole in the threadbare sock.

'What about Scott? He's our family too.' Amy reached across the table to put her hand over Jo's, her heart aching in sympathy. Ever since meeting her fiancé, Stephen, Jo had been happier than Amy had ever seen her. It was awful that their crappy childhood was returning to cause Jo unhappiness now, when things were going so well. Since she'd hooked up with Stephen, Jo had gone from strength to strength, quitting her job in the oil industry to set up the brewery with him at his family's winery.

'Yeah, but Scott is Stephen's cousin, so he sort of doesn't count in this case. Although I've been threatening to make him a brides-maid.' Jo's wide mouth curved up in a reluctant, wry smile. 'He's pretty enough.'

They shared a mutual grin at the thought of their six-foot-three friend wearing a frock.

'Pink for preference,' Amy chuckled.

'Hell, yeah.' Jo withdrew her hand and broke off a large chunk of chocolate cake, moaning with pleasure at the first bite. 'Hmm, Jesus this stuff is good.'

'I know, I made it.'

'No ego on you, Ames.' Jo chuckled. 'So you gonna get around to telling me about giving an opera singer the brush-off, or do I have to drag it outta ya?'

'Scott told you that too?' Amy felt a heated blush creeping up her cheeks.

'Mmm hmm,' Jo said, her mouth full of cake.

'He's such a tattle tale,' Amy grumbled. She'd Googled Alex Crane the minute she'd returned home with her hardware supplies and had quickly discovered Scott had been right; Crane was an operatic superstar. Even more embarrassing, he was in Perth for a huge sell-out production that was being advertised all over town. How she'd failed to recognise him from the billboards, the flyers and the TV ads was beyond her.

She'd also tried looking up his rude friend but hadn't been able to remember the man's last name. It was Ben . . . something. All she knew was that he'd featured in a really unpleasant dream last night.

She'd been back in the bar, but this time she'd been naked and Mr Thug had been sitting across from her, smirking, his ice-green eyes cataloguing every one of her faults before he'd started laughing.

She'd woken up feeling exposed, horribly vulnerable and, above all, confused.

She successfully interacted with men in her barbershop every day of the week. Despite her past negative experiences with her alcoholic father and a bevy of ex-boyfriends, Amy rarely had a problem talking or relating to men and frequently felt more comfortable in their company than she did around women, in professional situations at least. It didn't make sense that five seconds around this particular man had left her feeling like an overexposed piece of film. This morning she'd brushed the feeling off as the effect of too much wine, but that didn't stop her feeling anxious about him actually turning up on Monday morning.

'This is where you tell me what happened instead of staring into space.' Jo poked her gently with a finger.

'Do I have to?'

'Yep, or I'll sit on you and force you to. Tell you what though, how about I let you rip the hair off my legs while you do it? Come on, that way you can make me scream if I laugh. Remember last time?'

Amy chuckled despite herself, pushing the memory of taunting green eyes and nine o'clock appointments firmly out of her mind.

'Old Mrs Korrigan next door called the cops last time, thinking someone was attacking me. Yeah, alright, it's a deal. I haven't been sadistic in a while. I'll heat up the wax. Want your bite stick?'

'Hell, yes.'

Ben's ring tone assaulted his ears with all the force of an air raid siren. Clearly someone in his acquaintance had lost all sense of civility and had taken up torture for a hobby.

He snatched the phone off his bedside. 'What?'

'It's me,' Alex announced as if it were inconceivable that Ben could think it was anyone else.

'I gathered that. To what do I owe the pleasure?' He rolled over, pried his eyes open and peered blearily at the obnoxious red glow coming from his alarm clock. 'At eight a.m. *Eight a.m.*, Alex. I didn't get to bed until four. Neither did you. What fit of insanity inspired you to wake me up at eight?'

'Oh, I don't know. Something about a cut-throat shave.' Alex's smugness was almost tangible.

'You go instead. I'm tired. I've changed my mind. She wasn't all *that* interesting. I'll write about something else.'

'I can't go. I'm tied up getting ready for my flight. I'm in the kitchen. I've made coffee, so get your ass out of bed and come drink it.'

Ben grimaced, rasping his hand across his chin. It was covered in its usual dense, spiky forest of stubble, possibly the only thing he'd inherited from his father. 'You can drown yourself in that swill you call coffee for all I care. Then after you've finished doing that, you can untie yourself from getting ready for your flight and go get a shave. I'm staying here. In bed. Sleeping. Let yourself out quietly when you leave.'

'Oh no, you don't,' Alex said with an inhumanly good-natured chuckle. Ben never understood how his friend could be such a cheerful ass in the morning.

'You were the one who was a prick about making the appointment. I know you're feeling guilty, or should be feeling guilty, so get out of bed and go apologise to the nice lady.'

'I can't.'

'Can't get out of bed?'

'Can't go. Don't remember the name or address.'

'The store is named Babyface in . . .' Ben could hear paper rustling. 'Fremantle. Not far from here according to Google Maps. I'll see you in five minutes, or I'm coming in there, taking a picture of you and posting it online with your address so the paparazzi know where you are.' Alex hung up and Ben threw his phone onto the unattended pillow next to him.

'Bastard,' he mumbled to himself, cursing both Alex's sense of fair play and his own smart mouth. There'd just been something about the lady that had made him want to push her buttons to see which ones made her go. He knew he should be feeling a little remorse for his rudeness, and he was, but not enough to want to get out of bed. After all, she was only someone he'd offended once. There were numerous people in his life he'd offended on multiple occasions and he'd never bothered to get out of bed early to apologise to any of them.

Although . . . he hadn't yet come up with any material for his weekly newspaper column in the *London Enquirer*. Maybe the little blonde mistakenly identifying Alex as a sailor *could* be rounded out to produce an entertaining tale. He'd discounted it earlier because that one meeting didn't provide quite enough material.

Ben's personal experiences were frequently fodder for his column, albeit augmented with a generous sprinkling of the salt and pepper of literary free licence. That wouldn't change now that he'd relocated to Australia. In fact, after the recent unwanted media attention he'd received care of an ill-conceived fling with a publicity-hungry reality star, shining the light on someone else's world would be entertaining.

As much as he didn't want to get up, he couldn't pass up this golden – or more to the point, blonde – opportunity.

Forty minutes later, Ben studied the front of an old-fashioned barbershop, its window painted with bold white letters spelling 'Babyface' and garnished with a spinning red and blue pole. Next to the barbershop sat some kind of beauty salon with similar bold writing over its window declaring that 'Gentlemen Prefer Blondes'.

'Cute,' he murmured before pushing the door open. A bell rang in the shop next door but the long, narrow space before him was devoid of life. Well, almost. The silence was broken by an antique record player spinning the sounds of an old Muddy Waters classic.

Glancing around with a critical eye, Ben set about mental note taking, registering the dark green walls, scarred, dark wood floorboards and the two plush, deep brown leather barber chairs facing heavy square mirrors. On the wall directly behind one of the chairs, visible in the mirrors, was a framed print from Marilyn Monroe's famous 1953 *Playboy* spread. It hung next to an equally large black and white print of a young shirtless Rock Hudson, a cigarette dangling out the corner of his mouth. *Obviously catering to all tastes*, Ben mused with raised brows.

The room smelled invitingly of coffee and, if he wasn't mistaken, chocolate.

He turned around, wondering what the hell he was supposed to do now, when he spotted a discreet sign by the record player requesting that patrons *take a seat and wait for Amy*. Deciding to do just that, he took the chair affording the view of Marilyn and waited.

––––––

The bell rang announcing someone's presence in the barbershop and Amy paused in applying bleach to Jody Greave's inch-long hair to make a futile motion for Kate, her only other senior stylist, to take over. When Kate feigned blindness, Amy squelched the urge to throw a hair dryer at the woman's beautiful, sleek blonde head. She met her nail and beauty technician Marissa's sympathetic gaze and grimaced, cursing the circumstances that had left her short staffed.

On Monday the week before, Amy's other senior stylist and good friend, Mel, had quit for the third time in the space of a year. As always, Mel had cited personal reasons for leaving without providing any details. She didn't need to. It was obvious that she and Kate were on a downturn in their perpetual rollercoaster romance.

For her part, Kate appeared largely unaffected by the temporary split. Well, other than exploring her inner bitch and being a total drama queen, but that was kind of normal.

Amy had seen this particular soap opera numerous times now and knew that the two women would patch things up in a matter of weeks. Mel would ask for her job back and Amy would say yes.

As much as Amy knew she shouldn't forgive and forget, she would. Besides being a sweetheart, Mel was her only member of staff who could do decent weaves for Perth's growing community of African immigrants, and Amy was losing customers without her. Just once though, Amy wished it could be Kate who quit instead. Kate had only been with Amy for two years and, despite being adored by Perth's diva set, she was a pain in the arse and temperamental at the best of times.

Luckily, it was the first day of the winter school holidays and the next two weeks would be quiet. The only appointments due in the salon this morning were Jody and a performing arts student, Lilly, who was probably foregoing food for the next month to have an expensive style and colour done by Amy's junior stylist, Roslynn.

The barbershop was another matter.

The thug from the bar was the only nine o'clock appointment she had scheduled and someone was definitely waiting next door. No matter how much she'd told herself she was used to dealing with difficult people – her industry practically invited it – he left her unsettled. His apparent celebrity status just made her anxiety worse.

'Kate, can you take care of Jody for me?' Amy said finally, when Kate continued gazing out the shop window.

Kate heaved an overly dramatic sigh. 'Yeah, alright.'

'Thanks,' Amy said with forced cheer for her client's sake. She gave Jody's brawny shoulder, hewn on the hockey pitch, a gentle pat. 'I'll see you next time, toots. I've got a customer in the barbershop.'

'Catcha, Amy,' Jody said with an endearingly shy smile as she watched Kate's approach. Her crush was painfully obvious, and she only ever booked an appointment when Kate was temporarily single.

Amy felt a pang of sympathy over Jody's futile infatuation. She knew what it was like to be looking for love in the wrong places and, in crushing on a beautiful snob like Kate, Jody had picked the worst spot possible to park her heart. Amy just hoped she'd be strong enough to pick herself up when she realised that her affections weren't returned. Lord knew, Amy had had to do as much over the years.

Giving Jody one last smile, she braced herself to see to her first barbershop customer for the day.

Ben jolted awake at the sound of a door opening at the back of the barbershop. He stifled a yawn. He had no idea how long he'd been sleeping. All he knew was that he now had company. Chatty company.

A slightly breathless, melodic female voice pervaded Ben's consciousness. 'Good morning. Sorry to keep you waiting, Ben. It was Ben, right? I was just finishing up with a customer next door. I've brought you some homemade chocolate cake to make up for being late. Are we having coffee this morning?'

'I just woke up. What do you think?' Ben grumbled, rubbing his hands over his eyes.

'I think you're one of those.'

The blonde, Amy if he remembered correctly, approached and placed a tray bearing a steaming mug of black coffee, a small jug of cream and a pot of sugar cubes along with a generous slice of chocolate cake on a small inbuilt ledge in front of his chair.

'Thank you.' Ben looked up into a pair of china-doll blue eyes that were watching him warily, despite the smile stretching her fuchsia-painted lips. He paused momentarily to collect his thoughts. The woman was truly a polished piece of work, spectacular in fact.

The fifties pin-up thing was obviously an ongoing theme. Today, her platinum hair was styled in a high, soft ponytail with loose C-shaped curls framing her features. The rest of her wasn't so much cute as ridiculously sexy: a frilly, long-sleeved white blouse tucked into a navy below-the-knee pencil skirt that cupped her curvy little rump lovingly. Ben couldn't help but notice what her impossibly high red heels did for her calves as she walked away from him to collect a small trolley.

'You're welcome,' she said over her shoulder.

'What do you mean, I'm one of *those*?' Ben demanded.

'A grumpy bear in the morning. I'm used to your type.'

'You're not one of those disgusting morning people by any chance, are you? I heard you were a dying breed.' Ben reached for the coffee, added a dash of cream and took an experimental sip. It was good. Very good. Much better than Alex's dismal efforts, to say the least.

'Better?' she asked, draping an olive-green cape around his shoulders and tying it behind his neck.

'Marginally. This is good coffee.' Ben took a larger sip, feeling the caffeine zapping his neurons to life and kickstarting his charisma. He risked cracking his first smile of the day and was rewarded with one in return. No dimples though. It was obvious he'd have to try harder for those after his behaviour the other night.

'I know. It's fantastic, isn't it? It comes from a little place down south in Margaret River. I order it especially.' She smiled again, this time bringing out one dimple. For some inexplicable reason, the sight brought Ben out of his early-morning malaise like no coffee ever could. He couldn't quite fathom the why of it, but he was experiencing the first rush of purely physical attraction he'd felt in years.

Sex and relationships had come so easily to him for the past decade that he thought he'd long since graduated from the rampaging hormone-driven lust of his teens. Obviously he'd been wrong. That he felt it with this woman was perplexing and somewhat alarming in light of his recent disastrous, highly publicised affair. Been there done that, wanted a refund. But still . . . he hadn't managed to earn both dimples yet.

He broke off a chunk of cake and took a bite, moaning in pleasure the minute it hit his taste buds. 'I take back the dying breed comment. There needs to be more of you. This is amazing.' He reached for another piece, resisting the urge to lick his fingers.

Her eyes twinkled. 'Thanks.'

'Is this for a special occasion or just because you knew I was coming?'

She laughed and the sound coursed through Ben's system like quicksilver.

'No special occasion, but if it helps we can pretend. Is your birthday any time soon?'

'Birthday. No, that was a few months back. I don't celebrate those anyway.'

That earned him a shocked look. 'Never?'

Ben shrugged, running his finger across the plate to pick up the last of the crumbs. 'Never have. Not my thing.'

'What about when you were a kid?'

'Cake didn't feature high on my parents' list of priorities. Is this the scene of an inquisition specialising in torture through cake and coffee, or a barbershop?' His words came out sharper than he intended and he covered his gaffe up with a grin, running his hand over his jaw. 'Because as you can see, I currently resemble an extra in a low-budget detective flick.'

Other than an almost imperceptible pause, Amy didn't seem affected by his bad manners. 'Yeah, you do. What can I do for you today? I'm guessing just a shave since you keep this so short.' She ran her hand over the top of his head, regarding him in the mirror, her head cocked to one side.

Inexplicably, Ben fought the urge to purr. 'A shave please. As long as you can assure me I'm safe.'

'You ever hear the one about the fool who made fun of his barber?' She arched a blonde eyebrow.

'No, is it funny?'

'You'll laugh your head off,' she retorted. 'Now finish your coffee while I get the torture implements ready.' She met his eyes briefly in the mirror and he was struck once again by how blue hers were. They had to be contact lenses, surely.

'Order received and understood,' he said dryly, draining his cup while surreptitiously watching her work.

Amy went about the usual routine of heating water and collecting towels, shaving soap and her razor, trying her best to appear calm and professional. A tall order when her hands were faintly shaking and her insides felt jumbled.

She'd never had such a mixed reaction as this to a customer before. She didn't know what it was about this one. Well, maybe she did. The past two nights had brought bloody awful night-mares about him, and even though he wasn't making fun of her or laughing at her like he had in her dreams, she had the feeling the potential was there. His compliments over the coffee and cake, given in that icepick-sharp English accent, had given her a warm fuzzy moment, but he still looked like a thug – a handsome one with soft hair who reminded her of a big cat.

As she rested a hand on the top of his head and began lathering up his cheeks, she could've sworn he made a faint purring noise.

'What is it you do?' she asked, hoping he'd shed light on who the heck he was.

His pale eyes lit up and his mouth curved with a feline smile. '"What is it you do?" Ah, here we are. Barbershop small talk and the first step to categorisation. Why is that the first thing people want to know? Not, what's your favourite colour? Not, do you eat small fluffy puppies for breakfast? No, that one simple question, once answered, should tell you all you need to know. If I tell you I'm a lawyer, you'll have a whole barrage of generalisations at the ready. Same with doctor, dentist or nurse.' He tilted his head sideways when Amy began shaving with clean strokes down the side of his cheek.

'So are you gonna tell me or not? I do have a knife to your throat, you know,' Amy persisted.

'No, I don't believe I will. Do your worst. I hear face transplants are a new and exciting field of medical science. You can guess if it's that important. Or better yet, you can tell me about yourself. I find *you* absolutely fascinating.'

Amy looked up, startled to find him gazing at her with a disconcerting intensity. In an effort to appear nonchalant, she wiped her lather- and whisker-flecked razor on the towel she'd placed over his shoulder. 'How about I guess, then?'

'Pardon?' he murmured through stiff lips as she navigated around his nose. His breath smelled of mint and coffee. Amy felt her hand begin to shake with nerves again. She paused briefly, concentrating on Muddy Waters and the faint sound of female voices coming through the wall dividing barbershop and salon.

'Guess. I'll guess what you do,' she said, meeting Ben's enquiring glance as she scraped the razor along his jaw line again.

'Be my guest.'

'Well.' Amy stood back and regarded him with a critical eye. He should have looked comical with half his face still covered in shaving foam and the other baby-smooth, but he didn't; he looked at ease, like a tiger who knows it can eat you for dinner but is humouring you by letting you think it's a big softie.

'Well . . . you can't be a lawyer, although I'm guessing you keep them in business.' She moved around to the other side of the chair and started on his other cheek.

'True.' He shrugged unapologetically.

'You can't be a doctor or anything to do with medicine. I see enough of those here to tell them on sight. Tilt your head a bit this way. Thanks.'

'You don't think I'm intelligent enough?' He raised an eyebrow and followed her request.

'No, as rude as you are, you're not self-absorbed enough. I doubt you'd get a kick out of looking at teeth, so nope, not a dentist. I just can't see you taking direction, so definitely not a nurse.' Amy bit the side of her cheek to keep a straight face as he snorted, sending a large clump of lather flying.

'You've got lots of money.' She tilted his chin and began scraping the last of the whiskers on his neck away with a practised ease.

It was amazing what she could tell about men at this point. Most of them at least swallowed nervously at the prospect of having their throats accidentally cut by a cheerful blonde, but this one looked completely relaxed. In fact, she would swear he was watching *her* expression to see what the whole thing said about her personality.

She swallowed loudly and kept talking. 'That shiny spaceship car parked out the front is yours, right? I bet you spent a fortune on those clothes you're wearing too.'

He shrugged. 'The Aston Martin's mine. The clothes are moot. I don't know how much I spent on them; they were bought for me. I hate clothes shopping.'

'Ah.' Amy nodded and then swiped the razor down the under-side of his chin, deftly clearing away the last of his stubble. 'How did you get this scar here?' Without thinking she ran her thumb over a faint white line at least ten centimetres long that ran down his neck from just below his left ear.

'Skiing accident. How did you get that one on your lip?'

Amy paused, stunned. No one other than Scott and Jo, who'd been there when it had happened, ever commented on the inch-long hairline scar marring the upper left-hand corner of her mouth. The thing was usually invisible with the aid of a bit of artfully applied foundation, concealer and lipstick.

She looked in the mirror to see if she'd botched her make-up that morning, only to find Ben watching her. She forced her mouth to curve into her autopilot cheerful smile.

'Ah well . . . I'd answer you, but there's no time left.' She retrieved a hot damp towel and wiped down his smooth cheeks, before quickly rubbing some aftershave balm over them.

'Pity,' Ben replied, waiting for her to untie his cape before standing up.

He wasn't as tall as she'd first thought, but he was still a head taller than she was. Inexplicably, he made her feel small, which didn't make sense. She was used to almost everyone being bigger than she was – in the case of her sister and Scott, much bigger, and being around them never left her feeling this way.

'Yeah. Pity.' She recovered and took a quick step backwards. 'Anyway, that'll be thirty dollars.' She fully expected him to men-tion the free shave she'd offered his friend but he didn't.

'Hmm.' He reached into the back pocket on his jeans, retrieved the money out of a Louis Vuitton wallet and handed it to her, his expression thoughtful. 'I'd like to take you to dinner. Saturday night. What time do you finish work?'

'What?' Amy looked at him incredulously.

'Dinner. Where you put food in your mouth, chew and swallow. Most people do it daily. I'd like to do it with you.'

'Dinner? Ben. I'm not—'

'Good. I'll pick you up here at six,' he said, apparently deciding that he wasn't going to get the answer he wanted if he waited for her to finish talking. 'Wear something . . .' He gave her a very blatant up-and-down and his mouth twitched at the corner. 'Wear anything.'

He strode out the door before she could respond, climbed into his spaceship car and pulled out into the traffic.

She was staring out the front window when the door at the rear of the shop opened and Kate walked through and leaned against the doorframe with one hand propped on her hip.

'Who was *that*?'

'Ben.'

'What'd he want coming here? He looked like he was worth a mint.'

'Dinner,' Amy replied, cursing herself for once again not getting his last name. Bugger.

Chapter 3

BEN LEANED BACK in his chair, clasped his hands behind his head in a languorous stretch and regarded the screen in front of him with a sense of overwhelming satisfaction. The trip to the barbershop, combined with Alex's little case of being mistaken for a sailor, had produced comedy gold. He'd hammed events up and changed a few facts for entertainment's sake of course, but that was normal. He was in top form.

He made a mental note to bring a copy for Amy when he saw her for dinner. Or maybe he wouldn't. At the moment he liked the fact that she had no idea who he was, although she'd more than likely find out soon enough.

He had no doubt that Amy would find his writing just as amusing as the rest of his readership did, who expected witty satire mixed with a bit of the ridiculous with their Saturday morning crumpets and coffee. If his attitude was arrogant, Ben didn't care. He'd done the hard yards in his youth: stand-up in dingy pubs, writing for any infernal little publication that would pay and taking any job going to get to where he was now. His success had been earned honestly.

Today, he was particularly impressed with himself. Never in the entire history of his varied fifteen-year career as a writer, comedian, broadcaster, scriptwriter and columnist had he ever submitted work *before* a deadline. Incredible and, above all, improbable, which is exactly what his editor Ross would say when he received Ben's email.

To make matters even more unbelievable, it was before ten in the morning and Ben was awake and out of bed and had been since seven. He'd even managed to get in his daily hour-long swim before sitting down to work. He thought about calling a few of his friends in London to share this momentous achievement, then remembered the seven-hour time difference. *That* made him want to call them even more, but he decided against it at the last minute. As much as they'd all given him hell about his late nights and later mornings over the years, he was feeling far too damn peppy to be vindictive. In fact, he was in a better mood than he had been for months – and he knew the cause.

It appeared he had acquired a muse. An unlikely one with an abominably quirky sense of style and a penchant for holding razors to men's throats, but a muse nonetheless.

Rain gurgled through the rusty gutters of Amy's little Fremantle home, pitter patting on her bedroom window. Normally she loved the rain; it reminded her of the nights in her early childhood when she'd cuddled up on the bottom bunk with Jo in the postage stamp-sized bedroom they'd shared, safe in the knowledge that their dad wouldn't drive to the pub in bad weather. Amy had always slept the best those nights.

By rights she should be sleeping now, but something was stopping her. Well, not something – *someone*. Try as she might, she hadn't been able to get Ben last-name-still-unknown's dinner invitation out of her head. More to the point, she couldn't figure out *why* he'd invited her in the first place.

The man was good looking, rich, educated and, if Scott's reaction was anything to go by, famous. For the life of her she couldn't work out what his deal was. She'd analysed every second of his visit to Babyface time and time again and still couldn't come up with an answer, and that left her feeling wary.

She knew she was attracted to him, in the way that humans look at tigers and think they're cute until they get their heads bitten off, but what did attraction mean? If her past experience with men had taught her anything, it was that if they looked too good to be true, they were either married, gay or a total bastard. Her first experience having a boyfriend had been a nightmare. Since then, other than Tom Draper her no-show date, Amy had made a point of always sticking to the non-threatening variety of man: men who needed her more than she needed them, who couldn't harm her emotionally or physically.

That thought led her to the other source of her insomnia, her first disastrous boyfriend, Liam. It was the third week of the month, which meant that he would be home on his monthly rotation from the oil rigs up north. He'd no doubt visit the salon and try his best to scare the pants off her. He'd been doing it since she'd left him almost a decade ago, and it didn't look like he was going to stop any time soon.

Liam hadn't laid a hand on her since she was eighteen, but that didn't stop him from regularly making her life miserable. Usually, he just came to the barbershop and tried to intimidate her. Sometimes, he slipped abusive letters under her front door. The problem was that they both knew Amy couldn't, or more to the point wouldn't, do anything about it. If she went to the police and reported him, Jo might find out and that was unacceptable: in the early days, Liam had threatened to get Jo fired by spreading a couple of malicious rumours if Amy said anything. At the time, Liam had been Jo's boss and Amy had fully believed he'd do it.

Years later, Amy knew she'd been naive.

Jo had frequently complained about how much men on the rigs

gossiped and Amy knew that any rumour Liam could have spread would have been ignored. She hadn't known that at eighteen. At the time, she'd been worried about her sister's career and, much more importantly, her feelings. Jo had introduced Amy to Liam, thinking he was the antithesis of their dad, a good man who'd look after her, treat her well and keep an eye on her while Jo looked for a higher paying international oil and gas job. Amy had gone along with it because she'd watched Jo protect her for years, taking hits from their dad when they were younger, worrying about how to make everything work financially and emotionally after they'd run away from home. In Amy's mind it had been her way of giving Jo peace of mind, of giving her something back and setting her free to take her career to the next level.

Having to tell Jo she'd ended the relationship hurt Amy almost as much as it hurt Jo, but it was Jo's reaction that broke Amy's heart. Jo had been so upset, couldn't understand what had gone wrong, so she'd confronted Amy. The year of silence that resulted between them was easier to Amy's mind than telling her sister the truth about Liam. They'd only made up after Scott locked them in a room and refused to let them out until they'd formed a truce, with the tacit understanding that Amy's love life was well and truly off-limits in the future.

Jo would be devastated if she discovered that she'd pushed Amy into an abusive relationship, never mind the guilt she'd feel over that awful fight they'd had. There was no way Amy would put her sister through that, even today, especially not when Jo had physically put herself on the line so many times in the past to protect Amy, even getting shot last year in what had been the beginning of the end as far as Amy and Jo's relationship with their parents was concerned. Just the memory of what had happened was still horrible.

Jo had been visiting their mum, trying to convince her to leave their dad. Their mum had chosen to stay and Jo had taken a bullet to her thigh when leaving.

It had still taken a little while for the reality of what had happened to sink in, for Amy and Jo to realise that their relationship with their parents couldn't go on.

Amy had been devastated. The pain still hadn't left her and probably never would but it was preferable to what had been before; Jo always trying to protect her from their dad's violent outbursts.

The last thing Amy wanted was to see the worried look from their early years back in Jo's eyes and know she'd put it there. Anything was better than that.

Amy groaned in frustration, pounded her pillow into shape and closed her eyes again, but the neon-pink light from her Hello Kitty alarm clock burned through her eyelids.

It was no use. Might as well get up.

She threw herself out of bed and padded into the kitchen to make herself a cup of tea. The ritual of measuring tea leaves and boiling water calmed her down, as did the sight of the rain beating against her dark kitchen window. She contemplated doing some of the ironing that had been piling up over the week but decided against it. Her wardrobe was high maintenance, but she didn't mind. Her clothes were so much a part of the persona she'd created more than ten years before, she couldn't imagine not taking painstaking care to maintain them. Four in the morning, however, was not the time for ironing.

Once her tea was brewed, she arranged everything on a tray, added a few chocolate chip biscuits for comfort and wandered into her living room. Minutes later her favourite movie was playing on her ancient, boxy TV and she was curled up on her battered lounge with a purple crocheted afghan pulled around her shoulders. She'd forgotten to retrieve her glasses from her bedside, but it didn't matter. She knew every scene, every piece of dialogue and every song in the film by heart.

As Tony Curtis and Marilyn Monroe played their comical game of cat and mouse in *Some Like It Hot*, she felt her body relaxing and eyes getting heavy. It wasn't until halfway through the film that Marilyn's breathy voice and the beating rain worked their magic, and Amy drifted off to sleep.

By lunchtime on Saturday, Amy's feet were aching, her head was pounding and she was milliseconds away from closing up shop and going home. Roslynn had called in sick and almost every man in Perth had decided that today was the day he absolutely needed a shave and a haircut.

Thankfully, Amy's best friend, Myf, had raced to the rescue when Amy called, or more to the point howled, down the phone. While Amy was in the barbershop, Myf was helping Kate and Marissa by doing all the small, time-consuming tasks: blow drying hair, applying colour, buffing nails and, above all, keeping everyone sane.

Now, at five minutes past five, the end was in sight. When the bell rang signalling a customer in the barbershop, Amy added a dollop of cream to the coffee she'd just poured and sat it next to a generous slice of cake. Placing both on a tray, she nudged the connecting door between salon and barbershop open with her hip.

'You're late, young man. I was expecting you five minutes ago,' she chirped, fully expecting to be greeted by the smiling countenance of Terry Nelson, one of her favourite customers. He was a retired judge and visited every Saturday without fail to get his beard trimmed before his weekly dinner date with Maureen, his wife of forty-three years.

'This is a first. It's about time you were happy to see me.'

Amy almost dropped the tray at the sound of her ex-boyfriend's too-smooth voice. *Please, God, not today of all days.* She closed her eyes and sent up a silent prayer, but no one was listening. When she opened them again Liam was still there, bullish and menacing as he sprawled in the chair nearest her. His legs were splayed arrogantly apart, his heavily muscled arms resting on the arms of the chair, and there was a smug smile on the broad features she'd once considered handsome.

'Liam.' Her gut clenched painfully. 'I thought you were someone else.'

'Yeah?'

'Yeah. I've got a client coming then I'm closing for the day, so you're gonna have to leave.' She brandished the tray in front of her like a shield and prayed he wasn't going to be difficult. Not today. She was tired, she had a stress headache and she was fighting a colossal case of the willies about her date this evening with Ben, or more to the point, what she'd do and say if he actually showed up.

Liam looked around and shrugged a beefy shoulder. 'Your client's not here yet. You've got time for me. Besides, with that extra bit of weight you're carrying, you're lookin' good. How've you been, Amy?'

Just the mention of her name on his lips left her shuddering. 'Fine until you turned up.' She tried to keep her voice level. 'Look, I've told you before that you can't come here any more. Leave me alone, Liam. It was over years ago. It's over now. Please leave.'

She might as well have been talking to thin air. Other than a faint wrinkle on his brow, Liam's smug expression didn't change a bit. 'Nah. I'm a paying customer who wants a shave, so why don't you put that tray down and give me one?' It said a lot about the man that he didn't once think she'd slip with the razor.

'You know that's not gonna happen. Just leave. Please. My customer's here. You need to go.' She nodded towards Terry Nelson's white Jaguar, which had just pulled up at the kerb out front. Maybe God had been listening after all, she thought, ignoring the combined relief and apprehension currently causing her hands to shake.

Liam's expression turned stubborn. 'What's he here for? I'll wait.'

'A shave, and no, you can't wait. I told you, I'm closing up shop after. Just go,' Amy said, the faint plea in her tone making her furious with herself.

'What's in it for me?' Liam demanded.

Amy's words were cut off when Terry opened the shop door, ducking his head as he came through and calling out his usual greeting in cheerful, booming tones. 'Hello young lady, do you have time for me?'

'Liam,' Amy said softly.

'Am I interrupting?' Terry's sharp gaze took in the scene and his bushy salt and pepper brows beetled.

'No, Terry. I've got your cake and coffee here,' Amy said with forced cheer, feeling her knees wobble with relief when Liam stood up.

'She's all yours, mate. I just dropped in for a chat. She's a piece of work, isn't she?' His proprietorial expression made Amy's skin feel one size too small.

'The very best,' Terry replied warmly.

'Bye, Liam.' Amy suppressed a flinch when he brushed past her, his eyes clearly communicating that he knew full well she wouldn't make a scene in front of a client.

Nodding to Terry, he fished his keys out of his pocket and jangled them as he sauntered out the door, leaving the scent of cheap aftershave hanging in the air like a bad memory.

Aware of Terry's quietly watchful presence, Amy stomped the adrenaline coursing through her system into submission and refreshed her smile. 'So where are you whisking your lovely wife off to this evening?'

Amy only allowed her professional face to slip twenty minutes later as she waved Terry off. Giving in to the tension wracking her body, she gripped the back of the barber's chair and squeezed her eyes tightly shut as the sick feeling left over from being in Liam's presence crawled through her system on a thousand scurrying legs.

'Amy?' Myf's soft call came from the salon next door.

'Coming, m'love.' Amy opened her eyes, taking stock of her

appearance in the mirror. She grimaced. During the past few hours her lipstick had faded and the curls in her hair had begun to fall as flat as she felt. She'd have to fix those and soon. Ben was due in under thirty minutes – if he was the punctual type.

She took one last look around the barbershop to make sure everything was ready for Monday morning before making her way next door. The rest of her staff had gone for the day, leaving Myf curled up in one of the beauty salon's pink leather chairs reading a *Marie Claire*.

As always, Myf projected a lovely aura of serene confidence and acceptance that enveloped Amy the minute she walked into the room, making everything seem just that little bit more manageable.

In direct contrast to Amy's polished appearance, Myf radiated earth mother chic in recycled clothing splendour. Her wild fro of tight marmalade curls framed her narrow features and, as usual, she wasn't wearing any make-up. She didn't need to. Myf was perfect as she was, with her abundance of freckles, dark cinnamon brows and eyelashes, and incredible almost-black eyes.

'Hey.'

'Hey sweetie. You want a coffee? Or are you still doing that vegan detox thing?' Amy tottered on tired feet to the back of the salon to make a cappuccino. She was tempted to tell Myf about Liam's visit but held off. She had never told anyone about Liam's ongoing harassment. If she was honest, her silence wasn't only because of her fears Jo would find out; she was also deeply ashamed to admit she had effectively allowed someone to stalk and bully her for so many years. Myf would never judge her for it, but just the thought of speaking the words out loud made Amy's chest hurt.

'Coffee would be great,' Myf replied, oblivious to Amy's internal disquiet. 'All the detox did was make me crave chocolate.'

'I've got some of that here too. You want that instead?' Amy replied over the noise of frothing milk.

'Temptress.' Myf grinned. 'No, I think coffee is better after all the craziness this afternoon. I need the boost. Is it always this full-on nowadays?' She gestured to the shop. 'This is insane. When do you get time to centre yourself?'

'Worse and never.' Amy topped two cappuccinos with chocolate sprinkles, adding extra to Myf's.

'Really? You don't look like you're enjoying it as much as you used to. This is the third time Mel's quit on you. Have you thought of not taking her back?' Myf asked quietly, taking her coffee and drawing her finger through the froth and sprinkles before popping it into her mouth.

Amy just shrugged and took a seat next to her friend, giving her an apologetic half-smile. 'It's not that easy, petal. She's a good friend. You know why she does it.' She reached down and pulled her heels off, massaging her toes.

'And you tell me *I'm* too nice.' The words came as a kind rebuke.

'You are. You're here, aren't you? What did you sell your last painting for? Ten thousand?' Amy couldn't help but notice that her friend's bare arms and legs were generously covered with tiny specks of purple and green paint that blended in with her freckles. It made her smile. Myf was an artist, a highly successful one, whose explosive, violently dynamic canvases were a total enigma to everyone who knew her.

Myf waved a hand. 'Not important. What's important is the way you keep forgiving people when they do crappy things. You're going to have to draw the line some time.'

Amy sighed. 'I know, but you know what it's like. My friends are my family. Mel's family. I'm only doing what she'd do for me, right?'

Myf didn't look as sure. 'It doesn't work like that for some people, love. And you know better than anyone that sometimes you've got to let family go . . .'

Amy felt herself tearing up. She'd let go of so much in her life, she didn't want to think of giving up another person she cared about. 'Can we change the topic, sweetie?'

A flash of frustration crossed Myf's features but she hid it beautifully. 'Okay . . . so what are you wearing tonight? I take it you want me to stick around and check this guy out?'

'Of course. You're my bastard detector. I've got my blue party dress out the back.' Amy spun her chair around and leaned towards a mirror. How had Ben seen her scar on Monday? The man must have telescopic vision. 'He said wear anything, so I was tempted to wear jeans and a T-shirt.' They both knew it was a lie. Amy's appearance was her armour, and she never went anywhere without making sure she was fully suited up.

Myf chuckled. It was a warm sound, one that never failed to make people smile.

'What?' Amy demanded.

'You.'

'Me what? Look, m'love, if you're going to laugh, the least you can do is tell me the joke.' She swivelled her chair back around and prodded Myf with her big toe.

'There's no joke.' Myf tucked her knees up under her chin. 'You look lovely as is, but if you're going to change you'd better start. It's getting on.'

Amy glanced at the clock on the wall. 'It is too. Far out! Time to frock up.' She took a quick sip of her coffee then scampered behind the screen at the rear of the room to change.

'So where's this mystery man taking you?' Myf called out while Amy quickly got naked, put on clean underwear, slid on her stockings and stepped into her dress.

'No idea. Hopefully somewhere not too expensive. My credit card can't handle it. Give me a hand with my zip, petal?'

'Coming. Why are you worried? He's the one paying.' Myf

walked around the screen and zipped Amy the rest of the way up before stepping back and nodding her approval. 'I love this dress.'

'It doesn't make me look fat?' Amy looked anxiously down to her stomach. Liam's earlier snipe about her weight slithered insidiously into her thoughts. She'd always had a little tummy but had never thought it looked bad.

'Fat? No!' Myf bent down to brush the hem of Amy's skirt straight for her. 'It makes you look like a young Doris Day. Want help with your hair?'

'No, but you can keep me company.' Amy lightly rested a hand on Myf's shoulder as she slipped on her shoes.

'That I can do. So what's this about your credit card?' Myf asked, not willing to let the topic go. She padded after Amy to the front of the salon and resumed her seat while Amy heated up a curling wand.

Amy shrugged. 'It's nothing. Usually when I go on a date I pay. I'm used to it.'

'Seriously?'

'Yeah. I don't like being . . . you know . . .'

'No, I really don't.'

Amy waved a hand. 'Obligated. Food equals sex and I don't want to feel like I have to have sex with a guy because he's paid for dinner. It's easier if I pay.'

'Tell me you don't pay for their food too?' Myf asked, her eyes dark with concern.

Amy frowned at her reflection in the mirror, winding pale lengths of hair around her curling iron. 'Yeah. Why wouldn't I?' She reached for the hairspray. 'I mean, it just feels better that way. I don't have to worry about anything then.'

'Would you feel guilty or beholden if I took you out to dinner?' Myf asked gently.

'No, that's different.' Amy searched for some bobby pins in her work trolley.

'How?'

'I don't know, it's just different. You don't expect anything. You're my friend.'

'I bet you let Scott pay for your dinner,' Myf persisted. She and Scott were good friends and had held a number of exhibitions of their respective work together. Both women knew full well Scott would be mortally offended if any woman he'd asked out tried to pay for his meal.

'He's different,' Amy insisted. 'Can you see my bobby pins?'

'Different? Like not a man?' Myf asked, spluttering on her coffee in a burst of incredulous laughter. 'Have you *looked* at Scott any time recently? They're just here.'

'Thanks. Scott's not the same.'

'I'll make sure I tell him that next time I see him,' Myf said. 'I'll make sure I've got a camera with me to catch his expression while I'm at it.'

Amy opened her mouth to reply then thought better of it. Instead she popped a few pins in her mouth and began securing her hair back from her face.

'Amy?'

'Hmm? Look, I want to drop the topic, okay?'

'It's officially dropped. Does your gentleman drive something that looks like silver sex on wheels?'

'Yeah. It's an Aston Martin I think.' Bobby pins sprayed everywhere when she realised what Myf was saying. 'Oh bugger. Is he here?'

'If he's a sexy, built guy in a suit, I'd say yes.'

Amy followed Myf's gaze to Ben, who was prowling around his car to approach the door. He was early! 'Bugger! Can you stall him? I really have to pee and I haven't fixed my make-up yet. Keep him busy for a second or two, please?' She frantically scooped up her

make-up bag and sprinted as fast as she could to the bathroom at
the back of the salon.

'Sure,' Myf said in a laughter-filled voice as the bathroom door
slammed shut.

Ben pulled up outside Babyface, experiencing an unfamiliar sense of
anticipation. Checking through the barbershop window and seeing
it was empty, he pushed open the door of the salon next door.

The first thing that struck him was the scent he'd noticed on his
first visit. It was stronger this side. A combination of chocolate cake
and vanilla, mixed with the various faintly floral, ammonia and
acetone smells characteristic of the female beauty industry. The second thing he noticed was the décor, which managed to be blatantly
contrived, yet comfortable at the same time.

The pale pink walls contrasted with the white enamel skirt-
ing boards, shelves and window frames. The wall closest to him
featured a giant poster promoting the movie *Gentlemen Prefer
Blondes*, with Marilyn Monroe and Jane Russell displaying
maximum leg; the opposite wall held three ornate gilt mirrors
arranged a metre or so apart. Each mirror had a plush rose-pink
leather chair facing it. The back of the room was sectioned off with
a white screen featuring large polka dots.

The overall effect should have been cloying but it wasn't; it
conveyed the same level of welcome and comfort as the barbershop.
In fact, the only thing that *wasn't* comforting was the distinct absence
of the proprietor. Instead, he was greeted by a whippet-thin redhead
wearing the ugliest green dress Ben had ever seen. She was curled up
in one of the chairs, looking him up and down with a bemused smile.

'Anyone home?' He clasped his hands behind his back and wandered down to the back of the shop to inspect the area behind the
screen, which contained a small room, ostensibly for those beauty

treatments not fit for company, a small kitchen and another door, which was currently closed.

'I am. Amy will be back in a few seconds,' the redhead announced in a low, surprisingly strong voice. She had a more clipped, refined Australian accent than Amy's. It spoke of money, and lots of it, somewhere in the family tree. 'I'm Myf.'

'Myf?' Ben raised a brow.

'Short for Myfanwy. Before you ask, Mum's Welsh. I'm Amy's friend. You're Ben, right?' Her gaze was steady and Ben got the distinct impression his every movement was being thoroughly judged. Interesting.

'The man himself. Do you work here?' Ben examined a row of nail polishes mounted on a narrow white shelf set above a spindle-legged table with two chairs either side. He wondered why any woman would want pea-soup-green nails.

'Only as backup. Normally I'm an artist and yoga teacher, but both are too much fun to call jobs.' Myf gave him such a warm smile that Ben found himself wandering over and parking himself in the chair next to hers.

'An artist? Are we talking empty white rooms with used under-wear scattered around, great steaming piles of excrement turned into sculpture, or the more palatable stuff you hang on walls?' He propped an elbow on the arm of his chair and spun it around to face her.

Myf laughed. It was a warm, welcome sound. 'I do the wall stuff. I haven't advanced to any installation work yet.'

'Perish the thought.' Ben feigned a shudder.

'Ben?' Amy's voice was faintly muffled, coming from behind the mystery door at the back of the salon.

'At your service.'

'Just give me a few seconds.' There was the sound of something heavy thumping a wall and a muffled 'Oomph.'

'You alright, love?' Myf called out.

'I'm okay. Just give me a sec. I'm sorry, Ben. I'm running a bit late.'

'No problem at all. I'll just entertain myself out here with Myf and some of your quality educational reading material.' Ben winked at Myf before perusing a nearby shelf and selecting a magazine that advertised *Sex Tips to Send Your Man Wild*.

'Quality?' Myf let out a low chuckle.

'Of course,' Ben murmured. He flicked past countless outlandish advertisements for shoes, perfume and, if he wasn't mistaken, anorexia, until he found what was he was looking for.

'For example,' he said loud enough for Amy to hear. 'Did you know, and I have to tell you I didn't, that men like having toothpaste rubbed on their privates? Now this is definitely news to me. According to this article—' His words were stopped mid-sentence by Amy's shriek from the back of the salon.

'What!'

'Don't shoot the messenger. I'm just reading out loud.'

'Where are you taking her to dinner?' Myf asked in a low voice, leaning towards him, her eyes sparkling.

'I was thinking Christie's on the Beach in Cottesloe,' he whispered back. 'Good choice?' He raised his brows before saying much louder, 'Oh, no, *no*. I can't say I agree with this. It sounds horrifically painful.'

'What? Excuse me?' There was another thump. 'Oh damn.'

'Perfect choice.' Myf grinned. 'She'll love it. You're paying.'

'Excellent, and of course, worked my fingers to the bone to come up with the cash,' Ben replied, just as the mystery door behind the screen opened and he heard the clicking of heels. Enjoying himself, he deliberately kept his eyes on the magazine as he turned the page to be confronted with some rather fascinating illustrations of sexual positions the magazine promised would send one's man insane with lust. He snorted at the first improbable contortion and inhaled the scent of apples and bubblegum. 'Now this *is* fascinating.

I've never tried this one. I've always worried I'd damage a vital piece of equipment.' He tapped the page pointedly.

The magazine was ripped from his hands with a crackle of glossy paper and he looked up, fully intending on making a joke but simply stared instead.

The kewpie doll had curves – curves wrapped up in an impossibly cute blue and white pinstriped dress in a style last seen on a screaming teenager at an early Elvis concert. It curved down from a high boat-neck collar and capped sleeves to a tiny waist cinched with a dark blue ribbon tied in a bow before flaring out to a full circle skirt that fell just below the knee. Ben couldn't be sure from the front, but he was almost positive she was wearing French stockings. Her dark blue patent leather Mary Janes instantly kickstarted a few naughty schoolgirl fantasies he hadn't visited for a number of years.

'You look . . . fascinating.' He was aware that it might not be the most appropriate of compliments.

'Gee, thanks. You look nice too,' Amy replied pertly.

Ben was aware of Myf next to him, hiding a smile behind her coffee cup.

'Thank you, I do try, although I can't possibly compare . . .' He looked Amy's ensemble up and down again, resting finally on the loose curls framing her face. She was wearing fuchsia lipstick, the same colour she'd worn when he'd visited the barbershop on Monday. He was developing a penchant for fuchsia. 'For starters, I look hideous in blue and dresses have never suited me.' He was gratified to see a dimple appear in her cheek. Satisfied, he pushed himself to his feet. 'Shall we?'

'Yeah, sure,' Amy said, then turned to her friend. 'Are you alright locking up with your key, petal?'

'Not a problem.' Myf pushed to her feet and held out a hand to Ben. 'Nice meeting you, Ben.'

He took her hand in his and clasped it warmly. He liked this woman. She knew how to play along. 'The pleasure was mine. I look forward to viewing your work.' He turned back to Amy and gestured to the door with a flourish. 'Madam, your chariot awaits.'

'Are you comfortable? Impressed? Overawed? You're supposed to be.' Ben wore a devilish smile as he slid into the black leather driver's seat, buckled up and smoothly pulled out into evening peak hour traffic. The car purred with restraint. Amy had the feeling it would truly roar if he allowed it. Not that she was in any state of mind to contemplate the fact. Right now she was doing her best not to touch anything.

'I wouldn't say impressed so much as scared to death. This car probably cost more than my house.' She gingerly leaned down to make sure her heels weren't digging holes in the carpet at her feet.

'It's alright.' Ben shrugged. 'Gets me from A to B.' A faint smile played around his mouth.

'You're kidding, right?' Amy decided that she couldn't do much damage if she stayed very, very still.

'Never. And just in case you were wondering, I won't let you drive it even if you offer me exotic sexual favours designed to make my hair stand on end.' He said the words so casually that it took a few seconds for them to register.

'Excuse me?'

'You're excused. Just so you know, I've made reservations for Christie's on the Beach. You've heard of it? Yes? No? I hear it's good.'

'Christie's. Wow. Um. Okay. You don't have to take me there. We can go somewhere . . . more casual if you like.' She stopped herself from saying 'cheaper' just in time.

'When I'm looking so debonair? No. Definitely not. I'm told the view is excellent. Not that I'll be looking at it that much.' He slid her an appreciative sideways glance.

'The view is nice,' Amy said wistfully, ignoring the compliment. She loved the beach.

'Mind you,' Ben mused, 'places with a good location usually have dire food. London's atrocious for it. Many's the time I've gone to a restaurant in an excellent location expecting it to be amazing and . . .' He made a raspberry noise, comically out of character to his polished appearance. 'Shit.'

'Serious?' Amy laughed despite her worries. 'I've never been to London so I wouldn't know.'

'Oh?' Ben darted her a look that told her she might as well have admitted she had two heads. 'Well, that's probably wise of you. Hideous place. Crowded, overpriced and full of Australians. A bit like here really.'

'You don't like Australians?' Amy leaned against the door, regarding him with narrowed eyes.

'Oh, I like you all just fine. As long as you don't talk much.' He grinned when she snorted.

'You mustn't mind us that much if you're staying here.'

'I don't. I love this city. It's winter now and it's raining less than it does in the summer back home.' Ben turned off towards Cottesloe and they began driving along the ocean, huge mansions on one side, an endless expanse of sea and a vivid red sunset on the other.

'How long have you been here in Perth?'

Ben shrugged. 'A few months. My house is near here actually.'

Amy turned to study the mansions they were driving past. Cottesloe was a notoriously affluent suburb. Damn. She was definitely out of her depth and taking on water.

'You're quiet. I get the impression you're not often quiet.' Ben's clipped words cut through her panic, bringing her back to earth.

'What? No. I'm just blown away by the sheer sexiness of your car.'

'Oh?' Ben chuckled. 'Well, that's understandable. Embrace the shock and awe while I find us a parking place.'

Amy ran a finger over some polished walnut panelling. 'Do you do this often?'

'What?'

'Ask ladies you've offended out to dinner.'

His eyes crinkled at the corners as he pulled into an empty space. 'Offended? Not frequently, no. Usually they're far too busy consulting with their lawyers. I can honestly say you're my first dinner date offendee. Or at least the first one to accept an invitation. In fact, I do believe you should feel honoured.'

Amy pursed her lips, fighting a smile. 'Should I? Are you going to be nice tonight?'

He turned the engine off. 'Of course not. That wouldn't be in the spirit of the thing at all. Although I *do* owe you, so we might be able to bend the rules.'

'You owe me?' Amy's eyebrows almost hit her hairline.

'Yes. You inspired me. As a result I've been amazingly productive.'

'At being a dentist, you mean?'

'What else? I pulled out millions of teeth. Productive teeth. Fantastic teeth.' His white, toothy grin flashed in the dusky half-light. 'How was your day playing the female Sweeney Todd?'

'Busy. Exhausting,' Amy answered honestly and gazed over Ben's shoulder. The car park faced the ocean and was full of surfers stripping off their wetsuits and getting changed after catching some waves.

'Oh?' Ben regarded her with a faint frown. 'Tell me about it. Or better yet, don't. Wait and we'll have a little bit of social lubrication first so I can fully enjoy all the gory details. I'm all ears. And teeth.'

'Seriously?'

'Never more so. I have lots of teeth.' He shrugged. 'Pointy ones. But you might be a little more interesting.'

Amy laughed, giving in and deciding to enjoy herself. She'd find a way to resuscitate her credit card later. 'Alright, then. Lead the way.'

Chapter 4

'YOU KNOW, I think any man who isn't an Olympic athlete or a lifeguard should be banned from wearing those. They're an abomination.'

Amy followed Ben's gaze out the restaurant window, taking a moment to focus. The fading red sunset over the sea and white sand of Cottesloe Beach was spectacular tonight. She chuckled when she saw the object of his criticism, an intrepid senior citizen walking towards the water wearing a pair of faded red Speedos that left nothing to the imagination. Not that there was much to see, given how cold it was outside.

'What? You mean you don't have a pair?'

'Perish the thought.'

Amy grinned and reached for a wonderfully warm bread roll, slathering it with butter. 'You know what they call Speedos here?'

'No. Do tell?' Ben raised an eyebrow.

'Budgie smugglers.'

'What?' Ben guffawed. 'Budgie smugglers? As in a small parakeet?'

'Something like that,' Amy replied. 'And I've got some friends from Sydney who call them banana hammocks.'

'Banana hammocks,' Ben mused. 'Disturbing.' He feigned a shudder. 'If this conversation goes any further I'm going to need alcohol. Care to choose?' To Amy's complete surprise, he pushed the wine list towards her.

She internally grimaced. Her tried-and-tested technique in choosing wine was usually to order the second cheapest bottle on the menu. 'You know, it's probably better you pick. I'm pretty clueless about wine, which is a bit silly since I grew up on a winery.'

'A winery? You become more and more interesting.' Ben tilted his head to the side, studying her features in the soft light cast by the lone candle at their table.

'Yeah. I do.' Amy couldn't help a cheeky grin.

Ben waved a waitress over and ordered an Abbey Vale Chardonnay before turning back to Amy.

'Which winery and where?'

'Evangeline's Rest. It's only a short distance from Abbey Vale, actually,' Amy supplied. 'I don't know if you've heard of it.'

'I have.' Ben raised his eyebrows. 'Does your family own it?'

'Funny you should mention that.' Amy took a bite out of her bread roll. 'My sister is now engaged to a member of the family that owns it, but when we were kids my dad just worked there, so we lived on the property.'

'Oh? You don't look like any country lass I've ever met. Not enough beefy muscles, and I checked – your knuckles don't drag on the ground.'

Amy eyed off the basket of bread rolls, wondering what one would look like when it connected to the side of his head. 'You better behave, or I'm gonna be clumsy the next time you come in for a shave.'

'Ah.' Ben's lips curved into a satisfied grin. 'So you want my repeat business. I'm growing on you, aren't I? Admit it.'

'Maybe. Like a fungus.' Amy screwed up her nose. She opened her menu, saw the prices and experienced genuine heart palpitations.

'Fungus, eh? Well, I've always thought mushrooms were one of the tastiest foods in existence. Think of me as a rare truffle.' Ben perused his own menu, then glanced up. 'Although we can't all be truffle lovers. You look concerned. Nothing on the menu to suit your tastes? You have an explosive allergy to seafood?' In an unexpected gesture, he leaned forward and placed his hand over hers to gain her attention.

Amy's whole body felt electric as an unexpected jolt of pure lust hit her in the sternum. Inhaling sharply, she lost herself in the feeling for a few delicious seconds before drawing her hand away.

He cocked an eyebrow. 'Or maybe it's my company you're allergic to?'

'No! Everything's . . . fine. Marvellous.'

'Well, it's nice to know you think my company is marvellous, but we're talking about the menu.'

Amy let out an involuntary chuckle just as the waiter appeared with the wine. 'The menu's fine. *You're* a pest.'

Appearing faintly irritated at the intrusion, Ben didn't bother going through the usual glass-swirling, cork-sniffing ritual that went with wine in a high-end restaurant. Instead, he tasted it impatiently, nodded, then turned back to Amy. 'It's not vinegar.'

'Good to know,' she said, thanking the waiter and taking a sip. It certainly wasn't vinegar. Wow. Yum. She took another bigger sip, feeling the wine hit her empty stomach, untangling the giant knot of nerves there.

The still hovering waiter asked if they were ready to order and Ben gave Amy an enquiring look.

She longingly looked over the mouth-watering selection of seafood dishes on the menu before turning the page and locating the salad, thinking it would be the less financially crippling option.

'Give us a moment.' Ben politely gestured the waiter away and then narrowed his eyes. 'You know, speaking of allergies earlier, I have one I should probably tell you about.'

'Hmm?' Amy looked at him, still distracted by the restaurant's idea of a reasonable price for a bit of lettuce tossed in olive oil.

Ben winced, his features screwing up comically. 'Salad. I'm afraid if I see nothing but salad on a lady's plate I get this twitch and experience the overwhelming urge to force-feed her red meat. You aren't a vegetarian, are you? No? I hear the seafood here is fantastic.'

'It looks it.' Amy drew a bracing breath. 'The grilled snapper *does* look wonderful.'

'It does at that.'

'Mind you, I *am* feeling stubborn.' Amy pursed her lips. 'It sounded like you were just telling me what I could and couldn't eat.'

Ben sighed. 'No. Well, actually, yes but only to make sure you order something you'll enjoy. It's incredibly boring to see someone martyr themselves when there's good food on offer. Have I offended you?'

Amy feigned her best offended expression. 'Horribly.'

Ben smacked his forehead. 'Damn. Well, would it help if I just made a blanket apology for the entire evening? I'm probably going to offend you at least another twenty times before dessert and I can't even imagine what ridiculously stupid thing is going to come out of my mouth when I awkwardly suggest you come back to my place for sex later. I assure you that it will be hideously insulting. I apologise wholeheartedly in advance.'

Amy slammed a hand over her mouth to muffle her surprised peal of laughter but was still loud enough that diners at surrounding tables paused in their conversations to see what all the fuss was about.

'Does this mean you forgive me in advance?'

'Maybe.' Her lips twitched as she tried to hold back more laughter. 'Alright.'

'Good.' Ben leaned back in his chair, idly swirling his wine around the glass. 'Because now you've given me licence to misbehave later.'

Amy raised her brows. 'Who says I won't be the one misbehaving?'

'Oh? I hadn't thought of that. Well, I'm a generally magnanimous kind of guy. Give it your best shot and I'll try my utmost to forgive you.' Ben held her gaze for what seemed like hours, his smile slowly transforming into something more serious.

She turned her head and looked back out over the night-darkened sea. 'You never did tell me what you do.'

'No, I didn't. We'll come to that.' He paused as the waiter returned. 'Did you decide what you wanted to order? The salad? No? Oh good. I'll have the steak.'

Two hours and another half a bottle of wine later, Amy still had no idea what Ben did for a living, but that didn't seem so important any more.

'I'm not going to be able to walk out of here after that chocolate mousse,' she groaned, discreetly rubbing her tummy while blotting her mouth with her napkin.

'Don't worry. I'm sure they have a device for extracting over-fed customers at closing time. What do you think it's called?' Ben lounged back in his chair, looking effortlessly handsome and just a little bit predatory.

'A wheelbarrow?'

'Hmm, no.' He feigned thoughtfulness. 'It probably *would* be a wheelbarrow, but you're obviously not well versed enough with the tricks of marketing. It would have to have an attractive name. We're effectively talking about glutton extraction here.'

'Are you calling me a glutton?' Amy asked incredulously.

'You've forgiven me for all offence this evening, remember?

And no. Of course not. Perish the thought. A more effective way of removing you would be if I came around the table, threw you over my shoulder and carried you out of here. It would be incredibly manly. You'd be impressed.' He grinned.

'Or vomiting down the back of your suit.'

'There is that. No. Wheelbarrow it is.' Ben sighed. 'Shall we go?' He gestured to a passing waiter and requested the bill before turning back to find Amy rifling in her handbag.

'Everything alright?'

'Yes. Fine.' Amy found her purse.

Ben's eyes narrowed. 'Are you sure because, correct me if I'm wrong, you're brandishing that like you intend to pay.'

Amy shrugged, forcing a cheerful smile. 'Um, yeah. I don't mind. I've really enjoyed myself. Dinner was lovely.'

'So have I, and to keep it that way I'd suggest you put your money away.' Although he still wore a contented feline smile, Ben's tone conveyed obvious displeasure.

'Are you sure?' Amy bit her lip as he withdrew a wad of notes from his wallet and left it on the table, enough for the dinner and a generous tip.

'I'll pretend I didn't hear that. Otherwise I'd be mortally offended.'

Amy grimaced. Damn. Why hadn't she listened to Myf earlier? She should have known Ben wouldn't be like the men she'd dated in the past who'd let her pay without blinking. She'd offended him, which was the last thing she wanted to do after having so much fun tonight. Reaching out, she rested a hand on his sleeve. 'Thank you. Dinner was lovely.'

'My most profound pleasure,' he replied, tucking his wallet back in his pocket and then noticing Amy's downcast expression. 'Oh damn. You're not upset, are you?' He looked horrified at the thought. 'This isn't some ludicrous Australian ritual I've failed to grasp, is it?'

'No!'

'Are you sure?'

'Positive,' she insisted.

'Wonderful. Shall we go then?'

'Okay.' Amy heard herself say shyly, feeling a little derailed and not quite sure what was supposed to happen next. Normally she'd suggest going back to her place but right now that didn't seem right. She stood up and Ben placed his hand on the small of her back, proprietarily, scorching through her dress as they left the restaurant.

Ben opened Amy's car door and took advantage of her slightly tipsy state to keep his hands on her as long as possible as she climbed in. Somewhere in the last five minutes the evening had spun a little out of his control and he was at something of a loss. His original plan had been to wine and dine the lady and then end the night with the promise of seeing her again in the near future. He'd changed his mind. He was enjoying himself far too much to want the evening to end, despite the complete curve ball she'd thrown him by trying to pay for dinner. The meaning of Myf's earlier comment should have given him warning; he'd failed to grasp its significance, much to his peril.

His fleeting irritation had dampened Amy's mood and it was evident that he'd have to put in a bit of fancy footwork if he was going to get her somewhere private and see what she was wearing under that dress. How far would she take the look? Was she wearing old-fashioned sexy pin-up underwear too?

The woman was funny, fascinating, complicated, confusing and above all, unexpectedly fucking sexy. Even better, she had no notion of his celebrity. The latter was an incredible turn-on. He never slept with women on the first date, but he was certainly thinking of it now. In the past, he'd always preferred to commit to a short-term relationship at the very least before initiating sex. Not jumping into the sack gave him a chance to determine whether or not he was deal-ing with a raving star-fucker in disguise. Previous recent experience had taught him the perils of falling into that trap.

More importantly, he also liked to get a handle on a lady's likes and dislikes and what gave her pleasure. As far as he was concerned, a mixed bag of sexual tricks was all good and fine but it was just that – mixed, like the assorted sweets he'd bought in copious amounts as a boy. A lady might like the liquorice and chocolate buttons but abso-lutely hate the gummy bears and jelly beans. Better to have a tailored assortment. Funny thing, though, after his conversation with Amy this evening, Ben had a sense that he could spend years trying to figure her out and still wouldn't succeed. She presented a challenge, and a very intriguing one at that. Better than that, she inspired him.

'What are you thinking?' Amy's voice broke through the silence.

'About sweets, actually,' Ben replied honestly. He made a decision. 'I have an idea. It may be a hideous one, so feel free to scream if you don't like it.'

'What is it?'

'Well, the thing is . . . I have this large house not far from here.'

'Hmm?'

'And there's a spectacular thunderstorm raging off the coast if you look that way.' He glanced over and noticed she was smooth-ing her hands up and down her thighs; the movement was bloody distracting and he had to force his eyes back to the road.

'Yeah?'

'How do you feel about coming to my place and watching it with me? I have these monstrously large windows, a very comfortable sofa to sit on and, above all, a very nice body, have you noticed it? I hope so, considering the amount of work I put in to keep looking this good. I'm more than willing to let you snuggle up against me if you get scared of the thunder. You can even take advantage of me if you'd like. That's why you attempted to pay for dinner, wasn't it? So I'd feel obliged to sleep with you?' He checked Amy's expression for her reaction to his words and regretted his bloody fool mouth. Rather than looking amused, or even offended, she looked completely gobsmacked. Those brilliant blue eyes were wide above cheeks flushed with a blush that was visible even in the dull streetlight.

After two minutes of excruciating silence, during which Ben swore she'd rubbed a hole in her dress with the palms of her hands, she finally spoke. 'Okay.'

'Pardon?' It was Ben's turn to be surprised.

'Yes,' Amy said, her voice firmer now.

They pulled in to Ben's driveway five minutes later.

His sprawling white modern-style house was lit up like a beacon welcoming alien invasion, but that was nothing new. Ever since he'd been the brunt of a school initiation prank gone wrong, he'd hated the dark and avoided it whenever possible. Not that he'd ever admit he had an actual phobia or fear; he preferred to think of it as an aversion.

He owed the boys who'd locked him in a closet on his first night at boarding school his entire career. When they'd finally let him out, he'd cracked a joke that had made them laugh and hadn't looked back. Words would become both his best defence and weapon and they'd served him well ever since. Needing the lights on at all times was a small price to pay for the discovery of such a gift.

The illumination came in handy right now because it allowed him to catch every nuance of Amy's reaction to his new home.

Ben had been sold on it the minute his personal assistant, Colin, had sent him photos of this house showcasing its high ceilings, massive windows and open-plan, sunny white rooms seven months ago. The spectacular view over the Indian Ocean had been secondary. Colin had furnished the place with comfortable, contemporary furniture in warm earthy colours, but it had been up to Ben to finish things off with a few selected paintings and pieces he'd arranged to have shipped from London. He had a passion for graffiti artists and contemporary sculpture, and was particularly proud of the massive Banksy canvas hung on a two-storey blank white wall visible from the front door.

He watched as Amy peered up at the twenty-foot entry ceiling with its huge, cast-iron chandelier shaped into a sphere of interconnecting rings; his latest acquisition from an up-and-coming Brazilian artist. The lights twinkling through the gaps between the rings gave the impression that beams of light were being emitted from a slowly imploding star.

'Come in, take off your shoes if you'd like.' He led the way into a spacious open-plan stainless-steel kitchen, while pulling off his jacket and tie. Normally he avoided ties like the plague, but he'd had a feeling Amy would dress up for the occasion and hadn't wanted her to feel out of place.

'Would you like another glass of wine?' He pulled a bottle of Burgundy out of a small rack built into the wall, uncorking it before she could answer.

'A small one,' she replied, still looking around with open curiosity. Her heels clicked over the tiles as she wandered towards the wall of windows in the living room. They afforded a spectacular view over the ink-dark ocean, illuminated every few seconds by jagged flashes of iridescent lighting. Dwarfed by the room and the view beyond, she looked a little like a tiny, sexy Alice in Wonderland.

'Feel free to look around.' He poured the wine into two bulbous glasses. 'Just in case you're wondering, there aren't any torture implements in the cellar. Well, I don't have a cellar, but you get my drift.' He dimmed the lights, then wandered over and took a seat on the tobacco-coloured modular sofa facing the windows and the little blonde in blue.

He set Amy's glass of wine down on the coffee table and studied her profile. She was half facing the view, absently playing with the skirt of her dress while worrying her bottom lip between small white teeth. 'You haven't done this before, have you? Come back to some-one's place on the first date.'

'Nope. I'm not that good at it, either.' She heaved a sigh. It did interesting things to the bodice of her dress.

French knickers.

He hoped she was wearing French knickers and a garter belt. Just the thought alone had him casually crossing one leg over the other to hide the rather obvious effect she had on him.

'If it makes you feel any better, neither have I. Brought a lady home the first date, that is,' Ben replied, savouring a mouthful of wine.

'Really?' She turned to face him. Her eyes were huge.

'Really.'

'Why?'

Ben shrugged leisurely, running his eyes over those schoolgirl shoes, then up curvy little calves delineated by the seam of some seriously sexy stockings. 'I don't know really. I've never had the desire to. Until now. Although, I'm getting the feeling I'm doing it all wrong. You were supposed to be overwhelmed by my charming personality by now. Well . . .' He scratched his chin. 'Either that, or you were supposed to be taking advantage of me.' He raised his brows.

Amy snorted genteelly, then wandered over to the couch and sat down next to him.

Suppressing laughter, Ben looked pointedly at the space between them. 'You know, I do bite. Rather well, actually. I've been complimented on it in fact.'

Amy took the wine he offered her. 'I'm sure you do.'

'Hmm. But now, sadly – and this is going to be rather pathetic – I'm going to have to resort to trying to cop a feel while pretending to watch the view.' Ben theatrically feigned a yawn then stretched his arm out along the back of the sofa so that his hand rested just behind Amy's back. It felt naughty. Like he was a horny teenager trying to get to first base; quite novel in fact. He casually began to play with her hair, marvelling at how soft it was, and waited.

He was rewarded with a double-dimpled smile that unfortunately dimmed a little at the edges when she looked him in the eye.

'Ben?'

'Hmm.'

'I don't know how to do this,' she said in a small voice, nibbling on her lower lip in a completely endearing way.

'Define "this". If you mean just sitting back and relaxing with a glass of wine while I clumsily try to seduce you, I'm sure you'll manage.' He handed her a glass of wine before taking another sip of his own.

'Oh? Thanks.' She downed half of it in one go and Ben stifled a wince at seeing that much expensive plonk guzzled.

'You really are nervous, aren't you?' He moved his hand down to rub her back and shoulders, marvelling at how petite she was.

'Yeah. My boyfriends before always came to my place . . . not that you're my boyfriend yet . . . which is sorta weird. Oh bugger, this is awkward.' She wore such a comically concerned frown that Ben chuckled.

'Hey!'

'Sorry, but you really are being very adorable.' Ben grinned when her frown got more pronounced. 'If it helps, I'd be happy to just sit and enjoy this rather nice bottle of wine with you while watching the view.' It was a blatant lie.

'Really?' A flash of something, disappointment maybe, crossed her features. 'You mean you don't want to . . .'

'Obviously.' Ben looked pointedly down at the distinct pyramid in his trousers. 'But only if you'd like to.' He moved the hand on her back a little higher so that it rubbed the base of her neck. 'I tell you what – and bear with me here – why don't we try something and see if it works?'

'Hmm?' Amy let her head fall back into his touch.

'Why don't you kiss me and if it doesn't work, we'll call it a night?' Ben said solemnly.

'Oh?' Amy's gaze dropped to his mouth. 'Okay.'

'Whenever you're ready. I'm at your complete mercy.' He placed his wine glass on the coffee table, then closed his eyes and puckered his lips, gratified to hear her surprised giggle. 'No?' he asked with his eyes still closed, only to be surprised at the soft touch of Amy's mouth against his and then, unexpectedly, the dart of her tongue running along his bottom lip, tasting like wine and something sweeter. 'Hmm.' He opened his eyes.

'Was that okay?' Amy whispered, her eyes huge.

'Do it again and you'll give me something to compare it to.' Ben used his hand on her neck to urge her towards him. He nibbled leisurely at her bottom lip before darting his tongue out to meet hers. Encouraged by Amy's sharply indrawn breath, he deepened the kiss. She moaned.

'Bloody hell.' He pulled back. 'If you want to stop this, I'd suggest you speak up now.'

'I think I'm getting the hang of it. I might need to practise a bit more though. Tell me if I'm doing it wrong.' Her eyes tilted at the corners when she smiled and he lost himself in them for a few seconds.

'By all means, practise away,' he rasped, bringing his hand up to cup a delectably round buttock.

'Okay.' Amy grasped his shoulders and pulled him towards her, this time gently nipping and biting his lips before running a string of kisses along his jaw to his ear. 'If that's alright,' she whispered.

'Perfectly fine,' he breathed, bunching her dress up in his fist until he revealed an expanse of creamy coloured thigh delineating the gap between stocking and—

'Damn, I *was* right.' He was amazed at his good fortune.

'About what?' Amy's brow furrowed in confusion.

'Would you mind terribly if we got you out of this dress? I've been fantasising about your underwear all evening and I have a feeling it's going to more than live up to expectations.'

'Oh. Um. Okay.' Amy nodded thoughtfully, her eyes twinkling. 'But if I'm going to take off my clothes, you have to too.'

'With pleasure,' Ben purred. 'Ladies first.'

It was an incredibly awkward, sweet process that involved the location of hooks, eyelets and an invisible zip in between numerous stolen kisses, caresses and laughter, but eventually Amy's dress ended up on the floor next to her discarded shoes.

Ben leaned back to fully take in the sexiest woman he'd had the good fortune to see in the flesh nearly naked. She was kneeling on the couch next to him, her amazing little apple-shaped breasts cupped by a lacy cream bra finished off with tiny blue bows and a pair of matching French knickers and stockings.

'Your turn.' Amy's impish grin was framed by a tangle of white-gold curls.

'I'm shy.'

She laughed, leaning forward and pressing soft lips against his. 'You're a horrible liar.'

'I am.' Ben coaxed her onto his lap, wonderfully soft thighs straddling him as she settled her hands on his shoulders.

'Do you think this is alright?'

'No, it's awful.' Ben stroked his hands down her back, then along the outside of her thighs, caressing the satin-smooth skin above her stockings.

'Well in that case, we should stop.'

'Perish the thought.' Ben inched his hands higher, sliding his fingers under the lace at the edge of her French knickers. Amy's small undulation against him was delightful. 'You know . . .'

'Hmm?'

'I think you'd be so much more comfortable without all this

hideously constrictive underwear.' He flexed his fingers, cupping her backside, grinning with satisfaction when Amy arched against him again. 'What do you say?'

'I'm thinking about it.' She leaned forward and he took advantage of the situation, darting his tongue out, licking her bottom lip, anticipation a heady drug coursing through his veins. He'd let her run the show for a little while more, just to see where things would go. This was too good to rush.

His plans were harshly interrupted by the sound of his phone's infuriating ring tone blaring from where he'd put it on the coffee table.

'Ignore it.' He pulled her closer against him, enjoying the little gasping noise she made when he gently nipped at her bottom lip. He stroked his hands up her back, heading for the clasp of her bra.

His phone wasn't letting up.

'You can answer it.' Amy pulled back, twisting around in his arms to look for the source of the noise.

Ben stifled a growl of frustration. 'I'd really rather not.'

The phone stopped ringing only for his house phone to take up its cause. 'Damn. I *am* going to have to get that.' He reluctantly gripped Amy's hips and set her further back on his thighs. 'Sorry, sweetheart. The only person who has my home number is my PA and he would only call me at this time of night if it's something urgent enough to risk me killing him with a blunt object.'

He felt an acute sense of loss when Amy climbed off his lap. The feeling turned into pure unadulterated frustration when he saw how stilted her movements were as she pulled her dress back on, covering up all that lovely bare skin.

Cursing under his breath, Ben stalked over to the phone hanging on the kitchen wall and picked it up. '*What!*'

'Ben?' Colin sounded shocked, which wasn't surprising. In the ten years since Ben had hired Colin, he'd never once raised his voice at him; at other people yes, but never at Colin.

'This had better be good, Colin,' Ben snapped, watching Amy bend over to quickly put on her shoes.

'It's urgent. Jerry called. *Power to the Devil* is on hold. Cameron Bell is threatening to break his contract with Bright Star unless they get you in to rewrite his dialogue. He's saying the script diverges too much from your novel and isn't happy with the ending . . .' Colin continued talking at near-superhuman pace while Ben saw his evening disintegrating before his very eyes.

'Set up a conference call for a half-hour from now,' he finally interjected over the top of Colin's monologue.

'Well, actually, Ben, I've got everyone here now, including Cameron.'

'Bloody hell.' Ben ran his hand over his head. Despite washing his hands of the film rights for the book and making a tidy sum in the process, Ben had foolishly got involved in convincing Cameron, an old and dear friend, to do the film with Bright Star Pictures, a small, independent British film company. He'd been regretting it ever since. The writer Bright Star had hired to adapt his novel was better suited to working with vacuous commercial fodder for the Hollywood gristmill than a blackly humorous political satire. Now it looked like Ben would have to step in and pick up the pieces or face seeing one of his proudest achievements mangled. Cameron wouldn't be making a fuss if it wasn't necessary.

'Alright. Call me back in five.' He hung up the phone and swiftly walked over to stand in front of Amy, who was finger-combing her hair. To his dismay she'd collected her handbag and had just ended a call of her own.

'Something's come up?' Her expression was a strange mixture of disappointment and, if Ben wasn't mistaken, relief.

'Yes. I'm so terribly sorry. If you'd like to wait, it shouldn't take long.' He rested his hands on her shoulders willing her to stay, but she was already shaking her head, her expression far too serious for his liking.

'No. It's okay. I've got a taxi coming now and they said it was only a few minutes away. Actually, that's probably it.' They both heard the sound of a car horn. 'I'll see myself out.' She brought his head down for a soft kiss on the lips.

'No—' Ben began just as his infernal phone started ringing all over again.

'Bye, Ben.' Amy gave him one last shy smile before hiking her handbag over her shoulder and escaping out the door, leaving him standing in the middle of his living room with the shattered expectations of a spectacular evening lying at his feet.

'*Fuck.*'

Feeling more thunderous than the weather outside, he stalked back to the phone, ready to rain down a world of misery on the deserving few.

Chapter 5

AMY CLIMBED OUT of the taxi on wobbly legs and made her way down her tree-shadowed driveway, sidling past her faded pink 1970s Mini Cooper, barely noticing when an overgrown rose bush caught on the hem of her dress. All her attention and energy was focused inwards as she tried to work out what the heck had just happened.

She'd never before been able to free herself of her anxiety about getting things right long enough to be spontaneous around past boyfriends, but with Ben it had come naturally. His irreverence about everything had tempted her to be a little bit naughty. She felt a warmth spread low in her tummy at the memory of his expression when he'd watched her take off her dress. In that moment she'd felt so beautiful and sexy . . .

It had been perfect.

Distracted by her thoughts, Amy didn't notice her front door was wide open until she'd stepped onto her porch. Not only was it open, but half the lock was lying at her feet surrounded by splinters of mangled wood. Her living room was a dark gaping mouth framed by the open doorway.

Something rustled in the garden. Amy flinched, turned and squinted into the darkness before realising her back was to her open front door. Shuffling sideways, she backed up against the wall of the house until the heel of her shoe clinked against a potted plant; she scanned her ramshackle, overgrown front yard. She reached blindly into her handbag for her phone while her muscles tensed to flee.

At that moment a thumping noise came from inside and she made a decision. There was no way she was going to stick around to see who might be going through her house. Gripping her keys like the ineffective weapon they were, she sprinted to her car.

Thirty minutes later, Amy rang the doorbell on Scott's restored inner-city townhouse with a shaking hand. The weather had turned frigid and rain was beginning to spatter on the pavement around her but she barely noticed it.

Scott answered on the third ring, wearing only a pair of low-slung black pyjama bottoms and a dark scowl that changed to surprise.

'Ames? I just got your missed call. What's goin' on?'

'I think my house has been broken into,' Amy blurted, wrapping her arms tightly around her waist. 'I'm sorry for turning up so late, but the front door was jimmied open and I didn't want to stick around just in case someone was still in there. I tried to call but you didn't answer and I panicked . . .'

'What? Jesus!' Scott wrapped his hand around her upper arm and dragged her inside, all but shoving her down into a brown leather armchair in his living room next to a toasty warm gas fire. 'Are you okay?' He crouched down in front of her, running his knuckles over her cheek.

'Yeah, I'm fine.' Amy replied, giving him a tremulous smile. 'Just a bit spooked.'

'I'm not surprised,' Scott said. 'Have you called the cops yet?'

'Not yet.'

'Want me to call them for you?'

Amy shook her head vehemently. 'No, I'll do it. I just didn't want to stay there if they told me to wait for them and with Jo and Stephen away this weekend . . . I wanted to be safe, you know?' She was lying. Scott had been her first thought. When anything went wrong, her substitute big brother was the first person she turned to. Always had been.

'It's alright, squirt.' He stood up and rested a reassuring hand on her shoulder. 'Take a couple of deep breaths and warm up. I'll just get my phone.'

'Okay.' She tucked her knees under her chin, pushing her toes into the leather and trying not to think about all the things in her house that could have been damaged or taken. There wasn't a whole lot for them to take. She'd never owned anything really valuable in terms of money, but the thought of someone being in her home, her sanctuary, left her feeling physically ill.

Scott returned minutes later and handed her his phone. 'I've already dialled the number. It's ringing. I'll make us a cup of tea, eh?'

'Thanks.' Amy put the phone to her ear and watched Scott's broad back as he strode into his kitchen.

Ten minutes later, Amy ended her conversation with the Fremantle police station. They'd promised to send a car around to her place tonight to check it out, then meet her there in the morning.

She sipped the cup of sweet black tea Scott had just forced into her hands and tried her best to calm down.

Scott sat across from her on a low-slung divan, elbows resting on his knees, his brow furrowed. 'Did you ask them if they could send someone around there tonight?'

'They're sending someone now,' Amy said. 'Although they reckoned whoever it was would be long gone by now and I . . . I don't want to go back tonight even if they do catch him. I'm too freaked out. I'd rather go in the daytime. It's Saturday night. They've got way more on their hands to deal with than a house break-in. Is it alright if I stay here?'

Scott was nodding even before she finished speaking. 'Yeah, of course. Just let me sort things out for you upstairs first.' He flicked his gaze to the roof of the living room, directly under his bedroom.

A suspicion worked its way to the front of Amy's mind. There was something about the way he'd mentioned sorting things out. 'Scott?'

'Yeah?'

'I'm not interrupting anything, am I?'

'Nah, Ames. It's all good. Just . . . just let me sort some stuff out.' His flushed cheeks, visible even under his dark olive skin, gave him away for sure.

'Oh bugger. You've got a lady here, haven't you? I'm so sorry, sweetie. Let me call a hotel and I'll book in for the rest of the night.' Amy was out of her chair and halfway to the front door by the time he caught her around the waist. His hold was gentle but indicated he meant business.

'You're staying right here, or I'm gonna call Jo. You know she and Stephen will be in a car driving back to Perth even before she hangs up the phone. How about you start us on another pot of tea and I'll be back in a sec.' He firmly spun her around and pointed her towards the kitchen.

Amy nodded, giving in but still feeling awful. 'Alright. Tell your friend that I'm really, really sorry, yeah?'

'Be right back.' He gave her a quick, reassuring smile, then turned on his heel. Moments later she heard the heavy thud of his feet on the stairs followed by muted conversation.

Amy didn't even try to peek at the lady as he saw her out the door. Scott was notoriously discreet and it was a rare woman that he introduced to his friends. Amy kind of understood his reserve but she had a feeling Jo understood it better, since she'd been just as secretive about her love life until she and Stephen Hardy had got together.

Travelling internationally on a regular basis was hell on relation-ships and rather than getting embroiled in something long-term that would inevitably leave a partner feeling abandoned half the year, Scott opted to keep things casual and private.

'Did you apologise for me?' Amy asked as he strode back into the kitchen, pulling on a loose white T-shirt.

'Nope,' he said firmly in a tone that let her know the topic was closed, then took the teapot she was holding, setting it by the elec-tric kettle. 'There's a T-shirt and a pair of my old shorts on the spare bed if you want to get changed.'

'Thanks, sweetie,' Amy said with a relieved smile. As much as she liked the memory of Ben appreciating her dress tonight, it felt tainted by everything that had happened afterwards.

'Go on. I've left stuff up there for your contact lenses too.' Scott spoke over his shoulder while he sniffed the milk in his fridge to see if it was fresh despite having just used it. It was an automatic gesture that pointed to just how often he was away from home. 'You'll be able to see good enough without them tonight won't you?'

'Yep.' Amy walked over to Scott, hugging him tightly from behind. 'Love you,' she said against the smooth black hair hanging down his back.

'Love you, too. Go get changed,' he commanded. 'Then you're gonna tell me what the hell happened tonight in full detail.'

Amy gave him another tight squeeze. 'Tomorrow. I'm exhausted. Let's just have the tea and go to bed. The rest will wait.'

She smiled at Scott's grunt of reluctant agreement and tottered up the stairs to bed, feeling safe and very sleepy.

The feeling lasted until the next morning, when she shared the reason she'd returned home so late.

'You went out with Ben Martindale? Seriously? *Ben Martindale?*

The bloke we saw in the Norfolk last week? *That* Ben Martindale? Do you know who he is, Ames?' Scott's expression was dumbstruck. A glob of French toast fell off his fork and onto the table in front of him.

Amy flushed. 'Ben asked me out when he came by Babyface for a shave last Monday. He took me to Christie's for dinner then we went back to his place for a while but he had to take a conference call so I went home. It's not a big deal.' There was no way she was going to admit she actually hadn't asked Ben's last name or that she still had no idea what he did for a living. If Scott knew that, he'd develop an aneurysm. Strangely enough, those details just hadn't seemed important last night.

'Just wait.' Scott put down his fork with a thunk. 'You went back to his place on the first date? Like a one-night stand? *Jaysus Christ, Amy* – what were you thinking?'

'I'm not stupid, Scott. I just had a really nice night and didn't want it to end. It's not like you don't bring ladies home all the time, last night being a case in point, and I know Jo used to have flings all the time without you reacting like this.' Amy crossed her arms over her chest and gave him a good hard glare.

'Jo's different. I'm different,' Scott said, his jaw tense. 'She could take care of herself. She would have known the score. *You* don't. When's the last time you had a one-night stand? Never? Christ, Amy, you told me the other night that you don't even sleep with half of your so-called boyfriends, you just look after them like charity-case strays. When you said you were lonely the other night, I didn't think you'd go out and do something as outright stupid as this.' He threw his hands up in the air.

'Hey! Back off, precious.' Pushing away from the table, Amy stomped over to the sink with her plate. The arches of her bare feet ached from walking around without heels, which reminded her about her house being broken into and *that* put her even more on edge.

'I don't want to talk about this any more. I've got to get home. The police said they'd be around at nine.'

'It's only seven,' Scott said curtly, picking up his fork and finishing his French toast in a few angry bites.

'Yeah, but I don't want to look like this when they turn up.' Amy glanced pointedly down at the oversized pair of Quicksilver board shorts and comically large black T-shirt she was wearing. She'd scrubbed her make-up off in the shower and her hair was turning into the usual dandelion frizz it became when it dried without any styling products. She felt naked and didn't like it one little bit. Scott's continuing stare didn't help either.

'Give me five minutes, I'll grab my stuff and come with you.'

'I'm fine on my own. Thanks for last night,' she said stiffly.

Scott swore under his breath. Abruptly pushing away from the table, he walked over to Amy, hauling her into a warm hug, enveloping her with his reassuring sandalwood-and-Scott smell. 'Sorry, Ames. I didn't mean to step on your toes,' he said gruffly, giving her another squeeze before letting her go. 'Just promise me you won't do anything stupid. Ben Martindale's a big fish and he's got a reputation for being a total prick. You've never been around the world he lives in. It's nothing like yours. He'll eat you alive in one bite.'

'You're not helping my ego here, mister. What am I? Fish food?' She poked him hard in the ribs.

He just gave her another bone-crunching squeeze in apology, his tone turning gruff. 'You're small enough. Give me a minute. I'll follow you home in my car, eh? You've got your contacts back in?'

'Yeah, I do. Alright.' Amy gave in, feeling a little deflated. Was she really that backwards? Naïve? Maybe about some things. As much she didn't want to admit it to Scott, she definitely should have got more details from Ben. And as much as she didn't like the idea of snooping, she privately promised herself she'd Google him the minute she could get a few seconds' privacy, just to make sure her judgement wasn't truly as bad as Scott had implied.

It turned out that privacy was a long time coming. Someone, some *fiend*, had turned Amy's entire house upside down and inside out. She burst into tears the minute she walked through the front door and spotted her beloved photographs lying on the floor, the frames broken, the glass shattered. The tears kept coming as she walked from room to room with a furious Scott in tow, taking in the damage. All of her clothes had been pulled out of wardrobes and drawers, books had been pulled off shelves, even her bed had been pulled apart.

It didn't take long to ascertain that her laptop was missing, along with a bunch of vintage costume jewelry, a number of her shoes and all of her movies, including her treasured Marilyn Monroe boxed set. When she discovered the latter, Amy slumped down on her couch and let herself indulge in a few minutes of outright bawling.

Not quite knowing what to do to make things better, Scott called Jo and Stephen, who immediately started the three-hour journey back to Perth.

The police arrived on time and went through the usual routine of dusting for prints and asking questions before admonishing Amy for not having security screens on the doors and windows. There was nothing else she could do but nod and agree with them numbly before seeing them off. Then she called her insurance agent and got the clean-up underway.

'You don't have to do that, Scott,' she protested when she walked into the kitchen to find him pulling food out of her fridge and dumping it in a black garbage bag a while later.

'Yeah I do. Jo's going to be here to help soon too.' He didn't look up from what he was doing. 'Did they say why he took your shoes?' he asked, pulling out Amy's extensive collection of condiments and throwing them in the bag, where they clunked sadly against each other.

Amy looked on wistfully as a half-filled jar of saffron disappeared. She'd decided that everything in her fridge had to go the minute she'd noticed half an apple pie missing and a dirty plate on the sink. The police had agreed.

'The shoes? They said it happens all the time.' She rubbed her arms briskly to warm herself up. Although she was wearing one of Scott's hoodies over her blue dress from the night before, she still felt chilled to her bones. 'They said the thief probably has a girlfriend with the same shoe size.' She sighed. 'Either that or it was a woman or a transvestite with small feet. Whoever it was, I hope their toes pinch. Let me do that.'

'You go clean up the front room. I'll take care of this. If I don't keep busy I'm going to punch something,'

Nodding, Amy left him to it.

It took the rest of the day and a lot of hard work to get everything back into order. It would have taken longer, but Jo and Stephen arrived to lend a helping hand just before lunchtime, brandishing a couple of pizzas and a car full of groceries. While Amy was initially grateful for their presence, the feeling waned over the course of the afternoon as both Jo and Scott's outrage over the burglary migrated to a relentless barrage of nagging about Amy's reluctance to renovate. Finally, pushed to her limit, Amy retreated to her bedroom to curl up on her freshly made-up bed and indulge in a pity party that was cut short after only a few brief minutes.

'Amy?' Stephen's deep voice rumbled through the door. 'Can I talk to you a sec?'

'Just give me a minute, m'love.' Amy pushed herself upright and quickly wiped her eyes. 'Okay.'

'Does that mean I can come in?'

'Yeah.'

Stephen opened the door and let himself in, closing it behind him with a quiet click before taking a seat on the edge of Amy's bed. His big frame caused the old mattress to dip comically, but neither of them commented. Instead, Stephen's blond brows were beetled, his expression concerned as he took in Amy's appearance and her dejected expression.

Amy quickly ran her thumbs under her eyes to catch any smudged mascara.

'Don't bother,' Stephen said as she reached up to tidy her hair. 'I've seen you look worse.' He smiled wryly. 'Actually, a lot worse.'

Amy grimaced at the memory of the day he'd witnessed their family meltdown on her front porch the year before. She'd been a wreck that day. She and Jo had learned just how little they meant to their mother in the most awful way possible when she'd chosen their violent father over them. Their mum had walked away without expressing any remorse or regret that Jo had been injured trying to rescue her or that she was leaving devastation in her wake.

The memory was still fresh enough to stab through Amy's chest, bringing the tears she had just been fighting to the surface again.

'Although you're lookin' pretty scary now.'

'Gee, thanks.'

'You're welcome.' Stephen smiled gently. 'How're you holding up?'

'I'd be better if everyone hadn't spent the day acting like I'm some kind of idiot.' Amy reached over to her bedside for a tissue and blew her nose. 'Break-ins happen all the time, but Jo and Scott are behaving like I've been asking for this to happen.'

'Yeah, they've been pretty awful.' Stephen nodded thoughtfully. 'But you know they're acting like that because they're pissed off on your behalf and they're worried about you. So am I, for that matter, but it doesn't seem to be helping you much.'

'No, it's not. I know this is a lot to ask, Stephen, but could you get Jo out of my hair for a bit?' Amy asked. 'I mean, thanks heaps for driving up here to help, but I really need some quiet time right now to deal.'

'Say no more.' Stephen got up. 'Want me to get Scott out of here too?'

'Yeah.' Amy felt relief wash through her, followed immediately by a wave of guilt. 'I sound like an inconsiderate heifer, don't I?'

'Nah. Just someone who's had enough.' His eyes crinkled at the corners. 'I'll get the terrible twosome outta your hair if you promise me you'll get some security lighting and better locks. An alarm would be the best but I can see by the way you're already shaking your head—'

'No alarm.' Amy didn't want to tell Stephen she couldn't afford the cost of installation right now. Although her businesses were doing well, she still had salaries and bills to pay, not to mention the exorbitant cost of rewiring the building housing Babyface and Gentlemen Prefer Blondes earlier this year.

'I had a feeling you'd say that. So instead, I'm going to ask you to do something else for me.' Stephen looked up at the roof which, despite its current water fastness, featured the stains left over from the old leaks Amy had repaired.

'What?' Amy asked warily.

'If you're not gonna get an alarm, at least get a dog, eh? Something with a loud bark and big teeth.' He levelled a serious look at her that said he meant business. 'Not a wimpy little rat thing. A proper dog. Burglars usually check out a place they've done over a few months later to see if the owner's got a whole lot of new stuff. Make sure you have something that makes a ton of noise by then.'

Amy frowned. The police had said the same thing but still . . . a dog? 'I don't know . . .'

'You want me yelling at you too?' Stephen's tone turned no-nonsense, his expression shifting to a formidable frown.

'Nope,' Amy said straight away. 'I'll think about it. Does that work for you?'

'Nope. How about you just do it or Jo and I will get one for you?' He smiled but his determination was clear. 'Knowing Jo, she'll buy you a psychotic Doberman.'

'No thank you.' Amy grimaced. She climbed off her bed and gave her soon-to-be brother-in-law a peck on the cheek. 'Thanks, sweetie.'

'My pleasure. Take your time. I'll sort them out, alright?' With that, Stephen opened the door and stalked back down to the kitchen, booming, 'Jesus Christ! Give it a rest, you two. You're painful!'

Amy used the ensuing blissful minutes of stunned silence to pull herself together before venturing back out to the kitchen.

Stephen had snagged Jo around her waist with one well-muscled arm and was whispering something into her ear. From Jo's scowl, Amy guessed her sister wasn't too happy about what she was hearing. Scott was leaning against a kitchen bench gripping a cup of coffee and looking just as disgruntled. A foot shorter than everyone else in the room and dreading yet more confrontation, Amy forced a smile. 'Any coffee for me?'

Scott thrust his cup at her. 'Here.'

'Gee, thanks.' Her words were liberally sprinkled with sarcasm.

'Amy?' Jo asked, ignoring Stephen's squeeze around her ribs.

'Yeah.' Amy looked from Jo's face to Scott's, her stomach sinking. They'd obviously got themselves worked up again in the few minutes she'd been out of the room.

'What's this about you having a one-nighter with a British comedian?'

———

'Ben!'

'Colin.' Ben stalked across the Heathrow Terminal Five arrival hall to greet his personal assistant, who looked like a sharply dressed marshmallow in a black Paul Smith suit and strawberry pink shirt. Not bothering with pleasantries, Ben continued speaking. 'Before you ask, the flight was shit and I'm knackered, so you can save the excuses for why I'm here to fix this gargantuan cock-up until later.'

Well versed in Ben's moods, Colin nodded, smoothing a hand over his neatly side-parted mousy brown hair. 'I've got the car parked not far from here. Can I take that?' He reached out a hand for Ben's black leather Tumi carry-on.

'I've got it,' Ben growled, but thrust the duty-free bag he was carrying in his other hand towards Colin's chest. 'Laphroig Quarter Cask and a bloody massive Toblerone that I felt like an idiot buying. My gift to you.'

'And the moisturiser?' Colin enquired with a wide grin as Ben made a beeline for the exit.

The doors opened and Ben's scowl turned positively feral as the ball-shrinking chill and oppressive greyness of home sweet home greeted his senses. Summer in England, wasn't it grand? He spared some of his displeasure for his long-time friend and employee. 'In the bag too. Never again, Colin. I know you love the man but he's a sadistic fiend. You can tell Sharif that was the last time I buy him any duty free. If I had to rank excruciating experiences on a scale of one to ten – which way?' Colin gestured to the right. Ben veered off and continued walking at the same pace. 'On a scale of one to ten, buying male moisturiser in Dubai airport was a ten. Possibly the most unmanning experience of my existence.'

Colin chuckled, causing his second chin to wobble somewhat endearingly. 'Sounds like fantastic material to me. Sharif says thanks.'

'Yes. Well, there is that.' Ben came to halt in front of his Mercedes SLK Roadster and held out a hand. 'Keys.'

Colin handed them to him. 'I've set up a meeting with Bright Star for four this afternoon and Ross wants you to drop in and see him over lunch.'

'Ross say what was taxing his shimmering intellect?' Ben slid behind the wheel, waited for Colin to climb in, then roared out of the car park.

'Something about your last column getting a lot of positive atten-tion. Wants you to do a series of sorts. There was something else too . . . not sure what it's all about. He wouldn't tell me.' Colin averted his eyes from the road, wincing as Ben pulled out onto the M4 heading towards London and slammed his foot down on the accelerator.

'Next time, get out the thumb screws. It's what I pay you for and we both know Ross likes it,' Ben said with his first smile of the day at the thought of a gentle soul like Colin trying to go head to head with Ross Crankshaft, newspaper editor and amateur rugby player extraordinaire. 'What's the time?'

'Eleven.' Colin closed his eyes and clutched his pudgy hands around Ben's briefcase as Ben veered sharply around a slow-moving lorry.

'Add seven hours onto that . . . six p.m., she might still be there,' Ben mumbled to himself, pulling his phone out of his pocket and thrusting it at Colin. 'Look up Babyface in my contacts for me, will you? Thanks.' He cursed himself for not asking for Amy's phone num-ber, or her email address at the very least, before she'd scampered off on Saturday night, especially now that he knew she inexplicably had no social media presence. Now he was stuck trying to call her at work, the only number he had for her, with a seven-hour time difference.

He'd been looking forward to driving around on Monday and surprising her with flowers and a nice lunch if she was amenable, but instead he'd ended up trying to get sleep on an international flight back to the motherland. Not that he'd actually slept. Instead he'd been shadowed with a faint feeling of panic that in leaving

Australia so soon after Saturday night, he may have cocked up on a grand scale. It shouldn't matter after only knowing the lady for such a short time, but it did.

'Got it,' Colin announced. 'Want me to call on speaker?'

'Yes, please,' Ben replied curtly, then cursed a few minutes later when the call rang out.

'Try again?'

'No,' Ben sighed. 'Let's just get these meetings out of the way so I can get some sleep. I'll have to try again later. For now, I need a shower and a shave. Reschedule my meeting with Ross to two. If he complains tell him I'll have my lunch when I'm bloody well ready, then book me on a return flight to Perth tomorrow morning around ten. I don't care which airline. I just want to get back.'

'Ten?' Colin's incredulity was palpable. 'That means you would have to be up around six. Six a.m. Are you sure? You haven't been up before ten since you tried out breakfast radio for that week in two thousand and ten.'

'I have recently, as a matter of fact, and I'll have you know that I did two weeks for that breakfast gig . . .' Ben ignored Colin's snicker. 'And open that Toblerone while you're at it. I'm hungry.'

A few hours later, Ben strode into Ross Crankshaft's offices at the *London Enquirer* to find his editor lurking in his dull grey office, reclining on a decrepit leather chair, his feet up on a utilitarian desk as he munched his way through what looked to be salmonella in a pie shell. On the walls were framed, yellowing front pages that he kept around, along with his unnecessarily tired and weary furnishings, to fool the public into believing he was an impoverished, hardworking martyr devoted to spreading the truth to the nation. Ben knew otherwise.

'You summoned me, master,' Ben spoke from the doorway

before making his way to the desk and warmly shaking Ross's hand. Out of respect for their long-standing friendship, he did his best to refrain from grimacing at the tomato sauce that had inadvertently been transferred in the process.

'Ben, you bastard!' Ross grouched, picking up his pie again and settling into his chair. His wrinkled white Oxford cloth shirt had pulled out of his suit pants but he didn't bother to tuck it back in. 'We should be doing this in a posh pub.'

'At my expense, I bet.' Ben shoved a pile of books off a cracked and battered Chesterfield before taking a seat. 'What on earth have you been doing in here? It looks like hell after a nuclear holocaust. Suzy quit?' He referred to Ross's secretary of five years.

'She left me.' Ross's expression turned morose.

'A holiday, or eloping with someone with more hair?' Ben ran his hand over his own head to take the sting out of the jibe. Ross had started going bald when he was twenty and now sported a clean-shaven pate that actually suited his mangled rugby player features, complete with off-centre nose, cauliflower ears and soulful blue eyes that never failed to impress the ladies.

'Job over at the *Daily Mail*.' Ross grimaced. 'I'm still trying to replace her. Anyway, we'll do the pleasantries later. Colin said you were strapped for time so I'll get to the point.'

'Is that possible?' Ben feigned amazement as he propped an ankle on his knee and relaxed back in his chair.

Ross ignored him. 'Your column last Saturday, about Alex Crane and that barber woman – what did you call her? Babyface? – has received incredible feedback. The readers loved her and, as usual, loved to stick it up you. Gave you a complete roasting in the Letters to the Editor and in the Comments this week, both in print and online. It was brilliant. I want you to do more.'

'Oh?' Ben scratched his cheek thoughtfully. 'You mean as a sort of theme?'

'Something like that. As long as they feature the little barber, or characters like her,' Ross said with a decisive nod. 'Given the reception you got we may be able to turn it into a money spinner later, a sort of tongue-in-cheek anti-travel book about Australia. What do you think?'

Ben shrugged, immediately liking the idea but not wanting to appear too keen. It never paid to have Ross think his ideas were good ones. 'Might work.'

'Will work.' Ross thumped his desk emphatically. 'Get cracking.'

'That all?' Ben asked with raised eyebrows.

'No, actually, that was a side note. What I really want to talk to you about is an interview we're running with your ex next week.' Ross's expression turned faintly apologetic.

Ben groaned. 'Bloody hell, Ross. This has been going on for months. Hasn't she milked the cash cow dry yet? There has to be more interesting material out there than me.'

'Not with what she's just come up with there's not,' Ross replied darkly, pushing a few printed pages towards Ben. 'I said it at the time and I'll say it again: a reality star? What the hell were you thinking? They're so fame-hungry they'd shop their granny for lead story on the nightly news.'

'I know.' Ben picked the papers up off the desk. 'I wasn't thinking. Fit of insanity brought on by severe boredom and some pretty impressive cleavage.' He scowled, his expression getting even darker as he began to read. By the time he got to the end of the page, he was cursing inventively.

'She doesn't say you did the last one, but all the others apply.' Ross unsuccessfully tried to hide a smirk at his own joke. 'Don't worry about it, old man. It'll be great press for that travel book you're writing as of today.'

'You're as encouraging as ever.' Ben stood.

'You're welcome,' Ross said, not bothering to get up himself.

He spoke again just as Ben reached the door. 'Can you get me some duty-free single malt when you come back to London next?'

'Bye, Ross.'

Ben boarded a British Airways flight back to Australia the next day. He settled himself down in the nearly empty first-class cabin and did his best not to brood. He was normally philosophical about travel, usually enjoyed it as a routine part of his life, but not this time around. If the news of his ex-girlfriend's pending tell-all work of fiction hadn't been bad enough, the meal he'd shared with his parents last evening iced the cake.

Having been deposited in boarding school at the tender age of five, Ben could honestly say that at thirty-three he didn't know either of his parents any better than he knew the average man in the street. They were equally baffled by their genetic relation to him. Ben's father, a member of the House of Lords and an ultra-conservative, frequently threatened to disown him over his often scathing comments about the government and the monarchy. His mother, a senior administrator at Imperial College in London, chose to deal with her progeny's career by pretending it didn't exist. Ben had the feeling that Celia Martindale frequently pretended that *he* didn't exist too. He'd wondered idly over the years if that's why there weren't any childhood pictures of him in either of his parents' country or London homes. He liked to think of himself as their dirty little family secret.

Years ago he'd decided that he couldn't begrudge either his mother or his father; he owed them his entire career, after all. If it hadn't been for their appalling child-rearing skills, he wouldn't have been locked in that boarding school cupboard and developed the early ability to perform and entertain to fit into the cutthroat social hierarchy at school. That talent had led to numerous stand-up tours, several bestselling books, writing credits for three TV series, a weekly column and, if his friend Cameron and the Bright Star people had their way, a movie script. Not to mention a recent presence in the British tabloids that he'd rather not have at all.

He should have known better than to start a relationship with Marcella Black, but as he'd told Alex only the week before, she'd been like junk food: bland and generic but strangely addictive after the first bite. In that, she was nothing like Amy Blaine, his little Australian barber.

Requesting a Bloody Mary from a flirtatious flight attendant, he repressed a small half-smile, remembering his conversation with Amy that morning. He'd set his alarm for six and when it had gone off, he'd rolled over and reached for his phone before he'd even bothered to open his eyes, wondering the entire time if the lady was worth it. The breathless voice that answered the phone and his immediate rush of pleasure on hearing it told him yes, she certainly was.

She had sounded genuinely delighted to hear from him and even more delighted to agree to a mid-week dinner. In aid of advancing his cause, Ben had impulsively taken an hour out of negotiating with Bright Star to buy her a gift. With luck, it would achieve its purpose and the trip to London wouldn't prove to have been an annoying nuisance after all.

Chapter 6

AMY HADN'T STARTED her day intending to fall in love, but sometimes these things were simply inevitable. She stood in front of a concrete-floored wire mesh cage studying the object of her affection, who was currently wearing the most downcast expression she'd ever seen.

She didn't *want* to be in love. Not with this particular morose face. No. She wanted to be in love with the cute, fluffy white bundle of energy next door with perky, pretty features and an endearing grin. Unfortunately Cupid's arrow had struck her fair and square and now she had to live with the consequences. On the up side, at least those would be better than the last three sleepless nights she'd endured, lying in her bed thinking every bump and noise could be her burglar coming back for seconds. Never mind that going out to visit Harvey for nature's call had turned into a nerve-wracking, bladder-bursting experience. For the first time since buying her home, she was actually considering getting a loan to cover a bunch of renovations she really couldn't afford just now.

'Is it a he or a she?' she asked the burly middle-aged man next to her, who had minutes before introduced himself as Rowan.

'His name is Gerald. He's a three-year-old purebred bulldog as far as we can gather.' Rowan shoved a beefy hand into the back pocket of his khaki shorts. 'He came in a year ago. They found him wandering along the beach at Hillarys Boat Harbour. He was in pretty bad shape, not that you'd know it now. A few people have tried to take him so far, but no one's stuck.'

Amy squatted down closer to Gerald's eye level. 'Why? If he's a purebred surely people would love to have him.'

Rowan shrugged. 'Dunno. Especially since he's been thoroughly vet checked and doesn't seem to have any of the nightmare medical dramas his breed usually has, other than surgery for cherry eye when we first got him. The last people took him for their kids then returned him a week later. Said he wasn't active enough. The bloke before that said pretty much the same thing and complained that he got depressed just looking at him. I mean, bulldogs are normally pretty sedate, but Gerald here could write the manual for bone idleness.' He gave the dog an affectionate smile. 'I'm the one who named him Gerald, after my father-in-law.'

'Can I go in and meet him?' Amy reached through the wire of the cage, holding her hand out for the dog to sniff. In response he moved his front paws all of a millimetre forward on the concrete floor and snuffled at her half-heartedly before slumping down with a truly long-suffering sigh. No one could call this dog attractive. Even for a bulldog, Gerald looked like he'd lost the lottery in appearance. The combination of drooping, red-rimmed, brown eyes, massively pronounced overbite, white fur and pink skin stretched over a chubby loaf-shaped body were simply too ugly not to be adorable. There was also something charming about his complete disregard for social niceties.

When Rowan let Amy into his cage, Gerald let out a low 'oof' and snuffled loudly again before slumping down even further. His tiny stump of a tail wagged once, a sure sign of overwhelming enthusiasm, when Amy gave him a scratch behind the ear.

'Is he house-trained and good with people?' she asked, moving on to scratch the other ear. The dog wheezed and she took that as approval of the attention.

'Yes to the house-training as long as you drag him outside at least three times a day to do his business. If you call not moving and generally lying around like a lump good with people he's definitely grade-A.' Rowan let out a booming chuckle.

'What about being a guard dog?' Amy asked, having a feeling she already knew the answer.

Rowan gave Gerald a speculative glance. 'Well . . . I'll say this for him, he looks the part, but that's about it. Frankly, he's probably as useful as a taxidermied Rottweiler.'

'Ah.' Amy nodded gravely. Given her requirements, that should have solved her dilemma then and there, but true love was often irrational. 'He fixed?' She stood up and brushed her hands off on her skirt.

'Yep, but whoever owned him before gave him a bit of cosmetic surgery.'

Amy wrinkled her forehead in confusion.

'He's got fake nuts. Little rubber balls,' Rowan said succinctly. 'Never seen it before and it confused the hell out of the vet.'

'Seriously?' Amy regarded Gerald with amazement.

'Yeah, but even if they were real, he wouldn't have the energy to use them,'

Amy looked down at the dog and the dog looked up at her for a few silent seconds before she made up her mind. 'Can I take him today?'

Rowan looked surprised. 'Yeah . . . sure . . . as long as you meet our requirements. You look more like the type who'd go for Sprinkles, the little Maltese cross in the cage over there, though.' He rubbed his chin, openly taking in Amy's high-heeled black boots, red and white polka dot pencil skirt and cinched-at-the-waist black cardigan.

'That's what I thought too.' Amy smiled apologetically at the enthusiastic Sprinkles. 'But it's not gonna happen.'

'They weren't lying when they said you don't like exercise, boy. Come on.' Amy half walked, half dragged her new dog through the door of Babyface, awkwardly holding a paper bag full of doggy supplies under one arm. She looked down at him. 'It's a good thing I don't have anyone waiting for a shave or they'd be wetting their pants laughing. Come *on*, boy. Please?'

Gerald just looked up at her with red-rimmed eyes. He snorted, took a few lumbering steps into the barbershop towards a patch of sunshine by the window then collapsed on his stomach with a thud.

Amy put the paper bag on one of the chairs, then crouched down next to him. 'This is gonna be your new home, boy. Well, half the time. What d'you think? No, don't make an effort. I know ya love it.' She scratched him behind his ears and was gratified to hear an appreciative groan.

'What is *that*?'

Amy looked up to find Kate standing at the rear of the store, looking at Gerald like he was an outbreak of the Ebola virus come to pay its respects.

'He's my new guard dog,' Amy said with a cheerful smile, standing up and unpacking Gerald's new food and water bowls. In deference to his gender she'd gone for a hunter-green colour scheme.

'Guard dog?' Kate's eyes narrowed. 'He's not gonna be coming next door, is he? He'll get hair everywhere.' She looked down at her black *fleur de lys* maxi dress then at the very white and pink dog by the window.

'Sometimes.' Amy shrugged, not commenting on the fact that

Kate was a hairdresser who dealt with hair every day. 'When I'm next door. He's placid so I don't think we'll have any problems with our ladies unless some of them are allergic. Mostly I'll keep him in here with me on the boys' side. Unless you hug him, I don't think you have to worry about hair, m'love. Actually, I think all we'll have to do to keep the hair down is sweep around him once a day.' She spared her new canine best friend an affectionate smile.

Kate flicked a strand of waist-length blonde hair over her shoulder and grimaced. 'Better keep him in here. Anyway, enough about the dog. I need to talk to you. Well, not me. Mel needs to talk to you. She's next door. We've been waiting for you to get back for ages.'

'Mel?' Amy asked, simultaneously feeling a wave of relief and sharp stab of anxiety over the fact things were playing out exactly as they had every other time. Myf's words about the problem with treating friends as family ran through her mind but she ignored them for now. Mel hadn't completely let her down and that's what counted. That didn't mean Amy was going to be a total pushover. She couldn't afford to be. Myf was right. She had to put her foot down some time and in light of Kate's behaviour this past week, she never wanted to be down to one senior stylist again.

'Yeah. You gonna talk to her or not? She wants her job back,' Kate said briskly.

'You two back together again?' Amy asked.

Kate averted her eyes. 'Yeah. Last night. Anyway, you gonna talk to her or not?' Her voice had an edge you could cut wood with. This kind of attitude was nothing new and Amy usually ignored it due to Kate's exceptional talent as a stylist, but today it abraded her nerves like a cheese grater.

'Send her through. I've got Beau Jameson dropping by here for a shave in a bit so she can keep me company while I get ready,' Amy replied curtly.

'Yeah, alright.' Kate spared one last disapproving look at Gerald and went next door.

The minute Kate left the room Amy closed her eyes. 'You can do this, Ames. Toughen up,' she whispered to herself, then quickly rifled through her handbag, found her make-up case and began to touch up her lipstick and powder in the mirror.

'Amy?'

'Hmm?' Amy ran her pinkie along the edge of her lower lip to tidy up the scarlet gloss she'd just applied.

'Can we talk?' Mel walked into the barbershop, closing the connecting door behind her.

'Yeah, sweetie. Come sit down.' Amy gestured to one of the chairs and took the second, crossing one leg over the other. 'Kate just said you two got back together. Congrats.' She watched as Mel took a seat, noting that her friend had lost weight, which was a worry. Mel was one of the few people Amy knew who was actually shorter than she was. She had a straight up-and-down figure, which was made even more pronounced by the baggy trousers and loose-fitting vintage bowler shirts she liked to wear. She'd changed her weave since Amy had last seen her two and a half weeks ago. Mel's shoulder-length bob was now a ponytail of sleek mid-length red braids that complemented her caramel-coloured, lightly freckled skin beautifully.

'Thanks.' Mel gazed down at her hands, where she was picking at her cuticles. 'Amy? I know I'm asking a lot. And you can say no . . . but I wanted to know . . . did you still need someone to . . . ah . . .' She raised her eyes to Amy's and bit her lip.

'You want your job back?' Amy asked gently, fighting the urge to immediately say yes, knowing all the reasons why giving in quickly was a bad idea.

'Yeah.'

Amy abruptly pushed herself out of her chair, picked up a broom resting against the wall and began sweeping the already clean floor to stop her hands shaking. She hated, absolutely hated, this part of running a business. Confrontation had always been her sister's specialty, not hers.

'Amy?'

'It's been really hard, Mel. If you'd left it any longer, I would have had to advertise your job. Mrs Sadiq came in last week and I had to turn her away,' she said, referring to one of her most loyal customers, a Somali matriarch who had been coming monthly for two years.

'I'm sorry, Amy.'

Amy looked down at the scant pile of hair she'd swept up. 'Yeah, I know you are. But you were sorry the other times too. I love you, but I need to know you're not gonna do this to me again. Every time you and Kate split, this happens. You know, I was a bit worried when you two got together.' Her eyes met Mel's. She didn't say any more, knowing full well Kate had her ear pressed to the door. In Perth's small lesbian community, Kate had a reputation for being a jaded diva pillow queen, while Mel was in her first serious relationship after an extremely difficult coming-out to her conservative Kenyan family.

Mel nodded, her eyes darting to the connecting door at the back of the room.

'I just need to know you two can keep your private life separate at work. If you have another fight, you've gotta sort it out at home. Not here. I know it's hard, but you're gonna have to. I'm running a business here. This is the last time. You understand?'

Mel nodded again, biting her lower lip, obviously trying not to cry. Amy's tear ducts activated in sympathy.

'Can you *promise* me this won't happen again?'

The ensuing silence was only punctuated by the faint melody of Nat King Cole's 'Unforgettable' from the record player.

'I promise.'

Amy set the broom aside. 'Alright. Welcome back.' She held her hand up when Mel broke into a relieved smile. 'But you've gotta stick to your word. I missed you too much this time. It's not the same without you.' She approached Mel, pulling her out of her chair and giving her a warm hug.

'Thanks, Amy.'

'You're welcome, sweetie. Just please, please don't let me down.'

'Okay. I won't,' Mel said against Amy's hair before stepping backwards. Unfortunately she stepped back into Gerald, who didn't move a muscle. Mel landed on her backside with a thump.

'He *is* an effective guard dog,' Amy said in amazement, helping her reinstated employee to her feet. They were both chuckling as they checked that Gerald was alright when Kate reappeared.

'So you gave her the job back?' Kate demanded.

'Yes,' Amy said.

Mel gave her a relieved grin. 'When do you want me to start?'

'You free this afternoon?'

'I should be.'

'Now would be a good time.'

'Amy?' Roslynn poked her head around the door. 'You back, Mel?'

'Yeah,' Mel replied.

'You needed me?' Amy waved a hand to attract Roslynn's attention again.

'Oh, yeah. Um, while you were out a guy called and booked a last-minute appointment for five-thirty. I told him we closed then, but he said you wouldn't mind.'

Amy frowned. 'I kinda do. It's been crazy busy this week and I need a break. I think we're gonna have to cancel this one.'

'Alright.' Roslynn shrugged. 'I've left his number for you if you want to do it personally, otherwise I will. His name is Ben something.'

'Oh! That changes everything.'

Late that afternoon, Amy was humming to herself over the sound of her coffee machine when a warm mouth surrounded by bristly stubble kissed the point where her neck met her shoulder. She spun around, clutching her heart to find Ben standing behind her wearing a five o'clock shadow and a wicked smile.

'I missed you.' His words, clipped and sexy, reverberated up and down her spine a few times.

'You scared me!' Her pleased grin belied her words as she ate him up with her eyes. He was standing only a few inches away, too handsome for his own good in black jeans and a pale green jumper. She noticed he was holding a rectangular pink gift box in one hand.

'Did I? So sorry.' He didn't look the slightest bit repentant. 'Let me give you something to make up for it. Here.'

'Thank you. What is it?' Amy automatically took the box from his hands before looking down at it, stomach jittering.

'Something naughty,' Ben whispered, leaning forward and planting a soft kiss on her half-open lips. While she was momentarily stunned, he took the opportunity to pick up the coffee she'd just made herself and took a sip. 'Hmm, this is good. May I? Thanks.' He wandered over to a chair and sat down, legs splayed out comfortably in front of him.

'Naughty? What?' The man seriously scrambled her brain. She was still thinking about the kiss.

'Yes. Hurry up and open it so you can put it on and thank me.' He looked her up and down, no doubt noticing everything. 'You look . . . fascinating.'

Amy blushed. 'I hate to break it to you, but that's not really a compliment.'

'It is when coming from me.' Ben shrugged. 'Are you going to open the box or am I going to have to wait in suspense for – what the hell is that? Some sort of grotesque fur pillow?' He looked pointedly at Gerald, who was sleeping next to his chair.

'Oh. Meet my new dog.' Amy felt a pang of anxiety and cursed herself for it. Not so long ago, she'd given up joint custody of her sister's cat, Boomba, because her boyfriend at the time hadn't liked animals. The last thing she wanted to find out right now was that Ben hated dogs.

'A British bulldog?' Ben studied Gerald's prostrate form before leaning down and giving the dog a scratch on his wrinkled head. 'It seems I've inspired you. Hopefully not in the looks department. Although . . . I have to admit I do sometimes look like this in the morning before coffee.'

'Yeah? I could see that.' Amy chuckled. 'I'm not too sure your influence is a good thing, because I didn't mean to bring him home. I wanted to get something a little cuter and heaps more energetic, but he grew on me.'

'We do that,' Ben replied with a grin. 'Is it alive?'

Amy could see how he'd come to ask the question. Gerald's long pink tongue was hanging out the side of his mouth, his face was so folded and scrunched up that his eyes were invisible and other than the random thunderous fart, snore or half-hearted woof, he hadn't moved all afternoon.

'Yeah, he's just saving up his energy. He's my new guard dog.'

'How?'

'I haven't worked that out yet,' Amy admitted. 'I saw him this morning and he looked at me . . . and the rest is history. Do you like dogs?' She surreptitiously crossed her fingers behind her back.

'Love them,' Ben replied. 'I've never owned one though.'

'Not even as a kid?'

'No. Can't own dogs in boarding school and later I was far too busy working to own a pet.'

'Oh?' Amy asked, curiosity nearly overwhelming her. This was the first time Ben had openly referred to his career and she wanted to ask questions, but before she could form any his expression shuttered, replaced by his usual sardonic smile. 'Aren't you going to open my present?'

'Present? Oh. Yes.' She raised the box she was still holding and shook it lightly. A soft sound greeted her ears. 'Hmm.' She turned it over.

'Open it, woman,' Ben ordered brusquely. 'The suspense is excruciating.'

Amy was unfazed by his surly tone. 'It's my present. I'll open it how I want to.' She made sure she took her time peeling back the tape holding the box closed, enjoying the way Ben's frown became more pronounced and his eyes narrowed. The big scary tiger was worried she wouldn't like his gift.

'Do you like it?'

'I haven't seen it yet. Oh.' Amy was stunned as the box came open and an incredibly soft, sheer, pale blue negligee pooled into her hands. 'Agent Provocateur? Ben! This must have cost a fortune.'

'Irrelevant. Do you like it?'

'Yes. My God, how couldn't I?' She held it up against her, luxuriating in the softness of the fabric. It was calf length and looked like something Elizabeth Taylor would have worn as Maggie the Cat. Sexy and a little bit trashy. Amy loved it.

'I hope you don't think I'm horribly tacky. I was looking for something more respectable but I saw this in a shop window, thought of you, and the rest is history. As a matter of fact, if you consider the number of times I've imagined you naked over the last few days, it's quite appropriate,' Ben mused, his wry façade well and truly back in place, accompanied by a faint trace of smug satisfaction.

Amy grinned cheekily. 'You're easy. I shouldn't have bothered to strip the other night. I should have just told you to close your eyes and imagine. Anyway. Thanks. This is gorgeous. I really like it.'

'Don't thank me until you try it on and see if it fits. If I'd been able to actually see you naked, I'd be more confident now.' Ben looked her up and down in a way that made her feel a little achy all over. 'Care to appease my curiosity?'

For a few micro seconds, Amy considered it. After all, the salon and barbershop were empty, everyone had gone home . . .

'Later.'

'Does that mean what I think it does?'

'Maybe.' Amy folded the negligee up lovingly and slid it back into its packaging. 'Did you come for a shave?' she asked, deciding a change of topic was in order. Ben was giving her naughty thoughts about things that shouldn't play out in front of Gerald's delicate canine eyes.

'Would you mind? If you haven't noticed, I'm beginning to look like a cave man,' Ben said, rubbing his stubble.

'A handsome cave man. I think the stubble suits you. Not many guys can pull it off without looking scruffy. On you it sorta looks sexy,' Amy returned before she caught herself, knowing full well she'd just fallen into a trap.

Ben's grin was devilish. 'Nice of you to say so. I am a handsome bastard, aren't I? I'll pay of course.'

Amy pasted on a thoughtful expression. 'Hmm. I have a better idea. Why don't you come to my place and you can work off my services there?' She waited for Ben's smile to widen before she continued. 'Because my bathroom's a mess and needs cleaning . . . my shower needs someone to go over it with a toothbrush and I've got a leak under my kitchen sink. That should be worth half your face.' She leaned forward to drape a towel and cape over Ben's shoulders, deliberately pushing her breasts against his arm. She'd never played the tease before but Ben practically invited it.

His smile turned decidedly feline. 'What about the other half of my face?'

'We'll negotiate that later, after your trial run. You gotta do a good job though. Very thorough.' She gave him a cheeky peck on the lips.

'I humbly await your command.' Ben's voice had a husky edge to it that left Amy's knees wobbly and her tummy tingling with anticipation.

Chapter 7

BEN INSPECTED A small stone house that was barely visible through a mass of bedraggled gum trees and flowering plants. This had to be Amy's home. He couldn't imagine another sane human being who would own a prehistoric pink Mini Cooper. Certainly not one that looked like it had been through a series of crash-test-dummy trials before being sold and spray-painted by hand. He allowed himself a wry smile. It appeared the lady had a habit of taking in strays, both inanimate and canine.

He parked in the driveway, locked his Aston Martin DB9 and offered a prayer to whatever gods he hadn't offended lately that a storm wouldn't roll in from the coast, causing one of the over-hanging tree branches to fall and turn his pride and joy into an expensive silver pancake.

Taking one last look at his car, Ben climbed up onto a dimly lit porch, registering an ancient brown leather armchair and a wealth of plant pots ranging from chipped teapots to halved wine barrels, before noticing the front door had been recently tampered with. Along with two shiny new locks, there were a number of deep grooves in the navy-blue paintwork that indicated someone had been very determined to get inside. Making a note to ask what that was all about, he knocked and faintly heard Amy's voice calling out, along with the sound of feet swiftly moving over creaking floorboards.

'Hello.' The door was opened and Ben was confronted with a vision in a skin-tight, body-hugging art reproduction. She was wearing a velvet dress printed with Monet's water lilies that was molded to every inch of her delicious little figure. He stared for a few seconds, dumbfounded.

'You know, I don't think Monet's ever looked so good.'

Amy beamed. 'Thanks. Come in. It's cold out there. Is that the wine? I could do with a glass. Gerald and I have got everything under control, so you can spectate.' She plucked the bottle of red he was holding from his hands and led the way into a cosy, postage-stamp-sized living room complete with a sagging sofa covered with a crocheted purple rug, a red bean bag, wood floors and what was either a TV or a stone age artifact. Ben stared at it for a few bemused seconds before his eyes were caught by the plethora of remarkable black and white photographs hanging on the wall behind it. He skirted the sofa and walked over to study them. 'Watanabe did these?'

'The photos? Yeah. Scott did those for me. How did you . . . oh, you saw him at the pub that night we met. I keep forgetting he's famous. That one over there is my sister, Jo.' She gestured to a portrait of a strikingly attractive, short-haired woman wearing ragged jeans and a white T-shirt. The woman was in profile to the camera as she sat cross-legged on the floor of what looked to be a garage, inspecting the insides of a vintage motorbike.

'Your sister?' Ben looked at Amy and then back to the photo. 'She looks nothing like you.'

'No, she doesn't,' Amy said cheerfully. 'That one over there is

Stephen and Jo again. Stephen's Jo's fiancé.' She pointed to another photo that depicted her sister and a darker-skinned blond bloke emerging from the sea hand in hand, both carrying surfboards. Although Watanabe had captured them in black and white, the image conveyed an overwhelming feeling of warmth.

'Brilliant.' Ben's gaze skimmed further along the wall. 'Ah. There you are.' He moved to stand in front of an over-saturated colour portrait of Amy. She was standing in a kitchen, her hair up in a high, loosely curling ponytail. She was decked out in a frilly red apron and mixing something in a white bowl with a wooden spoon, her face wearing an adorably focused expression. Studying the image, Ben experienced an unexpected surge of jealousy towards Watanabe.

'Yeah, that's me. He took it last year.' Amy walked up behind him. 'I'm so used to Scott following me around and taking pictures that I don't notice any more. When we were kids, he'd hide out with us in the bush every summer and practise with his camera all the time. I don't know how many pictures he took. Must have been thousands.'

'How old were you when you met?' Ben asked, turning to study her expression. She was smiling softly, her eyes focused on what were obviously happy memories.

'Eight. Scott was ten and Jo was twelve. I've actually got the photo he took that day. This one here. He snuck up on us.' She pointed to a smaller image and Ben moved to study it.

'We look hideous.' Amy chuckled, but Ben saw the way she bit her lip when she thought he'd fully focused on the photograph. He did so now and was stunned by how much the image affected him.

It depicted two raggedly dressed girls from behind: one tall and overweight with a straggly brown ponytail; the other tiny and blonde with snarled hair falling to her waist. They were both standing under the shade of a large tree watching two other children playing in the distance, bathed in light. In the foreground the bigger girl was reaching out as if to comfort the small one, who had her little fists bunched at her side in obvious frustration and, maybe, longing. It was obvious they were outsiders, poor ones at that. Ben tilted his head to the side, feeling a sharp stab of affinity for the girls in the picture, knowing just what it was like to feel an outsider. It made him uncomfortable.

He pasted on a smile. 'I like the look. Urchin chic. One wonders why you changed your style?'

He was rewarded with a nudge in the ribs. 'You can insult me more later. Come keep me company in the kitchen.' She took his hand and pulled him behind her towards the irresistible hearty aroma of home cooking. 'Mind Gerald.'

'He's settled in fine.' Ben stepped over the dog, who was blocking the doorway to the kitchen, looking like a misplaced hairy log.

'Yeah, he has. Can you open this?' Amy thrust the wine back at him along with a bottle opener. 'I'm halfway through the risotto. You like risotto, I hope? If you don't, tough, it's what you're getting anyway.' She pulled on a blue and white spotted apron and went back to a large shallow pan simmering on a surprisingly modern stainless steel gas stove. Ben opened the wine and poured it into two glasses Amy had left on the counter.

Mission accomplished, he studied the kitchen, which was as quirky as its owner. A black and white tiled floor contrasted with fire-engine-red cupboards and white bench tops. The only furniture in the room was a tiny pine table with two mismatched ladder-back chairs. Ben contemplated sitting on one before deciding to lean against a bench and watch Amy instead. He was thoroughly and utterly entranced. Never in his life had he been in a house this small, or furnished this eclectically on what was obviously a tight budget.

Even in the Spartan accommodation at his college, his furnishings had been more modern, but they hadn't been nearly as inviting. He couldn't wait to share the details with his readers in his next column. His fingers were already itching to type, the words dancing across his mind. He'd centre the piece around what made a home maybe . . . or maybe he'd just write about Amy. She was far more captivating to his senses, and to his readers too, if their feedback had been any indication.

Amy reached for a half-empty bottle of white wine and poured a splash into the pan. 'Do you cook?'

'No, I burn things. I mainly rely on the kindness of others if I want a home-cooked meal.' Ben ran his fingers over a speckled sheet of paper on the counter, detailing the recipe for Risotto Milanese in dense feminine handwriting. 'Usually Colin's good for a meal or two. His partner Sharif is a chef.'

'He's your personal assistant, yes?' Amy retrieved a spoon from the counter, daintily taste-testing her dish with an approving nod.

'Hmm? Oh yes.' Distracted, Ben studied her profile. It was no doubt sexist and politically incorrect, but the sight of Amy cooking him dinner had him hornier than the Spanish Bull Run.

'You really are spectacular.'

Amy looked at him in surprise. 'Pardon?'

'You.' Ben reached out and ran a finger down the side of her flushed cheek, gratified by her soft exhalation of breath. 'I've never met anyone quite like you, and I've met a lot of interesting people.' He briefly touched her bottom lip, painted a tempting dark red.

'Thanks.' Amy's cheeks took on a deep pink colour that had nothing to do with the heat coming from the stove. 'I can safely say I've never met anyone like you, either.' She turned away and added some finely chopped herbs to her pan. 'So is it true you're a comedian?'

'Looked me up, did you?' Ben grinned. 'I'm sure it was all bad. I'm the one who wrote my own Wikipedia entry and I made sure it was suitably full of propaganda.'

'Really?' Amy laughed. 'No, actually. I haven't had a chance. My house was broken into on Saturday night and I've been too busy replacing everything, working and losing sleep to get around to digging up the dirt on you. It was Scott who told me. Well, actually, *he* didn't. He told my sister, who then told me.' There was an edge to her voice that told Ben dear Scott wasn't in Amy's good books. The thought heartened him until he replayed what she'd said just before that.

The short hair on the back of his neck bristled. 'Did I just hear you correctly? You had a break-in? On Saturday night? The same Saturday night you were with me?'

Amy nodded. 'Did you see the scratches on the front door?'

'I was going to ask you about them. What happened?'

'I got home and found the door open and noises coming from inside the house.'

'You didn't try to investigate on your own, did you?'

'No. I went to Scott's place and he came with me the next morning to meet the police and clean up.' She spoke as if she was describing a pleasant walk in the park, but the tension in her shoulders said differently.

Ben wasn't amused. Mixed emotions, alien emotions, bubbled through his system. Outrage at someone stealing from his little muse; horror at the thought of what could have happened if she'd walked in on whoever it was; and sheer blinding jealousy that she'd spent the night with Watanabe when she should have been with him.

'I'm alright, though,' Amy said quickly. 'I was upset because a bunch of stuff was taken but otherwise I'm fine. If you're thinking of having a go at me over being safe or something, don't.' Her eyes narrowed and she held her wooden spoon up threateningly.

'I wouldn't dream of it.' Ben feigned horror. 'Not when you're armed at least.'

'Good,' she replied. 'Anyway, it looks like insurance is going to cover everything and I've got Gerald now as a watchdog. He'll protect me.' She turned to regard her new pet affectionately.

Ben's expression was dubious. 'He'd certainly watch a burglar enter your property and steal your things, so yes, the name probably is apt.'

Amy snorted. 'Pass me that pepper grinder, would you?'

'Yes, ma'am.' Ben saluted. 'You look like a pro at this.'

Amy glowed at the compliment. 'Thanks. I love cooking. I know I can do it and it's one of the few things I do better than my sister. When we left home, I was the one who always did the cleaning and the cooking and Jo was the one who worked so we'd have money.'

Ben's interest was piqued but he kept his tone casual. 'How old were you?'

'Twelve, almost thirteen.' Amy took a sip of her wine. 'Jo was sixteen, so she worked after school. We lived in this complete dive of a share house along with two other guys. They were university students who spent all their time smoking pot and skipping lectures. The house was as rough as anything . . . I remember we had green carpet in the backyard instead of a lawn and the landlord didn't even care, and random guys would come by to use our housemates' bucket bong. Not that you want to know about all that . . . Are you hungry? Do you want some cheese or something to snack on to tide you over? I've just restocked the fridge, so there should be some brie on the top shelf if you want it. It won't be soft but it's still yummy. There's some crackers in the cupboard behind you too.' She gestured to the latter with her hip.

Ben just stared at her, stunned, trying to determine whether or not he'd just been fed a creative and highly imaginative tale of woe. It had happened to him before, most recently with Marcella, the media-crazed reality star, but there was something about the way Amy had spoken that told him she'd just been sharing an anecdote, nothing more.

What had she and her sister been doing, living on their own at such a young age? Where the hell had their parents been? And more importantly, how had Amy gone from such humble beginnings to owning not one but two businesses in a prestigious part of town and, if the pride he noticed was any indication, her own home? There was a story here. A damn good one. His fingers were itching again with the need to learn more and write it down, but common sense told him this was not the time to take notes.

'Ben?'

'Sorry.' He shook his head. 'Jetlag. I'm not my usual charismatic self, if you haven't noticed.'

'Oh?' Amy rested her fingers lightly on his forearm. 'I forgot you've just been to England and back. Sorry. I should be used to it with Jo and Scott travelling a lot. I've never flown before so I—'

'What?' Ben asked, incredulous. 'What do you mean you've never flown? As in on a plane? In the air?'

Amy flushed and returned to stirring the risotto with single-minded focus.

Ben immediately regretted his words. He opened his foolish mouth to apologise but she forestalled him by speaking. 'No. Not enough money and I run two businesses, if you haven't noticed.'

'I did.'

'So not many chances to travel. It's okay. I don't mind.' She shrugged, but there was a wistfulness in her tone that told Ben she well and truly did. 'Anyway, enough about me. Tell me about your job. Are you really a comedian?'

'Only to the people who find me funny.' Ben concentrated on locating the cheese and crackers in an effort to cover up his frustration over his gaffe. 'To everyone else I'm probably just a bastard who gets paid a lot of money to offend people. Which I do brilliantly and often, I might add.'

'Have you been on TV?'

Ben did a double take at her expression to make sure she wasn't playing with him, then remembered the old TV in her living room.

She mustn't be hooked up to digital or cable and didn't seem too fussed over spending time on the net, so there was a chance her question was genuine. 'Sometimes. Usually chat shows to promote something. I'll be doing the rounds in a few months no doubt to promote a film adaptation of one of my novels.'

'Really?' Amy spun around, her eyes wide.

'Hmm. Not a big deal. It's awful really, incredibly dull.' He located a cutlery drawer, sliced off some cheese, popped it on a cracker and held it out.

'You're lying.' Amy opened her mouth. 'Thanks,' she mumbled, chomping down.

Ben grinned. 'Yes, I am actually. *Power to the Devil* is possibly the best work I've done. They've recently pulled me in to take over rewriting the screenplay after the studio bollocksed it up.' His expression grew stormy at the memory of his recent trip to London.

'Oh?'

'Hmm. Anyway, I don't want to talk about myself. If you haven't gathered the fact already, I'm terribly neurotic.' He was gratified when Amy laughed, releasing both dimples. There was just something so *satisfactory* in making this woman laugh. It gave him more of a buzz than working a room of a few thousand people.

To his surprise, she leaned over and mischievously bit his lower lip.

'I don't know. You seem pretty marvellous to me so far. You know what would be even more marvellous though?'

'No, what?' Ben leaned forward to catch another kiss but missed when she ducked out of the way.

'If you could set the table.'

Amy watched, beaming with no small amount of eagerness and pride, as Ben took his first bite of the risotto.

'Good?' she asked, knowing what the answer should be. She didn't have a wide culinary repertoire, but the things she did make – good stick-to-your-ribs food and hip-clinging desserts – had been mastered to perfection. Or at least Amy's idea of perfection, which was to provide pleasure for the people in her life.

She wasn't disappointed.

Ben groaned. 'My God! Your talents are wasted. What are you doing with a barbershop when you can cook like this?'

Amy flushed with pleasure. 'Thanks, but you know, it's what I do for fun and for friends. If I *had* to cook, I probably wouldn't want to. It wouldn't be fun any more. I make cake for the customers at work and they seem to like it, but that's about it.' She took a sip of the red wine Ben had brought along and nodded with satisfaction. It went beautifully.

'Tell me more. We just covered me. I want to know about you,' Ben said, before popping another forkful of risotto in his mouth and chewing with a satisfied smile.

Amy waved a hand dismissively. 'Not much to tell, really. I'm quite boring.'

'I beg to differ.'

Amy averted her eyes to Gerald, who'd settled himself next to the still-warm stove. The sight of his comically ugly face, smooshed against the floor next to a puddle of drool, helped her regain her composure.

'What do you want to know?' she asked Ben, who was watching her with a disconcerting intensity.

'Everything.'

Amy laughed. 'Everything? You might regret that. How about I just give you a quick summary?' She tapped her chin thoughtfully with her index finger. 'I'm twenty-seven years old. I own my own business and the bank owns my house. I love my job most of the time. I have one older sister, Jo, who you saw earlier in the photos.

She's much more interesting than I am. She's amazing, really. She used to work all over the world but now she's setting up her own brewery with her fiancé. My friends are just as remarkable. You've already heard of Scott, right? So you know about him. Then there's Myf, who does the most amazing paintings. Her work is selling like hotcakes. So really, compared to them, I'm not that interesting. I'm just a small business owner.'

Ben set down his fork with a thunk. 'You've just managed to successfully tell me nothing at all.'

Amy shrugged a little self-consciously. 'That's because I'm not that interesting.'

'I beg to differ. Tell me about your little thing for the nineteen fifties.'

Amy ran her fingers over the stem of her wine glass. 'It's complicated.'

'I like complicated. That means it's an interesting story.' Ben leaned back in his chair and loosely crossed his arms. 'Spill.'

'If you fall asleep, you're not getting any dessert,' Amy admonished, only to have him impatiently wave his hand through the air.

'You're still not talking.'

'Okay, well, remember how I told that I used to live on a winery? We lived in this small house that only had two bedrooms and a combined kitchen and living room.'

'Smaller than this place?' Ben looked around the diminutive kitchen.

'Probably half the size.'

Ben contemplated that. 'In that case you weren't living in a house, sweetheart, you were living in a broom cupboard, but please continue.'

Amy pursed her lips. '*Anyway*. I shared a room with Jo. Some nights were pretty scary—'

'Why?' Ben demanded.

'Dad was an alcoholic. To distract me, Jo would get me to quietly sing all the songs I'd learned from the old daytime movies Mum liked. I didn't know they were from the fifties. I just knew they made me happy. I loved the clothes, the hair, the shoes – everything. The women were so . . .' She bit the inside of her cheek and looked out the dark kitchen window while searching for the right word. 'Neat, beautiful. Together. I used to dream about being like them and the minute I got enough money to dress like them, I did. When I turned fifteen, Jo bought me an entire Marilyn Monroe boxed set from a garage sale. All her movies. They got me through so many hard times. Meant so much to me.' Her eyes teared up when she remembered that her beloved films were now in the hands of whoever had broken into her house. 'They were stolen last Saturday. What someone wanted with some old movies, I'll never know but hey, that's life.' She blinked rapidly, forcing a smile. 'The rest is history. A few years later Babyface and Gentlemen Prefer Blondes were born.' She took a deep breath. 'So anyway, there you have it. Not that interesting, really.' She abruptly got up from the table, collecting dishes in one go and taking them to the sink.

'Do you want dessert?' she asked in the thickening silence.

'Would you mind terribly if I said no?'

Amy felt her stomach sink. Had she just been so boring that he wanted to go home already? 'It's apple crumble. I promise I won't poison you.' She grabbed a tea towel and pulled the crumble from the oven, setting it on the bench. 'It's from a recipe I've used for years. I've got it perfec—'

She gasped when two warm hands grasped her hips from behind.

'That does smell delicious, but I've got a better idea.' Ben whispered in her ear.

A shiver, part panic, part arousal, arced along Amy's spine and she went rigid. 'Yeah? Uhm, well . . .' she began, and then paused when Ben gently pulled her back against his chest and smoothed his hands around her hips, splaying his fingers over her stomach.

'Um, Ben. You don't have to do that.' She breathed out in a rush as he trailed a string of hot kisses up her neck to her ear before gently scraping his teeth over her earlobe.

'Don't I?' he whispered in her ear. All earlier worries evaporated.

'Hmm. Maybe you do.' She rubbed her backside against the hard bulge in his trousers and was rewarded with a low murmur of encouragement. His hands drifted back up to her waist and gently, firmly, turned her around before she could protest.

She found herself looking up into a pair of hungry feline eyes just before Ben's mouth covered hers in a voracious kiss. It was all she could do to breathe as his hands clasped her backside and pulled her flush against him, his arousal pressing against her stomach, her breasts flattened against his chest. This was nice. Very nice. She moaned and darted her tongue out to meet his. He tasted like red wine and something extra, darker and quite yummy. She reached her hands up to clasp the back of his head only to be foiled when Ben pulled away.

'I have a suggestion,' he said huskily, breathing heavily.

'Hmm?'

'Why don't we relocate the rest of our evening to somewhere more horizontal?'

'Oh. Hmm . . . Ben . . .'

'That's my name. I'll assume you're about to say, "Ben, horizontal is my *favourite* way to be,"' he said before distracting her with another hot, consuming kiss.

Maybe horizontal was a good idea. Her back arched as one of his hands worked its way up her side, coming around to cover her breast.

'My bedroom is just off the living room.' She bit the side of his neck, enjoying the way he purred in approval.

'Hmm?'

'Yeah.' She reached around his waist, running her hands down to clasp his backside and squeezing, enjoying the feel of tight muscle under her fingertips.

'I'll drive, you navigate,' Ben said against her lips with a chuckle, walking her backwards, across the kitchen, through the living room and into her bedroom before backing her against the wall just inside the doorway. A faint hint of stubble rasped against her cheek as he slid his hands down her hips, grasped the hem of her dress and pulled it to her waist, cupping a hand between her thighs.

'Bed?' The heel of his palm ground against her clitoris, his fingers stroking over satin before he nudged her tiny G-string aside and slipped a finger deep inside her.

Amy whimpered. 'The bed's right behind us.'

'Hmm?' His teeth scored a line down her neck, finding a pulse point and sucking while his finger began moving in a slow, lazy rhythm.

Amy grabbed his head in two hands and slammed her mouth against his, clumsily rubbing her tongue against his lips, her hips moving in a shaky rhythm.

Ben groaned against her mouth. 'Sweetheart, let's slow this down a minute. We haven't got to the horizontal bit yet.' He withdrew his hand and twisted them both away from the wall, taking the few steps towards the bed, coming down on top of Amy after a less than graceful stumble over a pair of her discarded shoes. They both laughed breathlessly.

'Sorry. No finesse.' Ben supported his weight on his elbows, his body pressed deliciously between her spread thighs.

'Don't let me stop you from continuing,' Amy said solemnly, her mouth twitching as she slipped her hands beneath his light wool jumper, running her hands up and down his sides, lightly scoring him with her nails. She was rewarded when his nostrils flared.

'I intend to,' he murmured, leaning down to gently bite the pale skin of her breast, just above the neckline of her dress, before giving the other one similar treatment.

Amy made a low humming sound.

'You like that.' It was a statement, not a question. He lightly kissed the spots he'd bitten, inhaling deeply. 'Apples,' he whispered. 'Who needs apple crumble when they've got you? Do you taste like this all over?' He shifted lower.

'Apples?' Amy felt a tug on her underwear.

'Fuchsia,' he said with a satisfied purr. 'And frills. I expected no less.'

'What?'

'These.' He nipped her through the lace of her underwear, his breath warm, unbelievably erotic.

'Ohhh.'

'Lift up, sweetheart. As lovely as they are, these really have to go.'

Amy obliged, closing her eyes with a wide smile when Ben's hands ran down the outside of her legs, taking her underwear with them, only to skim up the insides, pushing her thighs apart. Anticipation curled low in Amy's stomach. She felt Ben's thumbs delicately parting her hypersensitive folds and then . . . nothing.

'Ben? What are you doing down there?' She hiked herself up onto her elbows to look at him in the faint light coming from the open bedroom door. He was sprawled between her legs, studying her with a wide grin.

He sighed theatrically, keeping his thumbs right where they were. 'You're not going to be difficult, are you?'

'What do you mean?' Amy asked, wiggling her hips, hoping he'd get the message.

'One should never rush dessert. It's an insult to the chef,' he said solemnly. 'Now go back to what you were doing and leave me in peace.'

'What? Ohh.' Amy collapsed backwards on the bed, her hands gripping the duvet as he leaned forward and flicked her clitoris with a delicate lick, and then another before he really got to work. He sent her insane, exploring every inch of her, delicately at first and then more aggressively, his stubble rasping against the insides of her thighs, his tongue lashing, pushing inside her, his breath heated. He elbowed her legs wider, murmuring in appreciation when her whimpers turned to plaintive cries that filled the room.

'Oh *God*,' she wailed, her body taut, muscles straining.

'Yes?' He spared her a smug grin before doing something naughty with his tongue. 'Move your legs wider, sweetheart. That's better.'

She gripped his head, pulling him against her, trying to get closer as rippling sensation pooled between her thighs, condensing and crystallising with every movement of his tongue, as every growl of satisfaction he made in reply to her nonsensical pleas vibrated against her throbbing little clitoris. Her back was arched into a bow, legs wide apart, shaking and trembling as a feeling of acute pleasure-pain solidified.

'Come for me. You're so close,' Ben rasped as he slid two fingers inside her in one deft motion, hooking them upwards, hitting just the right spot.

Sensation intensified and Amy panicked; it was too much, too scary. She'd never felt like this before. Never felt this out of control. She abruptly jerked her body up the bed out of Ben's grasp, chest heaving, nerve endings electrified. 'I want you inside me.'

'I want that too, sweetheart, but I want to see you come first.' He watched her with narrowed eyes, his features taut.

'Inside me,' Amy repeated, tucking her legs together, begging him with her eyes. 'Please.' She pushed herself upright and scooted forward to where he was still kneeling at the edge of the bed. She leaned forward and gave him a hungry, frantic kiss, tasting herself on his lips.

'Come inside me.' She pulled at the hem of his jumper, anxious to feel his skin against hers. He resisted for a minute until she reached down and put her hand over the bulge in his trousers.

Ben didn't need any more persuasion than that. He impatiently pulled his jumper over his head before deftly unbuttoning his pants and coming back down onto the bed next to her, pulling her against him.

'Condoms?' he asked huskily, running his hands through her hair and holding her head in place as their tongues duelled. The taste and smell of their combined arousal surrounded them and their rasping breathing filling the room.

'Just wait.' Amy pulled back. She twisted around and flopped onto her stomach so she could reach into her bedside table drawer, fumbling around blindly until her fingers connected with a small foil packet. She tried to turn over again but found herself pinned to the bed with Ben's hot breath on the back of her neck, his arousal nudging her bottom.

'I want it this way,' he said against her ear. 'You have no idea how sexy you look spread out like this.'

'Okay,' Amy said shakily as he took the condom out of her hands and reared back for the few seconds it took to put it on, before his body came back over hers.

'If you don't mind,' he murmured, 'we'll dispense with the niceties.'

He reached down to position himself, then thrust inside with a sharp snap of his hips.

'*Oh*.' Amy's back arched at the sensation. It had been a while for her and the feeling was pleasure and pain combined. Her internal muscles clamped around him, although whether it was to push him away or hold him in she couldn't tell.

'Do that again,' Ben groaned, pulling out slightly and then pushing back in hard. Amy buried her head in a pillow and moaned loudly.

'Yes. Just like that.' Ben bent his head and fastened his mouth over the skin at the curve of her neck, biting, sucking hard enough to leave a mark as his hips maintained an even rhythm, pushing himself deep inside her over and over again.

It felt so good, so primal. Sensation began to build again. Amy's breasts felt heavy, constrained, and she resented the fabric of her dress between them as she pushed against Ben, widening her legs to receive his thrusts, wanting to take more of him, moaning louder as his movements got faster, deeper.

Groaning, his breath rasping, Ben hiked her hips higher. The angle catapulted her to the same terrifying stage she'd approached before, her entire body quivering on the edge. She tensed, internal muscles bearing down hard around him.

'Oh *God*. Amy, sweetheart, I'm not going to last if you do that,' Ben ground out through gritted teeth, making an effort to slow down his pace, obviously intending to last until she came. She didn't want that. She didn't want to feel this out of control. She wanted to feel him. This. *Now*.

Amy answered by slamming herself back against him. She was rewarded by a low, rasping groan as Ben's body went rigid, muscles straining, his cock pulsing inside her before he collapsed, knocking the air out of her lungs as his breath rasped in her ear.

Squashed under Ben's weight, Amy's body felt like someone had plugged it into a light socket. Her breasts felt heavy, her nipples were aching and a hot, hungry feeling roiled through her lower body but she did her best to ignore it, instead basking in what she and Ben had just shared. She'd never felt this close, this connected with a man before. Inexplicably, the thought brought tears to her eyes.

'That was incredibly devious of you, pulling my trigger like that.'

'Pardon?'

Ben withdrew and pushed himself off her. She rolled to face him, propping her head on her hand and giving him a tentative smile.

His harsh features were softer now, almost classically handsome, but his eyes were scanning her face intently. He seemed to come to a conclusion before he looked down her body. 'Damn.'

'Pardon?'

'I didn't even get you out of this dress. As sexy as it is, I really wanted to see you naked. Care to oblige?' He raised his brows.

'I don't have any energy right now. You wore me out.' Amy yawned massively to disguise her roiling emotions.

'Of course I did. Lethargy is a known side effect of good dessert. Even if you didn't finish all of it. Stubborn woman.' Ben's eyes lit with humour. 'Where's your bathroom?'

'Do you mean my shower or my toilet?' Amy asked, reaching out to stroke a finger down his chest.

'Toilet.' He looked puzzled.

Amy reluctantly sat up. 'Just wait – I'll get you a towel.' She pushed herself off the edge of the bed, smoothed her dress down her trembling thighs and teetered off to the bathroom with Ben's exclamation of confusion following her.

She returned moments later with a pink towel, a flashlight and a cheeky grin.

'Follow me.'

Chapter 8

'NO, I'M NOT SICK, so give over. You're being a total ball ache.' Ben held the phone away from his ear, wincing as Ross's booming guffaw of disbelief echoed around his study.

Only ten minutes before, Ben had filed not one, but *three* columns' worth of copy, freeing him up from the onerous task of meeting his weekly deadline for nigh on a month. Not even the knowledge that Marcella's tell-all interview was plastered on page three of the *Enquirer* today could put a dent in his mood. He was, quite frankly, on fire. However, Ross seemed to think he was, quite frankly, going potty.

He listened to Ross's laughter for a couple more seconds before his patience expired. 'And no, before you ask, I'm not delirious either. Just read the damn things and get your minions to edit them, and if Reg changes a word of my copy again without my consultation make sure you shoot him at point-blank range. Hurt and aggrieved by this attitude, Ross, hurt and aggrieved.' He hung up, marginally offended by his friend's incredulity but understanding it at the same time.

Over the length of Ben's varied career, writing had always been something he'd had to torture himself and sweat over. He'd never been able to plan what he was going to put on a page in advance. His fickle friend – Inspiration – wasn't that accommodating. In the past, he'd had to sit around twiddling his thumbs waiting for it to turn up and it was always, *always*, fashionably late. It seemed that had all changed now. Even though he'd got less than two hours' sleep the night before, ideas were zinging through his mind, not even bothering to politely knock before they blazed across his brain. They'd turned up the minute he arrived home and hadn't given him a moment's rest.

There was something about being with Amy that set his imagination on fire. He couldn't figure the woman out. Not one little bit. She confused him, intrigued him and left him feeling randier than a thirteen-year-old boy in the first thralls of internet porn-fuelled lust.

To make matters even more confounding, the devious wench had all but kicked him out last night after putting him through the indignity of traipsing out to her prehistoric outhouse in the rain, nether regions wrapped in a pink towel, bare feet slipping on mossy bricks.

When he'd returned from his ignominious excursion, she'd placated him with the most luxurious cup of hot chocolate he'd ever tasted, the flavour so intense it was close to a sexual experience. Then, when he'd been lulled into a near delirious post-chocolate, post-sex stupor, she'd politely mentioned that she had an early morning the next day and had given him the boot.

In protest, he'd done the necessary thing and kissed her senseless, trying his damnedest to get her out of that dress, but only succeeded in getting himself so fucking frustrated he was still brooding over the reasons why she'd stopped herself from coming – twice. It was bloody insulting. Or at least it would be if he was the kind of fellow to be insulted by that kind of thing. Which he wasn't. Much.

He frowned at the thought, pushing himself away from his desk and stalking into his kitchen.

He'd called her on it and would have said a whole lot more but her expression had been so tender and vulnerable when she'd looked at him afterwards that he simply hadn't been able to do it. Instead, he'd decided that the next time he got her underneath him, he'd bloody well keep her there until she screamed for Jesus Christ and his heavenly horde.

Contemplating that happy future event, he poured himself a coffee and ventured outside. It was a clear day; the air was tinged with the sea, salt and the faint ozone of last night's rain evaporating on warm tarmac. Although it was winter, there was a huge blue sky overhead and the sun was shining through a number of luxurious, fluffy white clouds only marred at the edges by a hint of grey.

The sea in front of him was choppy, but not enough to bring out the hordes of surfers that turned up when there was anything resembling a decent swell. Ben breathed in deeply and looked up at a seagull flying leisurely circles in the sky. Damn, but he liked this place. He'd like it a hell of a lot more if he could work a certain lady out. He had a sneaking suspicion that the more he tried to learn about her, the less he'd know.

Amy's revelation that her penchant for pinup clothing came from a desire to recreate the comfort of childhood escapism had truly surprised him, as had the other snippets of her past she'd unintentionally shared.

He'd found himself touched and feeling an uncharacteristic sense of anger on her behalf over the injustice she'd experienced at the hands of her incompetent parents. He'd wanted to demand she tell him more but had stopped himself in time. As impatient as he was to get to know her better, he now realised a subtler approach was required. He just had to work out what that approach was. If he pursued her now after her polite post-sex brush-off, he ran the risk of running straight back into the wall he'd encountered last night, but if he backed off too far . . .

A thought occurred to him and he grinned. Maybe playing a little hard to get was the way to go. Couldn't be too easy now, could he? Oh, he'd do the right thing and call this afternoon, but it was time for his kewpie doll to make the next move. If he was lucky, she'd make it wearing nothing more than an Agent Provocateur negligee and a sweet dimpled smile.

Amy inspected the Amazon package that had just been delivered to her salon with a furrowed brow.

'You gonna open that or just stare at it like a stunned guppy?' Jo asked. She was stretched out in a pink chair, her bare toes splayed apart with foam while her nails dried. It was just past closing time on a Friday and Jo had dropped by to get a haircut and be prettied up before she and Amy went to their favourite Italian restaurant for a girl's night out. Myf was supposed to be joining them but only minutes before, her housemate, Gavin, had called to warn Amy that Myf was caught up with a painting she'd just started, which meant that it was just going to be the Blaine girls this evening. When Myf was focused on her work she could go missing for days, sometimes weeks, at a time.

Amy didn't mind. She rarely got Jo to herself and Myf's absence had provided them with a chance to catch up. Not that they'd talked about much. Mostly Jo had gently teased Amy about her latest pair of shoes, a pair of lime-green pumps she'd picked up on discount from the mid-year sales. Jo had nicknamed them 'squashed frog' shoes. In retaliation, Amy had threatened to paint Jo's toenails baby-poo brown. The words had turned Jo's complexion a waxy grey colour.

She was still puzzling over that when Jo's voice broke through her thoughts.

'Ames, if you don't open it, I'm going to.'

Amy shook the package again. She hadn't ordered an Amazon

parcel. Using one of the cutthroat razors she kept tucked into the pocket of her apron, she sliced the box open.

'Oh!'

'What?' Jo craned her neck to see.

She stared down at the shiny new boxed set of Marilyn Monroe DVDs nestled in the packaging and felt her eyes begin to sting.

'Amy?'

Amy tilted the box sideways. 'It's a present,' she said breathlessly. 'A replacement box set. This one's even a limited edition. He must have ordered it the minute he got home for it to have arrived so soon.'

'Who's *he*?' Jo asked, brows raised, curious.

'Ben.' She tensed, waiting for Jo to say something. Much to her surprise, Jo averted her eyes to her drying toenails and kept quiet.

Amy relaxed, turning back to her gift. 'Oh, this is so lovely.' She stroked the picture of Marilyn Monroe in her iconic white dress from *The Seven Year Itch*. 'I've gotta call him.' Placing the box down on the chair next to Jo, she called Ben's number and waited for him to pick up. They'd talked a lot on the phone this past week, but had yet to see each other since the night he'd come to dinner. He'd called the next day and had left her laughing uproariously when he described exactly how much he deserved her apology for kicking him out so early after she'd inflicted Harvey on him.

Amy regretted pushing him out the door. At the time she'd been worried he'd want to further discuss why she'd held back in bed, or worse, joke about it. Thankfully, he'd been lovely and her worries now looked more than a little silly. She was beginning to wonder why she'd been so worried about being out of control around him in the first place. If he was sweet enough to do something like this . . .

'Don't think he's there, Ames,' Jo spoke while absent-mindedly flicking through a magazine, bringing Amy's attention to the fact she'd let Ben's call ring out.

'Oh well.' She looked back at her gift.

A goofy grin was still plastered across her features when the shop doorbell rang.

'Hey stranger, long time no see!'

She looked up just as Jo called out to the newcomer and felt her smile solidify.

'G'day, Jo. Lookin' good.' Liam strutted through the door as if he owned the place, his bullish body dressed to impress in tan chinos, a pale pink polo shirt and enough cologne to kill a rat at fifty paces.

'What the hell are you doing here?' Jo's expression was so ridiculously pleased, Amy felt ill. She wished she'd brought Gerald in to the salon today. Maybe he'd dislike Liam as much as she did and take a chunk out of him, or trip him over at the very least.

'Thought I'd check in on the little lady here,' Liam said, sounding for all intents and purposes like he was the white knight riding to the rescue.

Bile coated Amy's tongue, burning her throat as she swallowed it back down.

Jo's grinned widened, hope clearly written all over her features. 'Yeah? Ames didn't mention you two were still seeing each other.'

'We're not,' Amy interjected flatly.

'You know, I'd like that a lot, Jo, but Amy here's playin' hard to get.' Liam advanced on Amy, knowing full well she wouldn't push him away with her sister watching.

For Jo's sake, Amy suffered through the attention, holding her breath and clenching her fists at her sides as his lips connected with her cheek. Her stomach heaved as his peppermint-tinged breath assaulted her nostrils. 'Liam, we're going out now. You're gonna have to go.'

Jo immediately protested. 'No. No. It's alright. We can spare a few minutes, can't we, Ames? Take a seat, mate.' She moved Ben's gift from the chair next to her, sitting it on the floor by her feet.

'Great.' With a triumphant look at Amy, Liam settled himself down next to Jo, tapping his palm on the chair arm. 'Hey, Amy, while I'm catching up with Jo here, why don't you get us a beer from that little fridge you keep down the back?'

Amy froze. All she wanted to do was scream at Liam to get out of her salon and out of her life, but she couldn't bring herself to do it. Jo would want an explanation.

Jo broke the solidifying silence. 'So which rig you on now, mate?'

'*Sunrise* . . .'

Liam began a long, self-important monologue about his job that Jo interrupted to ask the odd question, nodding knowingly. To Amy, he was speaking a foreign language she didn't want to learn.

She let the conversation go on for five excruciating minutes before she cut in, wrapping her arms tight around her waist. 'Liam, we've got stuff to do and we're going out. You really have to go.' She gave him a tight smile for Jo's benefit. 'Now.'

'Aw, listen to it. Does she always order you around like this?' Liam simultaneously gestured to Amy and dismissed her with an arrogant wave of his hand.

'Always,' Jo replied, no doubt thinking he was teasing. 'You gonna be in town for a bit? Maybe we could all catch up. I'd love to introduce you to my fiancé.'

'Yeah, sure.' Liam gave Amy a wink. 'As long as Amy here doesn't object.'

'Why would she?' Jo did a double take when she noticed Amy's rigid stance and wooden expression. She paused and then spoke again, this time with a little less exuberance. 'Ah, actually mate . . . on second thoughts, how about I get back to you on the timing and stuff? I'm forgetting how busy Stephen's been lately. I'll give you a call. Anyway, we're just about to head out for a girls' night.'

'Yeah?' Liam looked disappointed, which was no surprise. With

Jo in the room, he'd probably thought he'd be able to stick around for ages.

'Bye,' Amy said brusquely. 'Jo, can you see him out? I've gotta get ready.' Without even waiting for Jo's reply, she hurried to the bathroom and locked the door, reaching the toilet bowl just in time to lose the coffee and cake she'd eaten. Breathing in deeply, she stumbled over to the basin above the sink and looked at her face in the mirror.

'You're not eighteen,' she reminded her reflection in a whisper, reaching for her toothbrush and toothpaste with shaky hands. Making sure she took enough time for Liam to be gone, she brushed her teeth, touched up her lipstick, straightened her floral green shirtwaist dress and matching cardigan, then walked back to the front of the salon.

'You right there?' Jo asked. She was leaning down to buckle up a tan ankle boot.

'Fine, petal.' Amy looked around. 'He gone?'

'Yeah.' Jo moved to her other boot. 'It was good to see him. What's up? You guys thinking of getting back together?' Her tone was hopeful.

'Nope. I didn't want to talk about it when we broke up and I don't now,' Amy replied, her voice too loud and higher pitched than usual, betraying her anxiety. She couldn't do a confrontation with Jo right now, especially not about this.

Awkward, stifling silence filled the room as Jo studied Amy's tightly clasped hands and rigidly set shoulders.

'Fair enough. Didn't mean to step on your toes.'

'That's alright.'

'Even if they're covered in squashed frogs.'

Amy felt herself almost puddle with relief. 'You should never be nasty to the woman who cuts your hair.' She forced a grin and lightened her tone.

'Easy, tiger.' Jo held up her hands. 'Or you're never riding on my bike again.' She was referring to her vintage Triumph. Amy loved riding on the back of it, but Jo rarely let her because she refused to wear anything but heels. It had turned into a long-running joke.

'Heaven forbid. Hurry up and get your stuff. I'm hungry.' Amy whisked around the salon, collecting her handbag and turning off the record player and the lights. 'If you don't get moving, I'm not letting you drive my Mini again.'

'Heaven forbid.'

'Come on, boy. You're driving me crazy here.' Amy stood on her porch watching Gerald's vaguely grey shape waddle around her front yard, sniffing and snuffling at every available leaf, twig and tree while he decided which particular spot to bequeath his business on.

She shivered as the chilly wind blowing in from the coast cut right through her wrap and thin nightie, triggering a run of goose bumps down her spine. A sharp cracking noise from somewhere in the dark startled her and she jumped, squinting through the trees, unable to see anything without the aid of her glasses or better lighting.

'Hurry up, boy. Why is two in the morning the only time you voluntarily want to go to the loo?' she called out to the dog again, shifting her weight anxiously from one foot to the other. Unfortunately, Gerald either didn't understand or was ignoring her in his quest for the perfect spot.

It took the dog another five minutes to finally complete his business and by that time Amy was twitchier than a fat chicken living next door to a KFC restaurant. Although she had every confidence in Gerald's ability to deter a burglar, she'd still much rather be inside in the warm with the door locked.

'You happy now?' she asked him as he lumbered through the front door, brushing past her legs. Her only answer was a wheezing sigh before he made his way over to the beanbag in the living room and clambered laboriously up on top of it before collapsing. Amy gave him a quick scratch behind the ear before turning on her TV and flopping down on her couch. She'd given up on sleeping tonight.

Her thoughts were a whirling mess and had been ever since Liam's visit to the salon. She knew that she couldn't let the situation go on, especially not since she'd come home after her dinner with Jo on Saturday night to find another abusive letter slipped under her front door. Normally she threw the letters out the minute she found them, but she'd kept this one. The minute she got a chance, she was going to take it down to the police station and see what they could do about him. With luck, it would be grounds for a restraining order.

As much as she wanted to protect Jo's feelings, Amy had had enough, more than enough. If she didn't do something now, who knew how long Liam would go on harassing her? It didn't seem like the idiot had a life. He'd been stalking her, in all senses of the word, for years. If she didn't do something there was a good chance he'd still be stalking her in her retirement home when she was ninety.

'Colin, as much as I find myself thinking fondly of you, I wasn't happy to see you in the flesh this time and I'll be a sight happier if I don't see you again for another few months,' Ben said as he walked through Heathrow Terminal Five's sliding doors and reached into his pocket for his passport.

'You shouldn't.' Colin trotted along behind him, just narrowly missing a collision with a large Pakistani family in the process of organising their luggage. 'That was the last of it. I don't think there will be anything more now you've signed on the dotted line. If I didn't say it before—'

'You did. Countless numbers of times.'

'I really am sorry.'

Ben heaved his overnight bag onto his shoulder, stopping

abruptly to scan the information for departing flights on an over-head screen. He had forty minutes until take-off but that didn't worry him. What was first class for if one couldn't arrive just in the nick of time?

'I've said it a million times and I meant it every time. You're forgiven.' He turned to regard Colin with affectionate exasperation, noticing for the first time his employee's lime-green tracksuit strain-ing at the seams around his generous midriff.

'Velour, Colin?' He winced.

'You only just noticed? It's comfortable,' Colin said defensively. 'And it *is* midnight.'

'Yes, I understand that. But really? Velour? What does Sharif have to say about this?' Ben advanced to the check-in counter with Colin bringing up the rear.

'He hates it.'

'I'm not surprised.'

'I like it.'

'You must do. Anyone who wants to look like he's a perambu-lating apple would have to.' Ben nodded his thanks to the woman at check-in as she handed him his passport along with a boarding pass. He turned and caught Colin's frown.

'A dapper apple,' he corrected, his mouth lifting at the corner.

'You're a prince, Ben.'

'Aren't I always? You know, once the media frenzy blows over you're welcome to come stay with me in Perth for a few weeks. Bring Sharif. You were saying the other day that he doesn't take enough holidays.'

'Sharif would love that, but you know I really don't like the heat.'

'Build a bridge and get over it, my friend.' Ben grinned at Colin's grimace and patted him on the shoulder. 'I'll talk to you soon and no offence, but unless you take me up on my offer, I don't want to see you or Dear Old Blighty for at least another six months.'

The minute Ben settled himself on the plane, he truly began to relax for the first time in four days. In an uncharacteristic cock-up, Colin had managed to let Ben's impending brief return to England slip out in conversation to a friend who just happened to work for one of the biggest muckraking publications in the country. Colin had then compounded things even more by leaving his phone at the table while he went to the restrooms, giving his Judas acquaintance a chance to get a hold of Ben's private number.

From the moment he'd returned to London, Ben had been beset by a barrage of calls from the baying British tabloid media demanding his response to Marcella's tell-all vomit, which artistically painted him as a sexually deviant, misogynistic sadist who stole sweets from children on his day off. As it was, he'd barely been able to make it to Bright Star Studios to discuss another round of revisions to *Power to the Devil*. Or more to the point, to discuss the paltry amount they were planning on paying him for what was, essentially, a total rewrite now that they'd decided that it wasn't just their movie star's dialogue that needed fixing.

He knew what their concerns were about. He knew they were on a tight budget, but that wasn't his problem. It hadn't been his decision to hire a Hollywood hack to work over his nuanced masterpiece, it had been theirs, and they could swallow their bitter pill and pay him to clean up their mess.

It had been a vicious dogfight, but Ben had ultimately won the war. In return for his services, Bright Star would be paying the modest fee he'd negotiated and sharing a generous cut of the profits, if any, that eventuated if the film actually ever made it as far as the cinema. All he had to do was hold up his side of the bargain, which wouldn't be hard. Unbeknown to his dear new friends at Bright Star, Ben already possessed a draft script for *Power to the Devil* that he'd written a few years before he'd sold the rights. At the time, he'd been harbouring grand plans to make the film himself before sanity had interjected. All he needed to do now was tweak it to best show off Cameron Bell's acting prowess and hand it over. It would be a week's work at most, which would free him up to spend his time on other, more pleasurable things – or more to the point, *people*. That's if the particular person he was interested in was still talking to him.

His little scheme to have Amy come to him hadn't quite worked out as planned, thanks to this nightmare trip. He just hoped to hell she hadn't been trying to contact him.

'Fuck.'

The word echoed off the walls of Ben's house as he saw he'd missed not one but three calls from Amy. One on Friday evening, one on Saturday morning and one from the day before. Given that it was just after midnight, he'd have to cool his heels until a respectable hour.

He ended up calling the minute he woke at ten the next morning.

'Hello?' Amy's voice was almost drowned out by the sound of chattering females and the whirring of a hair dryer in the background.

'Amy? It's Ben. I'm a shit. I didn't return your calls.' Ben rubbed a hand over dry, tired eyes. He'd managed less than twelve hours' sleep split over the past four days. He hadn't been able to locate the off switch for his mind and now he was paying for it.

'Ben? Are you alright? You sound strange.'

'Yes. Fine. Exhausted but fine. I just flew in from London.'

'*Again?*'

'Yes. More's the pity. I'd like to see you again. Preferably naked. Bear in mind I said preferably, not mandatorily.' He grinned at her stunned silence. She didn't take long to recover, however.

'I got the boxed set.'

Ben felt an acute rush of satisfaction. It had been an impulsive gesture but obviously the right one. 'You liked it?'

'I love it. Thank you.'

'Just how grateful are you?'

'Grateful enough to cook you dinner. I'll come to you. Tonight okay?'

'Tonight?' It was Ben's turn to be caught off-guard.

'I'll see you at seven.' She hung up.

Ben stared at the phone for a good few seconds with a bemused expression as the stress of the past few days flitted away. He then rolled out of bed and yanked open the heavy black bedroom curtains to reveal a spectacularly clear blue winter sky before making his way downstairs for a desperately needed coffee.

Despite his present state of exhaustion, he was feeling remarkably inspired to work. Not on the film script, of course. He didn't even want to think about that for another few days, but maybe Ross's idea of a travel book wasn't such a bad one. He could ask Amy to be his local guide to deciphering the peculiarities of Australian culture. He had a feeling she was something of an anomaly, but that didn't matter. That just made her all the more interesting.

Ben's latest column featuring his experiences with the outdoor toilet in a post-sex daze had certainly gone down well if comments on the *Enquirer*'s website were anything to go by. His readers loved Amy and he'd loved sharing her with them. He worried momentarily that she wouldn't be comfortable with the intimate details he'd alluded to, but squashed the feeling dead. He hadn't said anything that would identify her and besides, she'd no doubt be flattered and touched he'd devoted so much line space to her. His other lady friends would certainly have been ecstatic for the publicity – or understanding, at the very least.

He made a considerable part of his living off anecdotes from his private life and any woman getting involved with him knew that. Okay, so Amy didn't know much about his career other than what he'd shared, but was that his problem? One search on Google would reveal all there was to know about him. Come to think of it, one search on Google at the moment would bring up Marcella's tell-all story. If anything, *that's* what he needed to worry about.

Later that afternoon, Ben answered the door to a five-foot-tall, double-dimpled ray of sunshine. He blinked as he processed the sight of Amy in a pair of loose white linen pants and a soft yellow jumper cinched at the waist with narrow pink belt. He glanced down. As usual she was wearing heels. This time they were a yellow that matched the jumper. He'd never had a thing for women's foot-wear before, but he definitely liked the idea of seeing her clad in nothing but those shoes and her birthday suit. Sometime in the next five minutes preferably.

'Nice to see you, too. I missed you as well.' She stepped forward and kissed him. Apples and bubblegum greeted his senses.

'I'm being terribly rude, aren't I?' he murmured with a self-deprecating smile against her lips.

'Yep. Although I gotta say I'm feeling flattered by the attention. Can you take this?' Amy pulled out of his grip and pointed to a wicker basket covered with a red gingham tea towel resting at her feet. 'You've got an oven that works, I hope?'

'Last time I checked. Mind you, I've rarely used it.' Ben hefted the basket. 'What's in here? A couple of bricks and a bowling ball?'

'It's a surprise.'

'A good one, I hope. I'm terribly fragile.'

'You poor flower.'

'It's a trial.' He led the way into the kitchen and watched with amusement as she rubbed her hands together, surveying her surrounds with obvious glee. Her perky platinum ponytail swung jauntily as she kneeled to peer into the oven.

'This looks brand-new. Do you ever cook at all?' She stood and ran a finger over the immaculate stainless-steel stovetop.

'Never,' Ben said with relish. He lifted the towel off the basket and whistled at the array of fresh herbs and loose vegetables surrounding something that looked like lamb marinating in a Tupperware container with a cherry-red lid. Lurking off to one side was a large blue and white striped tin.

'Don't even think of opening that,' Amy warned, walking over and nudging him out of the way with her hip before beginning to unpack the goodies.

Curiosity roused, Ben reached over her shoulder and lifted out the item in question. It was heavy. 'What's the penalty if I do?'

'You'll get sent to your room.'

'Oh well. If you insist.' Ben reached for the lid.

'Without me.'

He heaved a dramatic sigh. 'Do I at least get a proper kiss now?'

'Oh.' Amy's drill sergeant demeanour melted. 'Sorry.' She turned and closed the space between them until they were only an inch apart. Damn but she smelled good. He decided dinner could wait.

'You know, I never did get to see you wearing my present the other day,' he said huskily, leaning down to lick at a delectably soft bottom lip. He'd been imagining her in that slinky scrap of lace every night since he'd bought it.

'No?' Amy breathed, leaning into him until her breasts pressed against his chest.

'No.'

'Hmm. Well, I did bring it. It's in my bag.'

His eyes widened. 'You did?'

'Yup.' She ran her hands down the sides of her thighs; it was an unconscious gesture that drew Ben's attention to the curves he'd like to be touching in the very near future.

'Do I get to see?' Ben reached out and gently grasped her hands in his, bringing them to rest on his chest, where they felt right.

Her eyes twinkled. 'You want me to put it on?'

Ben schooled his features into a serious expression. 'Only if you want to. If you *really* insist, we can just hang it on the wall and I can *imagine* you wearing it. However, I may have to see you naked for my imagination to truly do it justice.'

'You'd have to be naked too.' Amy smoothed her hands from Ben's chest down to his stomach.

'It would be a trial, but I think I could manage it. From memory we didn't get around to a few things last time. Terribly remiss of me.' He leaned forward, rubbing his stubble over Amy's baby-soft cheek as he whispered in her ear. 'This time I get to make you come.'

'What?' Her breath hitched as he caught the hem of her jumper in his fingertips.

'Lift up your arms, sweetheart.' After a moment's hesitation, Amy raised her arms and he unbuckled the belt at her waist, then swept the jumper over her head, revealing charming little breasts lovingly hugged by a buttercup-yellow bra.

'That's better.' He raised his hands to further extend his appreciation but Amy took a step back, narrowing her eyes and crossing her arms over her chest.

'Turn about's fair play. Strip.'

'If I must,' he sighed. His pullover hit the floor within seconds, along with the grey T-shirt he'd been wearing underneath it, leaving him in a pair of low-slung jeans. 'Now where were we?' He hooked a finger in the waistband of her trousers. 'You know . . . I think these can go too.'

The flush that spread from Amy's chest to her cheeks was utterly adorable, as was the way she pursed her lips thoughtfully. 'You first.'

'Oh no. I remember where that got me the last time you were here.'

'I liked where it got you.' Amy ran her eyes down his torso with obvious appreciation until they rested on the fly of his now rather uncomfortable jeans.

'No. I'm afraid I insist.' Ben undid the top button on her pants, then took his time pulling down the zip. He smiled widely at the sight of more yellow lace, slowly running his thumb over the petal-soft skin just below her navel. Her trousers slipped off her hips and pooled at her feet.

Amy's breath hitched. 'I can't draw this out, Ben.'

'Neither can I. Wrap your legs around me, sweetheart,' he commanded, drawing her hips against his and hiking her up his body. They shared a charged moment, revelling in the contact, before Ben swiftly walked to the sofa by the window and collapsed backwards with a groan as Amy straddled him. She trailed a string of warm kisses along his jaw, then sweetly fitted her mouth over his, promptly stealing his sanity.

'You know,' he said, coming up for air, hands flexing on her hips, 'I believe I was supposed to turn the tables on you this time.'

'You talk too much,' Amy moaned.

'You wear too many clothes,' Ben countered against her lips. 'Take them off.'

'Hmm?' Amy's fingers flicked over his nipples and he groaned.

'Now.'

'Alright.' Amy reluctantly slid off his lap to stand between his splayed knees. Her eyes met his as she first unclasped her bra, letting it drop to the floor before skimming those ray-of-sunshine panties down her thighs, kicking them off with a flourish and a grin.

'Leave the shoes on,' Ben purred as his eyes licked over lush little coral-tipped breasts, the adorable curve of her stomach, then lower. He opened his mouth to say more but Amy chose that minute to slide back onto his lap and the words flew away, along with what little was left of his sanity.

Without preliminaries, he pounced.

'Ben!' she shrieked when he drew one nipple deep into his mouth, sucking, biting, thoroughly enjoying the texture of her, the taste of her and the way she was squirming against him.

'Hmm?' He moved to the other breast, worshipping it with just as much fervour.

'What are you doing?'

'I thought it was obvious. Quality control,' he murmured against a tightly pebbled nipple. 'Have to check they *both* taste like apples and bubblegum.' He delighted in the way she writhed on top of him, pushing her naked warmth against the fly of his jeans until he suspected he was going to embarrass himself right then and there.

Raising his head, he looked up into her eyes just as he moved a questing hand to that delightful little patch of curls hiding his own personal nirvana. Her moans and the dampness that met his fingertips were the source of instant gratification. 'Nice to know I'm wanted.'

'You really do talk too much.' Amy reached down between them and fumbled with his fly. Seconds later her hand was wrapped around him, drawing him out of his jeans. A moment after that, all rational thought left him as she hiked herself up, braced her hands on his shoulders and, without preamble sank down, hot, wet, tightness engulfing him.

'*Christ*,' Ben groaned as his head fell backwards. Grasping Amy's backside with two hands, he braced his bare feet on the floor and raised her up, seeing white flashing light behind his eyelids as she sank back down with a slow undulation of her hips. She repeated the movement and Ben tightened his grip, losing himself in the wet glide and the sexy little whimpers she made each time she took his full length.

He allowed the torture to go on for as long as he could handle it, then moved his hands to cover her breasts, pinching her nipples hard enough for her movements to turn erratic as she ground against him, moving faster, slamming down on him harder.

Breath rasping, his control slipping, Ben reached down between them, placing a finger directly over her clitoris.

Amy wailed and tried to twist out of his reach, but he leaned forward and gently bit her shoulder, gripping her hip with his free hand just hard enough to let her know he meant business.

'Not this time, sweetheart. Faster.' He bumped his hips against hers, burying himself deep again and again. She tightened around him, fighting it until the last second then threw her head back, making keening cries, hips moving jerkily. He felt, rather than heard, her orgasm slam into her as she screamed, going wild in his arms, clenching down on his cock, shoving him into the abyss.

Feeling an unbelievable sense of accomplishment, Ben gave in to his own release, shouting triumphantly, his entire body wracked with pleasure.

He was still smiling smugly minutes later when Amy pushed herself away from his damp, sweaty chest.

'You look pleased with yourself,' she said in a kittenish, accusatory tone.

'Oh, I am.' Ben's expression was positively smug. 'This is where you tell me you enjoyed yourself.'

Amy narrowed her eyes and then yawned massively, pink tongue curling. 'Awful. I had an awful time.'

'So I noticed. About the time you were screaming my name.' He tenderly smoothed her hair away from her eyes. 'You were beautiful, you know.'

'Oh damn.' Amy's eyes watered up as she looked at him accusingly. 'I was doing well until now and then you had to say something like that.'

'Oh damn.' Ben pulled her back against his bare chest, loving the feel of her soft little body pressed against his, the feel of still being inside her. 'Is there some Australian etiquette I missed? Should I have insulted you?'

'Yes. No.' Amy burrowed her face against his neck. 'Thank you.'

'You're welcome.' Ben rubbed his cheek against her hair. 'Although I'd like to know what you're thanking me for.'

'You know.'

'No, I don't. I'm completely ignorant.'

'The thingy.'

'Thingy?'

'You made me thingy.'

'I did nothing of the sort. I believe I helped you come spectacularly but I *never* made you *thingy*. Sounds positively obscene.' Ben laughed when Amy began giggling.

She snuggled closer against him before tensing, rearing backwards in a sudden movement, her eyes wide with alarm. 'Oh bugger.'

'What's the matter?'

'We didn't use anything.'

Ben stifled a groan.

'You don't have any nasty bugs or diseases do you?'

'Bit late to ask that now, sweetheart.' Ben internally berated himself for his colossal stupidity but kept his tone light. 'I should have known you wouldn't have been able to resist me.' His expression turned serious. 'I'm all clear. Not that you should trust the word of a man who makes things up for a living.'

'So am I.' Amy's brow scrunched with a frown. 'I don't think we have anything to worry about. My period's due tomorrow.'

Ben nodded, mind whirring on the possibility of having just created a life before he shut the thought down. Best to wait and see. 'You *will* tell me if there's anything I need to know.' He searched her eyes for any resistance.

'Definitely.' She nodded, biting her lower lip.

'Alright, then. Spilt milk and all that,' he sighed. 'How about I take you upstairs, douse you under a nice hot shower, rub my hands all over your body then conduct an encore of my recent lauded performance, this time with protection, before we have dinner?'

Amy didn't give him a verbal reply. Instead, she hiked herself off his lap, grabbed his hand and pulled him towards the stairs. Ben followed along behind, grinning from ear to ear, admiring her naked form in sunshine-yellow heels.

Chapter 9

AMY PULLED A terracotta baking dish containing lamb and roast vegetables out of the oven and turned to find Ben leaning against the island in the middle of the kitchen, watching her with a heavy-lidded half-smile. She returned it, knowing she really should take him down a peg or two but feeling too good to bother.

Her legs still felt a little shaky. That was no surprise considering she'd managed a few poses in the past hour or so that would put a yogi to shame. Come to think of it, they put her to shame. To distract herself from that particular line of thought, she turned her attention to the food. She prodded the lamb with a fork and satisfied herself that it was done. 'Where are we eating?'

'Why don't we eat here?' Ben gestured to the island and the bar stools next to it.

Amy's look should have singed his socks.

He raised a black brow. 'Or maybe I could set the dining room table.'

'Don't forget the napkins,' Amy said primly. 'And where are your plates?'

'Ah.' Ben eyed the kitchen cupboards as if they were uncharted territory. 'May I assume you're looking for nice ones, not the usual everyday dross?'

'Preferably the nice ones. Knives and forks would be good too.'

Ben sighed theatrically.

'And glasses. Do you have any wine? A red would work.' Amy pulled the baguette she'd been warming out of the oven and deftly sliced it into rounds before arranging it on a serving platter she'd found lurking in an otherwise empty cupboard.

'Oh, and something to put this on. A trivet if you've got one.' She gestured to the lamb with a nod while breaking off a twig of rosemary and placing it on top for decoration. Maybe some rosemary butter for the bread . . . She was about to ask Ben what he thought of the idea, but the sight of him looking so lost in the middle of his own kitchen was too much and she ended up laughing instead. 'You know, I think I'd have more luck if I went looking for everything myself.'

Ben scowled. 'Hush. I'm strategising. Colin arranged for someone to stock the cupboards with the usual stuff and I haven't learned where everything is yet.'

'You've been here for months!' She took pity on him and pulled out knives, forks and glasses from where she'd spotted them earlier.

'Yes, but I don't cook other than heating up take-away. If you'd asked me where the microwave was I'd have more success,' Ben said, pulling cupboards open at random. 'Ah. Plates.'

'I've got the rest here,' Amy said just as he began to pull cupboards open again. 'Hurry up, mister. If my good lookin' hunk'a lamb gets cold I'm gonna be shirty.' She led the way into his dining room, which featured a rough-hewn, bleached pine dining table surrounded by eight high-backed white leather chairs.

'Have you christened this yet? You could fit at least twelve people around here.'

'No. You're the first. Alex was my only other guest and we mainly ate out.' Ben helped Amy set two places at one end of the table. He produced a bottle of Shiraz and poured them a generous splash each before pulling out a chair for her.

He took a seat. 'If I haven't said it already, I genuinely appreciate this.' The words contained such a rare sincerity that Amy felt warmth spread through her.

'Thanks.' She beamed, serving him up a generous portion of roast lamb and vegetables before serving herself. Her eyes sparkled as she watched Ben's usual decorum disappear as he ate with gusto. 'I wore you out, didn't I?' She chuckled at his sudden half-embarrassed, half-offended look. 'We'll talk later. I don't mind.' She gestured for him to keep eating, which he did, cleaning his plate in record time.

'Sorry. Terribly rude of me. It's been a big few weeks. And yours is the best home cooking I have ever tasted.' Ben leaned back in his chair, watching on as she ate at a much more sedate pace.

'Why did you go back to London this time?' She blotted her lips with a napkin and reached for her wine.

Ben's expression turned dark. 'Same thing as before, although this time was worse because Colin managed to drop me head-first in the soup.'

Curious, Amy raised both brows.

'An ex-girlfriend of mine has just sold her version of our time together to the tabloids. It's not flattering to say the least.' Ben paused as if gauging her reaction.

'Oh?' She played with her wine glass, deliberately keeping her expression impassive as she waited for him to continue talking. If her life had taught her anything to date, it was not to assume anything about people until you had all the information. Too often she'd assumed a man was worth her time, only to be disappointed. She'd never had it work the other way before, but if the kernel of dread sitting in her tummy was any indication, she was really, *really* hoping Ben wasn't going to turn out to be a dud. She had a sneaking suspicion she'd already managed to walk right past infatuation, straight to the deep and meaningful stuff. The thought of having it all blow up in her face was leaving her seriously queasy.

An awkward silence fell between them until Ben smoothed a hand over his head and loudly cleared his throat. 'Marcella has decided to use me to advance her career by making up a lot of unimaginative bollocks. I won't bother repeating it. Needless to say, she makes me look like the love child of the Marquis de Sade and Saddam Hussein. The British press are screaming for my blood, which they haven't been able to get since I moved to Australia but . . .' He took a sip of his wine. 'Colin let slip I was coming back to London to a member of the press. The long and the short of it is that you're probably going to see me plastered over a few of those magazines you stock in your salon, if you subscribe to any of the British ones at least.' Ben grimaced. 'Most of them feature me standing on my front door step, looking fit to kill.' He topped up Amy's glass.

'How long were you together?'

He scowled. 'Only three months, but you'd think it had been years given what she's written.'

Amy tilted her head to one side, searching his features for any sign he was lying. He certainly wasn't presenting his usual polished, glib façade. She relaxed a little. 'Can you give me a hint?'

'I'd rather not. It's pure fiction and badly written at that.'

'I could just look it up,' she pressed.

'That's not very sporting of you,' Ben replied indignantly.

'You're right,' Amy agreed. 'So I'll make it up instead.' She put her finger to the side of her mouth and frowned thoughtfully. 'Hmm . . . did she say you were really a woman? Because I checked. You're not.' She giggled at Ben's raised brows. 'Or did she say you were really a closet masochist who likes being spanked while doing the dishes? Because if you are, I can pencil you in. I'm quite good with the flat of my hand.' She clapped her hands together and was rewarded when Ben chuckled. 'That was a hint just in case you didn't notice.' She prodded him with her foot.

He feigned surprise. 'Really? No, no, I didn't notice the hint at all. I was actually seriously contemplating your offer. Dishes and spanking? I've never been *that* kinky but for you I would consider it.' His smile turned predatory.

Amy waggled her brows. 'After dessert.' She changed the topic. 'Do you have the whole paparazzi thing happening all the time?'

Ben shook his head slowly. 'No. This is the worst. There was some coverage a few years ago when I grievously offended a talk show host, Dermot Langston. Do you get him here? No? Well, he's a total wanker so I wouldn't feel bad about it. And then there was the time I ran my car into a stone wall in Lancashire, but that was just normal run-of-the-mill stuff. This was something else. I can't even begin to tell you how relieved I was to get on that plane and come back here, where I'm relatively anonymous. I missed you.' He reached across the table and ran his index finger over Amy's knuckle.

'Did you really?' she asked as the warm fuzzy feeling from earlier returned.

'Yes, actually. Surprising, considering how you boss me around. I'm positively brow beaten.' Ben laughed at Amy's indignant yelp and stood up, collecting plates and striding into the kitchen. 'I recall there was something I had to do with the dishes.'

'Keep this up, mister, and I won't give you the spanking to go with them,' Amy called after him, collecting the last of the things off the table and following along behind.

'Spoil sport. I'll settle for dessert instead. What's in the mystery tin?' Ben lifted it up and looked at Amy.

'Go for it,' she said with a wide grin, feeling faintly nervous and hoping that he liked her little present. From his surprised exclamation, he did.

'Where did you get this?' he asked, ice-pale eyes alight with amusement.

Amy beamed. 'I made it. It's a bit silly, but I saw the toy and thought of you . . .'

'Really?' Ben's harsh features softened. 'I love it.' He gently lifted the iced chocolate cake out of the tin and studied the small Matchbox Aston Martin perched on top of a ridiculously intricate marzipan racetrack.

'You said you never really celebrated your birthday. Remember that first day you came in to Babyface? Anyway, it sounded like you've had a pretty difficult few weeks . . . so . . . this is an un-birthday cake to make up for it,' she said in a rush, hoping, praying he wouldn't make fun of her for this and feeling relieved when he continued to examine the cake, turning it from side to side with a bemused smile.

'Un-birthday?'

'Yeah, well, since Jo and I didn't get to have our real birthdays a lot of the time when we were little, we'd pick another day and call it our un-birthday. You know, I think I had more than one some years when things were really crappy.' Amy smiled at the memory. 'Jo used to surprise me with them. We still do them every now and then – just had one for Myf a few weeks ago.' She watched his expression. He'd begun to frown so she kept talking. 'It's nice to pass it on. So . . .' She awkwardly shrugged her shoulders and smiled brightly. 'Happy un-birthday! Can I ask how old you are or do I have to guess?'

When Ben spoke, his voice was gravelly and his normal feline smile was a little less smooth than usual. 'I turned thirty-three this year but since this is my first *un*-birthday, let's say I'm one. That way I can be entirely selfish and keep the toy and have the largest slice of cake.' He plucked the tiny Aston Martin off the confectionery race track before retrieving a square of paper towel and painstakingly cleaning it off.

'Hmm, I'm not too sure about that. You only get to keep the toy if you're a good boy,' Amy teased, warm with pleasure that he'd understood.

'Look at this face.' He pointed to himself. 'Isn't this the face of a complete angel?' He licked the icing off his finger and then held out a hand for the knife Amy had just retrieved from a drawer.

'Nope.'

'I'm feeling grievously insulted. For that, you get a tiny, teeny piece of cake and I won't do any of those depraved sexual things you were hoping I'd do to you afterwards.'

'Depraved things, eh?' Amy tapped her chin, turned on and amused at the same time. 'Name one.'

'Hmm, for a start I wouldn't mind seeing what you look like wearing nothing but a few dabs of this.' He leaned over and smeared a small dab of icing on her nose before licking it off.

'*That* depraved?' Amy decided depraved might have potential.

'Mmm. There could be more.' Ben cut two generous slices of cake. 'But I haven't made them up yet. Want to help me ad lib? It's how my best work is done.'

Amy feigned thoughtfulness just long enough to keep him on his toes before grinning widely.

'Okay.'

Amy hugged a plush white cushion to her chest and covertly studied her sister, who looked stormier than the weather battering the windows of the fifth-floor apartment overlooking the Swan River.

If Amy didn't know better, she'd think Jo had a vitriolic dislike of the movie they were watching. Normally Will Ferrell flicks sent Jo into gales of laughter, but today she was sprawled out on her couch, furiously jiggling her splayed knees and frowning enough to give herself permanent wrinkles.

It didn't look like Amy was going to be enjoying the companion-able sister time she'd been looking forward to all week. The mood in Jo's living room was so miserable that both Gerald and Jo's cat, Boomba, had retreated to the kitchen to do their respective after-noon snoozing out of the blast zone.

'You know we don't have to watch a movie. We can go keep Stephen and Scott company at the pub,' Amy finally suggested when she'd had enough.

'Nah.' Still frowning at the TV, Jo stretched out her long legs and propped her feet on her glass and Jarrah coffee table with a thunk.

'Okay, maybe you can tell me what's wrong, then, instead,' Amy said briskly. 'It can't be the brewery, because you just told me yes-terday how much you're loving it. It can't be Stephen, because you were all over him when I got here. If I'm not mistaken, I interrupted you guys mid-hanky panky.'

Jo's generous mouth reluctantly curled up at the side. 'Maybe,' she grouched. 'Not that he deserves it.'

Amy raised her brows in surprise. 'So you *are* grumpy with Stephen? What's he done this time?'

Jo crossed her arms tightly over her chest and frowned even harder.

'Jo,' Amy prompted. 'I'm getting worried here, m'love. You want to tell me what's wrong?'

Jo rubbed her face with her hands. 'I dunno what to do.'

'About what?' Amy sat up straighter on the couch, genuinely worried now. This didn't sound like Jo at all.

'I dunno. Jesus. This really sucks.'

'What! What really sucks? Is it Stephen? Have you two fought?'

'No.'

'Then what?' Amy was on the edge of her seat now. For the first time that day, she noticed her sister's normally smooth, lightly tanned skin was pale. Really pale. 'You're not sick, are you?'

'Kinda.'

'What do you mean *kinda* sick? So help me Jo, if you don't tell me what's wrong I'm going to call Stephen and ask him.'

'*No!*' Jo's eyes were wide in alarm and the word reverberated around the room.

'Then tell me!'

'*Okay!* Fucking hell! I'm getting to it, alright?'

Amy watching in amazement as her solid-as-a-rock older sister began wringing her hands.

'Jo?'

There was a pause and Jo's features screwed up until she resembled a worried walnut.

'I'm pregnant.'

'*What?*' Amy launched herself towards her sister, pulling her into a bone-crunching hug. 'Pregnant? When? How far along? I didn't know you were trying. Why didn't you tell me?'

'*Omph*. Far out! You trying to strangle me?' Jo complained, but returned the hug with such force that her fingers bruised Amy's back.

'I'm going to be an auntie,' Amy said with a gleeful grin against Jo's hair.

'Yeah.'

'What's wrong?' Amy pulled away to look at Jo's expression.

'I just told you. I'm pregnant,' Jo repeated, scowling.

'Isn't that a good thing? Hold it. Was this planned?' Amy settled herself next to Jo on the couch, tucking her knees up under her chin.

'Nope.' Jo picked up the TV remote, pausing their movie.

'Then how?'

'Condom broke.'

'You're on the pill.'

'Yeah . . . well . . . I missed a few when I got that cold a while back and we used a condom instead, but Stephen got a bit enthusiastic and it broke.'

'Stephen, hey?' Amy asked, her eyes twinkling.

Jo pushed Amy backwards. 'Shaddup.'

Amy couldn't help her laughter. 'Sorry, precious. I know you're upset, but you have to admit this is funny.'

'No, it's not.' Jo's expression turned bleak. 'It's fucking terrifying. A baby? I always thought you'd be the one to have kids, Ames. You're the nice one. What happens if I turn out to be like Mum, or worse, like Dad?' She drew a shuddering breath.

'Aw, Jo.' Amy felt her sister's anguish like a kick to the stomach. She scooted back and hiked herself up onto her knees, pulled Jo's head against her shoulder and rubbed her back. 'You know you're nothing like them. No more than I am.'

'You don't know that. I've never really been around kids. I've got no idea if I'm going to be good at this.' Jo pulled back, her eyes swimming, her expression heartbreaking.

'Yes, you do. You raised me,' Amy said emphatically, fighting her own tears. 'Mum didn't. All my memories are of you, Jo. Do you think I don't remember all the times you put yourself between Dad and me when he was drunk?'

'That's different.'

'No, it's not.' Amy looked Jo directly in the eyes. 'You know it's not either. I bet Stephen's already told you all this stuff too, hasn't he?'

Jo averted her gaze.

Amy's eyes opened wide. 'You haven't told him yet, have you?' She leaned back to focus more clearly on Jo's expression. 'Jo?'

'Not yet.' Jo looked down at her fingers, which were again twisting each other into knots.

'Why not? Doesn't he want kids? Surely you guys talked about the chance of getting pregnant after the condom broke.' Amy remembered her own slip-up with Ben only a week before. Thankfully, her period had turned up like clockwork the next day so there had been no reason for panic, but it had never occurred to her not to have *some* sort of conversation about the potential of a baby.

'Not really.' Jo shrugged defensively. 'It just never came up. We still haven't got around to talking seriously about the wedding yet, let alone having a baby.'

Amy snorted. 'You just don't want a wedding because you hate to be the centre of attention.'

'Yeah, maybe,' Jo said in an uncharacteristically subdued tone.

'You're a wally. Talk to Stephen. He's gonna be really upset if he finds out you've told me first. How far along are you?'

'Almost three months. I went for a check-up yesterday that confirmed it.'

'So tell Stephen.'

Jo pursed her lips and went quiet.

Amy knew it was time to change the topic. 'Alright. I'll let it go for now, m'love, but when you finally stop being a scaredy cat, tell me so I can celebrate properly.'

Jo just grunted at that, then pressed play on their movie.

After giving her sister another tight squeeze, Amy settled back on the couch. As much as she wanted to get up and do a little party dance over the thought of a niece or nephew to spoil, she knew that Jo would more than likely aim the TV remote at her head if she tried. Instead, she found herself doing something she never ever did. She talked about a boyfriend with her sister.

'Did I tell you that I'm taking Ben down south next weekend?' she asked casually, leaning down to give Gerald, who'd ambled into the lounge room, a pat on the head. He uttered a loud groan at the attention but otherwise didn't move.

'Serious?' Jo asked, both eyebrows raised, her expression changing from brooding to incredulous.

'Yep,' Amy said with a wide smile. 'I'm really looking forward to it.'

'Hmph.' Jo ran her hand over her still-flat stomach with a pensive expression. Amy waited for her to say more, but when nothing was forthcoming, she turned back to the movie.

It wasn't until another half-hour had passed that Jo spoke again.

'Looked up your boyfriend online the other day.'

'What?' Amy's head spun around. An unfamiliar angry sensation welled up in her chest. Of course anyone could Google Ben's name, but the fact that Jo had looked him up *before* asking Amy's opinion of him hurt. 'Jo, you had no right to do that.'

'Yeah, I did,' Jo replied curtly. 'It was worth it, too. From what his ex-girlfriend is saying, he's a colossal bastard.'

'I don't want to hear this.' Amy was already calling herself an idiot. She should have known better than to bring Ben up.

'No? Well, you should already know about it. Have *you* looked him up yet?'

'No.' Amy raised her chin stubbornly, a look that usually told anyone who knew her well to back off. Jo however, wasn't in the mood to take the hint.

'Why not?' Jo demanded. 'I don't get it. Sometimes I swear you don't have a fucking brain in your head.' The words felt like a slap.

'Hey!' Amy physically reeled backwards, completely unprepared for the intensity of Jo's assault.

'What? It's true.' Jo's eyes flared, her body language screaming. 'I don't get it, Ames. You dumped the only decent guy you ever went out with and since then it's been a downward spiral. I've never got that. Liam was great. He's *still* great. He's educated, nice, and from what I saw the other day, he's still nuts about you. But do you take him back? No. Instead you waste your time with some half-arsed English celebrity who's using you because he's bored. There can't be any other reason. The man could have anyone he wants – and by the sounds of it, he has – so why would he want a hairdresser from Perth? Tell me that. He's using you, Amy. Why can't you see that? Why don't you *want* to see that? God! It pains me to say this, but when it comes to men, you're so much like Mum it's scary.' Jo's words punched through the air, angry, frustrated and hurtful.

Clutching at her stomach, Amy tried to speak around the solid lump in her throat. Nothing came out. There were no words. Never mind that Jo had no idea of what had happened with Liam or what Amy had gone through to protect her years ago, knowing that the truth would hurt Jo so much more than even a year of silence. And now Jo was saying Amy was just like their mum . . . *No.* No, she couldn't have meant that. Their mum had spent years being abused by their dad, ultimately choosing him over her daughters, not caring how much she hurt them in the process. Amy was trying to *protect* Jo.

Jo couldn't have meant it. There was no way she could have meant it.

Amy took a deep shaky breath and stood up.

Pregnancy hormones, that's what this had to be. Jo was just upset about being pregnant and looking for a way to vent. She wasn't meaning to be this hurtful.

'You know, I think I gotta go,' Amy managed to say, while frantically searching for her shoes then retrieving Gerald's leash from the dining table. Clipping it onto her mutt's collar, she snatched up her handbag and made it to the door, barely holding back the tears that were burning behind her eyes. Darting a look back, Amy saw her sister was now standing next to the sofa, her face pale as the reality of what she'd just said sunk in.

'Ames . . .' Jo began huskily, but Amy shook her head. She didn't want an apology. She didn't want to feel obliged to forgive when she was still hurting this badly.

By the time Amy got herself and Gerald settled in the car, she was shaking, Jo's words playing over and over in her mind. She couldn't process them. She couldn't believe Jo had said them. There's no way she could have meant them. No way.

Jo's distressed expression flashed across her mind and, despite her upset, Amy found herself reaching for her phone.

Chapter 10

AMY HURRIED THROUGH the dense crowd packing out the Subiaco hotel feeling underdressed and overexposed. She never, *never* went out in public dressed this casually. In her old pale pink tracksuit, minimal make-up and hair in a loose, messy ponytail, she felt naked. She wasn't even wearing her contacts, instead settling for her black rectangular-framed glasses.

She'd tried to call Stephen three times already but he hadn't answered once. If she couldn't find him in the next few minutes—

'Amy.'

Amy turned to see Stephen standing just behind her, big, blond and handsome in a soft grey pullover and old faded jeans, a pint of dark ale in each hand.

'Hey.' He gave her a warm smile. 'You girls decide to keep us company this arvo? Where's Jo?' He looked over her head, scanning the crowd.

'At home.' Amy had to yell over the noise. 'I tried to call you. You need to go home.'

'Home?' Stephen's expression quickly changed to a frown as he took in her appearance. 'Why?'

Amy shook her head abruptly, struggling to keep her emotions in check. She'd come intending to tell Stephen that Jo needed him then leaving immediately, but the minute she'd started talking, she knew she wouldn't be able to hold it together long enough to get back out the door. 'Where's Scott?'

Some of her desperation must have carried because Stephen looked over her shoulder. 'Over there. Follow me.' His baritone carried easily over the noise of the crowd. Sidling past her, he cleared a way to a window table where Scott was perched on a bar stool, people-watching. His lean body was dressed in green cargos and a loose black knit top, his hair in a long plait down his back.

'Scott,' Stephen boomed and Scott swivelled around to catch sight of Amy's casual dress and distraught expression, his warm brown eyes widening.

'What's wrong?' he asked, automatically accepting the pint Stephen handed him and setting it down on the table.

That was all it took. Eyes tearing up and breath hitching, Amy walked straight into his stunned embrace.

'Oh shit, this must be serious,' she heard Scott utter to Stephen. 'Babe? Talk to me, what's going on?'

Amy's throat was choked up with tears and instead of answering she burrowed herself against the comforting warmth of his chest.

'Amy? You said something about me needing to go home. What's wrong with Jo? Is she alright? Is she sick?' Stephen demanded.

'I can't tell you. She has to. If I talk any more, I'm going to lose it,' she managed to get out, her voice strangled.

'I'm gone,' Stephen said abruptly.

'Yeah.' Scott's hand came up to rub her back while speaking to Stephen. 'I don't know what this is all about, but it must be pretty bad. Message or call me when you work out what's up.'

'Yeah.'

Amy was vaguely aware of the noise of the crowd surrounding them before Scott murmured in her ear. 'Alright, squirt. Out with it. What's happened?'

'Not here. I'm embarrassing myself enough as it is,' Amy mumbled against his shoulder. 'Can we go somewhere else?'

'Yeah sure, but at least let me know how bad this is, eh? I'm getting worried here. Not to mention what you just did to poor Stephen.'

'Jo and I had a fight.' Amy's lip quivered despite her best efforts to maintain her dignity.

'Seriously?' Scott's incredulous expression said it all. Jo and Amy never fought. 'What about?'

'Can't talk about it now or I'll start crying again. Worse than I am now.' She reached up and swiped at her eyes behind her glasses. 'I need to get out of here. Did you drive?'

'No, I walked.' Scott frowned. 'But—'

'I'll drive you.'

She stayed silent on the short trip back to Scott's townhouse, deliberately ignoring his incredulous exclamation about the dog on the back seat, while she clenched and unclenched her hands on the steering wheel, keeping her eyes on the road. She managed to keep her composure until he opened his front door, gesturing for her to enter.

Uncharacteristically, Gerald didn't need any encouragement to follow her. He looked positively lively as he trotted through the door. That lasted all of three seconds until he located a small Persian rug in front of the stairs and collapsed with a huffing grunt, obviously exhausted with all the emotion crackling through the air.

'You gonna talk to me now?' Scott asked, closing the front door and leaning back against it, his arms crossed over his chest.

'I don't know where to begin.' Amy ran her hands over her gritty eyes. 'Jo said some stuff. Really hurtful stuff. She's keeping something from Stephen and . . .'

'This about her being pregnant?'

Amy's eyes opened to huge circles. 'You know?'

'Yeah. Stephen was wondering why she's been green around the gills lately and let slip he was worried about her. I put two and two together.' Scott shrugged. 'It wasn't hard. Not a lot rattles her, you gotta admit. That was the only thing that I could think of. Well, there's that, and the fact she wouldn't have a beer with me the other day, or a few weeks before that. Have you ever known Jo to turn down a drink?'

'No.' Amy shook her head, dazed. 'Stephen knows already then?'

'Nope.'

'But you do.'

'Guessed it.' Scott tilted his head and studied Amy's alarmed expression. 'Stephen hasn't yet. Ya think I should make up the spare bed here tonight? Am I expecting him?'

'I don't think so.' Amy leaned against a banister at the bottom of the stairs and put her hands around her waist. 'This wasn't really about that.'

'Then save me from the suspense. Either that or come help me make us some coffee. I just got back from a nightmare trip to Sydney for a fashion shoot. I haven't slept for a week. I swear I must have been insane to agree to it. Give me a war zone any day. You women are enough to send a guy mental.' Scott gently manhandled Amy to the kitchen.

Amy tried to get her thoughts together while Scott went about the comforting ritual of slamming cupboard doors, muttering to himself about forgetting to buy coffee and declaring that they'd be having tea instead. When there was a brewing pot on the table between them, she finally found her voice.

'I'm going to see the police about Liam tomorrow,' she said, avoiding Scott's eyes, adding two sugar lumps to her tea and stirring.

There was an excruciating silence, then Scott spoke in a deathly calm voice. 'By Liam, you don't mean the bastard who beat the shit out of you when you were eighteen, do you?'

Amy bit her lip and nodded, watching tea swirl around her cup. 'Yeah. He's been coming to the salon now every few weeks since we broke up—'

'And you didn't tell me this why?'

'Because I was worried you'd try and get involved or you'd tell Jo and *she'd* get involved.'

'So you thought you had to handle him on your own?' The words were a whiplash.

'I *have* handled him on my own.' She drew in a shaky breath.

'Yeah and how's that worked for you?' he growled. '*Jesus*, Amy! Between you and Jo . . . first it was your insane parents and now this.' He threw his hands up in the air, then focused on her like a hawk. 'Do you think Liam's dangerous?'

'No.' Amy hoped to God she was right. 'He's just annoying. He comes by every month and slips the odd nasty letter under my door. It's a control thing. For some reason, he doesn't want to let me go and I've let him get away with it until now because I was worried about him creating a drama and Jo finding out. But he came into the salon the other day while she was there and they were like long-lost friends and it was too much. And today . . . today Jo had a go at me for not being with him still . . . I can't do it any more, Scott. It's gotta stop.'

'You should have told her years ago.'

Amy gave him a level look. 'You know I couldn't have. Remember what she was like before she introduced me to Liam? She was so thin because she was always too worried to eat, she spent all her time stressing she'd screwed up in convincing me to leave home, she didn't sleep. All that changed after she introduced me to Liam. Even when we were fighting about me breaking up with him she wasn't as stressed out. Angry, yeah, but not stressed out and worrying all the time. Remember?'

'That was ages ago. Things are different now.'

'Yes? Now she's pregnant, and she'll blame herself for leaving me while she worked overseas for all those years. She'd be devastated that she was the matchmaker and that she's been nice to him all these years. Remember *your* reaction when you found out?'

Devastated wasn't quite the word. Scott had been homicidal when he'd dropped in to see Amy one afternoon and found her nursing a couple of bruised ribs and a split lip. He'd tried to pressure her into filing charges or telling Jo at the very least, but Amy had refused every time. In the end he'd let it go for her sake, but she knew the memory still upset him.

'Yeah,' Scott said heavily, pouring himself a cup of tea. 'Still doesn't mean I'm not right though. So keep talking. You told Jo about Liam and . . .'

'No, it wasn't that.'

He paused with his cup in mid-air. 'Then what was it? You mean there's more?'

'Yeah, we fought over Ben too.'

'Martindale? Why?' Scott was on full alert again.

Amy relayed the rest of the story, her voice thickening with tears as she came to the worst bit. 'She said I was like Mum, Scott.'

Her words were met with a stunned silence.

'No,' Scott said finally, shaking his head vehemently. 'Nah, Ames, you must have heard her wrong. Jo would never say anything like that. Fuck no.'

'She did.' Much to her frustration, she felt her eyes tearing up again and sent Scott on a search for a box of tissues. She had to settle for a roll of toilet paper and his apology because he hadn't had a chance to get to the shops.

He sat silently across from her, staring intently out his kitchen window, giving her the space she needed to pull herself together before speaking again. 'You want me to come help out with the police?'

'No.' Amy dabbed at the corner of her eyes with a square of toilet paper before putting her glasses back on, collecting their cups and taking them to the sink. 'I can take care of that.'

'You want me to kill him?'

'No!'

'Alright. So what are you going to do about Jo?' he asked. 'She needs to know about Liam and I reckon after the way she just behaved, you can step back a bit from worrying about her feelings and just tell her what happened.'

'I don't know, Scott. Like I said, she's pregnant and—'

'Yeah, and she'll deal. She's got Stephen to help her out, and we both know she'll be a fantastic mum so there's no worries there.'

'Yeah.' Amy nodded reluctantly.

'You trust Martindale?' Scott asked, abruptly changing the topic.

Amy considered this. Did she trust Ben? She thought she did. He was naughty, funny and sarcastic. More importantly, despite her initial wrong impression, he'd never once been cruel or mean. 'Yeah, I do.'

'You sure? Because you've made some pretty bloody awful decisions with men over the years. Remember that short, skinny guy? Keith, the *arteest*.' Scott rolled his eyes. 'You still owe me for the time he bailed me up in your bathroom and offered himself as a nude model for my portfolio.'

Amy's jaw dropped. 'He didn't! You never told me that!'

'I'm sure I did, and what about that other one – Clive, was it? The one that used to do all those self-help courses to find himself but got lost when he came bushwalking with us two years ago.'

Amy pressed her lips together and nodded. 'Okay, yeah. They were pretty atrocious.'

'Hell, yeah. Seriously weird shit, Ames.' Scott glanced sideways at her. 'At least the one you're with now looks like a real bloke. Sounds like one too.'

'He is. He makes me happy.'

'Yeah? Well as long as he keeps making you happy, I'll keep my nose out of things. I'm sorry for being a dick the other day. I was just pissed off over the break-in and worried about you. Forgive me?'

'In a blink, m'love.' Amy gave him a small smile that went south again when she remembered what Jo had said. 'I know this is probably a stupid question, but Jo was out of line, yeah?'

'So far out she's left the ballpark.'

'I've never felt this angry at her before.' Amy looked down at her hands in her lap.

Scott reached over and tucked a loose curl behind her ear. 'I know, squirt. But remember, you have a right to be. It'll be okay. Just give it a while, cool down and then make her really crawl when she gets her head out of her arse and says sorry.' He tweaked her nose. 'You feeling better?'

Amy hauled in a deep breath. 'Yeah.'

'Good, because I've got something I've been meaning to ask you . . .'

'Yeah?'

'What's with the slobbering lump in my hallway?'

The next afternoon, Amy was having her bimonthly coffee and gossip with Harry Lawson while Harry's hair treatment worked its magic. It was widely rumoured that Harry was a big player in Perth's criminal underworld, but as far as Amy knew, he was just a huge, somewhat hairy cupcake. Whenever he came in for his beard and hair trim, he made a point of bringing her flowers and tried, at least for the first two seconds, to curb his language. Knowing Harry's predilection to use the F-word as verb, noun and adjective, usually at full roaring volume, Amy always made a point of scheduling him at a time when business in Gentlemen Prefer Blondes was quiet.

Her phone rang, interrupting Harry's story about his son's latest run-in with the police.

'You want to get that, luv?' Harry asked while nibbling away at the chocolate cake Amy had just served him. Harry was the only one of her male customers who required a proper dessert fork to eat.

'Would you mind?' Amy wrapped a black towel around his thinning pate.

'As long as I'm eating, she'll be right. Besides, from what you've just told me, you've had a fucker of a weekend. This is fuckin' good cake by the way.' He took another delicate bite.

'Thanks, Harry.' Amy quickly fished her phone out of her bag, hoping it would be Jo calling to apologise. She squashed down a small twinge of disappointment when she saw it wasn't, then lit up like an electrical storm when she realised it was Ben. 'Hey,' she breathed.

'I'm looking for a petite sexy blonde with a shoe fetish, would you know if one's available?'

'I don't know. I'll see if we have any in stock,' Amy replied, grinning.

'See that you do. I'm in desperate need. Not that I can do anything about it. I've got bad news, I'm afraid.' In the background Amy could hear the sounds of traffic and some sort of public announcement.

'Let me guess . . . you have to fly somewhere and want to cancel coming to my place and enjoying my delightful company this evening?' They'd made plans, but with all the melodrama Amy had forgotten about them until just now.

'Unfortunately yes. I have to fly to Sydney for a round of meetings in addition to a few radio and talk show appearances to bolster my local profile,' Ben said. Amy heard a car door slam. 'It's either that or go back to London, and since Marcella's story's still hot, I'd rather be flayed alive.'

She smiled at the irritation in his tone. 'You gonna be back by Friday for our trip?' She crossed her fingers, hoping he'd say yes. On a whim – or fit of insanity, depending on how one viewed it – she'd come up with the idea of taking Ben on a trip to the country, more specifically to her hometown, George Creek.

She'd thought he'd be resistant since he was such a city boy. Instead, she'd been pleasantly surprised by how quickly he'd agreed to her plan. His interest had seemed so genuine, the last tiny bit of resistance she'd felt against falling hard for him dissolved. She trusted Ben and knew she was doing the right thing in not snooping about him. If anything, Jo's criticism had strengthened her resolve. Although it was so easy to find out information about people nowadays, looking him up still felt the equivalent of hiring a private investigator. It implied a whole lot of things she didn't want to have marring their relationship.

'If I'm not back by Friday, I'll be kicking some arse,' Ben growled. 'I have to go. See you soon. I do believe I'll miss you.'

'Miss you too.' Amy hung up, catching sight of her goofy grin along with Harry's curious expression in the mirror.

'You got yourself a new one, have you?' He'd been coming to Babyface for four years now. Over that time he'd managed to winkle a good number of details about Amy's life from her. She didn't mind. For all his gruffness and roughness, Harry reminded her of a favourite potty-mouthed uncle.

'Yeah, Harry. But only because you're married to your lovely lady, otherwise I would have snatched you up,' Amy said, referring to Tracey, Harry's wife of twenty years and a formidable woman to say the least. She checked his hair. 'Want to come to the back with me and we'll wash this out so I can make you handsome?'

'Whaddya mean? I'm already fuckin' handsome. Look at me.' Harry puffed out his beer belly and gave Amy a big cheesy grin, his snaggly, startlingly white teeth contrasting brilliantly with his bushy black beard.

Amy clasped her chest and fluttered her eyelashes. 'Smitten, Harry. I'm smitten. How about *more* handsome?'

'Too right, ya fuckin' are. If I get any better lookin' my missus'll not get anything done all day.' He beamed.

'Hurry up, Romeo,' Amy called out, gesturing for the basin.

'You got that shampoo for sensitive scalps you used last time?'

'Sure do,' Amy replied, settling Harry before getting to work giving him a head massage. She never skimped on spoiling her clients and had never once let a bad mood get in the way of good service. *This* was something she was good at. The attention to detail paid off. Most of her clients were regulars, or referrals from regulars. After the first year of opening her businesses, she'd never had to advertise and, more often than not, she had to turn people away.

Over the years, whenever she'd doubted her worth due to her father's abuse, her mother's apathy, or her own less-than-stellar track record with men, Amy'd always had her work to remind her that she was good at something.

To Amy, Jo had always been the real success story. Since Amy had been born, Jo had managed to raise her and shield her from their parents, and later got her to safety when they'd needed to leave home. After that Jo had got herself a chemical engineering degree between working shifts as a roughneck on the rigs up north, allowing Amy to get her hairdressing and barber qualification and open Babyface and Gentlemen Prefer Blondes.

Amy had always worshipped her sister. Jo had sacrificed so much for her – given so much. It had been the least Amy could do to shelter Jo from some of the more yucky things that had happened in her life. Surely Jo hadn't meant what she'd said yesterday? It was just worry about the baby. It had to be. She'd come around and apologise. It'd just be a matter of time. For now, Amy would get Harry taken care of and then do her best to dwell on the good stuff.

She and Ben were going on a holiday together. Like a couple. On holiday. Excitement washed over her as the reality of her situation sank in and her worry over her fight with Jo temporarily abated.

For the first time, she allowed herself to think of herself as being in a serious relationship with Ben Martindale. She had a boyfriend. And they were going on a holiday. Things were going to be alright.

Later that afternoon, Amy made sure the salon and barbershop were well taken care of by Mel before piling Gerald into the car and reluctantly making her way to the Fremantle police station. She was expecting a nightmare few hours of paperwork and a bunch of invasive personal questions but, much to her surprise, she was in and out of the place in only a short amount of time – albeit feeling only marginally relieved.

All the police could officially do was put Liam's abusive letter on file so that it could be used as evidence if he did anything else. Amy had felt disheartened at that until a wonderfully helpful senior constable named Kerry promised he'd go around and have a talk with Liam when he was next home from the rigs.

Amy hated to think what Liam's reaction was going to be. She doubted it would be pleasant but hoped he'd take the warning and back off instead of doing anything stupid. The last time she'd openly had a confrontation with him when he was angry, she'd stumbled away with a bruised jaw and two cracked ribs.

As if sensing her distress, Gerald hadn't wanted to sit on the backseat of her car and was instead perched next to her in the front, regarding her with a floppy-jowled expression that she liked to think of as wise. If wrinkles and bad teeth were an indicator of wisdom, Gerald had it by the bucket load.

'You gonna protect me if I have any trouble, boy?' she asked him as she turned the car towards her home, switching on the radio and filling the air with Lady Gaga. Gerald just noisily licked his nose and sniffed at the scents coming through the passenger side window. Amy had left it down a little for him while she was in the police station and small spatters of rain were now flying in and beading on his box-shaped head.

'I'll take that as a yes.'

She began determinedly singing along with the music but no matter how loud she sang, she still couldn't drown out all the worries rattling around in her head. Right now, Liam was the least of them.

It was going to be a long week until Ben returned on Friday, and Amy prayed things would be sorted out with Jo by then. As much as she wanted to, she knew she really couldn't buckle on this one. Jo owed her an apology. The problem was, she had a feeling Jo wasn't really in a state to come to the same conclusion any time soon.

Amy's heart ached for Jo, knowing full well how much her fear over her impending motherhood must be eating at her. At the same time, Amy experienced a surge of frustration that Jo was making things harder for herself than they needed to be. Heaving a sigh big enough to rival the ones Gerald specialised in, Amy pulled her car into her driveway, deciding to break out the ice cream and maybe call Myf, who would put a rosy glow on everything and make it all okay.

It took Jo three days to break the silence. When the call came, it was seven in the evening and Amy had arrived home after a futile attempt to take Gerald for a walk along the beach. Well, *walk* wasn't the appropriate word in Gerald's case. *Drag* would have been more fitting.

Jo started talking before Amy could even say hello. 'Amy, we need to talk. The sooner the better.'

'Okay.' Amy's heart skipped a few beats as the anger she'd been harbouring dissolved. 'You want to come over here?'

'Yeah. In about half an hour?'

'Okay.' She breathed a sigh of relief the minute Jo hung up. It was going to be okay.

She scooted into the kitchen, almost tripping over Gerald, who was sleeping in the doorway, and went through her cupboards to find the makings for peanut butter chocolate chip biscuits. They were Jo's favourite.

By the time she heard Jo's motorbike pulling up in the drive, her house smelled mouthwateringly good and she'd set the kitchen table with a pot of peppermint tea and Jo's favourite mug. Amy eyed the table speculatively and worried for a moment about napkins. Maybe she should put out napkins.

'Ames?'

'Come in. I'm in the kitchen,' she called out, pulling the biscuits out of the oven. They'd need a few minutes to cool down and firm up but she knew Jo liked it when they were all gooey. She turned at the sound of Jo's feet thudding over the floorboards.

'I made some bikkies,' she said, her back still to Jo, quickly grabbing two plates out of the cupboard and piling a couple of biscuits on each. 'There's tea there for you too.' She spun around with a smile that froze when she saw Jo's pained expression. Her brow furrowed. 'You feeling okay, or is the smell making you, y'know, morning sickness-y? Because if it is, I can open the back door.'

'No,' Jo said heavily. 'And by the way *thanks* for sending Stephen home on Sunday. He thinks I've got cancer or something and has been on my back all week. I'm here to talk, not to fuck around with food.'

'What? Oh?' Amy stood in the middle of the kitchen watching her sister warily. 'You haven't told him yet?'

'No, I bloody well haven't told him yet.' Jo impatiently ran a hand through her hair. 'If I'd told him, I wouldn't be here because I know for a fact he'd kill me before letting me ride my bike while pregnant.'

'Oh. Okay. So?' Amy ran her sweating palms up and down her legs. This wasn't working out how she'd expected and Jo seemed anything but repentant. She'd rehearsed telling Jo about Liam over a hundred times in her head these last few days. She knew it was time but she still felt sick at the thought of seeing the hurt on Jo's face.

'So I'm here to tell you I still really think you're making a big mistake but I screwed up saying it. I'm sorry about what I said the other day, about you being like Mum, I really am.' Jo met Amy's gaze before striding over to pull her little sister into a tight hug. 'I didn't mean it. You gotta believe me, alright?'

Amy drew a shaky breath, hugging her sister back. 'Yeah, alright. But there's something I need to tell you—' Before she could continue, Jo pulled away.

'But the other stuff I said still stands, Ames. You've got a shitty radar when it comes to men. It's dead obvious this new bloke is gonna treat you like crap like all the others. The sooner you realise it, the better. I'm only saying this because I love you and I've seen this way too many times. You know I care.' Jo's voice was earnest. 'Just go look this guy up. Do a bit of research and see what he's like. The last thing I want is for him to leave you a wreck. Seriously, I don't get why you go with all these arseholes when there's a good guy like Liam—'

'Don't go there, Jo.' Amy's entire body went rigid as the anger and hurt that had disappeared the minute Jo had called earlier returned to pool corrosively in her belly and the words she'd intended on saying evaporated. The thought of Ben in the same sentence as Liam was untenable.

Jo's eyes widened at the vehemence in Amy's tone. 'Alright. Okay, but since you're still friends and seeing him at the salon and stuff, I thought we'd be able to talk about this.'

'He's not my friend,' Amy said abruptly. 'He never was.'

'Then why's he hanging around? It was obvious he's still got a thing for you. He's a nice bloke, so what's the go?' Jo asked, obviously confused and confounded by Amy's resistant attitude. 'I mean, why are you bothering with this Brit—'

'Ben. His name is Ben Martindale.' Amy's hands were shaking so she clutched them behind her. 'And he's my boyfriend and he's lovely. I care about him and you're going to respect that. Alright?'

Jo just tightened her lips and her expression turned mutinous.

'Right?'

The sound of the oven trays plinking as they cooled down filled the small kitchen.

'Just tell me one thing, Ames.'

'What?'

'What's your problem with Liam?'

Amy felt something snap inside her. The way Jo had compared Ben and Liam and found Ben wanting was too awful to contemplate. She knew she owed Jo an explanation but not like this. Not when Jo was treating her like a child who couldn't make her own decisions. It felt wrong. Now Jo had turned the situation into something that would seem like retaliation if Amy told her about Liam right now, she'd think Amy was saying it to get back at her over their argument the other day. That was the last thing Amy wanted. This had all become so messy and right now, as far as Amy could see, it was Jo's fault. 'You haven't heard anything I've said, have you?'

'Yeah, I have, but none of it makes sense.' Jo's expression turned belligerent.

'No. No, we're not going there. I told you to drop it. You're going to drop it. We agreed not to talk about this stuff years ago. I don't want to talk about it. I've asked you not to talk about it and you're not listening. You owe me an apology. A proper one.' Amy let her last words sit heavy in the room while she battled the need to be sick. Silence fell in the room. She tried to keep eye contact with Jo to punctuate her point, but out of the two of them, Jo had always done confrontation better. In the end, Amy turned around and began piling the rest of the biscuits on a spare plate.

'I've got to get back to Stephen. I'll see you later.' Jo's voice was thick with emotion.

'You gonna tell him about the baby?' Amy asked quietly.

'None of your fucking business.'

Amy heard the front door slam and slumped against the kitchen counter, indulging in a good cry before washing her face in the sink, plastering on a smile for no one in particular's benefit and getting on with her day.

Ben considered not answering his phone. It was an obscene hour for anyone to be calling, but the blasted thing had been ringing for a solid thirty minutes so he supposed it could be urgent. Growling obscenities under his breath, he blindly fumbled on his bedside table, hoping to hell it would be a wrong number, or better yet a friend, so he could wish eternal damnation upon their inconsiderate souls.

'*What?*'

'How does a generous advance and a twenty per cent take on each sale sound?'

'Ross?'

'Who else? I was going to call Colin but thought, what the fuck, I'd tell you first instead. We've had an expression of interest for that travel book I talked to you about and you're going to bloody well do it because I need a new Jag. I get a cut too of course, being your go-between in this instance, and the *Enquirer* gets the exclusive rights to print bits and pieces of it as you go.'

'And this couldn't wait until morning because . . .?' Ben ran his hands over his eyes and yawned hugely.

'Because from what I've seen of your Australian press appearances recently, you're getting a bigger head than usual. If I called at a civilised time you'd just tell me to fuck off.'

'Fuck off, Ross.'

'Can't. I don't have a Jag. If I don't have a new Jag, the ladies don't love me. That's where you come in.'

Ben opened his eyes and sat up, squinting at the dull light coming from his dimmed bedside lamp and saw his alarm clock. It was four in the morning. 'Any reason for the urgency?'

'Your press. From the looks of it, the Aussies loved you and we all know how they like to read anything written about them.'

'Do they?'

'Yes. Anyway, that film of yours, what's it called? *Power* . . . something . . . is coming out in a year or so. It would be foolish not to capitalise on it. Think on it. I'll call you later this week to hear you say yes. Just remember, if you go straight to the publisher and not through me, I may have to cut your balls off.'

'You're all heart. Now I repeat: fuck off.'

'I'll call you Thursday.' Ross hung up and Ben glared down at his phone for a few minutes before rubbing the last of the sleep out of his eyes and getting out of bed. He was awake now. Might as well get some work done before he was whisked away to the countryside that afternoon.

Chapter 11

'DO YOU MIND if we change the play list?' Ben slanted Amy a sideways look. She'd been singing off-key karaoke for the past ten minutes and, amusing as it was, he'd reached his limit.

'Oh, sorry.' Amy's cheerful smile dimmed momentarily.

'Anything else is fine. Just no more Elton John doing Disney. It's an insult to my car.'

'That's what you said about Gerald.' Amy nudged his arm.

'He's an insult too. Thank God you didn't bring him along or he would have been howling at all this noise.'

Amy snorted. 'He loves my singing.'

'How can you tell?'

'He wagged his tail once. Be nice about my dog or I'll make you drive back to Myf's to pick him up.'

'Perish the thought. If I remember correctly, we weren't talking about the dog, we were talking about your abominable taste in music. Disney?'

'It makes me happy. Come on, everyone loves *The Lion King*.'

'I don't. Can't stand it. It's a tragic tale of death and woe overshadowed by a blatant marketing campaign. It says a lot that I've let you have it on this long.'

'It says you were too distracted doing indecent things to your car accelerator to notice anything else, I'd bet. What do you want to listen to then?' Amy flicked through her music selection. 'Cos most of my stuff is like this. Lady Gaga—'

'No.'

'Katy Perry—'

'Definitely not.'

'Britney Spears. Okay, I can already guess the answer to that one. This is all I have. I like happy music.'

'So do I. Britney Spears doesn't make me happy. She makes me want to pre-emptively burst my own ear drums. No more ditties from ladies who flash their titties. Time to search through my collection.' He was rewarded a few minutes later with a loud snort of amusement.

'Jay Z, Dizzee Rascal, 50 Cent, Wu-Tang Clan? Ben, you're white, sweetie.'

'Sort of pink in some parts too the last time I checked,' Ben said blithely. He had a passionate love for most forms of music and refused to let a little thing like the fact he was white and middle class get in the way.

'Jack Johnson . . . Ben Harper . . . Amanda Palmer. . . *This* is better.'

'How about something a bit louder? This is a very impressive vehicle and a very long stretch of road.'

'Okay . . . hmm. How about . . . this.' The sounds of Bon Jovi filled the car.

'That is *not* in my collection,' Ben exclaimed with horror. Even as he said the words, he vaguely remembered Marcella adding a few songs to his selection that he had yet to purge. It seemed she was haunting him.

'Yes it was. Look at this! Poison, Cheap Trick . . . I never would have guessed you had a thing for eighties cock rock?'

'I do not, and it can be purged right now.'

'Okay . . . how about this . . .' The Foo Fighters fired up and Ben grinned.

'*That's* better.'

An hour later, Ben was in leisure-driving heaven. He was coasting along a scenic road with sun-dappled wineries either side, birds singing in trees and a beautiful blonde in the passenger seat.

He'd been quick to accept Amy's invite to show him around her hometown. Although, after hearing the small amount she'd shared of her childhood, he had to wonder how much of a home it had provided her. Not that he'd pried. He was simply happy to be in her company at present, and she was obviously enjoying his.

It really didn't get much better than this after the stellar week he'd just had conquering the Australian media. His news from Ross this morning had just been icing on the cake. He was on fire.

Not only had he managed to lob a few witty salvos into the mix over the negative press he was receiving in the UK, he'd also found a receptive and appreciative audience for his work that he hadn't realised he had. Who knew that Australians had been following him for years? There'd certainly been a large amount of interest when he'd dropped a few hints he'd be writing about Australia in the near future.

Over the past week he'd wondered whether or not he should tell Amy about his plans for the travel book, which would no doubt feature her significantly, and had repeatedly changed his mind. It wasn't a concrete idea by any means, as much as Ross thought it was. If Ben didn't love Ross like a brother, he'd be considering bringing in a Colombian hit man to sort the bastard out for his devious manipulation. He made a mental note to call Colin and threaten him with a lynching, or better yet, a wardrobe burning, should he allow Ross to do anything stupid.

Speaking of doing something stupid . . . Ben glanced at towering straggly gum trees and green grassy fields on either side of the road and realised he had no idea where he was.

'You know, you haven't actually told me exactly where we're going yet.'

'Keep going straight.'

'Interesting turn of phrase. This road's starting to curve here and there. It would be easier if you tell me where we're going, so I can put it in the navigation system.'

'Or you could just enjoy the mystery and let me navigate.'

'Control freak.'

'I know you are but what am I?' Amy stuck out her tongue.

He guffawed. 'And adult too.'

'Last time you checked.' Amy giggled.

Ben realised that was the first time he'd heard her really laugh all day. All week, for that matter and he'd had enough opportunity given the amount of time they'd talked on the phone. Normally she was a cheerful little ray of sunshine, but lately, she'd been distant and pensive behind her smile. Even the impromptu singathon had felt a little forced.

'That's better,' he said.

'What?'

'You're laughing.'

Amy just smiled warmly, bringing out double-barrel dimples. 'Turn left up here.'

'Where?'

'That road just up ahead.'

'I can't see one.'

'That's because you just passed it.'

'Prepare to be fired.'

Thirty minutes later, Ben gingerly eased his exorbitantly expensive car along a rutted gravel road and winced each time he heard a stone flick up, no doubt chipping the paintwork. If he did write the damn travel book, it would include a chapter-long rant on this alone.

'This is why we should have brought my Mini,' Amy said with far too much I-told-you-so for Ben's liking.

'Sorry sweetheart, as much as I'm comfortable with my sexuality, I think I'd have to retire from the fraternity of heterosexual mankind if I drove that car.'

'Scott does all the time,' Amy retorted. 'It's just up here on the left, slow down. See that little cottage? That's ours.'

'Watanabe is either a greater or more foolish man than I, I can't quite decide. Is that a kangaroo?' Ben brought the car to an abrupt halt, scattering gravel everywhere as the large grey marsupial bounded across the road.

'Yup. There'll be plenty of them this time of year with all the green grass around. Along with cows, sheep and rabbits, thanks to your people. If you're really lucky, you'll get to see a couple of snakes and a whole lot of spiders too,' Amy said with glee.

Ben was still watching the retreating kangaroo with rapt fascination as every BBC nature documentary he'd seen as a boy darted through his mind. 'I've never seen one in the wild. Amazing.' He watched the kangaroo jump clean over a fence in the middle distance.

'It'd be a lot more amazing if we were watching this from the porch of our cabin.' Amy gently nudged his shoulder. 'Come on, or another one will turn up and scratch your paintwork. You know they attack cars right? They sharpen their teeth on the metal.'

Ben swivelled around to face her quicker than a possessed child eyeing off a crucifix. 'You're having me on.'

'I might be,' Amy said smugly before laughing. 'Come on, city boy, it's only a few metres down that track. Get moving.'

————

Amy sat on the edge of a beautiful white cast-iron bed covered in a blue and white patchwork bedspread and listened to Ben clunking through their cozy little cottage, lugging her second smaller suitcase into the bedroom where she was already unpacking her first.

'Thank you.' She grinned as he dropped her suitcase on the floor and eyed it balefully. 'Before you start, it's not just clothes and shoes. I've packed some other things too.' She resumed placing her under-wear in a simple unfinished pine dresser.

'Lead bricks? A contingency of overweight animals? A small surface-to-air defence system? We're only here for three days but I have a suspicion you've got enough in there to equip you for an arc-tic expedition,' Ben grumbled before wandering out of sight, back out into the cabin's cozy living area that was decorated in whites, blues and natural wood.

'Hey!' Amy exclaimed after him. 'You're not supposed to make fun of me until we've been together for at least three months. It's a rule.'

'Three months?' Ben repeated softly to himself in the other room, just loud enough to hear.

Amy cursed her big mouth and suppressed the urge to smother herself with a pillow. They hadn't had a relationship talk yet. Or an *anything* talk yet. She thought they were kind of serious, but she'd been wrong about stuff like this in the past.

'No. I can't agree with that.' Ben's voice from the doorway cut through her panic. She looked up from the drawer, now full of lacy underwear, into a pair of mischievously sparkling pale green eyes. His mouth was quirked at the corner.

'What?'

'Don't playground rules stipulate that the more a boy likes a girl, the meaner he gets to be?'

'What!' Amy snorted, despite her overwhelming feeling of relief. 'Who says we're in a playground?'

'Oh I don't know. I seem to remember someone poking their

tongue out at me on the drive down and threatening my car with a hopping rodent. And let's not forget that same someone's evil cackle when I overshot the first two turns to get here.' He sauntered into the room.

Amy stood up abruptly. 'I did not!'

'You did too.' Ben backed her up against the dresser.

'Ow.' Her rump connected with the drawer she hadn't closed yet.

'What?' Ben's expression changed to one of concern as he ran his hands from her shoulders to her waist and back up again.

'You've just bruised my bottom,' Amy said with an exaggerated grimace while rubbing the offended part of her anatomy.

'How?'

'You pushed me against the drawers.' She stuck out her lip.

'Oh? I'm terribly sorry.' Much to Amy's delight, Ben really did look contrite. 'Can I kiss it better?'

'You'd better.' She yelped when she found herself across Ben's lap, her face smooshed against the bedspread as he ran his hands up underneath her skirt. 'Ben! What are you doing?'

'Kissing it better. Shush, you're distracting me. What are these things? Tights?' he asked with indignation when his hands kept going, not making contact with bare skin.

'Leggings.'

'I hate them.'

'What?'

'As a matter of fact, I hate everything you're wearing. It has to go,' he said with enough playfulness to take the bite out of his words. Or maybe that was just his wandering hand, which had finally found the top of her leggings and was inching them down along with her underwear to bare the skin of her backside.

'You know this isn't exactly a dignified position.' She leaned on her elbows, twisting around to look up at him. 'I'm only staying like this so you can kiss my—'

'Hmm?'

'Ohh.' That sneaky wandering hand had decided to get up to mischief. Amy wiggled her bottom a little to encourage it.

'Is that better?'

'No, it's making it worse.' Amy tried to move but he placed his other hand on the small of her back, holding her still.

'Poor baby. Give me a moment. I'll do my best to make it all better,' he said and then proceeded to show her just how very good his best could be.

'So are you going to share what's been worrying you this week?' Ben's voice broke through the sated snooze Amy was enjoying a little while later. She was sprawled across his chest, cozied under the covers, listening to the sound of rain hitting the roof overhead.

'Why d'you want to know?' Amy nuzzled her cheek against the coarse black hair on his chest, savouring the heady combination of touch and his spicy citrus scent.

'Ah. Avoidance.'

'Yep . . . well, nope. I had a fight with my sister.' Amy went for a casual, one-shoulder shrug. 'And I'm having a bit of trouble with an ex-boyfriend. I had to go to the police and . . .'

'I beg your pardon?' She felt the muscles on Ben's chest and stomach tense as he lifted her chin up so he could look into her eyes. 'Is my hearing going in my old age or did you just say police?'

'Yeah, but it's not as bad as it sounds,' Amy insisted, desperately trying not to meet his gaze. She had a feeling if she did, she'd spill the whole story and she really didn't want to get onto the topic of why she and Jo had fought. Something told her that telling your boyfriend your sister thought he was a bastard might be a bit of a passion killer.

'Then enlighten me,' Ben insisted, steel in his tone.

Amy snuggled back against him. 'I don't want to talk about it.

I shouldn't have said anything in the first place. It's been a really bad week and being here with you is making it better. Can we leave it at that?'

There was a weighted silence while Ben contemplated her request. 'Are you in any physical danger?'

'I don't think so,' Amy replied truthfully. She was worried about Liam making a scene but she didn't really think he'd get violent.

'Are you lying just to make me feel better?' The deceptive calmness in his tone was belied by the taut muscles below her cheek.

'No. I'm really not,' Amy insisted. 'Can we leave it? I already feel enough of a loony as it is. I don't need you thinking I'm a colossal nut.'

'You're Australian, of course you're loony. Colossal goes without saying. What I'm more interested in is your safety.' He rolled over and pinned her beneath him, ice-green eyes boring into hers.

'It's all fine, Ben,' she said, trying for earnestness.

'Hmm. You know there's this relationship rule where you have to tell me the truth. It goes with the one that says I have to be nice to you for the first three months.'

'Can't we do something more fun instead?' She wiggled her hips against his and was gratified at his body's immediate reaction.

'That's not playing fair. You know, there's more than one way to get information.'

'Oh yeah?' Amy brought her hand up to stroke the side of his jaw. She smiled when he automatically rubbed against it like a big cat. 'What is it?'

'I vaguely recall you told me I talked far too much.' Ben inched himself leisurely down her body, his eyes narrowing with intent. 'I think it's far, far better if I show you.'

'Smelly socks with a hint of . . . no . . . don't tell me . . . ear wax. Yes? No? I'm right, aren't I?' Ben placed the small glass of Chardonnay he'd been sniffing on the table next to them and thumped Amy gently on the back as she spluttered. The six other people on their wine tour were not amused.

The tour guide, an overly tanned woman, embodying the Australian cliché in khaki shorts and shirt, cleared her throat loudly.

'When you're both quite ready,' she said in an exaggerated accent, while glaring pointedly at Ben and Amy, who were standing at the back of the cellar door of Leeuwin Estate, one of the region's largest wineries, laughing like two naughty school children. The guide's pronunciation of 'ready' as 'red-day' had Ben guffawing and it was all Amy could do not to thump him. The other members of the tour, two middle-aged American couples and a South African couple, added their censorious looks to the mix.

'My most *humble* apologies.' Ben bowed and smirked when Amy slipped her hand into the back pocket of his jeans and not so subtly gripped his tight backside in a warning.

'What?' he asked her, plastering on an innocent expression.

'Behave,' Amy whispered, the corner of her mouth twitching. 'You're offending my people.'

'Heaven forbid,' Ben whispered out the corner of his mouth as they watched the tour guide demonstrate how to taste wine in excruciating detail.

'I bet you have a wine cellar that's fully stocked, don't you?' Amy asked in a low voice a few minutes later while they were trying a too-young Shiraz.

'I'm quite proud of it,' he replied in an offhand manner, theatrically parodying their guide by swirling his wine around the glass. 'Good legs on this one,' he said, referring to the runnels of wine along the side of the glass. 'Rather sexy. A lot like yours. Although I have to say, yours taste much better.'

Amy prodded his side with an elbow and flicked a curl of her hair, left loose today, over her shoulder.

'Is there a line I just stepped over? You have an aversion to sexual suggestiveness in public?' he asked silkily.

'You stomped over it some time ago. Now be a good boy and gargle your wine.'

Later that afternoon, Ben watched Amy's stiff back as she charged ahead of him.

She was adorable when pissed off. It was like having a cupcake unexpectedly growl at you. Right now, he knew she wanted to growl at him to hurry up.

'You know, I think I have a new nickname for you.' He strode leisurely behind her, absentmindedly noting the lush green winter pasture mowed down to a few inches by a flock of sheep in the distance. Not that he was really focusing on the scenery with Amy's hips swaying in a pair of eye-wateringly pink skinny jeans. Her feet were encased in a pair of silly purple wedge-heeled sneakers of the kind that hadn't been seen since the Spice Girls inflicted them on the general public in the late nineties.

'Yeah?' Amy stopped abruptly and looked over her shoulder, her ponytail swinging round jauntily to hit her cheek.

Ben eyed off the shoes, wondering who had been insane enough to sell them. 'Yes. There are a few contenders actually. Pinup Spice? Sexy Spice? I like that one.' He made a mental note to log the name away for future reference. He'd decided this morning that he was going to make Ross's local Jaguar dealer very happy.

Over the past two days, without even meaning to, he'd begun mentally composing chapters for the book. Being shown around Western Australia's impressive wine region by Amy was far too good a subject to pass up. He was on holiday with his muse and his imagination was working double time.

'Walk or talk, your pick, smarty pants,' Amy said pertly,

oblivious to his thoughts as she turned back to stomping across the grass, deftly dodging sheep manure and the odd cowpat without even blinking.

'Do you own any flat shoes? Any at all?' Ben chuckled at the way her ponytail swished in irritation.

'No, they make my feet hurt.'

'Really? You really can't wear flat shoes at all?'

'I don't need to usually,' Amy said over her shoulder. 'I haven't worn proper flats since I was a kid.'

'After you left home you mean?' Ben skirted his way around a particularly large and pungent cowpat.

'Yeah. When I left here I promised myself I'd never go barefoot again.'

'Oh? You know, I never got around to asking why you left.' Ben tried to keep his tone nonchalant. He was now burning with the frustrated curiosity of both a lover and a writer. He'd worked out how Amy operated. It was bloody intelligent really. Instead of clamming up, she shared, but only what she was comfortable with, and she did it in a way that made any further prying seem rude.

'Less talk, more walk.'

He got the hint, realising that it would be better to temporarily change the topic. 'It's beautiful here.' He stopped walking and turned to look over a gently rolling panorama that could have been Mediterranean if it weren't for the eucalyptus trees lining the vineyards in the distance. And the smell. It was a uniquely Australian, tangy, earthy smell that communicated clearly that while it might be winter and green now, it would soon be dry, yellow and baking with heat. The smell crackled in his nostrils. It was hypnotic. Almost as hypnotic as the pensive lady standing a few metres in front of him.

'You haven't told me where we're going yet.'

'We're walking to the spot where my sister and I used to camp.' Amy rubbed her hands over her jeans and looked over Ben's shoulder. 'Oh?'

'It's about an hour away. This is Jeff's property, he's an old school friend. He and his sister own the cottage we're staying in. Anyway, just there,' she pointed to a fence a few hundred metres away, 'is the beginning of Evangeline's Rest. We lived here when I was little. Jo stays here a lot nowadays because she's engaged to Stephen. He's the third youngest son in the Hardy family. Remember I told you? Scott's their cousin.' Something flickered over her expression, fleeting but definitely there, at the mention of her sister. 'Remember the photo you saw on my wall, the one of Jo and me as kids? That's where we're going. With luck the stones from our old campfire will still be there so we can coal roast an afternoon snack.' She began walking again, gesturing for him to follow.

Before they'd left the cottage, she'd wrangled him into wrapping the oddest array of foods in tin foil, apparently to burn them to a cinder in a campfire. Ben was an urban beast at heart and had never camped in his life, so the prospect of charred vegetables wasn't exactly doing it for him. If it hadn't been for the opportunity of experiencing something he could write about, he probably would have vetoed this little trek and persuaded Amy to enjoy their surrounds from afar. From their bedroom window, preferably.

He stepped in something distinctly rural and scowled. 'Old campsite? You didn't tell me this was a pilgrimage back in time to the ruins of your wonderful childhood. Is this going to be where they publicly flogged you daily, or where they ritualistically tied you to a stake and torched the tinder?' Sarcasm dripped from his tone. The mention of Watanabe and Amy's close relationship didn't bring out the best in him.

Amy stopped again. 'Maybe this was a silly idea.'

'No, no. I'm a colossal ass.' Ben ran his hand over his head in a frustrated gesture before capturing Amy's elbow, bringing her round to face him. 'I'm terribly sorry.'

Her eyes were unusually shiny, as if she was holding off tears. The sight was like a punch in the stomach and he felt like a self-absorbed idiot, a two-inch tall one at that. 'How about I try that again?' He waited for an excruciating amount of time before she averted her eyes and nodded.

'Wonderful.' He felt relief course through him. 'Miss Amy Blaine, goddess of impractical footwear, I would be dearly honoured if you could show me the location of your childhood campsite.' He was gratified by a surprised gurgle of laughter.

'Okay, but you have to be nice. I'm not getting my shoes dirty for just anyone.' She gently shook free of his hold to lead the way again.

'*Your* shoes? You're not the one getting sheep dung on Gucci sneakers.'

'I told you to buy gumboots. What straight man wears Gucci sneakers anyway?'

'A straight man with a terribly label-conscious gay personal assistant who does his shopping. Besides, I had no idea what you were talking about when you said, and I quote, "gummies". I thought you were talking about confectionery, not footwear.'

'Not my problem, m'love,' Amy said breezily. 'Although, if you keep making fun of me, you'll wake up tomorrow morning tied to the bed with your feet covered in jam.'

'Kinky.'

'It won't be when the ants find you.'

And with that Ben decided to enjoy himself. It wasn't hard.

Amy was the perfect tour guide. Contrary to her immaculately polished appearance, she was entirely at home in this most rural of settings. The cool winter air flushed her cheeks pink and brought a sparkle to her eyes as she gradually relaxed and shared stories from her elusive childhood. She told him about playing hide and seek in the distant vineyards with her sister and Watanabe, and how they'd taught themselves to swim in a dam that was located near the campsite they were apparently walking to.

The way she talked, one would think she, her sister and Watanabe were the only people who'd existed in these parts twenty years ago. Amy never mentioned her parents. Ben knew better than to inquire. He never mentioned his either, unless under duress. He was curious, but that could wait. While not his strong suit, patience would serve him well in this instance.

'There's a restaurant at the winery here. It's called Evangeline's,' Amy said.

'Oh?'

'It's run by Stephen's sister Rachael. She's a chef. I've booked us in for later tonight. I'd like to take you to dinner for once. You don't mind?'

'Not at all. Why would I?'

'No reason. It's up there.' She pointed towards a dense clump of straggly trees and scrub next to a small gully dam.

'The restaurant?'

Amy frowned like an offended kitten.

'You mean the great pilgrimage is at its end?'

'Yep. I hope your fire-building skills are good because we're going to have to work fast to cook our snacks before the rain over there hits us.' She pointed to an incoming set of dark grey clouds, looking anything but alarmed. 'Although we might get lucky and it'll go the other way.' She took his hand and begun tugging him along behind her. The ground was wetter here and Ben's already soaked shoes got even more waterlogged. He noticed with ill humour that the tops of Amy's platform sneakers weren't wet in the slightest.

He was so focused in navigating his way across the increasingly swampy earth that he stumbled into Amy's back when she came to an abrupt stop.

'Sweetheart? Are you alright?'

'Yeah,' she said in a low, reverent voice. 'It's still here.'

'What is?' Ben looked around. They were staring at the edge of an overgrown clearing just inside the copse of trees. It was small, only about five metres across, and contained a circle of stones in the centre.

'The hideout I made with Jo nearly twenty years ago. I was eight when I made it. The last sheet we used must have rotted away ages ago but the supporting branches are still there.' She pointed to the branches propped against a gnarled and knotted tree trunk. A prickly-looking bush with leaves that reminded Ben of holly was sprouting healthily underneath them. 'We made it the summer Jo and I hung out here for the whole school holiday. Scott found us a few days after Christmas. He was standing where I am now when he took the photo you saw. We were watching the Hardy kids play.' She drew an audible, shaky breath.

'Care to tell me about it?' He raised a hand to brush her hair away from her cheek and then dropped it when she stepped away, her arms coming round to hug herself as she approached the decaying structure. The vivid splash of her clothing stood out in stark relief against the near-monochrome, storm-grey and khaki-green backdrop.

'We used to have this old tent we'd put here.' She gestured to a patch of bare ground covered in acid-scented eucalyptus leaves and twigs that were still saturated from the recent rain.

'Hmm?'

'And we used to swim over there.' She turned around and pointed to the clay bank of the dam before falling silent, her eyes blank as her mind rewound itself to a past Ben had no way of accessing.

He remembered the photograph, two girls, outsiders, watching other children play. He experienced the same pang of kinship as before. Memories of his own lonely childhood began to bubble to the surface. He didn't want that, so he did what he always did when things got uncomfortable. He spoke.

'This is all very moving, but you did say something about starting a fire before it rains. Or is starving us a part of this little retrospective?'

'Ben. Shh.' Amy's expression was calm, distracted.

Feeling strangely at a loss, Ben opened his mouth to speak again, then closed it, settling for taking a seat on a relatively dry fallen log instead, watching Amy as she wandered around.

He had absolutely no clue what she was thinking or what mood she was in and he didn't like it one little bit. He knew he had the perfect chance to ask more, to get her story, but seeing her in this space, caught up in her own thoughts, it felt like the worst kind of violation of her privacy.

Finally, desperately needing something to distract him, he rifled through the small backpack he was carrying and puzzled over how one lit a fire on damp ground.

Chapter 12

LATER THAT NIGHT, Amy lay on her side watching Ben sleep.

He was on his stomach, showing a broad expanse of pale, muscled back, both arms raised above his head, grasping his pillow. Even with his face mashed to one side, mouth slightly open while he snored quietly, the man was too handsome for his own good. In sleep, his harsh features softened until he looked almost boyish, particularly so in the soft light from the lamp he insisted on leaving alight despite Amy's protests about saving power. She'd asked him about it but he'd always changed the topic, distracting her with a joke or by deliberately sparking her temper. She'd noticed he always did that whenever he didn't want to talk about something, used words to deflect her as if he was worried she'd see something about him that he wanted to keep hidden.

She resisted the urge to reach out and brush her fingers over his cheek. She didn't want Ben awake right now. She needed to think.

She was feeling unsettled. Something inside her, something significant, had changed today, but she wasn't sure what it was, or why it had shifted for that matter. It had been years since she'd thought about the past but right now, she couldn't sleep for the memories.

Camping for days, and sometimes weeks, on end at Evangeline's Rest had been Jo's way of keeping Amy safe from their dad's drunken rages. Jo had put herself in the line of their dad's anger to protect Amy so many times she would never be able to repay her in one lifetime. Not that Jo'd ever admit she'd done as much. Jo had never wanted Amy to know what she went through to keep her safe and, in return, Amy had learned to paste on a happy smile and pretend everything was fine so Jo wouldn't feel bad.

It didn't take a genius to see the bruises, cuts and scars and add them to the instances when Jo had encouraged Amy to play outside. A few times it had even been past their bedtime when Jo had roused Amy from sleep, insisting she go out and hide for a game of hide and seek. Amy had always gone along with it, but as she'd got older, the guilt she'd felt over letting Jo take the brunt of their dad's abuse had become unbearable.

She'd finally cracked one Christmas after their dad had found out they'd gone to a Christmas party without telling him. When he'd taken a swing at Jo with a bottle in his hand, Amy had deliberately stepped in the way. She'd ended up with a slashed lip, but it had been worth it: it was the catalyst for them to leave home. With Scott's help, they'd escaped to Perth and started a new life.

Jo had been sixteen and a half, while Amy had been twelve. With Jo's height and maturity, she'd been able to fool their landlords and employers into believing she was legal. They had gone to school as normal, faking the presence of parents at home and generally keeping their heads down so their teachers wouldn't notice anything unusual. Even though they'd got away, they'd both felt guilty over leaving their mother and Amy had secretly travelled down to George Creek to check on her every few months.

She'd been devastated to learn last year that all those years of guilt and worrying had been for nothing. When Amy and Jo had given their mother the means to leave their dad, she'd chosen to stay with him, threatening their lives if they tried to rescue her again.

It had been heartbreaking.

The memory came with its usual stab of pain, but Amy let it wash over her, knowing she needed to feel like this to remind herself what she and Jo shared. She needed to remember that it was better to have Jo angry at her right now than constantly worried and stressed that she'd messed up, like she had been before. Anything was better than that.

Amy was grumpy at herself for not fixing things by now but also knew that she'd done the right thing in delaying the inevitable conversation until they were both calmer. She'd tell Jo everything but not until she knew Jo could handle it and, if she was honest, when she knew she could handle it too. She hated the thought of hurting anybody and seeing Jo's hurt was a thousand times worse than feeling her own.

She was happy she'd taken Ben along today. He was always so curious about her past. Since she couldn't bear explaining it all, she'd thought showing him would help. Despite him being a little grumpy here and there, she thought he'd somehow understood.

She looked down at him again and gave in to the urge to run her hand over the sleek muscles on his shoulder. He smiled a naughty half-smile in his sleep and the icky feelings were blown away.

She'd accepted today that she'd fallen in love with him. Looking at him now, bathed in the soft yellow lamplight, it wasn't much of a surprise. He was funny, intelligent, kind in his own weird way and a brilliant lover. She just hoped he liked her just as much as she liked him.

'I can hear your brain working from here.' Ben's eyes were still closed and he hadn't moved but there was still a faint smile on his lips.

'Am I keeping you awake?' Amy asked in hushed tones, taking the liberty to run her hand up his neck and over the top of his head, enjoying the raspy soft feel of his hair against her palm.

'You are now but keep doing that and I'll forgive you.' He opened his eyes and even in the dull light their pale green colour was startlingly vivid.

'Alright.'

He groaned as her hand drifted down to his neck again and she began lazily massaging the muscles there.

'Was I a bastard today?'

Amy paused. 'A little bit of one.' She patted his back to tell him it was okay.

'Do I need to apologise? It looked like you were having a difficult time of it this afternoon and you didn't say much over dinner at the restaurant. I was a little worried.'

'It's okay.' Amy ran her hand in wide circles over his upper back. 'Actually, I was just quiet because I was making sure I got to eat my share before you inhaled it all. That's the last time we order a tasting plate, mister. With you, I don't need to worry about dieting.'

'You calling me a glutton?' Ben abruptly rolled over, grasped her hand and pulled her against his chest. 'You do know that you're contradicting everything you said earlier about my magnificent body.'

'Magnificent?'

'Yes. Feel these muscles. Actually, don't bother with those ones. Feel this one.' He playfully dragged her hand further down his body.

Amy desperately tried for a poker face. 'Is it a functional muscle? It's not like the ones gym junkies have that look good but aren't useful, is it?'

'Functional? *Functional?*' Ben feigned offence, grabbing her hips and pulling her against him. 'I must be going deaf, because

I could swear I heard you telling the world just how functional I was a couple of hours ago.'

She suppressed a grin and ran a nail up and down his length, gratified by his badly disguised gasp. 'That was the wine you forced down my throat. My judgement was impaired.'

'Is it impaired now? Because you know this isn't a renewable resource, right? Who knows what could happen tomorrow. I may never be able to get it up again, so we better make the most of it.' He leaned forward for a slow, persuasive kiss.

Amy let herself enjoy it for a few moments before putting her hands on his shoulders. 'Tempting, but how about a hot chocolate instead?'

'Only a woman would think a hot chocolate is better than sex.'

'Well, I plan on making a *really* nice hot chocolate.'

'I'd much rather do this.' Ben pulled her back towards him, nuzzling her neck and then across her jaw to her mouth. 'You know you never did tell me how you got this.' He nuzzled the white scar above her lip, catching her off guard.

Since that first time he'd mentioned it, Ben had never brought the scar up and she'd always done her best to keep it covered. It was a physical reminder of her past. Lately, it had come to represent just how different her life really was from Ben's, and her growing fear that he'd realise just how improbable their relationship was. She was terrified that Jo was right. That no matter how far she ran, she was still a hairdresser who'd grown up poor, while Ben's every word dripped with old money.

'Let me up.' Amy pushed at Ben's shoulders.

He rolled onto his side and propped himself up on one arm, searching her expression. She waited for him to talk, say something funny, but at the same time didn't know what she'd say in reply. Instead she just sat up and hugged her knees to her chest and looked down at the rumpled bed covers in front of her.

'Amy?' Ben's voice, unusually serious and low, startled her back to the present.

'Hmm?'

'I meant it about the apology. Have I really been that much of a bastard?' He trailed a finger down her cheek.

She leaned into his touch, briefly closing her eyes when they began to prickle. 'No. I was only teasing before.'

'Well, that's something at least. So I'm correct in understanding this shift in mood isn't my fault?'

She took a few seconds to process his words. 'Yes.'

'Yes?'

'Yes. It doesn't involve you so you don't have to worry.'

'Now I'm really worried.' Ben sat up and swung his feet off the edge of the bed, giving his stomach a scratch and stretching.

'Why?'

'Because if it doesn't involve me, but it's serious enough for you to turn down what would have been spectacular sex, something is obviously wrong.' His expression was so comically disgruntled, Amy felt her mood lighten a little until he stood up and walked out of the room.

'Where are you going?'

'To get started on this hot chocolate, which is supposed to be better than sex, and then to find something to restrain you with.'

'Restrain? What?' She heard cupboard doors banging open and closed in the kitchen, then the sound of running water.

'Oh damn.' She looked around the bedroom floor and located one of Ben's T-shirts. It was black and had fit him quite snugly. On her, it fell almost to her knees. She had a funny feeling that Ben was semi-serious about the restraining her part. On top of all that, previous experience had already shown her the man didn't know how to make hot chocolate worth a damn.

———

'Talk.'

It was fifty minutes later and Amy was curled up with her feet propped on the edge of a pine chair, sipping her hot chocolate and trying to ignore the prowling tiger in the room.

'What about?' she asked, going for chirpy ignorance. It was mildly tempered with her complete exasperation at not look-ing her best. She was well aware that the make-up and concealer she'd sneakily applied before bed had worn off and that her hair was doing a pretty good impersonation of a bird's nest. Never in her adult life had a man seen her so undone so many times as Ben. Before now, the only people who'd ever seen her in any form of dishabille so often had been Scott, Jo and rarely, Stephen. Even Myf, Amy's best friend, had never seen her without make-up.

Ben straddled the other chair and regarded her over the top, his chin resting on his hands.

'Did he do that to you?' He gestured towards Amy's lip.

'Who?'

'This ex of yours. The one you went to the police about.'

Without even thinking, she shook her head.

'Then who did?'

'How do you know it's not just a childhood accident?' She raised her mug to her lips. The chocolate was still far too hot to sip, but she hoped it covered her scar at least a little bit. 'Ben, do we really have to do this? I'd much rather snuggle up with you back in bed.'

Ben cocked his head to one side. 'Why are you trying to hide it?'

'What?'

'The scar. If it was a childhood injury, you would have just told me. No one ever tries to cover up childhood injuries. They make for delightful stories, something everyone can cringe and laugh about. This is something you want hidden. You know, I've only just realised why you always sleep on the one side. It's to hide it from me just in case I wake up at night, isn't it?'

Amy sighed. 'You're not going to let this go, are you?'

'No. It's a mystery and I've never liked them. They niggle at me.'

Amy averted her eyes. 'Seriously, it's nothing.'

'I'll be the judge of that. If it wasn't the ex-boyfriend, that means more than one person has taken a swing at you.'

'How do you know it was a person?'

Ben gave her an exasperated glower. 'Because you would have told me if it was a wild, rabid, enamoured sheep or any other kind of four-legged fiend. Your story,' he nodded to Amy's lip, 'is one with multiple protagonists; you and at least one other person. I like stories. I assure you, I want to hear yours.' He took a sip of his hot chocolate and grimaced. 'You know, this is good but it's still not as good as—'

'It was my dad.' Amy was shocked at how small her voice sounded.

'Hmm?' Ben raised both brows but didn't say anything else.

'I was twelve and he'd just found out my sister and I went to a Christmas party without telling him.' She looked over Ben's shoulder, focusing on a small watercolour picture of an iris. 'He was drunk and lost his temper and beat me with a glass bottle.'

'And?' The word was sharp, terse.

Amy drew a deep breath as Ben's eyes swept over her features, over the rest of her body, as if looking for any more remnants of that night years ago.

'And we left home,' Amy continued. 'Scott helped us. He borrowed some money from his mum and we caught a bus to the city. The rest is history.' She shrugged again, hoping he'd leave it at that. She felt tears, never far from the surface lately, welling in her eyes, and bit the inside of her cheek in an effort to hold them back. 'I really don't want to talk about this.'

'Neither do I.' Ben spoke in a terse voice that Amy felt all the way down to her toes. 'It's not exactly easy to hear that someone

I care about has been on the wrong end of violence of any kind. It's also not pleasant to recall you let me get away with joking about you being beaten earlier today without telling me to shut it.'

'Ben . . .'

He sliced a hand through the air. 'Is your father still in your life?'

'No,' Amy said vehemently.

'Good.' When Amy jumped at his emphatic tone of voice, his expression softened. 'Sorry, sweetheart. Care to tell me about this ex-boyfriend now? Since we're on the topic of violence and why you think he's enough of a threat to talk to the police.'

Amy was already shaking her head before he finished talking. 'No. It's fine. Can we go back to bed?'

'Please.'

If he'd tried to crowd her it wouldn't have worked. If he'd tried to bully her it wouldn't have either. Although she was known for being far nicer than her sister, Amy had a streak of stubbornness that was bone deep and right now she was pushed to the wall and terrified of what would happen if Ben learned about her past.

Braced for fight then flight as she was, Ben's polite, single-word plea confounded her. Before she could even think, she heard herself saying softly, 'Alright.'

It took her a good half-hour to tell the story from beginning to end. How she'd been ridiculously naïve, never having had a boy-friend through high school because of the need to keep her home life a secret. How it all changed when Jo had introduced her to Liam, an engineer who'd been a few years ahead of Jo at university.

Trying not to think too much about the words as she said them, Amy told Ben about her first few months with Liam and how he'd tried to control every aspect of her life, getting physical when she fought with him. She shared how she'd broken it off after that one violent episode and how she'd kept it all from Jo – everything up to the present day.

The sun began to rise over the vineyards outside, bathing the rolling landscape in purples and pinks, and her words finally came to a halt. As she finished, she realised that the tight ball of nerves that had lived in her chest for weeks, maybe years, was now a whole lot looser, unravelling gently with each calm breath she took. She gave Ben a self-deprecating smile.

'Not much of a puzzle, really.'

Ben didn't say anything. Sometime in the past little while, he'd started slowly pacing the kitchen while he listened, eventually coming to rest in front of the sink by the window. Amy took in his profile. His features seemed sharper, much more inscrutable than usual. The sleek muscles of his bare back and arms were tensed as he braced himself against the counter.

'You're a twit, you know.'

She blinked in confusion. 'Excuse me?'

'A complete twit.' His accent became more clipped as his words got louder. 'With the self-preservation of a guppy in a piranha tank. Tell me, when you cross the road, do you look both ways so that oncoming motorists won't have to deal with the mess you'd make, splattered on their windshields?'

'What? What do you mean?' Amy asked, stunned.

'You don't know? She doesn't know,' Ben repeated softly to himself and the scenery at large.

'No, I don't,' Amy said slowly, feeling that fleeting sense of peace she'd experienced only moments ago evaporating.

Ben turned around and regarded her with incredulity. 'From what I understand, and correct me if I'm wrong, you've just effectively told me that you would do anything to keep the people around you believing that your life is rosy, peaches and cream, all flowers and puppies. Am I right?'

'Yes, well, no. Ben—'

He held up a hand. 'So given that you've shown quite a bit of affection for me of late, how am I to know you wouldn't keep me in the dark over something equally serious? If you won't tell your own sister, the woman that you've just admitted means more to you than anyone else, that this Liam,' he spat the name, 'is an abusive bully who delights in making you squirm, how do I know that you wouldn't keep something equally significant from me?'

'This isn't about you!'

'It bloody well is.'

'No, it's not! It's about me and my family, and you asked! All I did was try to make you happy by telling you what was wrong.'

'See? That's the thing right there, isn't it?' Ben resumed his pacing, a lion trapped in a too-small cage. 'You tried to make me happy.'

'Ben.'

'No, no. I want to explore this.'

'I don't,' Amy said tightly. 'I don't understand what I've done wrong. This isn't making sense.' She sniffed loudly and wiped her eyes with the back of her hand.

'Doesn't make sense,' Ben said as if trying to work something out himself. He stopped mid-stride. 'No, it doesn't.'

'No, it doesn't,' Amy repeated. 'Can we drop this? I could do with a hug right now. I'm feeling pretty horrible again.' She gave him a watery smile. 'See? I can tell you when I'm unhappy.'

Ben just looked at her blankly before inhaling deeply, looking down at the floor in front of him for a moment, then back at her. 'Well, I guess that's something.'

Amy nodded.

He ran a hand over his jaw before seeming to come to a decision. 'You know . . . I'm not quite sure how this is done correctly, but I do believe that if I do this,' he held out his arms, 'you're supposed to fit quite nicely here.' He glanced down at his chest and then back up at Amy again, his expression intense, his words tight despite the levity they were supposed to imply.

Amy studied him, feeling a little lost for a few seconds before pushing herself shakily to her feet and into his arms.

It was the faint relaxation in his shoulders that gave him away. She realised he hadn't known how to come to her, but he was doing his best.

'It works. You do fit.' He pulled her close and buried his nose in her hair.

'I do.' She nuzzled his chest. They stood in the middle of the room, holding each other for a long time as the day got brighter and the landscape woke up.

'Promise me something,' Ben murmured against her hair.

'What?'

'Don't give a fuck about my feelings. If you're ever feeling sad or, heaven forbid, in a dangerous situation, think about yourself and for God's sake tell me.'

'Ben—'

'Promise me or I'm never, ever doing what I did to you yesterday morning again.'

Amy nuzzled his chest a little bit more. 'Oh, well in that case . . .'

'Yes.'

'I promise but—'

'Now this is where *you* shush and I repeat yesterday's performance. All you have to do is take off that T-shirt and put on those little pink heels you were wearing last night. Some of that pink lipstick would help, too.'

Chapter 13

BEN'S FIRST IMPRESSION when he opened his front door and immediately switched the lights on was that his house was cold, and the second was that it was empty. It was something he'd never minded before, but now it felt wrong.

The houses he owned had never meant all that much to him. His happiness had always been supplied by his friendships more than material possessions. It didn't take a psychoanalyst to work out why. His rather abysmal childhood had taught him that a friend at one's back was worth far more than a comfortable pillow. After all, the dorm bully could try to smother you with the latter.

All he could think of right now was that he could really do with that comfortable pillow after all, and someone to share it with. A specific someone in this instance.

Toeing off his shoes and leaving them by the front door next to his overnight bag, he padded towards the large windows in the living room. The sea was a stormy confusion of dark greys and greens today. Snarling white caps were slamming into the beach and the sky was the darkest and murkiest grey he'd ever seen.

For the first time since he'd begun visiting Australia five years earlier, he believed all the stories of the rips present just off the coast that could drag an unsuspecting swimmer far out to sea, drowning them if they didn't know how to get away. He'd avoided them so far during his morning swims, but had listened attentively when he'd been told one had to swim sideways to escape a violent current.

The advice was counterintuitive; simple but not the first option someone gasping for breath would consider. So they drowned. Usually they were tourists who didn't know the rules. Foreigners. He felt like a foreigner in more ways than one at the moment.

This past weekend had taken him far from shore and despite being a bloody good swimmer, he felt like the more effort he made to keep from being pulled under, the more he stayed in the same place. It seemed Amy had hidden depths. She fooled everyone with that perfect and polished three-dimensional façade she presented – but not him, not now. The clothes, the impeccable make-up, the chirpy personality, were all smooth waters over untold dangers. If you weren't careful you'd have spent all your time marvelling at the pretty colours on the surface without thinking about what lay below.

The thought, although fanciful, left him with a cold coil of dread in his gut. The last time he'd even vaguely trusted a woman, she'd plastered details both intimate and fabricated across the British tabloids for the titillation of the masses. That had been a mild irritation. He hated to think what Amy Blaine could do to him.

Not that she'd intend on doing anything. No, that was the crush of it right there. He knew if he let her, she'd daze him with her pretty surface, keeping everything even vaguely distasteful to herself, to be dealt with alone. Every now and then he'd have a faint suspicion that her sunny smile was a little forced, but it would pass. He'd never know how she really felt, what was really going on. It'd be like that ocean his parents put between them when he was a small boy, only this time more devastating, because this was one he wanted to dive into.

He snorted. Only a month or so after meeting the woman and he was already forecasting doom and destruction. Not that it was surprising. They were coming up to the two-month mark soon. His past relationships had rarely lasted more than three and he'd ended every one of them. That he didn't want to lose Amy was giving him the cold shakes.

'Live in the moment, you stupid bastard,' he said to himself, imitating Ross's booming voice, taking one last look at the view before stalking to the kitchen to make some coffee.

'Live in the moment is all bloody good and fine,' he muttered moments later while locating some fresh grounds from the freezer, where they kept a solitary bottle of Grey Goose vodka company, 'but it's not much of a life preserver when it all goes to shit, is it?' Oh well, his navel gazing could wait. Thanks to his trip with Amy, his imagination was whirring and he had a script to mail off and a travel book to write.

If Amy thought going away for the weekend would bring any form of clarity to her home situation, she was gravely disappointed. In fact, she returned more confused than ever and pitifully thankful for the immediate mundane tasks pressing for her attention.

The minute Ben had dropped her back at home, she drove to Myf's place to pick up Gerald, only getting the chance to give her friend a quick hug before Myf ran off to teach her weekly community yoga class.

'Did you miss me, boy?' Amy asked Gerald as he settled in the passenger seat.

Red-rimmed eyes looked at her disapprovingly.

'Myf put you on vegan dog biscuits, didn't she?' She gave him a conciliatory pat on the head. She could have sworn he nodded. He certainly gave a doggie sigh.

'I'm pretty sure we can stop off at Costa's Deli and get you something better.'

She ended up treating Gerald and herself to a round of steak and Sara Lee cheesecake, which they ate while curled up on the couch watching *The Maltese Falcon*. Amy had contemplated turning off her brain with some trashy reality TV instead, but just couldn't do it. There was something about Bogart's cool in a crisis that always left her feeling like nothing was too hard. If he could do it, so could she. She looked at her phone sitting on the coffee table. Jo was only a short call away. Bogart would call Jo and have things out. He wouldn't let things lie.

'Maybe after I've had another slice of cheesecake,' she said to both Gerald and the TV.

The next day she woke up from a deep dreamless sleep with a faint headache and an overdramatic sense of impending disaster. The feeling didn't get any better as she made the short trip to work, narrowly avoiding an accident with a cyclist and being honked by a line of cars when she missed a set of traffic lights going green.

Then an unexpected sight intensified Amy's sense of foreboding. Standing in front of Gentlemen Prefer Blondes and peering through the windows was Jody Greaves. Jody, who only made appointments when Mel and Kate were fighting.

'No, no, *no*.' Amy pulled into the disturbingly empty parking lot behind her salon and wrenched her car door open. Mel, who was supposed to be opening for the morning, hadn't arrived yet and Amy hoped to hell she'd imagined spotting Jody out front, because there was no way in heaven she wanted the reality.

She ran to the front of the salon as fast as her three-inch black pumps and Gerald's lagging pace would let her.

Jody greeted her with a wide smile. 'Hi, Amy.'

'*Fuck*,' Amy whispered, startling all three of them. Jody, Gerald and Amy herself. She never swore. That was her sister's job. And she *never*, *ever* insulted customers, which is what she'd potentially just done. Damn, bugger and blast.

'You right there, Amy?' Jody stepped back, her brow wrinkling in concern. She was wearing her usual navy-blue hoodie and baggy jeans and gave the impression of a big hug waiting to happen. Amy needed one if her hunch was right.

She went for a plastic smile, trying to cover up her slip. 'Jody, m'love, I wasn't expecting you. Are you just here for a visit?' She couldn't keep the plea out of her voice as she scrambled through her purse for her keys. It was two minutes before opening time and the sleep-in that morning meant she was running late. Mel was supposed to be here, dammit.

Jody blinked. 'Ah, no. I'm here for an appointment.'

The bottom dropped out of Amy's stomach as her worst suspicion was confirmed. 'Appointment?'

'Yeah. With Kate. I made it Saturday.' Jody's face transformed with a shy smile.

'Saturday?' Amy repeated, unlocking the door. 'Who did you talk to?' Remembering her manners, she ushered Jody in first, followed by a long-suffering Gerald.

'Kate.' Jody hesitated at the entrance. 'Look, uh, if this isn't a good time, I can go.'

'*No!*' Amy drew a deep breath, counted backwards from ten to one in her head and refreshed her smile. 'No, sweetie. It's fine. Sorry. It's me. I'm running late today and am not my best. It's wonderful to see you.' She patted Jody's shoulder. 'Do you want some coffee? I'm sorry but I don't have cake for you. I was away this weekend, but we've probably still got some giant chocolate-chip bikkies if you want one.'

'That'd be great.' Jody took a seat and looked around the salon with open curiosity.

It was no wonder. To Amy's recollection, this was the first time a customer had ever seen the place without it being in perfect order. She'd only left it for two and a half days, but a lot had obviously happened in that time, none of it cleaning.

Magazines were piled haphazardly, hair dryers and trolleys weren't stowed where they should be and a coffee cup sat unwashed in front of the station Amy used when she was in the ladies' side of her business. Even worse, the record player was silent, leaving the place eerily quiet. In short, nothing was right and it rattled her to her bones.

'Great, a bikkie it is,' she echoed. 'Just make yourself comfortable and I'll be right with you.' She flashed Jody another smile, then escaped behind the screen at the back of the store.

As expected, there was a note waiting for her by the microwave. True to form, the messy scrawl was blurred in places as if splashed with water or tears. Probably tears.

Amy didn't need to read the words to know what the note said.

It seemed that Mel and Kate's newly minted reconciliation had run its course in record time and she was now short staffed. Again.

She'd had enough. This was the fourth time, the last time. Every other time she'd been so *nice* about things. So pathetically sweet and understanding and look where that got her – let down by someone she cared for, who'd made her a promise, *again*. Myf had been right; no matter how much she expected people to treat her the way she treated them, sometimes they didn't and never would. Enough was enough.

Screwing up the paper, she threw it as hard as she could against the wall where it connected with an unsatisfying *thak*. Self-righteous anger became a bolt of electricity zinging up and down her spine with nothing to earth itself on. Opening her mouth wide, she balled her hands into tight fists and allowed herself a silent five-second scream of frustration before drawing in a deep breath and repeating her count from ten.

'Black or white coffee this morning, m'love?' she called to Jody in a perfectly calm tone.

'Black, please,' Jody replied from the other side of the screen. 'What's your dog called?'

'Gerald.'

'He new?'

'Yeah, I got him as a guard dog.' She managed to keep up the small talk through gritted teeth as she went through the ritual of grinding fresh coffee beans and setting up the machine.

When she could finally trust herself to keep smiling for Jody's benefit, she made up a tray with coffee and two biscuits and purposefully strode to the front of the store, stopping briefly on the way to start up the record player. There was a record ready to go, and within a few seconds, 'Perhaps, Perhaps, Perhaps' by Doris Day filled the room, suiting her mood perfectly. If she could just hold it together, perhaps she would get through this week without committing murder, and perhaps she'd work up to firing a staff member and *perhaps* she'd finally have some peace. This was the last time, absolutely the last time.

'Are you sure I'm not too early?' Jody asked as she accepted the coffee.

'No, love. Of course not.' She softened her tone. It wasn't Jody's fault her presence indicated Amy's business had taken a wrong turn down a dark alley in the middle of the night. She ran her hand gently over Jody's short-cropped hair with a professional eye. It had grown half an inch since she'd last come. That half-inch represented a small oasis of calm, now unfortunately over. 'What can I do for you this morning?'

To her surprise, Jody blushed. 'I was wondering if you could colour it red.'

'Red?' Amy took in Jody's broad, florid features, her own worries momentarily forgotten. 'Are you sure? The blonde streaks look really nice. They make you look sexy,' she said with all honesty. Blonde suited Jody's short hairstyle and fair colouring beautifully.

'Well, uh . . .' Jody shyly looked down at her coffee. 'When I talked to Kate on Friday night she said I needed a change, so I called and made the appointment first thing Saturday.'

'Oh?' Amy asked, a sharp edge entering her tone, her lips thinning.

'Yeah.'

Amy drew a deep breath and placed her hands on Jody's shoulders. 'Do you *want* to go red, sweetie? I mean, seriously, the blonde is lovely.'

'I'm sure,' Jody said earnestly. 'Kate said—'

Her words were interrupted by the door of the salon opening as Kate breezed in, platinum hair whipping around a sleek black shift dress. Kate spared a venomous glare for Gerald, who had formed his dozing loaf shape by the window, before directing a wary glance at Amy.

'Hi Kate,' Jody called out, her shoulders tensing beneath Amy's hands.

'You get the note?' Kate asked Amy, ignoring Jody's presence entirely.

Amy nodded shortly, turning back to study Jody's hair in the mirror again.

'And?'

'Later.'

'But—'

'I think Jody looks gorgeous with the blonde streaks, Kate. Was there any reason you suggested red?'

Kate strode to the back of the salon to store her handbag before reappearing, her stilettos clicking over the floor as she tied her apron. 'The streaks are boring.'

'Boring?' Amy asked tightly.

'Well, yeah.' Kate shrugged defensively.

'I don't think they're boring. Are you really, *really* sure you want to change your colour, sweetie?' Amy turned back to Jody.

Jody gave Kate a look of pure adoration. 'Definitely.'

Amy scrunched down the urge to have a good yell, knowing full well the only reason Kate had suggested the change was because she was manipulating Jody to prop up her own ego. Not for the first time did Amy think her employee should come with a warning label.

'Alright,' she said reluctantly. 'Kate, I know you'd love to take care of Jody, so I won't get in the way.' She shot Jody a soft smile and patted her back. 'It was marvellous to see you, sweetie, but I have to go next door for my first appointment. We'll catch up soon, alright?'

'Yeah, sure, Amy,' Jody replied happily.

Amy didn't even bother to wait for Kate's response. Instead, she purposefully strode into the barbershop and made a call to post an advertisement in the *West Australian*'s employment pages while outrage still zinged through her system.

She was so caught up brooding, she almost didn't hear the knock on the barbershop door moments later.

She peered out and saw Keith, a fireman from the local station, waiting with a grin, pointing at the locked door. He was one of her regulars and only ever came in for a haircut when his wife threatened to divorce him or his superiors threatened to fire him. Castigating herself all over again for not having things together, Amy forced yet another smile and began her day in earnest.

It turned out to be a truly hectic day that didn't stop until a quarter to six that evening. Finally waving off the last of her customers, Amy limped into Gentlemen Prefer Blondes expecting to find it empty after Roslynn had ducked her head into the barbershop fifteen minutes prior to say goodbye. Instead, she found Kate sitting in one of the salon chairs, reading a magazine.

'Can we talk?' Kate asked as Amy walked past her with a tray full of dishes, setting it down next to the small sink at the rear of the shop.

Amy paused, mentally braced herself, then turned to face her employee.

For the first time in her recollection, Kate looked vulnerable. Her mascara was smudged, her lipstick faded and she had dark shadows under her eyes.

Amy squashed the feeling of sympathy that immediately came to the fore. She was a lady who well and truly understood the importance of outward appearances and in any other circumstance would have gently hinted that Kate's façade was a little cracked, but this wasn't one of those days.

'Yeah. We do need to talk.' She turned back to the sink and began running hot water. 'Or more to the point, *I* need to talk to *you*. Could you clarify something for me, Kate?'

'Yeah. What?'

'Why does Mel always leave every time you two fight? Why not you?' She didn't bother looking up when Kate didn't immediately reply. She was done with worrying about how her words affected other people in this particular instance.

'Why d'you ask?' Kate's voice had an edge to it. It was the same edge she always got at the first hint of criticism, no matter how gentle.

Kate's over-defensiveness had always grated on Amy but this time, for the first time, she felt the need to react. No more being nice and making excuses for someone else's crappy behaviour. She'd had enough. One look at Jody's hopeful, infatuated expression this morning, the expression of a good lady, a kind lady, wanting a bit of love in return and being strung along, had been the final straw.

'Because your job depends on it,' she said calmly.

'What?' Kate exclaimed. 'What do you mean my job depends on it? I wasn't the one who quit. Mel quit! Not me!'

'And apparently Jody needed a different hair colour too, even though it looked horrible when you finished.' Amy submerged her hands in soapy water, rubbing a plate so hard she was vaguely worried it would break.

'What's that got to do with it?'

She finally turned around. 'Everything.'

As expected, Kate didn't appear the least bit repentant. In fact, she was looking at Amy as if she'd grown a second head, a pair of horns and a tail. 'In all the time you've worked here, have you ever seen me, or Mel for that matter, let a customer walk out of here looking like Jody did today?'

Kate looked baffled. 'I'm not following you.'

Amy sighed. 'I know you're not, because you don't get it. I hope Jody gets it though. I hope she's got a good friend who'll tell her she looked better before and I *really* hope she'll trust me enough to come back and let me change her hair back when I call her and tell her she's won a free cut and colour next week.'

Kate just stared at her.

It was no use. Amy took her hands out of the water and dried them on her apron. 'Kate, you're a brilliant, talented hair stylist, God knows how I'm going to replace you, but this can't go on. I can't deal with your need for drama and I have a feeling your friends won't be able to for much longer, either. I'm letting you go.'

She watched Kate absorb her words. It was like witnessing someone being punched in the stomach in slow motion.

'*What?*'

Amy desperately wanted to turn back to doing the dishes so she didn't have to face Kate's upset, but didn't. Although she was really angry, furious even, with both Kate and with herself for not fixing things sooner, she didn't want to trivialise what was happening.

'I'll pay you out for the rest of the month,' Amy said, her voice soft. 'But I think it would be better if you took the time off. I think you should know I'll be calling Mel tonight and offering her her job back.'

'*Mel?*' Kate shrieked. 'She quit!'

'Because you didn't give her the choice, did you? What was she going to do? Come back in here this morning to watch you putting on a performance with Jody? That's why you lined Jody up to come in today, wasn't it? Just in case Mel wanted to keep her job.' Amy knew she was right when Kate opened her mouth to say something and shut it again with a snap.

She squashed down the urge to say more, to rail at Kate for manipulating someone who deeply cared for her into repeatedly quitting her job, making sacrifices for her and looking foolish, just as Kate had left Jody looking foolish today.

Kate would have to learn that you could only push people so far before they pushed back and right now, as hard as it was, Amy was the person who had to do it.

She braced her shoulders and waited for Kate to say something, to begin the inevitable tantrum that usually accompanied a challenge to her status quo. It wasn't long coming and it was just as ballistic as Amy had been dreading.

'You fucking bitch!' Kate began a long tirade against Amy's faults, her failure as an employer, her taste in décor, clothes, friends. She even stooped so low as to rant about Gerald, who chose that moment to finally recognise his name, woofing quietly when it was yelled at full volume accompanied by a tirade of unrepeatable insults. The more Kate yelled, ranted and raved, the calmer Amy grew.

For years – forever – she'd done anything she could to divert or avoid angry confrontations completely, but she refused to back down now. She owed it to Jody, she owed it to Mel and she owed it to herself. She should have done this years ago.

She skirted around her hysterical ex-employee, picked up a

broom and began sweeping the salon in long purposeful strokes until Kate finally found the sense to calm down, collect her things and storm out. Amy didn't bother asking for her key just now. She'd sort all that out later.

The minute Kate left, Amy set aside the broom, sank down on the floor next to Gerald and gave him a pat. When her composure was restored, she retrieved her phone to hire herself back a brilliant hairstylist. She had a gut feeling that if she convinced Mel to come back, this time she'd be here to stay.

Ben was living in a blur of grey as ideas and inspiration sleeted by him in the form of tiny black words, thousands of them, all surrounded by a haze of white noise. The first night after his return from his weekend with Amy, he'd woken up with the opening line of his new travel book and hadn't moved from his computer other than to order take-out, drink, shower and answer the call of nature for days, maybe weeks.

The phone rang a few times, probably more than he noticed, but he ignored it. Anyone who knew him would understand, eventually.

The only person he thought to call was Amy. Every morning he woke up with a picture of her in his mind, then the ideas would come again and he told himself he'd call her after he got the next chapter written, and then the next. He'd never had the words come this strongly and he had a furiously frantic feeling that if he didn't get them all down at once and in order, they'd disappear and he'd never be this lucky again.

Ross wasn't going to be happy. This wasn't a travel book, not in the usual sense, certainly. It was something completely different. Autobiographical even.

Without even realising it at first, he'd found himself including anecdotes from his childhood in boarding school, about his awkward relationship with his parents in chapters that only passingly mentioned his relocation to Australia. In fact, other than mentioning a certain little blonde as the source of his inspiration, his manuscript took a direction that was entirely and extremely personal.

There was no structure in his work to speak of, but an insane hunch told Ben he was writing his best stuff yet and he didn't want to stop. He could edit it all later and get rid of the bits that bared too much of his soul.

Despite his public persona, he'd always been an intensely private man and this would be rolling over and exposing his belly to the press for a disembowelling. At the moment he didn't care. It took him a little over two weeks to finish his first draft and when he finally came up for air it was with a gasp.

Amy.

When he reached for his phone, the battery was flat. How long had it been like that? He shook his head. Couldn't be that long. It wasn't until he charged it up and saw the date, along with eighty-three missed calls, that he realised how much of a hideous faux pas he'd committed. It was one thing to be incommunicado for a week, quite another to be off the radar for two.

Some time during the sleep-deprived haze of the past seventeen days, he'd forgotten that the woman in his head wasn't the woman who inspired him so completely, who he was so eager to talk to, see, smell, touch, right now. *That* woman, the real Amy, probably wasn't too happy about his absence from her life for so long without a word. Damn.

Bracing himself for an onslaught of abuse, Ben procrastinated enough to have a shower and a shave, run a pair of clippers over his head and make himself something more substantial than a bowl of cereal to eat before he gave her a call.

'Hello? Ben?'

'Forgive me?' he asked, then winced at the ice-cold silence that greeted him for the next few seconds.

'No,' she said softly after a while. 'Not yet. Where have you been?'

'Here.' Normally good with words, he didn't really have any at the ready right now. 'I, ah . . . I was writing and I lost track of time.'

'For over two weeks?'

'It's embarrassing, really. If it helps, I thought to call you, I thought of you every day but I know that's probably not much of a defence. I don't know how to make it up to you.'

'Neither do I,' Amy replied in a tone that Ben couldn't decipher. He resisted the urge to punch himself. 'Why didn't you call me back? Or answer the door when I came by?'

'My phone was flat and I genuinely didn't hear the bell.' He grimaced at the poor excuse, vaguely remembering his doorbell ringing at some time or another. 'I didn't realise so much time had gone by. It's never hit me like this. The ideas came and I got so busy . . .' His words trailed off into silence. It was a silence Amy didn't help him fill. 'If it makes you feel any better, I didn't call *anyone* back. My editor wants to cut my throat, my agent wants my liver and my PA, who's a vegetarian pacifist, wants to chop me up into tiny little bits.'

His words hung in the air for an excruciating minute before he heard Amy take a deep breath.

'So you were writing the whole time?'

'*Yes*. I completely, utterly lost track of the time. Please forgive me. I assure you, I promise you, it wasn't intentional and I mean it. I really did think of you. Every day.' Ben had never grovelled in his life but he was doing it now. He knew that leaving it two weeks without a by-your-leave after their holiday was nigh on lynching material. He just prayed she'd find clemency.

There was a further silence during which all he could hear

was the sound of his own pounding heart and some miscellaneous blurred background noise on the other end of the phone.

'You're lucky, you know.'

'Am I?' He held his breath.

'My best friend's an artist. I'm used to her. She gets distracted, too.'

Ben exhaled in a rush while making a note to buy every painting in Myf's next exhibition. 'Thank God.'

'But never for this long.' Amy fell silent again. There was none of the usual bubble in her tone and that genuinely worried him.

He didn't quite know what to say. She wasn't giving him anything to work with. It was excruciating staying quiet and waiting for her to talk again, but he had a feeling he could quite easily put his foot in it and didn't want to risk it.

'Did you really lose track of time or were you lying?'

'Despite what you'd probably believe, I'm a terrible liar. I'm rarely in a situation where I feel the need to explain myself,' Ben said truthfully. 'I can show you my manuscript if you'd like, if that's what it takes, and I never, ever show anyone my work at this stage of the game.'

'I'll think about it.' She sounded tired, exhausted, as a matter of fact. Ben said as much.

'I am. Things have been crazy lately. It's probably a good thing you've been busy.' An ounce of her usual cheer returned to her tone and Ben felt the muscles in his back and arms relax.

He let go of the tentativeness; it didn't suit him anyway. He was still feeling like a colossal shit, but there was no use dwelling on the negative. 'If I prostrate myself before you in your barbershop and beg your humble apology, how forgiven does that get me, and more importantly, do I get into your pants?'

Amy let out a shocked burst of laughter. 'Pretty presumptuous of you, given how hurt my feelings have been lately.'

'I'll make up for it later. I promise.' He tried to inject as much sleazy innuendo into his voice as he could. He really needed to work on the Groucho Marx eyebrow wiggle. He had a feeling she'd appreciate it.

He was rewarded when she sighed. 'I can't believe I'm saying this, but I think I believe you.'

'Wonderful.'

'But I'll believe you even more if you cook me dinner. At my place. And sleep overnight with no complaining about Harvey *or* mentioning how much nicer your house is.' To Ben's surprise there was a genuine authoritarian edge to her tone he'd not heard before, with the exception of when she was cooking.

'Your wish is my command.' He grinned. He hadn't expected to be let off this easily. Although he had a feeling that, with Amy, things were never as simple as they seemed. He was proven correct by her next words.

'It better be. While you're at it, bring a copy of *The Lion King*. I feel like some escapism. I've had a horrible few weeks and you haven't helped.'

'Do I have to? Oh wait, don't answer that.'

'Bye, Ben.' She hung up.

Ben looked towards the heavens. 'You really do have it in for me up there, don't you?'

Chapter 14

BEN WAS AMAZED to find himself fighting a pang of anxiety
as he pulled into Amy's driveway. He'd just spent the previous
hour trying to find a copy of a Disney movie. *Disney*, for God's
sake. Downloading the damn film wasn't an option – Amy's television had probably been made when Churchill was convincing
the troops to storm the beaches, so it wouldn't have any facility
to connect to anything but the most basic technology. As it was,
Ben had actually been surprised to note she had a DVD player
until she'd mentioned that her sister had bought it as a present
years before. He had no idea how she'd hooked it up to the tube.
Probably through a complex series of adapters that defied all
logic.

He knocked on her door and was stunned by the sound of a dog
growling. Maybe the mutt had learned to be a good guard dog after
all. He reconsidered when he tried the handle, found it unlocked
and let himself in, making a mental note to redden Amy's backside
for being so trusting.

'Hello?' he called out, looking censoriously at the bulldog dozing in a beanbag to his left. 'One growl? What was that supposed to do? I'm hardly shaking in my socks.'

The dog just snuffled indignantly and closed his eyes.

'She would have been better off with a cat.' Ben stomped through the house calling for Amy with no answer, only to find her in the courtyard out the back. She was watering a motley assortment of potted plants arranged against the mossy bricks of her walled backyard, wearing a white shirtwaist dress dotted with tiny pink roses and a pair of impractical pink heels with pompons on the toes.

Ben thought, not for the first time, that Amy Blaine had been born in the wrong era. With her colouring and style she would have been considered a bombshell in the forties and fifties. Deciding to wait for her to notice him, he held out the ridiculous piece of Disney fluff as a peace offering and waited.

Amy's mind wouldn't shut up. It had been a truly horrible day, horrible week, horrible month. If she was the kind of lady to pull her hair out and howl at the moon, she would have done it weeks ago. Mel had finally returned after two weeks of deliberation. Her studious, calm presence served as a daily reminder of just how great Amy's lapse of judgement had been in keeping Kate on for so long. As much as she knew she'd made the right decision about firing Kate, it hadn't been easy finding someone to replace her. In the end she'd settled on Ted, a quiet, soft-spoken 24-year-old stylist from Sydney who showed a lot of promise.

In addition to the workplace stress, there'd still been no word from Jo.

Amy had tried calling twice, but the phone had rung out both times. In the end, she'd decided that she'd done all she could and it was now Jo's turn. Scott was overseas again, so she hadn't had anyone to talk to about the problem and didn't want to burden him any more than she already had in any case. Myf would have been her other best option, but Amy hadn't wanted to interrupt her friend when she knew Myf was madly trying to build up a big enough portfolio to hold a solo show at the end of the year.

Add Ben's two-week absence to all that and it was an understatement to say she hadn't exactly been Little Miss Perky of late.

She'd tried to stay optimistic about Ben's radio silence, but around the one-week mark an all-pervasive hurt had begun to gain momentum. It had mixed insidiously with a dread that hung around her like a dank cloud as she'd waited for Liam to return from his usual stint on the rigs. The nice senior constable from the police station had said they'd visit him soon after he returned, which would be either today or tomorrow. She could only imagine how he'd react.

All in all, if someone were to tell her there was an evil genius planning to blow up the world at any minute, she would have said, *Fine, at least I get a sleep-in tomorrow.*

'I think they've had enough water, don't you?' Ben's voice startled her so much she screamed and spun around, only just managing to not trip over the hose.

'Ben?'

'Yes, but it could be your neighbourhood serial killer for all the security you have here. Correct me if I'm wrong, but weren't you burgled only a few weeks ago?' His expression was anything but apologetic, despite the brightly coloured DVD clasped in one hand.

'Yeah but . . .' Amy began and then shrugged. The hose was still running, leaving a growing puddle of water on the paving at her feet. 'I forgot and I knew you were coming anyway . . .' She let the words trail off as a feeling of immense relief washed through her, leaving her knees weak and her hands shaky.

She hadn't been wrong. Jo hadn't been right. He hadn't walked out and left the minute she'd got a little bit serious. The DVD in his hand proved it. For a man who hated all things Disney, even revealing to her one night that he'd received legal threats from the massive corporation for parodying their products, she knew he must really care if he'd got her one of her favourite comfort movies. And he looked so good. Her tummy flip-flopped. She knew she was being a pushover, she knew she should be grumpier with him but . . .

'*The Lion King*?' Her features split into a wide grin.

'If you ever tell anyone about this, I *will* have to kill you,' he answered with narrowed eyes.

Amy ignored his words, took two seconds to turn off the hose and then threw herself at him, glorying in the feel of hard muscles and his warm citrus smell. It felt even better when his arms wrapped around her in a tight hug.

'I take it you missed me,' he said wryly.

'Nah. You're horrible,' she said into his cream-coloured cricket jersey. 'I don't miss horrible boyfriends who don't call for weeks.'

'Sorry about that.'

'You're not forgiven yet. What are you making me for dinner?'

'Take-out.'

'Not good enough.'

'I brought cake too. From a bakery. A good one. It's as home-made as I get, I'm afraid.'

'That's almost good enough. What flavour?'

Ben pulled back and gave her an incredulous look. 'Chocolate. What else?'

'You're forgiven. For now.' She grabbed him by the hand and led the way back into the kitchen. She had a feeling he didn't often apologise, so she'd do her best to make the most of it.

'Do you have a spare water bottle?' Ben asked the next morning. He was lying on his back in Amy's bed and she was curled up next to him, her head nuzzled against his shoulder. Her alarm clock

said it was around seven but neither of them were going anywhere. It was a Sunday after all.

'You need a drink of water?' Amy mumbled.

'No, I need to piss and you have this insane fetish for outdoor
toilets.' Ben growled indignantly when Amy giggled.

'Tough. Put on your big boy pants and go out there.'

'Care to hold my hand?'

She gave an outraged squeal when he pulled the covers off her.
'NO!'

'I think you do.' He took the time to tickle her tummy before
bracing himself for the elements and venturing outside.

Amy howled with laughter as Ben let loose with a string of
obscenities as his bare feet made contact with the cold, rain-damp
paving seconds later.

'It's alright for you!' he snapped indignantly when he returned,
standing at the end of the bed wearing only a pair of black boxer
briefs. 'You're used to it. My poor feet are practically blue.'

'Aww.' Amy rolled over, stretching like a contented kitten.
'You don't look *that* hard done by.' Her eyes rested on his boxers.
'Although, I gotta say, your ego's deflated a bit. Want to come back
to bed?' She yelped when Ben answered her invitation, promptly
pulling her warm little body against his cold one, rolling her over
until she was blanketed by him.

'Vigorous activity, sweetheart. It's the only thing that's going to
prevent my hypothermia.'

'I'll take the hypothermia!' Amy shrieked, protesting until he
managed to distract her enough with the vigorous activity.

They were still cozied up in bed a while later when Ben's phone
rang and kept ringing.

'You gonna pick that up?' Amy asked after the ten-minute mark.
She'd already noticed Ben's habit of ignoring his phone as often as
possible, for as long as possible.

'No.' Ben nuzzled a naked nipple, then looked around for its twin. 'I'm otherwise occupied.'

Amy glowered down at him. 'Want me to answer it?'

'Hmm? Why not?' Ben nibbled his way down to her belly button as she twisted sideways and picked up his phone.

'Hi, Ben isn't—'

'It's about bloody time, you lazy prick!' A booming voice that was unmistakeably English echoed around the room. '*Two fucking weeks* and not a by-your-leave. Anyone would think you don't love me. I'm out a fucking column for this week thanks to you. I had to put in some tripe you wrote last year about touring in Cardiff. *Wales*, for God's sake. Bloody awful.' Amy looked wide-eyed down at Ben, who met her gaze briefly, then went back to ignoring Ross's rant, preferring to concentrate on her navel instead.

'Ben?' she whispered.

'Give him another few minutes to calm down.' He inched himself down even further. She was so soft. He really couldn't get enough of her.

'Don't you dare!' Amy whispered, trying to scrunch her thighs together with a complete lack of success.

'And where is this fucking book you promised me?' Ross roared over the phone. 'You get my reading public fired up and then you fuck off without a trace. I was this close, *this close*, to reporting you missing. If I didn't know you weren't more than likely balls-deep in that little blonde barber—'

Ben snatched the phone out of Amy's hand. 'Ross, you ass, put a sock in it. The next time you want to insult me, make sure I'm the one on the other end of the phone,' he snarled. He was still sprawled over Amy's lower body. She tried to wriggle away but he was bigger and heavier than she was and he'd be damned if she was going anywhere until he could explain his friend's hideously rude behaviour.

'Let me up!' Amy whispered, but he shook his head.

'What do you mean, make sure you're on the end of the phone?' Ross demanded.

'Ross, in your sweetest, most dulcet tones, I'd like to hear you apologise to Amy for your absolutely atrocious display of bad manners just now. She heard every word.' Ben spoke calmly, his tone viciously polite.

'Amy? Who the hell's Amy?'

'The lady you've just crassly insulted. She answered the phone and didn't quite catch your good side. It's rather early in the morning here in Perth and we're still in bed. If you'd bothered to check your bloody watch, you would have worked that out.'

'Fuck.'

'No, Ross. I'm afraid that's not going to happen now you've put your foot in it.' Ben caught sight of Amy's shocked, hurt expression and winced, realising he'd now stepped over the line himself. 'Here she is now. Play nice.' He held out the phone and when she didn't take it, held it up to her ear. 'Start talking, Ross. She's listening.'

'Amy, is it?' The booming voice was gruff and a lot quieter now, but still no doubt loud enough for people walking on the street outside to hear.

'Yes.' To Ben, Amy looked like a kicked puppy.

'I thought you were Ben.'

'That's alright.' Amy spoke quickly. 'I'll put you back onto Ben now.'

'I'm so—' Ross began, but by then she'd managed to twist herself out from underneath Ben, collect her robe, and leave the room.

Cursing under his breath, Ben moved to the side of the bed and rested his elbows on his knees. 'You can forget about the rest of the apology. She's gone.'

'Oh. Well,' Ross said in an abashed tone and then recovered true to form. 'Where the hell have you been?'

'Writing, you idiot. I had a screenplay to polish and I've finished your bloody book. Or the first draft at least.'

'What? Oh. When do I get to see it?'

'When it's edited to my satisfaction.' Ben stood up and looked around the floor for his discarded jeans, pulling them on with one hand.

'Is it any good?'

Ben paused with the phone in the crook of his shoulder as he buttoned up his fly. 'Yes, actually. Not what you were expecting possibly, but I think it's good.'

'The blonde – Babyface – in it?'

'Yes. Her name is Amy and you still owe her an apology. You owe me one too considering how much you've just bollocksed things up for me.'

'I'm not going to say I'm sorry to you. If you'd bothered to call, you wouldn't be in this mess.'

It was an indicator of just how pissed off Ben was that he hung up at that, not even bothering with pleasantries. Locating the cricket jersey he'd worn the night before and yanking it over his head, he went out to find Amy, only to be foiled by the discovery she was taking refuge in that abomination in her backyard.

Deciding that he'd let her have a few minutes of peace and quiet before prostrating himself at her feet and begging forgiveness, he collected his keys and went out to get the overnight bag he'd thrown in his car the day before.

Ben's roar of outrage snapped Amy out of her brooding commune with nature. Hearing the anger in his voice, she pulled her clothes together and sprinted through the house as fast as her shoes allowed.

'Ben?' she called, urgently looking around. An inventive round of swearing from her driveway told her exactly where he was.

'Ben?' She came to a dead stop, placing her hand over her mouth in shock.

Ben's Aston Martin was a putrid mess. During the night someone had upended every rubbish bin in the street over the top of it. The bits of the car that weren't covered with slimy leftovers and miscellaneous detritus looked scratched and battered, as if someone had run keys along the paintwork.

'Oh no,' she said quietly.

'*Oh no?* Is that all you can say?' Ben was standing in the driveway in bare feet, hands on his head and every muscle tensed for a fight as his eyes shot icicles.

Amy gripped her robe tightly around her body. 'Let me get dressed and I'll help you clean it.'

'Clean it?' Ben exclaimed with cut-glass precision, gesturing to his car. 'It's a fucking disaster! Some bastard managed to destroy my car and you think we can clean it up just like that? Call the bloody police. Better yet, I'll call them.' He strode past Amy back into the house, fury emanating from every pore.

She jumped out of his way, feeling sick to her stomach.

Ben was right. It was a disaster. It smelled worse than it looked, too. Whoever had done this had made a point of spreading her next-door neighbour's dirty nappies across the windshield. She was about to turn away to follow him back into the house when a folded, relatively clean, piece of paper trapped behind a windscreen wiper caught her eyes. She reached for it.

The word 'BITCH' written in large black letters greeted her eyes.

'Oh *no*,' she repeated, feeling ill. The friendly senior constable must have got around to paying Liam that visit.

She quickly refolded the piece of paper and unthinkingly scrunched it up in her hand when Ben returned.

'Don't touch a thing,' Ben barked, coming back to glare at his car. 'The police will be here soon and I don't want a bloody thing touched. Just go back in the house and leave it the hell alone. As it is, I'm going to have a hard time explaining to them about the alarm system being off last night because I was under the misconception that no one would dream of trying anything like *this*.' His words were clipped and his expression pure fury. Amy found herself shrinking away without even realising it.

'I'm sorry, Ben.'

'So am I,' Ben growled. 'I should have bloody well known better than to park it here. What was I thinking? Look at it.' He turned around and gestured to Amy's little house, her pride and joy. 'The place should be condemned. You don't even have proper facilities, for God's sake. Bloody tin-pot, working-class piece of shit.'

'Ben?' Amy tried again, feeling every one of his words like a knife blade.

'Just go back inside and put some bloody clothes on.' He sliced his hand through the air. 'The last thing we need is for you to be arrested for indecent exposure. A mess. A bloody mess.' He turned away from her as he said the words.

Looking down, Amy felt a wave of mortification sweep over her. She wasn't wearing any make-up. Her hair wasn't done. She was only dressed in the lacy black wrap she'd put on to go to the toilet minutes before and had been standing outside flashing her legs and almost everything else to the whole street. Feeling her traitorous lip begin to quiver, she turned and hurried back to the house, stopping only long enough to grab a curious Gerald by the collar and haul him back through the front door.

It took ten minutes for a patrol car to stop by, their reaction time no doubt sped up by Ben telling them the car in question was an Aston Martin DB9.

Ben barely managed to keep his cool as he answered the woefully inept questions directed at him by a pimple-faced teenager masquerading as a policeman while a middle-aged policewoman, the brains of the operation, walked around the car, taking down notes. Ben knew it was all for show and was just about to go from being barely civil to downright aggressive when the policewoman asked him if he owned the premises.

'No, but I can get the lady who does.' He gestured impatiently for them to wait and then strode inside the house.

Amy was in the kitchen furiously beating the hell out of what looked to be cake batter, her shoulders rigid enough to be cast concrete.

'The police need to talk to you,' he said without preamble, still feeling the fury boiling in his veins.

It wasn't just about a damn car. It was the bloody principle of the thing. Some bastard had damaged his property, offending him to the core. It had been years, *years*, since he'd been the recipient of this kind of bad behaviour and, unsurprisingly, he wasn't taking it any better now than he had then.

'I'll go see them.' Amy carefully rested the wooden spoon she was holding against the side of the bowl and walked out of the room, collecting a small piece of scrunched-up paper from the kitchen table on the way.

'What's that?' Ben demanded, eyes narrowing.

Instead of answering, she kept walking. A few seconds later he heard the front door bang.

He followed her, fully intending to see what was going on, but didn't account for Gerald, who'd taken up his usual post across the kitchen door. By the time he'd collected himself from the floor and threatened the dog with stuffing and mounting, Amy had returned.

'They've got the report ready for you to sign,' she said curtly, brushing past him and stepping daintily over Gerald as she returned to the kitchen. Her expression was unreadable but her body language screamed upset and Ben's pervasive sense of outrage departed long enough for him to realise that he'd probably have a considerable amount of grovelling and apologising to do in the near future. He didn't have the time or the patience for it now though. She would simply have to understand. Someone had just ruined his bloody car. If anything warranted behaving badly, surely this did.

He finished up with the police as quickly as possible, collected the police report and put a call through to his insurance company.

Marginally relieved that his beleaguered car would be taken care of, if not his offended sensibilities, Ben returned to the kitchen to find Amy still looking as wooden as the spoon she was using to scrape the batter from the bowl into a cake tin.

'A tow truck's coming along with a replacement car within the hour.' He took a seat at the kitchen table, one knee bumping up and down with pent-up energy. He stared at Amy's back, waiting for her to say something, but she didn't. Instead she opened the oven and slid the cake tin inside.

'They said I should have it back within the week if the damage is only superficial.' He waited for a response but still got nothing other than her shoulders tensing even more under the crisply ironed white shirt she was wearing.

He noticed, for the first time, that she'd dressed impeccably in a shirt, chocolate-coloured pencil skirt, seamed stockings and dark brown leather heels. Her hair was done up in one of those impossibly difficult-looking bun things she favoured, and her make-up was immaculate. Red lipstick. Black eyeliner. If clothes were armour, she was dressed for war, and the frilly pink apron she was wearing was a breastplate.

'It's a Sunday.' He watched as she began running water to wash the dishes. 'Why the full regalia?'

Amy's hands stilled in the sink. 'I didn't want to look like a mess.'

'A mess?'

'Although since I live in a *tin-pot, working-class piece of shit*, it doesn't really matter, does it?'

Ben sat back, stunned at his own harsh words coming out of Amy's mouth. He'd never heard her swear before and it didn't suit her. It sounded positively obscene.

'I wasn't talking about *you*,' he said with both shock and irritation.

'No, you were talking about my house.' Amy turned and he saw for the first time that she was genuinely, extremely upset. 'I work really hard for this house, Ben. It's mine and I put every cent I earn into it. I make my payments every month. Everything that needs doing, I do it. It's all I ever wanted in my life and for you to just act like it's nothing—' Her face crumpled.

Ben knew he should react but he didn't. He couldn't work out what had happened. One moment he was furious that his car had been vandalised, possibly beyond repair, and the next minute he felt like he'd kicked a sack full of puppies. Rather than focus on the latter, he took refuge in his earlier self-righteous fury.

'Someone vandalised my car. In front of your house.'

'Yeah, but—'

'So I think that entitles me to be a little pissed off, don't you think?' The words cut through the air between them.

'It does, but—'

'Or do you think it's amusing that the rich Brit bastard got taken down a peg or two? For *your* information, I worked hard for that car. I never asked for money from my parents and I worked my arse off for every cent I made, everything I own. Forgive me if I'm wrong, but you seem to be acting like *that's* nothing.' He stood up, catching the chair before it toppled backwards with an impatient gesture.

He wanted a bloody fight. He wanted to find the bastard who had dared to ruin what was his and beat the living hell out of him, but instead the only target in sight was Amy. It all felt wrong, terribly wrong. Amy's kitchen, Amy's house, was suddenly too small. He had to get some air.

'I'll be waiting outside,' he said abruptly, storming out to the front of the house with a growled '*Move*' to Gerald who, for once, got out of his way.

As luck would have it, the people from the insurance company pulled up only moments later. His car was loaded on the back of a tow truck and the forms signed for the loan car within a matter of minutes. Ben snarled at the tow truck driver when he had the temerity to snicker, but it gave him little satisfaction.

He palmed the keys of his temporary rental, a rather lacklustre BMW Z4, and watched the tow truck retreating, then considered returning to the house before thinking better of it. He was still bubbling with fury. It would be better to go home, cool down, get some sleep, then call Amy later. Surely she'd understand. If she could forgive him for a two-week radio silence while he was writing, she'd surely understand why he needed time to himself right now.

He climbed into the car and pulled out of the driveway, only just missing the sight of Amy standing in the doorway, watching him go.

Amy waited two hours after Ben left, foolishly expecting him to come back and apologise so everything would be alright again.

When he didn't, she got angry. Really angry. She wasn't sure who she was angrier with: herself, Ben or Liam, who'd decided to pick last night to truly get nasty.

She hadn't told Ben about the note, intending on showing the police first to verify if there was anything they could do. She knew it was wrong not to tell him but this was something she had to resolve herself. Liam was *her* problem.

Sergeant Thomas, the police officer writing up Ben's police

report, had taken the note with the intention of comparing it to the other one Amy had given the police, but had said there wasn't much hope for getting a decent match.

Since it had been left in the middle of a pile of garbage, there was no way to confirm it hadn't just been a random scribble someone had thrown away.

Sergeant Thomas had admitted that vandalism was one of those small crimes the cops couldn't waste much of their time on of late, much like unarmed robbery. If Liam had *stolen* Ben's car it would have been another matter entirely, but that didn't seem to be his style. He wasn't a criminal in the most common sense of the word, just a garden-variety bastard out to make a point. That point had more than likely ruined any chance Amy had of making things work with Ben.

How dare Liam do this to her. *How dare he.*

And Ben . . . she didn't even want to think about how much his words had hurt. Not to mention his leaving without saying goodbye. The worst bit was that she couldn't really blame him. She deserved his anger. If it hadn't been for her cowardice in dealing with Liam, his car wouldn't have been damaged.

Liam was out to hurt everything she cared about – her home and her salon. Her stomach lurched. Would he target her businesses too? No, surely he wouldn't. That would be going too far . . . Before Amy's thoughts got any further than that, she was snatching up her keys and sprinting for her car.

Chapter 15

'OH NO. NO, no, no, no, *no!*' Amy wrapped her arms around her waist as she paced from the front of Babyface to Gentlemen Prefer Blondes and back again as cars slowed to a near-crawl on the road nearby, rubbernecking at her misery.

Both salon and barbershop had been doused with a tarry sludge that obscured the lettering on the windows, marred the paintwork and formed shiny black pools on the pavement. Whatever Liam had used was still sticky and he'd been devious enough to throw it over the back door that served as an emergency exit as well. This time the idiot hadn't even bothered to cover his tracks, literally: there were a number of clearly delineated sticky black shoeprints all over the concrete paving and the car park.

There was no way Amy would be able to get inside without getting herself filthy. Stepping around the garbage bins Liam had overturned in front of the back door, Amy spotted a white piece of paper stuck to the black goo and pulled it off. Imaginatively, this one said 'BITCH' as well, in Liam's distinctive blocky handwriting.

If she'd been furious before, it was nothing compared to how she felt now. Idiot. Absolutely bloody controlling *male* idiot. A surge of sheer indignant rage saturated Amy's system. What had she done to deserve this other than try to keep people happy? *What had she done?*

She was the *nice* one, dammit. She was really beginning to understand why her sister used to strategically lose her temper when she worked on the rigs just to keep the men around her on their toes. Amy had a feeling that if she'd lost her temper a lot earlier with Liam, none of this would have happened.

How *dare* he.

The police came and went within the hour. They took things a lot more seriously this time around. It seemed vandalising a rich foreigner's car was one thing but vandalising a local business was another.

In the end, they came to the same conclusion she had: that Liam had thrown some sort of goop at her store, left a note, then driven off. Because he'd done it all early on a Sunday morning, there were no immediate witnesses. Liam had conveniently left a couple of black tarry fingerprints along with the shoeprints so, at the very least, there was enough evidence to give Amy the grounds to apply for a restraining order. With luck, he'd end up in court for vandalism.

It would take days to get the black gunk cleared away from the doors and for the painting contractor endorsed by the insurance company to get things back to normal. There was no way Amy could subject her staff or clients to paint fumes while the work was under-way, so she cancelled her appointments and gave her staff some time off. By the time she climbed into her car at the end of the day, she was determined to end this once and for all. She'd had enough.

She hit the road and floored the accelerator. As she drove east towards the hills surrounding Perth, her fury grew. By the time she got to Liam's place, her hands were shaking on the steering wheel and her head was pounding.

The seventies bungalow with its stained cream bricks still smelled of bore water and claustrophobia. The meticulously mowed front lawn was bare with the exception of a lone pencil pine.

The fact that nothing, absolutely nothing, had changed just served to make Amy angrier as she pulled into Liam's cracked concrete driveway, then climbed out of her car, stomping purposefully to the front door.

Liam answered at the second knock. He was shirtless, his barrel chest bare, wearing only low-slung jeans and a stunned expression that quickly changed to amazement as Amy found her voice.

'You *bastard*,' she screeched, advancing on him until only an inch separated them, her hands clenched at her sides in tightly balled fists.

'Amy?' Liam stumbled back into the recesses of the house, his expression as gormless as a guppy's, as Amy took another step towards him.

'*Leave me alone!*' She poked his chest with her finger, her nail leaving a satisfying red crescent. 'I don't want to see you *ever again*. I'm never, *ever* going to be your girlfriend again and if you come near me, my house or my business again I'll . . .' She paused as shockingly violent images flitted through her mind featuring various parts of Liam strewn across his front lawn. She drew a deep breath. 'Go to the police again. But before I do that, I want to say something I should have said years ago. I don't love you. I never loved you. I don't want to be with you and I never will. Ever. Leave. Me. Alone.'

Her eyes narrowed on the red flush spreading from Liam's chest to his cheeks. She recognised that look. It was the same one he'd worn the last time he'd taken a swing at her, but this time she wasn't scared. It made her even angrier. 'And if you even *think* of hitting me again, I'll bloody well hit back. These are four-inch stilettos I'm wearing and I *will* use them.' She reached down, wrenched off a shoe and held it up in front of her, pointed heel aimed at him.

'*What the fuck do you think you're doin'?*' Liam roared, taking another step backwards, his expression incredulous.

'Warning you off, you *idiot*!' Amy's voice, not suited to this much strain, came out as a squeak. 'You've vandalised my business! You've destroyed my boyfriend's car! What the heck do you think I'm doing?' She punctuated her words by waving her shoe around so much that he threw his arms up in front of his face to defend himself.

'You sent the police after me!' Liam bellowed, trying to step forward but stopping when faced with a flailing shoe.

'Because *you scared me*! You wouldn't leave me alone. You *hit* me, Liam. Don't you remember that?' Amy asked incredulously, watching with amazement as Liam deflated right in front of her eyes.

'Yeah. But that was years ago.'

'And how does that make me feel any better? How was I supposed to know you wouldn't do it again? How do I know you won't try again *now*? You scare me every time you come to my work. You don't take no for an answer. You even left notes calling me a bitch in the wreckage last night!' Amy paused as a suspicion began to take form. 'You were behind the burglary, weren't you?'

Liam puffed up again, his face nearly purple. 'You went to the cops! What else did you expect me to do? And whaddya mean burglary? What burglary? Who burgled you?' He had the temerity to sound outraged, which just set Amy's blood back on the boil again.

'For the love of God!' She threw her hands up in the air, shoe and all. 'I went to the police so you'd leave me alone. I know you're not stupid. You're university educated, you hold a good job, so why can't you get this through your thick head? It's been nearly ten years. *Ten years.* Get yourself some therapy and get a life. You don't need me. You never really even wanted me when you had me. I have no idea, *no idea*, why you're still hanging around now. The only answer I can come up with is that you're pathetic and you can't let go.' She felt the anger that had propelled her to Liam's doorstep abating enough for her to speak calmly. 'Look, if you're lucky, the police won't charge you with vandalism over Ben's car and my shop, but I doubt it. *And* I'll be applying for a restraining order against you first thing tomorrow, so you'll have to accept that you can't see me again. Forever. I know it's not easy working offshore and it's hard to meet people, but you've gotta move on. I can't believe I'm saying this, considering how upset I am with you, but I feel sorry for you. Move on and get a life.' She turned on her heel and hobbled back to her car, not even bothering to replace her shoe or caring if one of her favourite French stockings was being irreparably damaged.

She didn't wait to hear him saying anything else. The adrenaline from being so angry was wearing off and was quickly being replaced by a serious case of the shakes and the urge to vomit.

She'd just climbed in and turned the key when Liam thumped her window, his face disturbingly close to hers on the other side of the glass as he gestured for her to wind it down.

Amy felt a jolt of fright and immediately began reversing down the driveway, wanting to get away as soon as possible, only to relent when she heard a muffled 'Please.'

'What?' She slammed her foot on the brake and wound down the window a couple of centimetres.

'Did I really scare you?' Liam's voice was a mixture of outrage and something else. Maybe if she was going temporarily insane, she'd think it was disbelief.

'Just now? *Yes!*'

'No, I mean before.'

'*Yes.*'

'Serious? I wasn't doing anything. Just dropping in to say hello,' he said petulantly and then stepped back at Amy's look of fury. 'Well, until last night.'

'Bye, Liam.' Amy started to wind her window up again.

'Stop.' Liam tried to jam his sausage-like fingers through the gap so that she had the choice of trapping them there and taking him with her, or waiting to hear what he had to say. She looked at him through the glass, eyebrows raised.

'I didn't mean . . . aw, fuck . . . I didn't mean to get outta hand last night, or those other times I left you letters. I had a few beers – a lotta beers – and was gonna come round and ask you why you went to the police and—'

'You were *stalking* me!'

'Yeah, well I wouldn't go that far . . . then I saw the car and knew it was some other bloke's . . . I was good to you!'

'*You abused me, Liam!* You threatened to get my sister fired from her job when I wouldn't come back to you! What part of "stalking" don't you get?' Amy looked around for her discarded shoe.

'Yeah, but I said sorry.'

'No, you didn't. You never did.'

'Didn't I?'

'No,' Amy said tightly.

'I'm sorry, Amy.' His face was pressed grotesquely up against the window, a parody of contrition.

'Not good enough. You don't just owe *me* an apology now. You ruined my boyfriend's car.' The memory of the fight she'd had with Ben and the words he'd said washed over her. 'That's if he's still my boyfriend.'

'Yeah, well . . .' Liam stepped back, crossing his arms over his chest. He didn't look so threatening now. Instead he appeared strangely lost and despite everything, Amy found herself feeling sorry for him.

'Liam, it's over. It was over a long time ago. Just leave me alone. *Please?*' She felt tears rising to the surface but was damned if she'd show them. Instead she ran the heel of the shoe she was wearing over her ankle hoping the physical pain would prove a distraction. It worked, but she knew it was only temporary.

'Was I really that bad?' he asked plaintively.

'Yes. Yes, you were.' Amy sighed. 'If Jo hadn't introduced me to you and if I hadn't been so worried about hurting her feelings, I probably never would have gone out with you.' As she spoke, she realised the words were the truth, and it devastated her. How could she have been such a doormat? Self-disgust came thick and fast, along with the need to get away. 'Move back, Liam. I've got to go. I don't ever want to see you again.' She made eye contact with him and held it for long enough to convince herself she'd made a stand. Later she'd be able to pinpoint the exact moment when he realised it was over and accepted it.

His shoulders drooped and his expression crumpled. 'Amy . . .'

Amy didn't want to hear any more. She didn't even bother to look in her rear-view as she reversed out of the driveway and drove off. She'd had enough of the past haunting her.

When she'd driven a good ten minutes, she pulled over on the side of Reid Highway, opened the car door and promptly lost the small amount of food she'd eaten that day. Never in her life had she confronted someone like that, not even her own parents, and contrary to what she'd expected, it hadn't felt liberating. It had just felt sad and pathetic.

Resting her head on the steering wheel until her nerves settled down, she waited for the self-recriminations and anger to abate before heading home. Tin-pot little house or not, she'd never felt the need to be there more than now.

Amy was jarred out of a fitful sleep the next morning by a loud banging on her front door. Whoever it was either wanted to talk to her badly or had a thing against doors on principle.

Her first bleary thought, accompanied by a healthy dose of dread, was that Liam had decided to turn into a deranged psychopath. Her second thought, a much more welcome one, was that Ben was here to make up.

The last person she expected to see when she opened the door was her sister looking like she'd gone a few rounds with a combine harvester. Jo's hair, the colour faded, was standing on end and her blue jeans and purple-and-white Perth Glory football jersey looked slept-in. Not that she'd been doing any sleeping if the huge black circles under her eyes were any indication.

Amy barely had time to feel concerned before Jo pulled her into a bone-crunching bear hug, lifting her feet off the floor. 'You're alright. Jesus Christ, I was worried.'

'Oomph.' Amy automatically returned the hug, inhaling the scent of her sister's faintly floral perfume. 'I'm fine, but I think I'm missing a few ribs now.'

Jo didn't let her go for a few more seconds, then released her gently, pulling back to look her up and down. 'You look like shit.'

'Gee, thanks.' Amy pushed her dishevelled hair out of her eyes and pulled Ben's T-shirt, the one she'd found on her bedroom floor, further down her thighs. 'You want a coffee?'

'Yeah.' Jo studied her features with a worried frown. 'Are you seriously alright? I just saw the salon and—'

'I know,' Amy interrupted, collecting the crocheted afghan off the back of her couch and wrapping it around her to ward off the chill before leading the way to the kitchen. 'It happened yesterday. I've got to go down there and supervise the painters this afternoon.' She located her coffee beans along with the chocolate cake she'd made the day before while trying to calm down after Ben's outburst.

'Did you call the police?'

'Yeah,' Amy said curtly, not wanting to dwell on the details. 'Hey, are you sure you want coffee?' She looked pointedly at Jo's stomach, currently obscured by her jersey.

Jo grimaced. 'I'm allowing myself one a day and the withdrawals from cutting back are killing me. It's the smell I miss more than anything. Although I might pass on the cake. I can't stand the smell of chocolate at the moment.'

'Oh. Okay.' Amy couldn't imagine not being able to eat chocolate. Out of deference to Jo, she repackaged the two slices she'd just cut and set them aside so Jo could take them home for Stephen.

A light spring shower began pitter-pattering on the roof.

'I had my first big ultrasound three days ago.' Jo's voice was unnaturally loud against the muted rain.

'Yeah?' Amy drew a shaky breath and added boiling water to her coffee plunger. 'Everything okay?'

'Yeah. Stephen was with me,' Jo said gruffly. 'I brought the pictures if you want to see them.'

Amy bit her lip and counted to ten. 'Yeah,' she said in a choked voice, still not wanting to turn around. She poured out the coffees. 'That'd be great.' Squeezing her eyes shut, she took another deep breath before carrying the coffees the short distance to the table, placing Jo's in front of her.

'So do you know who did it?' Jo asked, playing with the handle of her cup.

'Pardon?'

'Your salon. Do you know who trashed it?'

Amy averted her gaze to a pile of mail she had yet to open. She ran her finger over the RSPCA logo on what would no doubt be a request for money.

'You *do* know. Who did it? A pissed-off customer? Who, Ames?'

Amy sighed. She raised her eyes to look at her sister. 'No. Nothing like that. It was Liam.'

Jo's expression froze. 'Liam?'

'Yeah. He didn't react too well to the news I'd reported him to the police. They must have visited him when he got home from the rigs on Saturday and—'

'*Liam?*' Jo's voice rose in volume. Unlike Amy, Jo had a good voice for shouting. Amy hoped her future niece or nephew hadn't developed little ears yet, or there was a good chance they'd just been stunned.

'Yeah.' Amy tried her best to keep her voice calm.

'What *the fuck*! Liam? What do you mean, *Liam*?' Jo demanded, leaning across the table. 'We're talking the same Liam right? Your ex-boyfriend, my *friend*, Liam?'

'Yeah.' Amy's chin came up at the disbelief in Jo's tone.

Jo sat in stunned silence, twin flags of red riding high on her cheekbones as she processed Amy's words. When they finally sank in, she exploded.

'And you were going to tell me about all this when?' She stood up abruptly, looming over Amy, her chair scraping across the floor. It toppled backwards, clattering against the wall. Jo righted it with an impatient gesture.

Amy started to defend herself and then stopped.

No. This wasn't how it was going to go. It couldn't work like this any more. A cool calm sensation washed over her. It wasn't quite anger; it was something far more complicated.

'Sit *down*, Jo,' she said calmly and was just as shocked as Jo when her sister complied. Jo opened her mouth to speak but Amy held up a hand. 'I need to tell you something. I'm going to talk and you're going to listen. Alright? Some of the stuff I'm going to tell you might hurt your feelings, but you're gonna have to deal with it.'

Jo stared at her as if she was possessed. 'What's this all about?'

'There's a bunch of stuff I should have told you about years ago . . . about Liam and what happened between us.' Amy paused.

Jo's mouth flattened into a grim line but she didn't say anything, just nodded curtly for Amy to continue.

'Liam was like Dad.' When Jo's features blanched, Amy had to fight the urge to stop talking right then and there, but the memory of how awful the past weeks had been kept her going. 'I broke up with him after he hit me the first time. I didn't tell you about it because he threatened to get you fired from your job and, more importantly, I didn't want you to feel bad.' She gave a dismal shrug. 'It was silly. I know that now, but that's how I felt. You did so much for me. I didn't want you feeling guilty about working away and not being there.'

'All those years ago when I blasted you for breaking up with him . . . why didn't you say something? We didn't talk for a year!' Jo exclaimed in a croaky voice, her expression stricken.

'Yeah. Well at the time – up until just recently – I thought that was better than you knowing. I didn't want you feeling like this, feeling like it was your fault.' Amy averted her eyes, her heart breaking at the pain mapped on her sister's face.

'So, what? So since then he's been – you let it get bad enough that you had to go to the police? *What the fuck has he been doing?*' Jo's voice rose until it cracked.

Amy looked down at her hands wrapped around her coffee mug. 'He didn't do anything other than turn up to work. It was the last time I saw him. It was the time when you were there. I knew it couldn't keep going on like that. He'd come in at least every month and stress me out; sometimes he'd leave notes under my door. You being there just showed me how stupid it was to let things continue. I know it was silly of me but I wanted to protect you.'

Jo made a quiet keening noise. 'Ames—'

'You didn't know, so don't go there, sweetie,' Amy said gently.

'Why didn't you tell me?' Jo asked, her expression pleading, her eyes watering. 'I would have done something. I woulda warned him off. I can't believe you kept this to yourself.' If anything, she looked more hurt than before. 'Did Scott know? He always told me to back off over this. He knew, didn't he?'

Amy nodded reluctantly. 'Yeah. But only because he saw me after Liam—' Her words bled into the stream of profanity Jo rained down on the kitchen.

Flinching every now and then, Amy just waited until Jo drew a breath.

'It's over now, Jo. I saw him last night and it's over.'

'*Last night?* Is this *after* he trashed your shop? Fucking hell!'

Amy abruptly stood up. 'Enough! I'm a big girl, Jo. I dealt with it. I'm not five any more, okay?'

'I know but—' Jo began but Amy interrupted her.

'And if you respect me and love me, you'll trust me and believe me.' Amy's voice wobbled but she kept going. 'And don't you dare be angry with Scott, because he wanted me to tell you about it years ago.'

'Too bloody right you should have,' Jo said, but her words didn't have the bite they had seconds before. Instead she looked defeated, her shoulders slumped, her wide mouth turned down at the edges.

'I needed to stand up for myself this time. It took me a long time, but I did it. I don't want you trying to see Liam. I've talked to him already and the police are more than likely going to take care of him. You didn't do anything wrong.' Amy tried to keep her voice firm, but the tears running down her cheeks probably diminished some of her authority. She didn't care. If she couldn't cry in front of her own sister, she might as well be dead.

'Amy.' Jo shook her head, eyes damp with her own tears. 'I . . . Just give me a bit to process, alright? I can't believe . . . How badly did he hurt you?'

'Not as bad as Dad used to hurt you,' Amy said softly. 'And you always kept that a secret.'

'But that was different.'

'No, it wasn't. You didn't want me to worry about you. I didn't want you to worry about me. Same thing.' Amy expected Jo to object, but she kept quiet, studying Amy with shadowed eyes until the silence in the room became unbearable.

'I don't know what to say,' Jo said eventually in a low, husky voice. 'I'm so sorry.'

'So am I.' Tears fell in earnest now as Amy launched herself towards Jo, who met her halfway. 'I don't want us to fight like this again.'

'Neither do I. I hate it.' Jo pulled Amy tightly against her. 'I wanted you there at the ultrasound but I was too bloody stubborn. I'm so sorry. I told Stephen the other day and he – he was so happy. I wanted you there too, but I didn't know how to call or what to say. I need you. Please don't keep stuff like this from me again.'

'I won't, but I need you to trust me. I'm a big girl. I don't need you trying to protect me any more. Yes?' Amy pulled back far enough to look Jo straight in the eye.

'Yeah.' Jo inhaled shakily before continuing. 'There's something else we need to talk about before we settle this fully. I know you don't want to, but it's about this guy you're going with.'

'Ben?' Amy abruptly pushed away from Jo's grip. 'I told you I didn't want to talk about this.'

'I know, but this is important. Please, *please*, check out what his ex-girlfriend's written in the papers. I don't want you hurt again.' Jo's voice was devoid of any of its earlier over-protective self-righteousness.

Amy felt herself soften. 'Ben's already told me all about it. I trust him.'

Jo grimaced. 'Alright. At least I know I tried.'

'You really shouldn't have bothered.' Amy shook her head. 'Just leave it, okay?'

Jo bit her lip, obviously torn. 'Alright. Still, I really wish you'd—'

'No.' Amy's voice sliced through the air. 'Leave it. And sniff your coffee.'

Jo's mouth curved into a half-smile as she sat down. 'Yeah, alright. I won't bring it up again. Sorry, Ames.'

'Apology accepted.' Amy took her own seat, reaching across the table to put her hand over her sister's. 'Let's change the topic to something much more important. Am I having a niece or a nephew?'

'Dunno yet,' Jo said with a genuine, tired grin. 'I told the radiographer I didn't want to know. Stephen wants a girl because he reckons it'd be hilarious since I'm such a tomboy, but I want a boy. What would I do with a girl?'

Amy squeezed her hand. 'You'll do just fine. Although . . . if the kid gets your temper, you're in biiig trouble.'

'You saying yours is any better?'

'I don't have a temper,' Amy said primly, allowing herself to forget the previous forty-eight hours for a few seconds and simply enjoy her sister's company. 'Anyway, where are these ultrasound pictures you promised to show me? I want to see if my new niece is going to be as tall as her mama.'

Chapter 16

'I'VE BEEN FOLLOWING your column lately,' Alex drawled. He'd called Ben from his dressing room post-show in New York.

'Oh?' Ben leaned back in his office chair, massaging his temples to dispel the lingering hangover from his ill-advised interlude with a bottle of scotch the night before.

'Hmm, I couldn't help but notice how unoriginal you are. Couldn't find your own girl so you took mine?'

'Don't know what you're talking about,' Ben protested.

'The blonde from the bar, remember? Or "Babyface" as you refer to her. You know you're a real asshole, don't you?'

'What do you mean, *asshole*?'

'Has she *read* any of this?'

'What's *this*, Alex?' Ben scowled and sat upright in his chair.

'What you've written about her. It's not exactly flattering. I would have called you on it earlier if I hadn't been so goddamn busy this past month,' Alex said distractedly, voice distinctly disapproving. 'Some of the things you've said were just plain nasty.'

'What the hell are you talking about? I haven't been nasty at all.

Quite the opposite. People love her. I love her.' Ben said the words glibly, ignoring the sharp pang in his gut as they came out.

'Huh. That's interesting, because if she read any of this, I doubt she'd love *you*,' Alex retorted. 'Where was I? What did you call her in that first one that featured me? Here it is. *A comical facsimile of a nineteen-fifties pinup who would be much more attractive if she weren't patently trying so hard.*' He impersonated Ben's clipped accent, making the words sound cold and harsh.

Ben winced. 'You're taking that out of context.'

'Yeah? How about what you said about your visit to her house: *Slumming in a charmingly antiquated convict-built hovel.* I'll admit you said it was charming, but no one likes to have their house referred to as a hovel. And I haven't even started on the one you wrote about the time you slept with her. *Babyface shares the curse of all women in that they think far too much at the most inopportune moments, often resulting in disappointment for all parties present.* Dude.'

'I was thinking that it made great comedy if you bothered to read the rest of the piece.' Ben did his best to ignore the memory of Amy's hurt expression the last time he'd seen her. The words *tin pot, working-class piece of shit* had echoed over and over in his mind for the past twenty-four hours. He wished he could take them back. In fact, he intended to apologise the minute he no longer saw red when he thought about his car. If his current simmering fury was any indication, that wouldn't be for some time.

Alex emitted a noise that conveyed the maximum amount of scepticism. 'Yeah, the rest of the piece *is* funny if you don't know it's written about a real person with feelings. Remember those? I hope to hell she knows about your stage act or you're toast, my good friend.'

Ben feigned disinterest to hide the fact Alex's words were causing small tendrils of apprehension to worm their way through his veins. 'You're boring me.'

'I'm so sorry,' Alex said sarcastically.

'So you should be. I think this conversation would be better served if you shut up so I can tell you how my car got wrecked. Then feel free to shower me with all the sympathy I so rightly deserve.'

'The DB9?'

'What else?' Ben said dryly before commencing his tale of woe.

'Did they catch the guy who did it?' Alex asked after sharing Ben's opinion that the perpetrator should be shot, revived, shot again, drawn, quartered and then fed to starving dogs for good measure.

'No. I doubt anyone will. Amy doesn't live in a highly vigilant area. It's more a nesting site for retired hippies and the hipster set. To make matters worse, she has a forest of trees for a front yard, which obscures the house and anything parked in the driveway from view of the street.'

'You're referring to the convict hovel, right?'

'I'd really rather you didn't repeat that out of context.'

'So I take it this is serious?'

'What's serious?'

'This thing you've got going with this girl, Amy, Babyface. Because you've featured her, or more to the point *insulted her*, for one . . . two . . . three . . . four . . . *five* weeks out of the last three months. That's got to be a record. From memory, you only wrote about Marcella—'

'Never mention that name in my presence.'

'—once.'

Ben frowned and opened his mouth to tell Alex to shove his pithy observations up his arse when his friend cut in, tone thoughtful.

'Can you give me Amy's details again? An email address would work.'

'Email address? Why?' Ben pushed himself out of his chair and prowled over to the window.

'Because when she kicks your bitch ass out the door, I want her number. And seriously? If she reads any of this, you *are* history.'

Ben's inventive and thoroughly disparaging opinion of Alex's request filled the room before he hung up, his friend's laughter echoing in his ears.

Instead of putting his phone down, Ben kept it in his hand as he debated calling Amy. Something about the assuredness of Alex's words left him feeling uncomfortable, even a little worried. It was still early in the day so she'd be at work . . .

No, best to leave it. It would be much better to call her later in the evening when she was alone. She'd have cooled down by then and he would have time to get his usual charming veneer back in place.

He would have to be a total prick not to realise he'd royally cocked things up in losing his temper earlier, but he also knew that it wouldn't take much for Amy to forgive him. It was obvious she cared for him, probably even loved him, so it would just be a matter of apologising before things were back to normal. Ben snorted – whatever *normal* was in their context.

In the interim, he had a massive number of phone calls to make to atone for his recent absence from humanity. Once all that was finalised and out of the way, he'd be able to devote some serious time to getting down on his knees and looking properly repentant. He might even extend to another Disney film and he'd never, *ever* consider that for another woman. Amy should think herself lucky.

'So tell me about Ben.' Jo turned her head from side to side and inspected the new, edgier pixie cut Amy had just styled for her. She was keeping Amy company while the painters finished the front of Gentlemen Prefer Blondes and Babyface. Earlier, they'd picked up drive-through KFC for lunch and were now digesting huge quantities of lardy, chickeny goodness. Well, Amy was. Jo had just managed to stomach a few fries.

'I thought we'd agreed not to go there, m'love.' Amy tucked her scissors away in her apron pocket and reached for a hair dryer.

'No, I just want you to tell me about him. Normal stuff.' Jo shrugged, looking abashed. 'It just occurred to me I haven't asked you anything about him, just got pissed off and made a bunch of assumptions.'

'Yeah, you have,' Amy said softly. 'And it's not worth believing the stuff you read on the net. No.' She held up a hand before Jo could speak. 'Keep it to yourself, sweetie. Ben and I had a fight the other day and I'm really upset about it, but otherwise he's been lovely. He cares for me and he makes me laugh. He's a lot nicer than any other boyfriend I've had and I think—' Her voice caught. 'I think I'm in love with him.'

'Serious? So why do you look like you're going to cry?' Jo asked in exasperation.

'We had a fight—'

'Yeah, you said. So are you gonna tell me about it or just stand there looking like a soggy chipmunk?'

'You won't try and make him into the bad guy?'

'Out with it, woman!'

Much to Amy's surprise, Jo listened quietly while she shared what had happened, only pursing her lips to whistle when Amy described Liam's radical makeover of Ben's car. Amy felt better for sharing it all. Ben's words and actions didn't seem so extreme or intended to hurt her feelings on the retelling, they just seemed like the way any man would react if his valuable property had been damaged.

She wasn't sure what to make of his friend's comments on the phone from earlier that morning, though. She wanted to believe they had nothing to do with Ben; she *hoped* they had nothing to do with Ben. Her chest tightened a little as she glanced at her handbag, wondering if she should check her phone. Maybe he'd already called and she'd missed it.

'I hate to say it, because what he said was harsh, but he had pretty good reason to blow his top. I know I probably would've reacted just as badly if someone had trashed my car like that. It was probably just a vent and he most likely didn't mean any of it.' Jo interrupted Amy's runaway thoughts.

'I know.' Amy's mouth turned down at the corners. 'I'd be really angry, and I *am*, especially after what he said about my house, but I know how much he loves that car. Plus I'm feeling really guilty since it was Liam . . .'

'Yeah, I get that,' Jo said curtly. 'Okay. So tell me more about this guy. I'll pretend I know nothing about him.' She leaned back in her chair, cocking a brow at Amy in the mirror, waiting for her to begin.

Feeling lighter than she had for a while, Amy did.

Later that night, bolstered by Jo's new supportive attitude, Amy decided that, for once, she was going to be the one to take the initiative in a relationship. She'd had enough time to think now and realised that she owed Ben an apology just as much as he owed her one. His words had been awful, yes, but if she'd stood up to Liam earlier, none of the drama would have happened.

Determined to speak to him and talk things through, she braced herself and called Ben's number, only to reach his answering service. She debated trying again but then thought better of it. All he had to do was check his messages and call her back. She'd made the first move.

She spent the next few hours whisking through her house, manically cleaning every surface in sight before giving a very long-suffering and rather smelly Gerald a bath, all the while listening out for her phone. That done, she tried watching a movie, then attempted to read her favourite Zadie Smith novel. In the end, restless and tetchy, she picked up her phone and called Scott. He'd been out of the country for nearly a month now and she'd missed him.

He answered on the second ring, voice unexpectedly sharp. 'Amy?'

'Hey, stranger. Where are you?' she asked, enjoying the warm feeling she always got at hearing her friend's deep voice.

'London at the moment, but I'll be home in a couple of days.' He sounded tired and agitated. 'I've been trying to call you for two days. I was just emailing you now. Why haven't you returned any of my calls?'

Amy frowned. 'I haven't received any, m'love. Not that I've seen at least. Are you okay?'

'Yeah, I'm okay. That old Nokia you have is crap, Ames. I've been telling you that for years. It never tells you when you've got messages. Anyway. Ah shit . . . I didn't want to be the one to have to do this, but I'm going to email you something. You're not going to thank me, but someone had to tell you,' Scott said, his voice heavy.

'Tell me what?' The worried feeling she'd been fighting all day coalesced into a tight knot of tension in her chest.

'I looked up Ben Martindale's column in the *Enquirer* out of curiosity last night. You've got to read it.'

'Is this the same stuff Jo wanted to show me? Because we made up. I told her I'm not reading anything about Ben off the internet. I promised myself. He said he's had some bad press and I know none of it is true.'

'Yeah. Well. I don't think Jo knows about this stuff or I would have seen the explosion from here. She just read up on his ex-girlfriend bagging him out. This is different, Ames. This is *me* telling *you* that you really need to look at this. It's not press. It's stuff he's written himself. There's no other way to say this, but it looks like he's been using you from the start. He's been writing about you nearly every week in a column he does, and it could be grounds for defamation. He doesn't exactly use your name . . . he calls you Babyface, but anyone who knows you can tell who it is.'

'*Defamation?*' Amy sat down heavily on her couch as the air whooshed out of her lungs. 'What do you mean?'

'Just read it? Then call me back. I'm seriously sorry about this.'

'Why? Scott?' She was talking to herself. She stared at her phone, stunned.

Ben writing about her? *Her?* Why? And *defamation?* Amy's first impulse was to call him. She was put straight through to his answering service again. Instead of hanging up this time, she left him a short message.

'Ben? I, ah. It's Amy. I've just learned you wrote some stuff about me. I'd really rather hear about it from you, but Scott's forwarding it to me and I'm reading it now. Okay? Call me back if you get this soon.'

Amy waited another hour, hoping Ben would call her back and explain, but he didn't. Her mind was left replaying Scott's words over and over again. Using her? Defamation? No. No, Ben wouldn't do anything like that. He cared about her. He'd shown it in so many small ways. Surely he couldn't have faked it. Surely . . .

She might have left it, might have still waited for Ben's call, but the phone call she'd accidentally intercepted began playing through her mind.

The way the man, Ross, had called her the 'little blonde barber' sounded like something flippant Ben would say. The man had referred to Ben doing some writing for him and had sounded like someone Ben worked for, or with. Surely Ben wouldn't have written about her without telling her about it. She'd been too busy the past couple of months and admittedly a little wary about doing a search online for fear she'd see something she didn't want to in relation to his ex-girlfriend, but . . . No, he would have told her if he'd written about her, wouldn't he? The question played over and over in her mind as she paced through her house. Gerald watched on without interest from his beanbag in the living room.

Eventually, when there was nothing else to do and still no call from Ben, Amy gave in, sat down with a cup of tea and followed Scott's link to a newspaper called the *London Enquirer*. The page was titled 'Hello, Sailor' and featured a photo of Ben at the top sporting his familiar feline grin.

She began to read. It didn't take long for the mocking tone behind the words to register. It was Ben's recounting of the night they'd met. She read about how he'd thought her clothes were contrived and her apology to his friend was awkward. The name 'Babyface' jumped out at her, laughing at her from the screen. He'd portrayed her as a ditsy idiot, some sort of bimbo who was two brain cells short of a single-figure IQ.

Feeling as if she'd been publicly stripped naked, Amy read on to the third column, which was about Ben's first visit to her house. While this one wasn't quite as awful, Ben still referred to her as Babyface, a clownishly naive female who lived in a hovel and impersonated a fifties housewife. It wasn't until she got to his fourth entry, a comedic description of the first time they had slept together where he said he'd been disappointed, that she spun away from her laptop, clutching her chest, gasping for air. She felt sick. Gut roiling, she made it to the kitchen sink just in time, heaving until the contents of her stomach were long gone and the reality of the last few months sank in.

She'd been living in a dream world. None of it had been true.

If Ben had stripped her naked and ridiculed her in public, it wouldn't have hurt this badly. It was obvious he'd never once considered her feelings. It was obvious she'd never meant more to him than some sort of fuel for his creativity, someone he could ridicule for his readers' amusement.

Amy's own culpability, her complete gullibility in this whole affair, came crashing down on her. How stupid could she have been? She'd trusted him. She'd defended him and deliberately kept herself in the dark about the rumours surrounding him, hoping that, this time, she wasn't going to end up falling flat on her face. *Stupid.*

Yeah, sure, a millionaire celebrity wanted to spend time with her, she thought cynically. Jo had been right. With Ben's looks, charm and money, he'd be able to be with anyone he wanted, so why had she believed for a second that he'd be serious about a hairdresser? A nobody. She'd just been an amusing little detour. *A try-hard pinup wannabe* with sexual hang-ups who lived in a *hovel.*

It turned out that he'd written five – *five!* – pieces about her, the most recent focusing on their weekend away. That one had been even worse than the others. Using a flippant, wry tone, Ben turned Amy's bittersweet return to her childhood home into a hike through the Australian countryside with a manic pixie in Spice Girl shoes, who had a messed-up white-trash relationship with her ex-boyfriend.

His writing was entertaining, sharp and . . . wrong, so incredibly wrong. How could he have turned something so private into public fodder in such an awfully hurtful way?

Why would he do this to her? Why would he put so much effort into making her believe he cared and then do this? Somewhere along the way, while reading and re-reading his words, seeing herself being made fun of with such obvious disregard for her feelings, Amy's disbelief and hurt transformed into a roiling, volcanic outrage that put anything she'd felt for Liam in the pale.

She surged to her feet.

This wasn't something she could swallow and smile about tomorrow; this was too big, too horrible to have sitting in her, leaving her feeling this violated. Hands shaking, she called Ben's number again, then threw her phone across the room with a shriek of pure rage when it went through to voicemail.

Startled, Gerald barked at the noise, scampering out of the way when Amy swept through the house, galvanised into action. This time, *this time*, she wasn't going to be some shrinking violet who let another arrogant bastard make her feel like crap for years on end. She hadn't deserved this and by God, Ben was going to know about it. She reached her front door before realising she didn't have her car keys, then turned and strode into her bedroom where she'd last seen them, throwing clothes out of the way and dumping books, make-up and shoes onto the floor. Finally finding them in the pocket of her dress from that morning, she turned to leave again, then caught sight of her reflection in the dresser mirror.

She looked like a wild woman, eyes unnaturally shiny, face pale and streaked with mascara and clothes far too casual. This wouldn't do at all. She'd be damned if she'd give Ben any more ammunition to write about next week. If she was going to do this, she'd bloody well do it *right*. Ben had already found more than enough in her behaviour to write up for the amusement of his readers; she'd be damned if she'd give him anything else.

Ben stood up, rubbed his hand over his jaw, stretched out his muscles and threw his phone onto his desk. He'd been stuck on a conference call with his lawyer and Colin for the past two hours and had reached the limit of his civility. What did the French call small-picture people? *Fuckers of flies* – that was it. He'd have to share that with Colin later, who'd been just as exasperated as he had in having to go through the tedium of a lawyer dissecting the draft of Ben's manuscript to determine whether or not it contained anything that would invite litigation.

Ben knew it was a completely unnecessary process since he was the main subject matter. Everyone else, even his own parents, were kept strictly in the realm of pseudonyms and nicknames. He normally wouldn't dream of doing all this until the final draft, but in this case he didn't want to bother polishing something he'd have to omit in the long run.

His doorbell rang and he looked at the clock. Nine at night was a little late for Mormons, and his few Australian friends knew far better than to drop in unannounced.

He opened the front door to find Amy standing on his doorstep. He blinked to make sure he hadn't conjured her out of his imagination. His imagination surely couldn't do the vision in front of him justice.

She was stunning in a calf-length, figure-hugging red dress with a neckline that showed enough cleavage to set his imagination alight and a pair of black boots that Ben had never seen before but definitely wanted to see again, often. He finally raised his eyes to her face and took in perfectly coiffed hair, blood-red lips, cold blue eyes and white, white skin. Too white. Something was seriously wrong.

'This is for you. It's the T-shirt you left at my house.' Her voice was all wrong, too. It was as flat and cold as her expression. She thrust the plastic bag she was holding towards him and he took it automatically, noting that her hands were trembling.

'Is everything alright? I was just about to call you.' He reached for her, intending on drawing her against him but she took a quick step backwards out of his reach.

Her killer lips curved in a humourless smile. 'Too late for that, Ben. You should have picked up earlier when I tried to call you. I left you a message.'

Ben tried once more to reach for her, but her entire body stiffened, her eyes narrowed and he dropped his hand, immensely confused and beginning to genuinely worry. He knew she was upset over what had happened at her house but he hadn't expected anything like this.

'Come inside.'

She shook her head. 'No, I have to go. I just wanted to tell you . . .' She drew a deep breath and clasped her hands together so tightly in front of her that her knuckles turned white. 'I've read what you wrote about me in the *London Enquirer*. I don't understand why you would do something so cruel, but I'm not going to let you do it again. I don't want to see you any more, Ben. It's over.'

He watched the beginnings of tears form in her eyes and his stomach flipped, his skin dampening with sweat. She couldn't mean it. *Didn't* mean it. She was just upset. All he had to do was get her inside and they could talk.

'Amy. Sweetheart—' He stepped towards her just as her cool façade shattered.

Her eyes flashed pure, unadulterated fury and her hands curled into tight fists at her sides as she erupted, a vengeful porcelain doll wading into battle. 'You *bastard*! How *dare* you call me sweetheart after what you did? Scum, Ben. That's what you are. You used me and laughed at me behind my back – *publicly* – and then you have the nerve to call me sweetheart like you care? Fuck you,' she spat.

Ben flinched at how ugly the words sounded. He opened his mouth to talk but she held up a shaking finger.

'I let you into my life. I trusted you. I cared for you and you . . . you *screwed* me. Quite literally, didn't you?' Her mouth twisted into a horrible semblance of a smile. 'I bet you enjoyed writing that week. "Let's make fun of the silly bitch who thinks too much to come." Did you laugh, Ben? Did you?' Tears filled her eyes again before she impatiently swiped them away. 'How long was this going to go on? Until you ran out of things to make fun of every week? Oh, just wait. It's pretty endless with me, from my shitty house and novelty businesses to my pathetic clothes and my hilarious – what did you call it? – *bloody-minded inability to relax and enjoy the moment*. You made it sound like a mystery. Well, I'll tell you what it was all about. I didn't trust you enough to let myself go. I should have stuck to that but instead . . . instead I thought you cared. Stupid me . . .' She heaved a shaky breath, her face crumpling. 'Stupid. Stupid me.'

'Amy. Come inside,' Ben commanded, panic rising in his chest.
'No.'

'Come on. You're upset and overwrought right now. Come inside and we'll talk about this rationally.' He immediately regretted the words. The condescending tone was all wrong. He regretted them a sight more when Amy's fist came out of nowhere, sucker-punching him in the solar plexus, leaving him doubled over and gasping on his own doorstep.

'*That's* being overly dramatic, you bastard. You told me to tell you if there's ever anything wrong – that I shouldn't care about your feelings. Well, I'm doing it now. This is the second time this week I've had to tell a man in my life that I never want to see him again. The first time was easy, so easy compared to this, because I didn't care about him. You . . . you've just torn me to shreds and all you can say is that I'm *overwrought*?' She took another step towards him, eyes blazing, and Ben had the good sense to step backwards. 'I felt so guilty about your car and blamed myself when the whole time you were using me like some kind of comic prop. I hate that you did this to me. I loved you and you ruined it.' Before Ben could say anything more, potentially ramming his foot further into his mouth, she spun on her heel and ran to her car.

Stunned, hand over his bruised abdominals, his chest feeling like it was about to explode, Ben braced himself against the door frame and watched her go.

Chapter 17

'AMY?' STEPHEN ANSWERED the door to his and Jo's apartment, his sun-bleached hair messy, eyes open wide. Given the late hour, his surprise was understandable.

Amy managed a tremulous smile. 'Hey, sweetie. Um. Is Jo here?' Her breath hitched at the words and she fisted her hands at her sides, digging her nails into her palms.

Stephen stepped back out of the way. 'Yeah, yeah. Come in.'

'Thanks.' Amy walked inside, looking around blindly at Jo's simply furnished apartment with its cream couches, large-screen TV and densely packed bookcases off to the far wall.

'You want a drink or something? Jo's just in the shower.' Stephen's bare feet padded on the floor as he headed for the kitchen.

'No,' Amy managed. She could hear the shower running in the hallway bathroom. All she had to do was hold it together for a few more minutes until Jo—

Stephen paused, turning back to study her. 'Everything alright?'

Amy curtly nodded her head.

'You lyin'?' Stephen asked, bending at the knees to better see Amy's expression.

She bit her lip. 'Maybe.' She felt herself losing it and bit her lip harder but it didn't work. The first sob started and then it was all downhill from there.

'Oh hey, uh, *Jo!*' Stephen yelled as he wrapped his arms awkwardly around Amy, overriding her protests.

'WHAT?'

'I need you here. *Now*,' Stephen bellowed back, all the while roughly patting Amy's back and possibly breaking some ribs in his effort to offer some form of comfort.

'Stephen, I'm fine,' Amy managed to say in a waterlogged voice just as the bathroom door opened, the smell of hot, damp air and shampoo filling the room as Jo stepped out.

'What's so bloody urgent? Ames? What are you doing here? Stephen, what's going on? What's wrong?'

'I dunno. She just walked through the door and . . .' Stephen shrugged helplessly.

Amy stepped away from Stephen, trying to collect herself. 'I'm *fine*.'

'You don't look fine,' Jo said, holding a large red towel around her, her soaked hair dripping down the sides of her face as she looked Amy up and down. 'Don't even try and tell me it's nothing because there's no way you'd be here at this time of night looking miserable if it was nothing.' She turned to Stephen, who was still hovering by Amy's side. 'Can you put the kettle on?'

'Definitely.' The relief in his voice would have been comical if Amy weren't so upset.

'Talk to me,' Jo ordered as Stephen disappeared into the kitchen.

Amy drew a deep shuddery breath. 'Give me a minute.'

'Yeah, alright.' Jo raised a hand and ran a thumb under Amy's left eye, then her right, collecting her running mascara. 'I hate to break it to ya, but you'd make a crap goth.'

Amy managed a watery laugh. '*Damn*. And I always wanted to be one too. Sorry, I didn't mean to barge in here like this.' She gestured to her face with a flutter of her fingers.

'Don't be.'

'Tea or coffee?' Stephen asked from the doorway.

'Tea, please.' Amy looked around Jo's shoulder to catch his worried expression. 'Sorry, Stephen.'

'No worries.' His half-smile didn't reach his eyes.

'Amy?' Jo asked again.

'It's Ben,' Amy blurted.

'Ben,' Jo repeated, expression resigned.

'He's been writing about me. Did you know he was writing about me in a newspaper column? About everything we did together?'

Jo shook her head slowly. 'No. The stuff I wanted to show you was an interview with his ex-girlfriend. I didn't know he'd been writing about you. Where?'

'The paper's called the *London Enquirer*. Probably better I show you.' Amy borrowed Stephen's laptop and pulled up all five of Ben's columns featuring her.

She hugged Boomba the cat, burying her face in his soft grey fur so she didn't have to look at the screen. She'd read the words so many times by now that she'd memorised them.

The room was dead silent with the exception of Boomba's purring and Stephen's odd exclamation of outrage.

Amy looked at Jo. Her sister's eyes were narrowed and her lips were thinned into a narrow line. 'You finished?'

'Yep.' Jo snapped the laptop closed. 'I—' She began but Stephen put his hand firmly on her shoulder and she stopped. The two of them exchanged a series of pointed looks until Jo heaved a massive sigh. 'I dunno, Ames. This looks bad. What are you gonna do about it?' she asked eventually, the words sounding forced.

Amy stared at her, mind temporarily blank. She'd expected

shouting, yelling, even threats of revenge. That Jo would respect her space enough just to let her share her problem without trying to fix it had been too much to hope for.

Jo must have noticed her shock. 'I want to kill him for you, but I can't. I promised to stay out of your love life and I'm trying. *Fuck.*' She stood up and stalked around the living room once before coming to face Amy with her hands on her hips, her towel barely holding together. 'Please tell me you're going to kick this son of a bitch's arse or I'm seriously going to be pissed.'

Amy gave her a small, humourless smile. 'I punched him. Really hard.'

Jo snorted. 'Was he still breathing afterwards?'

'Yeah.'

'Not hard enough then.'

'Babe,' Stephen rumbled.

'Yeah. Alright.' Jo darted a look at her fiancé and grimaced. 'This really sucks Ames. I can't even imagine what you're feeling right now.' She rolled her shoulders, tightened the towel and unclenched her jaw, forcing her words out. 'How . . . can I – we – be there for you?'

Amy felt a little lost until Stephen's large warm hands settled on her shoulders, grounding her. She pulled herself together. 'I could do with another hug and maybe, if it's okay, staying here tonight. I don't want to go home right now. I'm feeling pretty crap.'

Jo nodded. 'What about your dog?'

'I'll go get him,' Stephen volunteered.

'Thanks. Stephen . . .' Amy looked up into his kind blue eyes and felt herself tearing up again.

'Not a problem.' He ruffled her hair gently before disappearing down the hall to the bedroom.

Amy turned to Jo. 'About that hug?'

———

'*Ben? I, ah. It's Amy. I've just learned you wrote some stuff about me . . .*' Ben listened to Amy's voicemail message for the fourth time, his gut twisting in knots as he cursed himself, Colin, his lawyer and everything else that had prevented him from taking her call earlier that evening when she still sounded as if she cared for him.

He tried calling her again. She wasn't answering her phone and she definitely wasn't home. He knew because he was standing on her poorly lit porch now. He stared at her locked door, trying to work out what to do. Her car was gone and there was no sight or sound of her dog. He waited around for five minutes until he realised how pathetic he was being, then drove past her salon, foolishly thinking she might be there even though it was now fast approaching midnight. The sight that greeted his eyes made him go cold.

Amy's business had been vandalised. Recently. He slammed on his brakes, impatiently switching on his hazard lights and getting out of his car, feeling sick with dread.

The façades of both barbershop and beauty salon were freshly painted but the pavement in front contained more than enough evidence in the form of some kind of black muck to tell him the damage had been significant.

The knowledge that something so horrible had happened to her and that she hadn't felt she could call him tore him apart.

'*Fuck.*' The profanity echoed along the empty street as he looked through the windows, the sharp tang of fresh paint stinging his nostrils. Nothing looked damaged inside and there was no police tape to indicate anything more serious had occurred but he couldn't think past the panic. His gut hurt where she'd punched him and his chest ached as if he were about to have a heart attack.

He knew she was alright. This had to have happened before she'd come to see him but the fact she hadn't told him about this just emphasised how much he'd obviously fucked up.

If he could only talk to her, he'd be able to find out what had happened. He'd be able to make it alright. Words were his forté and without them he was lost. He just needed to get her alone so they could talk.

He climbed back in his car, sparing another look at the black marks on the pavement before returning home, sending yet another text message asking her to call him. Afterwards, he paced the length of his kitchen, trying to work out what could have upset her so much. Obviously he'd stepped over the line at some stage, although he had no idea where or when.

He knew his brand of comedy could easily be taken the wrong way if read out of context, but he couldn't believe anything he could have written would warrant the devastation he'd seen in Amy's expression. Or the anger. She had actually sworn at him, had even called him *scum,* which was somehow so much worse than the profanity. He felt the impact of her words all over again like a wrecking ball.

Finally, when he couldn't come up with any answers, he retreated to his study and pulled up all the copy he'd filed with the *Enquirer* over the past few months.

It didn't take him more than a few sentences to realise just how much he'd fucked up. Line after line, his words jumped off the screen, words he'd thought were so amusing, that he'd arrogantly believed Amy would find amusing too once he got around to showing them to her. They really didn't seem funny now. In fact, Alex was right. They were nasty, even downright cruel in places. Oh, they were funny in an abstract sense, and he could certainly see why Ross had said his reading public had fallen in love with Amy and loved to despise him, but they also, undeniably, set Amy up as Babyface, a character he'd created on the page to fuel his own ego.

He recalled a critical review he'd read of his first sell-out show at the Edinburgh Comedy Festival. He'd read the review so many times, he had it memorised.

Ben Martindale's humour is naughty when it's mediocre, delightfully cutting at its very best. He has mastered the art of staying your friend while insulting you to your face and you'll keep coming back for more, paying for the privilege because you know deep down that Martindale's a lovely chap at heart. You never once think that his jokes could possibly be at your expense. And maybe you laugh all the harder to quieten that little voice that asks, 'Or could they?'

Ben had revelled in the review, knowing the writer's description was bang on the money. Over the years he had become so adept at satirising people while simultaneously charming them that he now did it automatically. It was a skill he'd picked up during his early years in boarding school and honed to a fine art. He never *really* hurt his victims' feelings; they knew the score – they understood what he did for a living and enjoyed being a part of the process. Only, Amy hadn't known. There was no way she could have anticipated that he would write about her because he'd selfishly kept that information to himself. He knew now that he'd been worried all along she'd ask him to stop.

He began reading the column he'd written about Amy's home. It wasn't long before he was cringing with stunned disbelief at how he'd arrogantly reduced something he knew Amy loved and cared for into a pithy little vignette. He moved onto the piece he'd written after the first time he and Amy had slept together and felt his gut drop to the floor.

He had well and truly – unforgivably – fucked up.

He walked downstairs, noticing for the first time he hadn't turned on the kitchen lights when he'd returned home. The entire

bottom floor of his house was dark with the exception of the moon-
light filtering in through the windows. His fear of the dark, it
seemed, had been obliterated by the realisation that it wasn't the
dark he was scared of. It was being left alone.

The next morning Amy did something she'd not done her entire
working career: she called Mel and arranged to be away for a week
before turning off her phone and booking herself into a beachfront
holiday cottage south of the city.

She staunchly refused to notice the twenty-three missed calls and
fifteen messages from Ben. She didn't want to talk to him right now.
He was too good with words and she was scared she'd give in and
forgive him far too easily. Instead, she bundled Gerald into her car,
threw in a minimum of clothing, and set off for the country.

She pulled up at the rear of a small weatherboard cottage three
hours later. Climbing stiffly out of the car, she took in the panorama
of white sand dunes, olive-coloured saltbush and massive waves
breaking on the beach a few hundred metres away. There was a
strong wind blowing off the ocean, bringing with it the tang of salt
water, seaweed and an incoming rain shower.

After letting Gerald roam free, she propped the cottage door
open with her suitcase, saw to putting out some food and water for
her dog and collapsed on the double bed facing the view, giving in
to the emotional exhaustion she hadn't allowed herself to feel for
nearly three days.

When she opened her eyes next, it was dark outside and freezing
cold. The sea breeze had transformed into a groaning and howling
wind that was presently whipping around the room.

She squinted through the dark with eyes that felt grainy from
wearing contacts too long and saw Gerald's boxy silhouette blocking
the entry door. 'Hey, boy,' she croaked.

He snuffled in reply and wagged his stub of a tail once, which told her just how much he'd missed her company for the past few hours.

It took her at least another ten minutes to haul herself off the bed, close the door and get some food for herself and the dog. By that time she was exhausted all over again. Sleep was what she needed. Sleep meant she wouldn't have to think about the fact that the happiness she'd felt over the past three months had been a sham, a joke at her expense. Not even bothering to change into pyjamas, Amy kicked off her shoes and crawled back into bed, passing out.

The next days disappeared in a blur of sleeping, waking up to walk Gerald along the beach, answering the call of nature, eating then sleeping again. She was just *so tired*. It was as if she hadn't slept for a lifetime. Every time she tried to think about what had happened, sort it out in her mind, she felt exhausted all over again. She finally turned on her phone on Saturday and was shocked at how much time had passed – almost a whole week gone already. She had only one more day left before she had to return home and she'd barely got out of bed.

This couldn't go on. She'd gone out with Ben for less than three months. The thought of him brought a familiar pang to her gut but instead of burying her head under the covers, she climbed out of bed, straightened her shoulders and injected some steel into her spine.

So what if her now ex-boyfriend had exposed an entire newspaper readership to her most intimate fears and worries? So what if he didn't really care about her? It wasn't as if she hadn't had people make fun of her before. She'd survived her childhood, she'd survived her parents, she'd survived Liam (along with countless other pathetic ex-boyfriends) and she'd survive Ben Martindale – and have good hair while doing it, dammit.

The last thought deflated her a little when she caught sight of herself in the bathroom mirror. Her hair was a limp and greasy tangle, her face was puffy from far too much sleep and she had what was hopefully not the permanent imprint of pillow wrinkles on her cheek.

'I should have known better than to get a bulldog! You could have told me I was beginning to look like you, Gerald.' She gave her snoozing dog a prod with her toe then looked back at her reflection. 'Amy Blaine, what were you thinking?' Her reflection wasn't forthcoming with answers, so instead she undressed, wincing at how hairy and scary she'd become, and climbed into the shower.

Amy was packing to go home when her sister got hold of her.

'Ames, I don't want to step on your toes and I know you're having time out but I think you might want to see this. Can you check your email where you are?'

Amy looked out at the view in front of her. The sea was calm today, a lot calmer than the night before. She took a gulp of her coffee, feeling it slowly awaken her sluggish senses, alerting her to Jo's worried tone of voice. 'What's this about?'

'He's published something else. I didn't want to tell you but . . . ah . . . fuck it, I *wasn't* gonna tell you but Stephen thinks it's up to you how you deal with it and I agreed to back off.'

Amy squeezed her eyes shut. Why couldn't he just leave her alone? 'What is it?'

'An apology. Kind of. You might want to look at it.'

'Alright.' She wouldn't let herself hope. Not yet. 'Send it through.'

'Yeah. Alright. You sure?'

'Yeah.'

'You okay?'

'Yeah.'

Later that afternoon Amy stopped at a roadside café and checked her email, following the link to Ben's *London Enquirer* column. A fragile bubble of hope expanded in her chest when she saw the heading, 'Forgive Me, I've Sinned.'

She read on. The words jumping off the page were so obviously Ben's she could almost hear him.

Anyone who's read me would well know that I'm not a man who apologises lightly. In fact, I say this with a heavy heart. I owe the delectable subject of my most recent entries into this esteemed paper an apology. A grovel if you will. I had no intention of hurting her feelings, making the erroneous assumption that she'd understand, as you do, dear reader, that I'm a complete bastard but a soft-hearted one at that. In the months I've known my little blonde barber she has brought light to my life like no other . . .

The bubble popped within seconds. Glib, funny, contrite and so, so horrible. This was an apology, yes, but it was also a performance. It was meant for everyone but her and it wasn't what she needed.

Three words. If he'd just said he'd loved her, then she might think about this differently, but they were conspicuously absent.

She'd laid herself on the line for him, heart on the table, and he was incapable of understanding that, for her to truly forgive him, he had to lay himself just as bare. She'd given him her love. That's what she'd needed in return. And no matter what Ben thought, this wasn't enough. It wasn't nearly enough.

'Colin. I don't care. Tell them that if they don't like the script they can fuck themselves with their own towering incompetence and get someone else in,' Ben snarled into his phone, glowering at the other patrons of the open-air beachfront coffee shop he was currently bunkered down in.

'I don't think that's going to work, Ben,' Colin replied in a painstakingly calm tone.

'Well fucking *make* it work.' Ben hung up, grimacing at his own hideous behaviour. He made a mental note to apologise and give Colin a week-long five-star holiday somewhere nice for putting up with him. He'd earned it.

He swore under his breath and lit up a cigarette, abruptly putting it out again. He settled for glaring at the few intrepid surfers braving the spring temperatures and frigid water.

His public apology to Amy in last week's column hadn't worked. Despite the fact he'd published a mortifying, soul-baring piece of sentimentality, Ben hadn't heard a thing from her. He'd left voicemails, emails and text messages. He'd dropped by her house and her salon numerous times only to be put off by a pitbull-stubborn employee who wouldn't let him through the door.

He was lost and out of ideas. His column had been his best effort and it had been published six days ago. He didn't even know if she'd read it, despite the fact he'd slipped a copy under her front door like a pathetic stalker.

He'd wanted to do more but he'd had to make an emergency trip back to London for a meeting with Bright Star. The trip had turned into a nightmare that made the furore over Marcella look like child's play. The tabloids had been having a field day speculating over the identity of Babyface and wanted the story. Luckily he'd managed to elude their vermin by doing all his business in the early mornings, shocking his acquaintances one and all, before departing back to Australia.

So here he was now, having reached rock bottom and having no option but to acknowledge he couldn't get Amy back on his own. As much as he hated to admit it, he needed help.

'Martindale.' A deep, unfriendly voice pulled him out of his brooding and he looked up to see Scott Watanabe standing by his table accompanied by a striking red-haired Amazon wearing blue jeans, a black T-shirt and scuffed, no-nonsense boots.

Watanabe was doing his best impersonation of a modern-day samurai in frayed jeans and a long-sleeved black linen shirt; the woman just looked pissed off and out for blood.

'Watanabe,' Ben said crisply, removing his sunglasses before turning to the woman. 'Jo Blaine, I presume.' He stood up and gestured to the other chairs at his table.

The woman nodded, acknowledging that she'd seen the chairs and would sit when she felt like it. 'Give me one reason why I shouldn't kick your balls through the back of your head,' she growled in a startlingly husky voice.

Ben internally winced but kept his voice and expression cool. 'Did you read my column? I sent it to Watanabe here,' he said as the man in question took the seat across from his, sprawling out with deceptive casualness. 'I apologised and gutted myself publicly in the process. She won't call me back, she won't see me. What more can I do?'

'After what you wrote, you expect another bit of writing to make it better? A single apology shared with every man and his dog?' She glared at him with the intensity of a blowtorch.

'No,' Ben admitted. 'But writing got me into the mess I'm in, so I thought it would be a start.'

'Writing didn't get you into this mess. Your lack of empathy, decency and brain cells got you into this mess.'

'Sit *down*, Jo. We agreed to hear him out, so let him speak.' Watanabe spoke quietly but his words acted on Amy's sister like a stun gun. Snapping her mouth shut abruptly, she hauled out the chair next to Ben's and sat down, long legs splayed apart, arms crossed over her chest.

'Thanks.' Ben felt the word grate on his very soul. He knew Watanabe and Jo were his last links to Amy, but that didn't mean he didn't feel jealous about it.

'Start talking,' Jo snapped, but again Watanabe interrupted.

'Coffee first.' He waved down a passing waitress and the two of them ordered.

Ben had been nursing his espresso for the past half-hour and it was cold but he didn't want another one. Instead, he played idly with the packet of cigarettes on the table. 'How is she?' he asked once they were alone again.

'Crap, thanks to you.'

'She's been better,' Watanabe said at the same time, shooting Jo a warning look which, amazingly, she seemed to heed.

'Has she read it?' Ben asked, valiantly managing not to squirm under Jo Blaine's death glare.

'Yeah. I told her about it.'

Watanabe heaved a sigh. 'I think it worked a bit, but it wasn't enough. She's a private person. Trying to fix this in public wasn't the smartest thing you could have done.'

Ben swore under his breath in frustration.

Watanabe tilted his head to the side. 'Why'd you contact me?'

'Because everything I've tried, with the exception of camping at her front door, hasn't worked,' Ben said tightly, his frustration palpable. 'If it's not already obvious, I want her back.'

'Bullshit.'

'Jo,' Watanabe warned.

'Seriously, Scott, this is crap.'

He studied Ben's expression for a long while, no doubt taking in his three-day stubble, pallor and red-rimmed eyes. 'No, I don't think it is. I was fully ready to kill him until I read what he wrote in the *Enquirer*.'

'Yeah, but how do you know it wasn't a lie?'

Ben began to defend himself but Watanabe spoke first. 'Why would he bother?'

'Exactly.' Ben felt his shoulders relax a little. It seemed Watanabe was on his side. Although he had no idea why until the man's next comment.

'I've seen you live, Martindale.'

'Oh?' Ben raised a brow, keeping his expression impassive.

'You're funny. Or you were until you picked Amy to make fun of.' An edge crept into his words and his mouth tensed around the edges. 'Why'd you do it?' he asked, breaking his eye lock with Ben to briefly thank the waitress who'd arrived with the coffees.

Ben waited until the waitress left to answer. 'Believe it or not, it wasn't intentional.'

'What was it then, mate? Because whatever it was, you screwed up big time.'

'She inspired me.' Ben regretted the words when Jo snorted in disbelief. 'My readers loved her. Ross, my editor at the *Enquirer*, wanted more and I gave him more. I never thought she'd read any of it, and if she did I thought she'd find it funny.' He met their incredulous expressions, trying to inject as much sincerity into his tone as he could. 'I realise that was a stupid assumption. I care for her a lot. I've tried to make it up to her, to explain, but she won't see me, let alone talk to me.'

'You'll need to do more than that,' Watanabe said.

'I'm fully prepared to apologise in person. I just need to be given the chance.' Ben levelled his gaze at the man across from him. 'If you're willing to help out on that front.'

'You can't be serious,' Jo interjected, her tone incredulous.

'Extremely so,' Ben said simply, feeling his pride crumbling at his feet. 'I'm in dire need of inspiration. I love your sister. I need help. The fact that I'm here asking you for it when I'd rather be digging my eyeballs out with a teaspoon says just how desperate I am.'

He waited, watching Watanabe's entirely unreadable expression for a few seconds before lighting another cigarette from habit.

He managed to just get it to his lips when Jo snatched it out of his hand and ground it out. 'Not helping your cause, mate. I'm pregnant.'

'Apologies,' Ben said curtly, pushing away from the table. 'I'll be right back.' He walked outside, hoping to hell he wasn't setting himself up for yet another roasting. Through the open café windows he could see Watanabe and Amy's sister talking heatedly. Her expression was furious at first, then, as the minutes went by, she appeared to calm down and sit back in her chair as Watanabe leaned forward and spoke to her. Ben gave them nearly fifteen minutes before he rejoined them.

'Well?' he asked, looking between the two of them, trying to ignore the tension shooting shards of ice up and down his spine.

They looked at each other for a few seconds, communicating with a series of frowns and raised eyebrows until Watanabe sighed loudly.

'Alright. I can't believe I'm saying this, but tell us what you want to do and then we'll decide if we can give you a hand.'

Realising he only had a small window of time before Amy's sister untangled herself from whatever hold Watanabe had over her and launched herself across the table at him, Ben talked fast.

Chapter 18

AMY WAVED GOODBYE to her final customer for the day, placed her hands on the small of her back, stretched, then collapsed in a chair, pulling off her shoes to massage her exhausted feet.

Everything ached – her head possibly the worst of all. It was closing time on a Friday, her staff in the salon had already left and she was ready to drop. The last few weeks had been a continual, emotionally draining blur and right now she'd do anything to turn off the world even for a few seconds.

The shop bell jingled and she stifled a groan. All she wanted to do was get home, put on her pyjamas and snooze on the couch.

'Amy?'

She looked up. Her breath caught as her heart tried to beat its way out of her chest.

Ben was standing in the doorway with one hand shoved into the back pocket of a pair of blue jeans, the other tightly gripping a large brown envelope. The sardonic smile he usually wore was absent; instead his ice-green eyes were shadowed with uncertainty, sucking her in.

'Are you open still?' he asked, his normally self-assured, clipped accent sounding tentative. 'I desperately need a shave. I've got this incredible woman to impress and I don't want her thinking I don't care enough to look my best.'

'We're closed.'

'Oh.' Ben's shoulders slumped a little. 'Are you sure? Because I've really made a hash of things and I need to ask her to forgive me. I wrote some things that were unintentionally unflattering and have tried to apologise both in person and in writing but she simply won't give me the chance.'

Amy felt her eyes prickle and looked back down at the foot that she was massaging, slipping her shoe back on.

'I said we're closed.' She felt her heart breaking all over again.

'I'm sorry, Amy.'

'So am I.' She kept her gaze on the floor.

'Did you read my apology?'

She had read it at least twenty times. 'Yes.'

'I meant it. Every word. I'm sorry, Amy.'

'Don't,' she said, her voice cracking.

'And after trying everything I could think of to convince you that I really am certifiably crazy about you, I've decided that I'm going to give you a chance to kill me.'

'What?' Her eyes snapped to his face, taking in the dark shadows under his eyes.

'A cut-throat shave.' He walked further into the shop.

'I'm closed,' she repeated. 'I don't want to see you, Ben.'

'I think you do. I think you'd relish the idea of cutting my throat. So come on.' He sat down in the chair next to hers, placing the envelope he was holding on the ledge in front of the mirror.

'I don't want to see you.' It hurt so much right now, there was no way she was going to touch him.

'Well, I'm not going anywhere.' He regarded himself in the

mirror and then gave her a forced smile. 'And you have to admit it would be pretty bad advertising for you if I walked out of here looking like this.' He gestured to what had to be five days' worth of scraggly, overgrown stubble. 'Think of all the damage you could do without actually killing me.'

'Why are you here? Surely you have better things to write about,' Amy said, voice flat.

He turned his chair to face hers, his expression deathly serious. 'It will never happen again. Somewhere over the past few years I've become terribly arrogant and egotistical. It never occurred to me that you'd be upset. I . . . I don't do declarations or emotions that well. I'm not used to showing people I care. Pathetic really, for a grown man, and terribly clichéd.' His mouth quirked in an unhumorous smile. 'You inspired me so much. I wanted to write about you. I wanted to share you with others. You might not know it, but my stage persona is a total bastard who makes fun of other people. It's something I've done my entire life. Believe it or not, I was a shy child. Humour, *my* kind of humour, worked. Until recently.' He looked away. 'Half the reason people come to see me is because they love to hate me. It never occurred to me how that might look to someone who doesn't have that context.'

Amy abruptly pushed herself out of her chair and walked over to stare blindly out the window at the congested evening traffic.

'Please, Amy.'

She squeezed her eyes tightly shut. 'Just go, Ben. I can't do this.'

He sat there behind her for almost five minutes, the feeling of complete dejection in the air palpable, before getting up and walking silently out the door.

Not wanting to watch his departing back, Amy turned back to tidy the barbershop and saw the envelope he'd been carrying lying on the ledge in front of his abandoned chair. She picked it up, intent on throwing it in the rubbish, but her sister's unmistakable handwriting scrawled across the front stopped her.

Amy, read this and give him a chance. Both Scott and I think he really means it when he says he's sorry.
   Trust yourself.

Amy's brow wrinkled. Jo? What would Jo have to do with this? Leaving the thought unfinished, she up-ended the envelope and a heavy block of paper fell out.

She looked at the first page. It was a manuscript, entitled *Laughing at the Dark*. She turned the page. The words 'For Amy, I love you with all my heart,' were typed and centred, stark and unadorned. For a couple of seconds it felt as if someone had kicked her in the chest. A sob tore through her body. Then another one, her vision blurring.

Hope, so terribly small and fragile, sparked as she swiped at her eyes. He loved her. He hadn't said it before but for some reason he'd said it here.

She knew, in that moment, that she couldn't let him go without knowing if it was the truth.

The manuscript dropped from her fingers, pages fluttering as she turned and ran for the door. Ben was walking towards his car, his shoulders bent, truly looking like the devastated man he'd professed to be.

'Ben!'

Ben turned. If he'd thought it had hurt to walk away just now, it was nothing compared to this. She was crying, tears creating muddy smudges in her make-up. She'd never looked more beautiful.

'Yes?' He heard the raspiness in his voice, bracing himself for another blow, watching as she rubbed her hands up and down the hot pink pencil skirt she was wearing. They were shaking.

'Come back here. Please.'

He took a few seconds to process the words. 'Why?'

She swiped at her eyes, only smudging her make-up all the more as she drew a shaky breath. 'Did you mean it? The dedication?'

'Yes, every word.' He nodded slowly, trying desperately to understand what was going on. Her sister had said that he should put how he felt front and centre but it couldn't be just that.

He watched her expression crumple. 'Why tell me you love me now? Why not before? Why now?'

Ben cleared his throat, trying to search for words but none came. The sound of heavy traffic on the road behind him intruded but he didn't give a damn who was watching. This was too important. 'I honestly don't know.'

She looked over his shoulder as a bus screeched to a halt at a nearby stop. 'Come inside.'

He stared at her, trying to decipher what was happening. He wasn't stupid enough to hope this was a second chance. 'Why? Because, honestly—' He shoved his hands in his pockets, taking the time to force his damn brain to come up with the right words. It had never failed him before but now, nothing was forthcoming but pure honesty. 'I don't want to hurt you any more than I already have and—'

'Just shut up and come inside, Ben. I really don't want this to be any more public than you've already made it.'

She walked back inside the shop, leaving the door open. He stepped through it, letting it close with a loud click. The bell above it tinkled in the quiet.

He glanced at his manuscript scattered on the floor, disregarding it. 'What do you need from me?'

She leaned against the arm of one of the barber's chairs,

wrapping her arms around her waist. 'Why didn't you say this to me earlier? Why did you have to write that horrible thing in the newspaper instead?'

If Ben had felt small before, it was nothing compared to now. 'It was the only thing I could think to do. You wouldn't talk to me. You wouldn't see me. I was desperate.'

She turned her head, closing her eyes tightly. 'Do you love me?'

'You read the dedication in my manuscript, didn't you?'

'Do you love me? I need to hear you say it out loud.'

This shouldn't have been so difficult. He'd already admitted his feelings to her sister, to Alex, to Ross, and he'd typed them on one of the sheets of the manuscript at their feet but that had been different. For some reason, saying the words out loud right now to a woman who held his future in the palm of her hand was too much. He felt more open and exposed than he had since he was a young boy, before he'd learned to cover up his true feelings with wit. He had no wit now, no pithy comment to offer.

A humiliating prickle started up behind his eyes and he willed it away. 'I – ah . . . Yes. Yes. I love you.' The words felt wrenched from his chest. His fists clenched at his sides as he watched tears course down Amy's cheeks. 'Amy—'

'What you wrote was horrible, really, really horrible, and that apology in the paper was even worse.'

'I know. I realise that now. If I could take it back I would. I was too stupidly arrogant to consider the fact you didn't know—'

'You can't do that, write about me again, ever.' She looked directly at him, pressing her lips together before speaking again, the tremor in her voice telling him just how close she was to breaking down. 'If you wanted to apologise, you should have done it to my face.'

'I tried. Believe me I tried.' Ben injected every bit of the sincerity he felt into his tone, fighting every instinct that told him he was about to be gutted, that he wasn't safe. 'And if that's what you want, I'll agree to your terms, any terms. Just tell me we've got a chance.'

'And you'll have to apologise to my house. I know it sounds silly, but my house means a lot to me. I work hard for it. It's mine and I love it. I love the life I've built for myself. I love who I am. If you can't accept me as me, we . . . we can't do this.'

Ben felt a wave of hope, so strong it almost crippled him at the knees. 'This? Are you giving me a second chance?'

She kept speaking as if she hadn't heard him. 'And if you mean it, if you want to be with me, you've got to follow through. Words come too easily to you, Ben. You use them to push people away. You used them to push *me* away. I need to see you trust me enough that you won't do that again.'

'I mean it.' Ben tried for his usual sardonic smile but even without looking in the mirror, he knew it was a poor facsimile. 'Amy, I'd appreciate it if you made this clear for my feeble mind. Have you forgiven me?'

She looked at him for a long time and he felt every second of silence as a hard thud in his veins. 'Not yet.' She paused again and the wait was excruciating. 'But I will if you behave. You're on six months' probation.'

Ben reeled back, confusion mixing with hope and a hint of elation. 'Probation?'

She nodded, heaving in a shaky breath. 'Six months, living at my house, sharing my life and no complaining, no making fun of anything. Can you do that? I'm going out on a limb here – I need you to meet me halfway.'

'Six months?' Ben mentally baulked. All the reasons why he couldn't live in such a small place raced through his mind: the outdoor toilet, the abominable garden, Amy's lack of decent television or internet. He'd have to temporarily get himself a cheaper car, one that wouldn't be stolen or ruined. He'd have to find some way of talking her into upgrading her television. He'd have to – what was he think-ing? Of course he'd do it. He'd do anything. He spread his arms apart, leaving himself open. 'When do you want me to move in?'

He was rewarded with a pint-sized blonde barrelling into him, tears wetting the front of his shirt. His own eyes gave up the fight momentarily as he buried his face in her hair, inhaling apples and bubblegum, the most wonderful woman who'd ever walked into his life, and it looked like she was crazy enough to be his.

'As soon as possible. Now get into the chair. If you're gonna be my probationary boyfriend, you can't go around looking like that.'

Relieved laughter shook Ben's body as he rubbed his cheek against Amy's, earning a squeal. 'I thought you liked me like this.'

She poked him in the ribs, her voice radiating the relief he could feel shaking through her small frame. 'I like you better quiet with a razor against your throat. Now sit in the chair and behave.'

Ben leaned back so he could see her face, taking in every detail. 'I love you, you know.'

He saw the impact his words had, marvelled at them and then watched with relieved delight as baby-blue eyes, still shimmering with unshed tears, narrowed. 'You can love me even better when you don't look like a scruff. Sit.'

'Your wish is my command.'

'It better be.'

'Unless your command shows a severe lack of judgement.'

'It won't. You're moving in tonight, by the way.'

'Tonight!'

'Sit in the chair, be a good boy and be quiet.'

Ben took one look at Amy, hands on her hips, glaring him down, her mouth twitching, and felt pure joy course through him. His laughter echoed around the room.

'Whatever you say, sweetheart. Whatever you say.'

Epilogue

'THIS KIND OF heat should have a warning label on it. Remind me why you decided to traipse us all the way down here mid-week just to make me walk cross-country in an inferno?' Ben squinted his eyes against the blinding white sunlight and took in the panorama around him. To the left stretched rolling, sun-baked vineyards featuring some large, miscellaneous, chugging machinery, and to the right stood the copse of trees and the gully dam he'd visited with Amy seven months before, looking almost unrecognisable through the heat haze.

'It's Australia. It's supposed to be hot. Deal with it.'

'That's what I said to you when we visited Alex in New York last month.'

'That doesn't count. It was snowing. If it's hot you can always take off more clothes or go for a swim. If it's cold, you die of hypothermia. How are your silly shoes going?'

Ben looked down at his irreparably ruined Gucci sneakers, still showing signs of trauma from the last time he and Amy had made this trek. At least the ground wasn't soggy with water. Instead, it was packed hard and dry, the green grass of late winter frizzled away to crackling gold stubble, chewed down by livestock.

The air was still. Ben felt a continuous trickle of sweat run down his back and his torso and thanked God that he'd worn a baseball cap, otherwise his head would look like a tomato, seventy-plus sunscreen or not.

The months spent living in Amy's little sweatbox hadn't prepared him for this. He could only be thankful they'd be driving straight to his house when they got back to Perth on Sunday night. The six months of his voluntary exile from the modern world was over. Never would he take air conditioning and an indoor toilet for granted again.

'Do you think it's possible to die of thirst out here?' he mused, knowing full well there was plenty of water in his backpack.

Amy stopped abruptly and turned to look at him with an exasperated frown, hands swooshing the skirt of her filmy yellow sundress. 'Don't start, mister. I know you're enjoying yourself. You only complain this much when you're really, *really*, enjoying yourself.'

She was right but that wasn't the point. 'Care to tell me *why* we're doing this in the heat of the day rather than at a more sensible time?'

'Because I promised Jo we'd look after Tiffany. It'll be the first night she and Stephen have had a breather for ages and I want to spend a bit of quality time with my niece before we leave for your book launch in London.' She gave him a pointed look, then flicked her ponytail over her shoulder, marching towards the trees and dam in the distance again.

Ben was momentarily distracted, watching her pert little backside moving from side to side before he snorted and caught up, long strides eating up the ground. 'Quality time? The child's seen so much of you, she's probably confused who her real mother is. Don't even think of getting any ideas. We discussed this.'

'Hmm?' Amy's voice was all too innocent as she paused to open a homemade wire and ring-lock gate, letting Ben through, then deftly closing it again.

Ben didn't like the sound of that. 'I'm not impregnating you until you get off your high and mighty horse and agree to marry me. That damn dog of yours is more than enough for now. One of these days I'm going to break my neck falling over him instead of merely bruising my ego.'

From the back he caught Amy's cheeks plumping out as she chuckled and felt the urge to grin back, despite his exasperation. *Four times*. He'd asked her to marry him four times over the past six months, and every time she'd turned him down, saying he had to do his time in purgatory, living in her house, before she could agree.

He'd jumped through the hoops, passed the bloody test and she was going to agree to marry him today or he was going to do something unspeakable, which would more than likely result in him getting something Australian stuck in a crevice or two when he got her underneath him until she said yes.

He was prepared for a long siege. He had the engagement ring he'd picked out six months ago in his back pocket. He'd brought a picnic blanket this time and, unbeknown to Amy, he'd arranged for a gourmet packed lunch and a rather lovely bottle of champagne, currently residing in a compact chiller providing a blessedly cool patch on the otherwise overheated skin of his back.

It took them another ten minutes to reach the relative cool of the clearing next to the dam. Like last time, Amy inspected it in silence before walking forward. Taking his baseball cap off to smooth a hand over his damp scalp and letting the backpack slide off his shoulders to rest on the ground by his feet, Ben watched on as warmth bloomed in his chest. Damn, but he loved this woman.

'Ben?' Amy turned and held out a hand for him. She was standing right next to the gnarled tree she'd told him was the site of her old childhood hidey hole.

He walked forward, wondering at the sparkle in her eyes while being completely charmed and gratified by the happiness in her expression. He'd been a little worried that this place would still hold shadowy memories for her, not only of her childhood but of his much more recent stupidity that had nearly been the end of them.

He took her hand. 'Are you happy?'

'Yes.' She nodded emphatically.

'You're not feeling down about the partnership?' he asked, referring to Amy selling forty per cent of her business to her friend and colleague, Mel. The decision had been a hard one but both Ben and Mel had finally convinced Amy it was the right thing to do, along with hiring a second barber, Cathleen, who was turning out brilliantly.

Be that as it may, Ben couldn't help but notice that Amy had experienced a few pangs of anxiety during her first ever trip overseas last month to see Alex in the opening night of Gaetano Donizetti's *La Fille du Régiment* with the Metropolitan Opera in New York.

'I was feeling a bit flat, but I'm not now,' she replied. 'I've done the right thing.'

'You have.' Ben saw she was rubbing her thigh with the palm of her hand, the way she always did when she was nervous or anxious. Something was up. He couldn't quite put his finger on it. Even after six months of close proximity, he was still not fully versed in all her moods. She kept him on his toes.

'Ben?' She looked up at him, her expression earnest. Too earnest.

'Yes?' he asked warily.

'There's something I want to ask you. Could you promise me you'll be quiet for a few seconds and not say anything?'

He felt a small curl of apprehension. 'This isn't going to be depressing, is it?'

She shook her head, a small smile playing around her mouth. 'Nope.'

He nodded. He would have shut up for a bloody year if she'd keep smiling.

She pulled her hand out of his, looked up into his eyes, then bit her lip. 'Close your eyes.'

He opened his mouth to protest but quickly snapped it shut when she raised her brows. He heaved a massive sigh instead and did what she'd asked, feeling a full wave of apprehension wash over him.

'You still with me?'

He nodded and felt two warm hands pressing on his already overheated chest through his T-shirt. His mind was buzzing. What the hell could his little barber be up to?

'Will you marry me?'

It took a few seconds for the words to register and when they did Ben's eyes snapped open, his words coming out in an indignant roar. '*You devious wench!*'

Amy's wide grin turned into hearty, full blown, head-to-toes laughter. 'You're supposed to say yes.'

'*No!*' Ben exclaimed in outrage. Six months he'd been asking and now the woman springs this on him. As if he hadn't been sweating bricks the entire time. He shook his head emphatically. 'Oh no. No way. You made *me* wait for six months and turned me down four times. *Four* times. And then you—' He paused, momentarily lost for words. 'Apoplectic, sweetheart, there's no other description for how I feel right now. Start running because when I catch you, your backside's going to be too damn sore for you to move for weeks.'

'So yes, then?' Amy stood on tiptoes, planted a quick kiss on his firmly closed lips, then turned to sprint away, her laughter trailing behind her.

Ben let her get a little bit ahead to keep things interesting, then gave chase, hounding her steps through the trees, across a patch of dry grass and up along the bank of the dam. Amy ran ahead of him, her head thrown back, her gleeful laughter filling the air, ending with a choked giggle as he picked up his speed, grabbed her around her waist and threw her over his shoulder.

'Put me down!'

'No. I'm afraid you're getting what you deserve this time.' Ben strode determinedly down the bank. 'It's not like my shoes aren't already ruined, so trust me, this is going to hurt you far more than it does me.'

It took Amy a few seconds to gauge his intent before she really started struggling. 'No! My hair—'

'Will bloody well survive, never mind that my ego is in tatters,' he said indignantly, holding her just at the water's edge. It did look blessedly cool. 'I want a "yes" in retrospect. No, bugger that. I want *four* in retrospect, or you are going to have a bath within the next thirty seconds.' He made as if to let go.

Amy squealed. 'Yes, yes, yes and yes – now put me *down*.'

'Okay.' Ben promptly dropped her in the water.

When she finally picked herself up, spluttering and cursing him, he was sitting on the bank only a few feet away, holding up a ten-carat diamond engagement ring between thumb and forefinger. 'Love me?'

She stood on one foot, pulling off one sodden sneaker, then another. Her hair was a bedraggled mess around her cheeks; her dress was plastered to her body. She was perfect.

Ignoring the ring, she sniffed. 'I can't answer that until I get an answer to *my* proposal.'

He pretended to look thoughtful, angling the ring so the diamond caught the sunlight and sparkled. 'Which one was that?'

His answer was a massive splash of water fair in the face, then another that hit his chest. Before long he was dripping wet, feet sliding on the slippery clay bank as he struggled unsuccessfully to get to his feet.

'Yes, *yes*. Bloody well stop – stop that! *Yes!*' he managed, spluttering in between the laughter, hands coming up to shield his face.

The water abruptly stopped.

'Good.' With a satisfied nod, Amy walked over, plopped herself in his lap and took the ring, sliding it on her finger while Ben watched on in a blissfully silent moment of pure happiness.

Acknowledgements

A massive thanks to my wonderful editor, Sarah Fairhall, for believing in Amy's story. You are, as always, amazing. Also an equally huge thanks to Carol George for being so supportive over the years and for the chats about the cats!

Tony Johnson, thanks so much for putting up with me, for kicking me up the pants when I need it and making me belly laugh every single day of this journey.

Anja, Theresa and Jo thanks for your honesty and awesomeness.

Rex Kingston, you're a legend. An extra special thanks for the advice about Ben's car.

And finally, my all-encompassing gratitude to everyone who has supported me over this book's journey. You're all exceptional, extraordinary people and my life is so much better for having you guys in it.

About the Author

Georgina Penney first discovered romance novels when she was eleven and has been a fan of the genre ever since. It took her another eighteen years to finally sit in front of a keyboard and get something down on the page but that's alright, she was busy doing other things until then.

Some of those things included living in a ridiculous number of towns and cities in Australia before relocating overseas to Saudi Arabia, Bahrain and Brunei Darussalam.

In between all these travels, Georgina managed to learn to paint, get herself a Communication and Cultural Studies degree, study Psychotherapy and learn all about Hypnotherapy. In the early days she even managed to get on the IT roller-coaster during the early noughties boom, inexplicably ending the ride by becoming the registrar of a massage and naturopathy college. There was also PhD in the mix there somewhere but moving to Saudi Arabia and rediscovering the bodice ripper fixed all that.

Today she lives with her wonderful husband, Tony, in a cozy steading in the Scottish countryside. When she's not swearing at her characters and trying to cram them into her plot, she can be found traipsing over fields, gazing at hairy coos and imagining buff medieval Scotsmen in kilts (who have access to shower facilities and deodorant) living behind every bramble hedge.

Don't miss *Fly In Fly Out* by Georgina Penney

'What the hell?'

Jo Blaine's motorbike helmet bounced off antique pine floorboards with a dull plastic thud as she took in the state of her Fremantle penthouse apartment.

This was so not the way she'd left it when she'd flown out to her offshore oil job in Mauritania. No way.

There was a rumpled tartan throw rug and a pillow on one of her cream leather couches, a bright-red coffee cup – her favourite damn coffee cup – was sitting on her hand-cut glass-and-jarrah coffee table and the books in her bookshelves looked as if they'd been rifled through.

She took a step further inside, kicking a pair of expensive-looking, size-fourteen men's leather shoes out of her way, and immediately felt a cool breeze against her cheek.

The sliding door leading to the balcony was wide open, letting in the scent of a recent summer shower on bitumen. The sounds of distant traffic and boats going up and down the Swan River filtered in, an incongruous backing track to her growled exclamation.

Definitely not how she'd left it before.

'Hello? Anyone here?' She turned back around, narrowed eyes searching for a coffee-loving, couch-sleeping, male Goldilocks but only saw her massive silver Maine Coon cat, Boomba, who chose that moment to waddle past with a pair of men's undies firmly clasped in his mouth. His fat furry backside moved side to side as he disappeared into the kitchen, where Jo could see stacked Domino's pizza boxes on the counter. Her temper, always on a short fuse after a long, sleepless flight, began to sizzle and fizz as she put the clues together.

She only knew one man with size-fourteen feet. That same man had a key to her apartment and was about to experience the flaming wrath of a jetlagged woman. 'Scott? Where the *hell* are you?' She called out her best friend's name as she kicked off her steel-capped boots and reached into her pocket for her phone. She held it to her ear, hearing nothing but dial tone, feeling herself getting more and more worked up.

Boomba waddled past her again, chirruping around his mouthful. His expression said clearly that as far as he was concerned, she should forget her house invader, admire the thing he'd killed and give him a pat.

'And what the hell are you doing here, fuzz ball?' Jo reached down and plucked the underwear out of his mouth, throwing it away. 'You're supposed to be at Amy's. Want to tell me what's going on?' The cat gave her his usual entitled feline stare and then butted his head into her shin.

'You're no help.' She walked through the living room, kicking a pair of socks out of her way, and stopped short in front of the vibrant blue-and-green abstract painting she'd bought last time she was in town. It was askew, as if someone had knocked it, and she felt something inside her snap.

This was not cool. *Not. Cool.* Her house was supposed to be empty. Her cat was supposed to be at her sister's and there wasn't supposed to be a . . . *man* anywhere within a good twenty metres of her right now, even if he was her best mate. She'd spent the last sixteen weeks surrounded by Y chromosomes and all she'd been looking forward to was a blessedly empty, *male-free* environment.

Scott finally answered, his tone suitably shocked. 'Jo? What time is it over there?'

'It's eight in the morning. I'm home. In Perth. Where are you?'

'*Home?*' Scott's deep voice momentarily took on choirboy heights he hadn't achieved since pre-puberty. 'You're supposed to be on holiday in Brazil!'

Jo squeezed her eyes tightly shut. 'Yes. Home. I cancelled the holiday because I wanted to be *home.* You know, that place I like to come when I'm not on some rusting oil rig in the middle of nowhere? You know that place? The place you were looking after. The place currently being lived in by someone who has feet the size of yours. The place currently containing my cat, who should be at Amy's.'

'Ahh. Yeah. About that.'

'Yeah, about what? What the *hell* is going on?'

There was a moment of silence and then a dull thud as if something had been hit, quite hard. 'I'll explain, but it's probably better I do it in person.'

'What? Why? I just want an answer and I want it now!'

'You'll get one . . . just . . . just stay there. I'll be there in fifteen minutes. We'll get all this sorted out. I'm sorry, Jo.'

Jo scowled, turning around, taking in the disorder and feeling a renewed sense of outrage. 'You bloody well better be. And bring me some goddamn coffee. I haven't slept properly for days and all

I wanted was to have a shower and fall into bed and instead—'

'Ten minutes,' he said with an edge of frustration in his tone that had better not be aimed at her. Given the mood she was in at the present moment, she'd be able to take Scott on one-on-one. They didn't call her Krakatoa out on the rigs for nothing.

Jo hung up, looking around until her eyes settled on her bedroom door.

There was no way Scott would make it in ten minutes, let alone fifteen, and she was *tired*.

Shooing Boomba out of the way with her foot, she headed for her room.

The feeling of tiredness was blasted to smithereens the minute she pushed the door open, took in the contents of her bed and roared with rage. '*Who the hell are you?!*'

'AAGGHH! *Gnph.*' The very naked, very buff and all-over tanned blond man who'd until that moment been sleeping spread-eagled on her bed shouted in surprise, leapt to his feet, tripped over Jo's cat and fell facedown on the floor.